In the sky the larks still sing

In the sky the larks still sing is the second book in
The Charlotte Series by Lindsay Inkster.

It is set in Shetland, Scotland, including West Aberdeenshire,
Edinburgh and Glamis and,
parts of North-east France during the First World War.

Also by Lindsay Inkster,

Lassickie

Writing as Lindsay Reid

Scottish Midwives: Twentieth Century Voices
Midwifery: Freedom to Practise?
Midwifery in Scotland: A History

Lindsay lives in Fife, Scotland and has three sons,
one daughter and five grandchildren.

www.lindsayreid.co.uk

In the sky the larks still sing

By
Lindsay Inkster

BLACK DEVON BOOKS
Dunfermline

Author's Note

Any resemblance to any character, alive or dead, is purely coincidental.

I take full responsibility for any errors, factual or historical.

There is a small amount of Scots dialogue in the book. To help with the meanings of some of the Scots words, there is a Glossary at the end.

Lindsay Inkster
August 2014

First published 2014
By **Black Devon Books**
Dunfermline
Scotland

Cover artwork by Vivien A Reid
Printed by Airdrie Print Services
ISBN 978-0-9557999-3-8

British Library Cataloguing in Publication Data
**A catalogue record for this book is available on request from
The British Library**

For

Our grandchildren who are the future:

Shona, Caitlin, Jenny, Fergus and Jamie

Acknowledgements

While writing *In the sky the birds still sing* I have received a great deal of interest and encouragement from friends. For this, I should like to say a very big 'Thank you'. The push to keep going is not just from within me. It also comes from a word here, an indication of understanding there and an overall interest which is almost tangible at times. I should also like to thank:

Yvonne McEwan, Project Director of 'Scotland's War 1914-1919', the Centre for the Study of Modern Conflict, University of Edinburgh. What seems a long time ago, I visited Yvonne in her office in Edinburgh. Her generosity, of time, knowledge, information, sandwiches, books to read and absorb, and, infectious passion for her subject, is unparalleled. Yvonne I shall return your books – thank you.

Jeanne Sledmore, for her equestrian advice and information, and readiness to help.

Viv Reid, Artist, for listening to what I wanted, brainstorming, making changes where necessary and accomplishing the artwork for the cover of *In the sky the larks still sing* within a tight timescale with talent, patience and grace.

Michael and Trish Oatts, for being persuaded to model for Viv.

Jenny Macleod for her immediate response and expert help with French grammar and idioms.

Ruby Inkster, for her in-depth Shetland knowledge and always being there to help.

Anne Cameron, for her helpful contribution to Scottish baptismal traditions.

Mike Ward, Curator of Grampian Transport Museum, Mike Cooper and Keith Fenwick, for their emailed helpful input into the Strathdon buses discussion.

Alison Webber, Assistant Librarian of Alford Academy for her help in researching secondary schools of the day in the Donside area.

Ruaraidh Wishart, Archivist, Aberdeen City Archives, for further research and shedding light into Secondary schools of the day in the Donside/Deeside areas.

Jim Paterson and his colleagues at Airdrie Print Services, for their expertise and willingness to help with all problems.

Daphne Tullis, for her constant encouragement over numerous cups of tea and coffee.

David, Ruth, Ewan and Robert, who, each in their own way has contributed.

David, my husband, partner and best friend – for finding and looking up books, reading, pointing out errors, giving encouragement, listening to me going on about 'the book', patience and just being there. Thank you, David.

Abbreviations

AChD: Army Chaplains Department
ADS: Advanced Dressing Station
CCS: Casualty Clearing Station
CEF: Canadian Expeditionary Force
CGH: Calgary General Hospital
CO: Commanding Officer
GMC: General Medical Council
HMHS: His Majesty's Hospital Ship
ID: identity
L/c: Lance Corporal
MO: Medical Officer
NCO: Non-Commissioned Officer
QAIMNS: Queen Alexandra's Imperial Military Nursing Service (aka QA)
RAMC: Royal Army Medical Corps
RAP: Regimental Aid Post
SWH: Scottish Women's Hospitals
TC: Tunnel Companies
VAD: Voluntary Aid Detachment

In Flanders fields the poppies blow
Between the crosses, row on row,
That mark our place; and in the sky
The larks, still bravely singing, fly
Scarce heard amid the guns below.

John McCrae (Ypres 1915)
Published (1919) *In Flanders Fields and Other Poems*

Chapter 1

Near Vimy Ridge, North East France

9 APRIL 1917

Snow, driven on by a bitterly cold westerly wind, covered trenches and everything and everybody in them by half past four that morning. Padre James MacLeod Army Chaplains Department (AChD), arrived at the Regimental Aid Post (RAP), stamped the snow off his boots, ducked his head at the entrance and went in.

Robert Duncan, Medical Officer, stood discussing proceedings with his Royal Army Medical Corps (RAMC) Sergeant Willie Bissett, an experienced man who had seen much in his army years. Over forty now, hair greying, weather-beaten face becoming lined, Willie Bisset was well-known for the support he gave the young doctors. Also there, were three RAMC other ranks, medical orderlies, soldiers who trained and worked within the RAMC in peace-time and who expected to assist the Medical Officer and give first aid to the wounded in war.

RAPs could be situated anywhere suitable near the Front line. Dugouts, communication trenches, old ruined buildings or even shell-holes if they were deep enough were used. They were, of necessity, temporary affairs, even if the men who staffed them often knew each other well and could do their job anywhere.

This RAP was in an old dugout. It was situated just behind the Front line, reinforced with extra sandbags and roofed with heavy wooden planks with sandbags on top. There wasn't much room to move around. The orderlies moved efficiently, organising in this small space the necessities required to give speedy first aid to an as yet unknown number of wounded men. The facilities were only sufficient to carry out first aid before the wounded were sent on to the Advanced Dressing Station (ADS). Anti-tetanus serum was high on the list. It was given to all the casualties because of the previously-ploughed and now war-torn infected and damaged battlegrounds. There were also different bandages and gauze, shell and field dressings, various ointments, cotton wool, army blankets and stretchers.

In one corner stood a small table with a shoogly leg, supported by a piece of wood. On this stood the all-important stove, with another in reserve beneath. Beside this were the 'stores' : brandy, cocoa, Oxo and Bovril and biscuits. An assortment of chairs stood along the wall. Along the length of another wall, but with space to work from both sides was a long table for laying a stretcher on. Boxes of replacement equipment were piled up against another wall.

Records were not officially kept in the RAP although most MOs recorded, if possible, the name, rank and number of any man who came to the Aid post, his wounds and his condition. A man's details were very important but officially recorded at the next port of call, the ADS.

1

James went up to the group and saluted. 'Good Morning.'

'Morning Padre. Have you had any sleep?' Robert Duncan eyed him.

'No. Have you?

'I don't think anyone has. Now, this is the way we'll have to work today...'He launched into a precise description of the way he wanted the RAP to run. As he finished he looked over at James.

'Can you manage that? We appreciate your being here. We're also aware that you'll have pastoral duties as well.'

'Let's just do it and see how we go,' said James. 'Put me wherever you want me to be. When does the whistle go?'

'Zero hour is at 05.30. It's a quarter to five now.'

'Listen, I hear the bagpipes. Faintly above the wind the sound came, a light, happy tune.'

'Yes,' said Robert. 'It's Dougie MacLean – he's a veteran now, they say. Been around for ages. Listen to what he's playing. One of the jigs,' he commented. 'Lifting their spirits. He'll take them forward too.'

James peered out into the driving snow.

'What devastation. This used to be beautiful, before the war. They may have tucked themselves in behind their new Hindenberg Line but they've managed to make a fine mess of the area they've pillaged into the bargain. And messed up our tactics too, I hear.'

'Mind you,' said Robert Duncan. 'Our boys have managed to do a good job of wrecking some of their Front lines in the last week or two's bombardment. But, then again,' he added pensively. 'Look at the cost.'

As if on cue, eight soldiers arrived. 'Morning sir. Stretcher-bearers sir.'

'Ah, well done. Good morning. All present?'

'Yes Sir. Not many of us Sir – but there are more up the line.'

'Right then,' Sergeant Bisset said. 'Stretchers over there. Had breakfast, have you?'

'Yes, Sergeant, thank you.'

'Got rations with you, just in case?'

'Yes, Sergeant.'

'Right. Stand by.'

The minutes crept on. Then...

'Listen. They've started the bombardment,' said James.

'They're ready for off. Dear God, what a noise. It's like the Somme all over again.'

'The visibility's terrible.' James strained to see through his binoculars. 'How on earth are they going to manage?'

The whistles blew. Immediately the noise levels raised by the 51st Highland Division grew, with their cheering and yelling audible to those at the RAP even above the noise of the advance bombardment. All along the line as far as they could hear, and further, with the Canadian Corps on their left and the 34th Division on their right, officers ordered, urged, shouted, and otherwise persuaded their men to climb the scaling ladders up and over the top of the trench and walk towards the enemy under cover of a creeping barrage of Allied fire. This part of the Front line was 3000 yards widening to 4000. Their end objective, the southern shoulder of Vimy Ridge, lay some 5,500 yards, over three miles, away.

In response, from the enemy side came a counter barrage of heavy artillery accompanied by fireworks from star shells, flares and billowing clouds of smoke – multi-colours reflecting their destructive source and temporarily highlighting what was going on below.

Judging from the speed with which the hundreds of soldiers disappeared from view into the driving snow it was obvious to the observers that visibility was going to be a problem. Still dark, still snowing, drifts rose up to meet them, unseen hollows opened traps for the unwary. Tree stumps tripped them up.

They could not hear – the enemy or each other. The howling wind, the noise of the barrage, the ear-covering knitted woollen helmets worn under their tin helmets and woollen scarves around their mouths and noses combined to see to that. In this devastated, rutted snow-drifted landscape, with poor vision and hearing, and clumsiness and confusion brought about by severe weather, and the conditions underfoot, each man could only do his individual best. Within this isolation he had to trust that his mates were somewhere near. Yet, at last, they were doing something. The waiting was over. For the moment, they were no longer rats in the trap of the trenches.

They could hear one sound, however. All along the battle lines, the pipers with their bagpipes, ahead of the pack, advancing, stumbling, coping with the snowdrifts as best they could, but still there, played them on. The listening men in the Aid Posts could hear the high notes of the bagpipes diminishing, their sound whipped away by the following wind towards the enemy lines.

'Right, stretcher-bearers,' shouted Sergeant Bisset. 'Go now. Spread out. Watch where you're going. Keep listening and looking. Take care. Make use of any cover you can get.'

'Yes, Sergeant.' The stretcher-bearers set out at a walk as fast as they could manage.

Willie Bisset turned back, grim-faced. 'That's a dangerous job if ever there was one. They're as brave as any man. They've gone.'

'That's it,' said Robert. 'Now, we wait.' James looked out into the whirling snow. Not a soul could be seen.

They did not have long to wait. Slowly a trickle of returning wounded became a flood as the men drawing closer to within the enemy's range were caught in the counter-barrage of gunfire and shrapnel. The first two, both wounded and holding each other up, staggered into the RAP well after day-break.

'Well done.' Robert Duncan went over. An orderly was already at their sides. 'Now, what have we here?'

'How are things out there?' Bates, one of the orderlies asked. 'Many down?'

'Yes, there was a huge barrage for a bit and a lot of us were caught. Some are in shell holes.'

Two stretcher bearers from another platoon came in. 'Can someone take this one please?' They put their burden on the waiting table and skilfully pulled out the poles.

'Careful now.' James went over to help.

'Morning Padre. If you hold him when we roll him over then we'll get the canvas out…that's it… now back again.' The man on the table screamed. 'Right that's fine thanks.'

'Has he had any morphine yet?'

'No, not yet.'

'Could you give him a quarter-grain to begin with James, and an anti-tetanus?' Robert's voice came over. 'I'll be with you in a moment.'

'Right. Check please.' James held the morphine up.

'Yes, thanks.' Robert turned to his walking wounded. 'Now you two need to get to the ADS. Can you walk? It's only just up the road about half a mile, back beyond the support lines. Here are your initial chits. They'll see to you and tell you what to do next.'

'Thanks.' The men stood up gingerly and moved their legs cautiously. 'That's a bit better, Sir.'

'Right, good luck.'

It went on all day. The price of initial good progress was the inevitable loss of life and limb. Stretcher bearers went out into the snow to return a long time later, hand over their burden to the care of the staff and go out again immediately. The staff in the RAP did what they could. Their job was to add to and build upon the initial emergency field dressing done at the point of injury. In better weather it was usual practice to find as safe a place as possible, like a shell hole, to wait for help. But, the weather conditions that day made it more urgent for the wounded to get under cover. Significant first aid with further immediately imperative life-saving treatment and decision-making happened in the RAPs, the first in a chain of workers whose *raison d'être* was care of the wounded stretching from the battlefields to hospitals at home.

By late afternoon the news filtering through was marginally positive. Those who were able were unanimous in their telling of the blown-up German barbed wire and many ruined German trenches – achieved in the pre-battle bombardments.

'I've never seen anything like it before,' said one Sergeant, gritting his teeth as Robert Duncan did some emergency suture-work to a big gash in his leg. 'Their barbed wire is in pieces in places. Well-done whoever did that.'

On the other hand, the enemy's long hold on Vimy Ridge since 1914 was not to be given up lightly. Eventual Allied success cost many lives.

At 18.30 the barrage stopped.

'Listen, Padre,' Bates said. 'Listen, there's nae noise.'

'Except for the racket you're making, telling us,' Jackson said. He turned back to his patient, a heavily build Lance-corporal with a badly swollen ankle. 'Sorry we can't make this into a Blighty one for you. I don't even think it's broken. What do you think, Captain Duncan? Bandage and on to the ADS?'

Robert looked. 'Yes, you'll need to get it X-rayed but I think you've probably sprained it. Never mind, you'll be off for a couple of weeks,' he said. 'Give you a break – and not your ankle,' he nodded at Jackson's laughter. 'Sorry for the pun, totally unintentional. Now then, who's next?' He turned to his next patient who came limping in holding a fallen branch as a staff with his right hand and with his left arm tightly bound to his side.

'Come on then,' Jackson started bandaging the lance corporal's sprained ankle. 'Then we'll see if there's a truck going up to the ADS.'

Bates pumped up the primus stove. 'It's surely nearly time for rations. Dinner anyone? What have we got today?''

Dusk fell.

'Now we need to wait. Where are my binoculars?' Robert and James looked out, surveyed the scene. Slowly it grew darker.

Then, they saw them. Slowly moving irregular shapes, low down, crawling to safety. Every now and again they heard sporadic rifle fire from an enemy sniper with an immediate response from the Front line.

'Stretcher bearers, to me, please.'

'Yes Sir.'

'Right, men, we've got more casualties out there. Are you prepared to go out and bring them in?'

'Yes Sir.'

'Thank you very much. I'll send a messenger along to the guard to inform that you are going out, and to provide cover.' Robert scribbled a basic dispatch.

'Bates.'

'Sir.'

'Take this. Inform the guard that stretcher bearers are going out. We require cover please.'

'Sir.' Bates went off at the double. Robert watched a minute and then turned to the stretcher- bearers.

'Please go now. Keep down. Use all cover you can. Good luck.'

They saw them, bent double, going out as quickly as they could to the crawling bodies in no-man's land, taking advantage of all the shell-holes, rough dugouts hastily created by past soldiers, dips in the ground, heaps of snow drifted into the side of a fallen tree.

The sniper-firing continued. The men with the stretchers disappeared.

Then, 'here's one lot,' said James. They came, with a heavy burden. Heads down, running for home at the end as the fire from both sides continued all around them. Panting, they laid their stretcher on the table.

'This one wasn't going to make it. Look at his legs. Give us the poles and we'll get another canvas and go out again. Some are trying to come in by themselves but there are some still alive who can't move without help.'

Robert and James turned to the first man. His legs were useless. Blood oozed through the field dressings from shrapnel wounds.

5

'We don't want to disturb this now. We'll bandage on top of the field dressings. A quarter-grain of morphine please, James, and tetanus. For a start. Then we can get him up to the ADS.'

'Hello,' James said to the soldier. You've been shot-up a bit. We're just going to give you something for the pain and more bandages and get you up to the ADS.'

'My legs…'

'Yes, we know. Here's your injection.' James, now long-practised, gave the morphine, rubbed the man's arm briskly. 'Can we have some help here please?'

'You go Bates,' said Willie Bisset attending to another man just in. 'Here's another one coming. Jackson, will you take this one coming in?'

'Sir.' He turned to the next patient, screaming and rolling on his stretcher. He was very young.

'I want my mother.' His hands clutched frantically at the wound in his side.

'They all say that…it's so sad.' Robert turned to James as the first man was carried in the direction of the waiting truck. 'Could you take him please?'

'Yes.'

'Mother,' shouted the soldier.

'She can't be here just now,' said James, 'but I bet she's thinking about you.'

'Do you really think so?'

'I know so. I'm sure you're never out of her mind.'

'I need her here.'

'Ay, I know. Now, come on, let's have a look. I'll give you an injection for the pain. What's your name?' he asked, undoing the soldier's battledress at the same time.

'Moffatt. Oh, oh,' he gasped. 'The pain, it's terrible. I can't stand it. I don't want to die without my mother. I'm going home.'

James held the writhing body still.

'Moffatt, listen. You're here so that we can help you. Think about going home to see your mother.' Bates quietly appeared at his side with morphine ready made up for him and anti-tetanus serum.

'Thanks, are you…?'

'Yes, I asked for re-inforcements. We have another body here to help.' He exposed the man's arm and gave the injections. 'There, that should do you for a bit. You all right here, Padre?'

'Yes, I'll hold on here.'

'Padre?' said Moffatt. 'Padre?'

'Yes, that's me.'

'Here with the Doctor?'

'Yes.'

'That's the full team. That's what the men say. "Body and soul".'

'Well, we try to help each other. We work together a lot.'

'Oh, oh,' the boy's voice grew softer as the morphine began to take effect. 'Body and soul, body and soul…working together…I like it…' he stopped rolling about…drifted off into his own world.

6

'Let's have a look now.' James and Bates viewed the destruction of Moffatt's right side held together with field dressings.

'Frankly, I don't know why this lad's still alive. He must be very determined.'

'Yes Padre. Some of them just seem to hang on.'

'Well, we need to get him up the road. Let's pack this up further. You never know, once they get an intravenous going and warm him up, alleviate the shock, he *could* make it…the mind does amazing things.'

Later, when they looked out over no-man's land, the snow had stopped. The sky was clear, a beautiful star-lit night. It was icy-cold. Frost glittered across the terrain in the cold light of the rising moon two days past full. The stretcher-bearers were out again hunting for wounded. They could still hear occasional sniper fire and quick replies from the home side.

'See that,' Robert said. 'What a moon. Lights up everything doesn't it? Beautiful, yet treacherous.'

'Yes,' James concentrated on his binoculars. 'There,' he said, 'I knew I heard something. Now I can see him. There's someone else out there. Someone trying to get in on his own – in trouble. Look, see, ten to twelve, past that broken tree. There he goes again.' A faint cry carried in the stillness. 'I'll go out.'

'No,' Robert said. 'You can't.'

'Yes I can. You can't stop me.'

'But, but…'

'Don't you see, I *have* to go. You lot can't go. You must be here. I'll just get my bag. I'll get him in and you can take over.' Robert stopped arguing.

'Bates,' he ordered. 'The Padre's going out after that casualty. Go to the Guard and ask for fire-cover for him. Keep your head down and run. James,' he turned to him, 'I know I have no authority to stop you, so, thank you. Take care.'

James, tin helmet and haversack on, stepped quietly out into no man's land.

To begin with all went well. He loped, well bent-over, between anything that could provide cover. The bright white moonlight lit up contrasts in the terrain. Boulders, tree-stumps cast shadows masking shell-holes and old furrowed dips. Twice he tripped over bodies and had to check to see if the man that had inhabited the body was breathing. Neither was. Twice he said a perfunctory prayer over the body, twice he removed the man's dog-tag, and moved on. The sniper fire continued. Each time he ducked, waited and carried on. Responding fire was immediate, always giving an extra few seconds of time.

The cries and moans became clearer. He was in the right direction. He suddenly saw a head above a boulder. A hundred yards, fifty, twenty. He reached the boulder.

'Ss-h!' he said. 'Keep your head down. I'm here.' He crawled round the boulder into the shadow.

The man lay on his side. His right leg was shot off below the knee. He wore a clumsily applied field dressing. He had a large bruise on the side of his head; his face was covered in blood.

'What's your name? Can you move at all?' James examined the bloody field dressing.

'Grant. I've been trying to crawl. I somehow got missed. There's someone else over there.' He pointed to the right. 'I'm pretty sure he's alive.'

'All right, I'll attend to you first. Is this your own field dressing?'

'Yes.'

'Who put it on for you? Where is he?'

'My mate.' Then a hesitation… 'He's dead now. Got caught in the fire.'

'I'm sorry.'

Grant sighed. His head drooped.

'Let's get another dressing on. I have a couple here.' James wrapped his own field dressing round the stump on top of the other.

'Now, listen. The RAP is over there.' He pointed. 'See?'

Grant nodded. 'Uh-hu.'

'We'll make for that. I'll give you a lift on the right hand side. But,' he warned, 'there are snipers out there. We need to crouch, move from cover to cover. The moonlight shows up everything but there are some shadows. We'll make for them. Can you give it a go?'

Grant made to sit up, suddenly saw who his rescuer was and said, 'Yes, Padre.'

'Slowly does it.' A sniper's bullet sang over to their right. 'Careful now.'

They got themselves into position in the shadows. Then,

'Come on now. Keep low. Make for that shadow over there.' Leaning heavily, Grant moved one leg.

'That's it. Use me as a crutch.'

They made it to the first shadow without attracting attention.

'One minute to catch your breath,' said James. 'Now, d'you see that dark area over there?'

'Yes, I think so.' Grant sounded tired and doubtful.

'We need to give it a go.' James moved under Grant's right oxter. 'Arm round my shoulder. That's right. Come on, move.'

Together they stumbled across to the next shadow. The sniper's bullet shot past. They stopped, crouching, trembling. Reply fire came from the Guard on watch.

'Come on.' They reached the next point.

They became very tired. I feel we've been at this for hours, thought James. It can only be a few minutes.

'Now,' he said. 'Look, we're nearly there.'

'Thank God for that.'

'Now, do you think we can do this last bit in a oner? There isn't anywhere else to stop. We'll have to keep very low but it's not for long.'

'All right.' Grant took a deep breath. 'Let's do it.' Once again he tightened his grip round James's shoulder and leant over him as they crouched together.

'Let's go.'

Robert Duncan and Bates could see them coming from the RAP. They held their breath. Nearer, nearer – suddenly there was a rattle of fire with immediate response. The stumble towards safety became a crawling rush. They could hear the moans of the injured man as James half-dragged, half-carried him over the last section.

8

'Here they are now. Well done James. We'll take over now. Get your breath back.' Willing hands lifted Grant on to the table. He sank back in relief.

'Padre,' he said. James stood by him. Grant put out his hand. 'Thank you,' he said. 'I wouldn't have made it on my own.'

'You've earned a break, Padre,' said Sergeant Willie Bisset.

'No, I can't do that yet. There's someone else out there. I know where he is. I'll need another field dressing.'

'But you can't go out again, Padre. That's not on. You're exhausted.'

'I said to Grant I would. I must. There's a wounded soldier out there, within reach. He's not making any noise but Grant says he's alive.'

Once again James commenced his dangerous dodging journey out into no man's land. He moved more quickly, more surely this time, retracing his steps to where he had located Grant. There he stopped and considered.

He looked over to the right where the soldier should be. There was no sound but James could just see a faint heap – difficult to make out. The area between looked flat, bright in the moonlight, unshaded. James looked up at the moon. A few small clouds hung around. If I wait – I might just make it when the cloud goes over. He watched, munching a piece of his chocolate ration as the minutes ticked past. Here we go now, he said to himself. The cloud edged up to the side of the moon. Slowly, as James watched, in no hurry, it gently moved over the face, hiding the moon from view.

'Go, now,' he whispered. He crawled forward. Inch by inch, keeping as flat as possible, he went across to the stranded soldier under the cloud shadow. Just after he got there, the shadow lessened and in seconds the terrain was white with light again.

He looked at the man. He was unconscious. James could see a faint rise and fall of his chest. He was breathing. He found the pulse in the man's neck. Quick, thready, he noted. I've got to get him back in. I'll have to carry him. But first, this head. The man's face was badly bruised with shrapnel wounds on the side of his head.

'You've had a right clout there,' James murmured. 'I wonder if you got caught in the sniper-fire.' He took out a bandage, put it on as best he could. 'Any more wounds? Ah, his foot.' The man's left ankle, still in its boot, was turned out sideways. 'I'll leave that as it is. Now, I need to get you up.'

With some difficulty he heaved the unconscious weight of the soldier up and over his right shoulder. He staggered to his feet, his burden hanging helplessly down his back.

'Come on now,' James said. He could not go back to his last point. His friendly cloud had gone. On the other side he could see shadowed areas here and there. As fast as he could he moved from one to the other. With every step his burden became heavier. He moved the soldier to his left shoulder. His breathing grew short and painful. The firing continued. He felt as though the sniper was playing games with him. He was sure whoever it was knew he was there, drawing him on in some horrible dance. He would not give up.

He was nearly at the end of his strength when he paused and looked. There was the RAP only a few yards away. Not far… not far. He gripped the soldier tightly, bent double, took a deep breath and walked forward. The sniper fired from the right hand side. Immediately there was responding fire. In the distance there was a cry. James heard both the fire and the cry. He felt the thump on his right side. No pain.

9

Slowly his knees gave way. James and the soldier he was rescuing went down into the snow.

'They're down. I'll get the stretchers,' Bates shouted.

'Right everyone,' Robert Duncan said. 'Careful now, watch out for that sniper. We've maybe got one. I heard a cry out, but we don't know how many there are. Let's go. Do not get up.'

They crawled with their stretchers out to James and the soldier. The few yards seemed much further than that. It seemed even longer bringing the laden stretchers back.

James was conscious. He smiled faintly as Robert expertly cut open his uniform jacket.

'That cost money. It's my one and only.'

'Too bad. Now what have you got for us?' He surveyed the exit wound in James's chest.

'Hmm, Let's have a look at where the entry wound is.' Willie Bisset came alongside.

'Tetanus, Sir, and a quarter-grain of morphine?'

'Yes, please, Sergeant, and then we'll do a quick roll-over to see what the other wound is like. How are you feeling James?' he said, noting the pallor, the bluish tinge around James's mouth, along with the blue fingernails, the intermittent cough, the blood stained sputum.'

'Breathless,' James gasped.

'We'll be quick. Need to see the back.'

Then, 'That'll do for the moment. We need to clean both wounds,' he said to James, suiting his actions to his words immediately, cleaning the entry wound with antiseptic before putting on a sealing dressing. 'This is much the smaller of the two. Now, back again please. I want to look at the front.'

'James,' he said, 'can you hear me?'

'Yes,' said James. 'A bit woosy but I can.'

'James, you've been caught in the sniper fire. In your chest. The exit wound's at the front. The bullet's caught your right lung and that's why you're so breathless. Now, we need to sort this. I need to clean it as well. I'm sorry,' as James gasped and coughed. 'I know it's painful. Can you breathe out now and we'll seal your lung as much as we can before we take you up to the ADS.'

'Yes, I'll try.'

'Right, here we go.' Willie Bisset was ready with the dressing. 'Ready, breathe out, now.'

They quickly put on the sealing dressing in an effort to prevent any air getting into the torn lung and thereby collapsing it even more, then firmly bandaged around James's chest for support and protection.

'Now away to the next step,' said Robert, and, 'James,' he added, 'you did an excellent job today. Apart from all the work you did here, you saved two men's lives.'

'How is he, that last one?' James wheezed. 'I haven't heard. He was unconscious. Did he get hit, that last time?'

'No, no, you protected him. I think he'll be OK. He's going to have a sore head but I think he'll make it.'

'Thank God.'

'Yes, and thank you.'

Willie Bisset watched, shaking his head as the truck carried James away to the RDS. Slowly he walked back in to the RAP.

'What would you give for his chances?'

Robert looked up soberly. 'I just don't know. All I know at the moment is that there goes one very brave man.'

Chapter 2

Birkenshaw

1904

A fine, bright Shetland spring day. New lambs in the fields. Leaves bursting open on the saplings at Birkenshaw. Birds nesting. Warmth in the sun at last.

Charlotte Sinclair ran down the front steps to the pram in its sheltered spot. Three month old Hannah Margaret still slept. Charlotte gently felt the back of the baby's neck for warmth. Hannah was born in a snowy night in February of that year 1904 and as usual for Shetland winter babies in that era, kept inside for weeks until the fine weather. This was Hannah's second time napping outside and as well as her traditional Shetland shawl she was happit up in layers of clothing and well-nigh invisible.

Perhaps Charlotte was more anxious than most. She released the brake of the new high perambulator and walked along, the big modern wheels making light work of the gravel on the path. Granpa and Granny in Towie wrote telling her not to worry so much but after what she had been through, how could she not?

Charlotte and Alexander married six years previously in 1898. This was the culmination of a time of change for Charlotte when she came to Shetland as teacher at the Jarlshavn School. As junior schoolmistress she lived in Da Peerie Skulehoose and soon became friendly with the local folk and in particular the Sinclair family. Alexander and Margery Sinclair lived with their children Magnus and Christina in Harbour House, designated house of the Jarlshavn harbourmaster. Margery, terminally ill with consumption, died the following February. Three years later Alexander and Charlotte married and the family moved to newly built Birkenshaw on the outskirts of Jarlshavn.

Charlotte prevailed upon Alexander to agree to her continuing teaching although he had his doubts. He was of the old school: if a man's wife went out to work there was an implication that he couldn't 'keep her'. Charlotte enjoyed teaching. She also wanted to justify her training. Besides, she had a long-held feeling that women should be seen using their talents in the workplace for the sake of women as a whole.

Ten months on from her wedding day Charlotte was sure she was pregnant. She cornered Maggie the Jarlshavn howdie, on her way home from school.

'Christina, would you like to run on in front? I'll just be a minute. I'll catch you up.'

'All right Mother.' Six year old Christina liked to walk by herself sometimes. It made her feel grownup and important. 'See you in a minute.'

'Maggie,' Charlotte turned to the midwife. 'I need to ask you – do you think I could be well – you know – pregnant?'

'Well,' said Maggie. 'Do you think you are?'

'Well, I think I might be.'

12

It didn't take long for Maggie to agree that Charlotte was indeed probably pregnant. The two parted with Maggie's promise to call up and see her soon.

Alexander was pleased about her pregnancy. Pleased, but apprehensive as he remembered what had gone before. He and Margery had been through the deaths of three of their children. While Margery had been fine during all her pregnancies, except with wee Kenneth whose birth had been premature and who died soon after, he kept thinking about the vulnerability of it all and how many babies and children were lost.

Charlotte was fine to begin with. She was delighted to be pregnant and coped well with morning sickness. Edie and Meg were a great help. While Meg took over Christina's morning routine, Edie took early tea with arrowroot or ginger biscuits (which were reported to be just the thing for morning sickness) to Charlotte in bed. Once up and properly breakfasted, she was still in time to walk Christina up to school and carry on with her work. Christina had no idea why their usual morning pattern had changed and probably didn't even notice.

Alexander usually left for work quite early and took no part in the morning school routine. So he was away when Charlotte at fourteen weeks pregnant, experienced pain and bleeding as she was dressing. Fortunately Edie was not far away.

'Edie, Edie.'

'Yes, Miss, I mean Mrs Sinclair.' Edie had never grown out of the habit of calling Charlotte 'Miss'. She ran through.

'Oh Edie, there's blood. There shouldn't be blood. Oh Edie, my baby…'

'Right Miss, back to bed. I'll get Meg.'

Charlotte miscarried later that day. Dr Taylor and Maggie both appeared as soon as they were called but when they saw what was happening, they shook their heads.

'Mrs Sinclair, you're losing this one. I'm very sorry. Did you have any pain before today?'

'Only a wee ache last night. I went to bed early.'

'Hmm. That was probably the beginning of it. Now we'll just have to let it happen. Stay in bed for now.' He consulted with Maggie.

'Maggie will see you later this morning and Meg knows where she is going to be, just in case she needs to send for her. I'll be in again later on. I'm very sorry.'

Edie took Christina to school that day and broke the news to Ina Manson, the head teacher.

'Oh I'm sorry. She was doing so well too. I'll be down to see her in a few days when she's feeling like a visitor.'

Edie also had the job of telling Alexander.

'I'll be right there.' He slammed the Harbour office door shut, put up his OUT notice and almost ran back to Birkenshaw. He arrived home to the news that Charlotte had indeed miscarried.

'Oh my love.' He held her hand as he knelt by the bedside. 'That you should have to go through this. How can I help you?' Charlotte smiled at him through her tears.

'Just by being there,' she said. 'Are you all right?'

'Och, I'm just so worried about you.'

'I'll be fine. But – but I'm so sad about our baby.'

13

'So am I.' They wept together.

Downstairs the business of running Birkenshaw carried on.

'Where's mother?' Christina came in from school. 'Why wasn't she at school today? I missed her and so did everybody else.'

'Your mother isn't very well today.' Meg took her hand. 'She's in her bed. Would you like to come up and see her?'

'Mother what's the matter?'

'Oh just a sore tummy. I'll be better tomorrow, you'll see.'

'When are you coming back to school? We have the reading to finish and the Nature table to do.'

'Who helped you today?'

'Mrs Manson. She was very busy. She stayed mostly in our class and ran through to the big ones. Then she put Frank Adamson in charge of them and Ann Baxter came and she helped us with our reading and spelling.'

Magnus, home from his final year at school in Lerwick for the weekend came in. By this time Charlotte was up and sitting in a chair. Alexander met him in the front hall.

'Magnus, come in, I need to tell you something.'

'Father, is everything all right?'

'Well – that's what I wanted to speak to you about – it's Charlotte she's …'

'Is she all right,' Magnus burst out.

'Yes, she will be, but she was expecting a baby, and I'm afraid she's lost it this time.'

'This time – you're surely not going to let her go through it again are you?'

'Magnus, I think that's up to Charlotte and me.'

The boy took a deep breath. Don't have a row. *Don't* have a row. He swallowed hard.

'Yes, yes, of course. I'm sorry. How is she?'

'Well, very sad of course but she's making steady progress.'

'When did it happen?'

'On Tuesday. She's in her room. She'd like you to go up if you want to.'

'Does Christina know?'

'No. Not necessary.'

'No, she doesn't need to know. Can I go up now?'

'Yes, go on. She'll be glad to see you.'

He opened the door softly and looked at her sitting there. She turned the page quietly. Then, sensing the hovering figure she looked up, saw him and smiled.

'Magnus, come in. Don't stand at the door.'

'Charlotte, I'm so sorry. Was it very bad? Are you all right?' The questions of a schoolboy, knowing, yet not knowing. He went forward and held her hand.

'Magnus, I'll be fine. It's sad but, we just, get on with it.'

'What can I get you? Water? Tea? Anything?'

'Nothing thanks. It's good to see you back. Sorry you returned to bad news. Now, tell me about your week. What have you been doing? How's Lowrie?'

Ina Manson came to visit. She was Charlotte's superior and mentor at school and therefore had to see that Charlotte's work at school was covered until she could return. They were also great friends – had been since Charlotte arrived in Shetland in 1894.

'You just take your time in getting fit.' Ina sipped her tea. 'We'll manage fine.'

Charlotte smiled. She knew Ina Manson would say something like that. But she also knew how busy she would be and how tired she would become with two classes to see to.

'I'll be back as soon as I can.'

'You just take your time.' Ina stood up and brushed the crumbs off her skirt into the fireplace. 'See you in a few days.'

Six months later Charlotte was sitting in the same chair in the same situation. This time Alexander was adamant.

'Charlotte, I don't want you going back to school.'

'But Alexander…'

'But, nothing. Look at you. Two miscarriages in one year and you look exhausted. This time you must listen to me. Look.' His tone took a persuasive turn. 'I know you want a baby. I want one too. But you have to look after yourself. Give yourself a chance.'

Charlotte gave in. She had to give notice to Ina Manson and the School Board. Alexander as Board chairman returned from the meeting when her resignation had been discussed. He reported that the Board was very sorry to lose her but quite understood.

Charlotte cried, talking to Ina about it. 'I did so love teaching and knowing and caring for all the children.'

'I know,' said Ina. 'But maybe Alexander has a point. It'll do you good to have a break with only home things to think about. And you'll be really rested and fit for when you fall again.'

'Fall,' repeated Charlotte, smiling. 'It's a funny word used like that.'

'Thought that would make you smile. I wish people would just say "become pregnant".'

'Ina, I don't know when you'll manage that without folk going all embarrassed.'

'Aye, but we're all mixed up with ideas of sin and fornication and such-like things. Never mind. I'll look forward to hearing of you being fit and pregnant again soon. There, I said it.' She went away smiling, to make arrangements for another teacher to take over Charlotte's class. Charlotte's third pregnancy ended in a stillborn baby boy born five weeks early.

'Poor wee man.' Maggie sat with her as she cried. 'Why did he not breathe Maggie?'

'Some babies just don't. Maybe something happens before they're born, or during labour. Looking at him, I don't think his heart had been stopped for long.'

'I wish I could see him.'

'Well why don't you. It might help you. He's lying in the wee room through there – all dressed.'

'Yes,' Charlotte sat up. 'But Maggie, Alexander should see him too. Could we do it together do you think?' A few minutes later, she heard Alexander's step at the door.

'Hello.' He leant over and kissed her tear stained face.

'Alexander, I want to see the baby.'

'I know. Maggie's gone to get him. We'll see him together.'

'Do you still want to call him "Alexander"?'

'I don't see why not. That's what we planned and he should have his name. "Alexander John", after your father too.'

The door opened and Maggie entered, carrying the small bundle.

'Here, my dear.' She placed the still baby into Charlotte's arms. 'I'll leave you for a few moments.' Charlotte looked at the wee face, undid the shawl, examined the tiny hands and fingers, the perfect features.

'Wee Alexander.' Again they cried together. But this time, they could see and remember for whom they were crying. That here was someone real was made all the more so when Maggie came back with something.

'I don't know how you feel about this.' She hesitated. 'Not many people do this, but when I was washing him I made hand and foot prints for you to keep. I wasn't sure if you'd want them but now I see you with him I think you might like to have them.' She held out the blue card with the tiny prints.

'Oh Maggie, how kind. We'll keep those for ever. Thank you, thank you.'

Alexander was unable to speak. He put out his arms and held his wife and baby. They sat together until Charlotte stirred.

'I think we should let this boy go now.' She kissed the little face, handed the baby to his father who held him closely for a moment before handing him back to Maggie.

The door clicked gently behind her and their baby was away, leaving them not quite empty-handed but with a tangible memory on their looking back on that day.

Now she had little Hannah. She hummed to herself as she walked along towards the Birkenshaw gate. Perhaps the next would be a boy. She was so happy with her girl but she knew Alexander had wanted a boy. He'd admitted it before the birth..

'A son would be perfect, Charlotte,' he said one dark evening just after Christmas. 'Just perfect,' he repeated. Charlotte looked at him.

'But, we can't choose. You wouldn't be too upset if it's a girl, would you?'

'No, no,' he said hastily, 'but, well you know, a man needs sons…'

Charlotte was silent. There was no point in arguing. Sometimes it was like this with Alexander. You couldn't argue with very set ideas – it just led to sore feelings. So Charlotte just waited.

The baby was a girl. Maggie was in attendance as usual, along with Dr Taylor. The labour was short and sharp. When the baby was born Maggie swiftly dried and wrapped her in warmed towels before handing her to her mother. The wee girl looked at her mother with wide eyes. Charlotte loved her instantly. She wondered what Alexander would say.

'Well,' he said later after he had been called in. 'Well, she's very nice. I would have liked a son, but, there's always a next time and she's a pretty little thing.'

Christina was much more enthusiastic. 'Mother, she's lovely. A wee sister. Oh I always wanted a sister. Can I hold her?'

Magnus had written from Aberdeen:

I am so happy for you that all has gone well this time. Now please go slowly, don't do too much and take care of my new little sister for me. I'll see you all in the holidays.

16

Yours affly., Magnus.

Now the little girl was thriving, smiling at the adoring admirers who peeped at her, held her when allowed, and was learning fast that one squawk brought Christina or Edie or her now quite won over father rushing to her side. In vain Charlotte said, 'You'll spoil her'. The baby was the darling of the house. In the meantime, Charlotte had recovered so well that she could almost contemplate having another baby. Not quite yet, but well, sometime in the future.

Chapter 3

'Mother,' Christina popped her head round the door. 'I'm back.'

'Hello, how was school today?'

'Oh, fine, but Mother, don't you think I could go to school in Lerwick after the summer holidays. I'll be twelve and a half and everybody else is going.'

'Everybody?'

'Yes, well nearly everybody. Well I know Gertie Laurenson isn't going but she doesn't want to go. And I do. It would do me so much good.' Christina was very serious. 'I really need to do this. Mrs Manson was speaking about it today and says it's very good to widen our horizons. If Mrs Manson says that, can I go please?' She looked at Charlotte pleadingly. 'Please Mother.'

'But Christina, it's six miles, and you couldn't go there and back every day.'

'But I could stay in the new girls' boarding house. Just like Magnus stayed with Mrs Blance. Mrs Blance still takes boys but Mrs Manson says that Mrs Blance's cousin, Mrs Anderson, is going to be taking girls from August. Oh Mother, please.'

'Well Christina,' Charlotte got up from her seat and looked out of the window at Hannah's hands waving around in the pram. 'Christina, I can't say anything without Father. You know that.'

'Yes I know, but if *you* feel 'yes' it will help *him* to say yes.' Christina looked at her. Charlotte had to laugh.

'You're a wee besom. Well I don't know…'

'Mother,' Christina felt she was winning. 'Look, you know I want to be a nurse?' Charlotte nodded. 'Well I really need the extra education.'

'You've been listening to Mrs Manson.' Charlotte knew Mrs Manson felt this way about girls' education: that girls should be given the same chance as boys. In theory she agreed – she had always felt this way. She had not been able to go to secondary school and had worked her way up, staying on at the primary school, doing extra subjects, becoming a pupil teacher before finally going to teacher training college in Aberdeen. Now things were moving on. Why shouldn't girls get the opportunity?

'Mother?'

'Right,' Charlotte said. 'I know what you want and I can only sympathise. I would have liked that for myself, I suppose. But you must understand that Father will have the final say.'

'Oh Mother, thank you.'

'Don't smile too soon. You're not there yet.'

'No, but, you know, if you say you agree … Well I'm sure he'll…'

'Don't count your chickens. Father will maybe give you an outright "no". Anyway have you thought this through? Do you really want to be away from us all week? Won't you be homesick?'

'Oh yes, I expect so, we've talked about this…'

'Oh you have, have you?'

'Yes, Jeanie and Mamie and I particularly want to go but we are a wee bit worried because we haven't been away from home before. But we thought if we were together we would be able to help each other and be company for each other. Mother we've been through the whole school together. We all started on the same day. It would be so good to go on together.'

'What do Jeanie and Mamie's parents say?'

'Well,' Christina hesitated, 'I think they're thinking about it.'

'Certainly not.' Alexander's voice was firm.

'Oh Father,' Christina pleaded. 'Please, this is what I really want to do.'

'But you're just a little girl. The idea of your going away to Lerwick at the age of twelve. It's just ridiculous.'

'But it's not away, away. It's only six miles, and I would be home at the week-ends. I'm not really so little. I'll be thirteen in October. Please Father. I really will work hard.'

'Charlotte,' he appealed. 'Don't you agree with me? Christina's too young. She'll get all the education she needs here in Jarlshavn.'

They were sitting in the parlour after tea. Hannah was in her cot for the evening. She looked at Alexander. He looked very stubborn. Inwardly she sighed.

'What about – what about …'

'Well?'

'Well, if you like, I could go and have a chat with Mrs Manson. This is all pretty new, to have a girls' boarding house in Lerwick. They must have discussed it up at the school.'

'Hmm, well now come to think about it, the Board did talk about some such thing at the last meeting.'

'And what did the Board think?'

'Some of the Board thought it was quite a good idea. Some thought it was rubbish – giving girls ideas above themselves. Some think girls should stay at home. As long as they can read and write, count and cook and sew, yes and maybe play the piano a little. Then that's enough.'

'And what do you think?'

'Ach, I'm married to you. You've made me think that girls can go further. But…' he looked at Christina. 'Not yet. Christina's far too young.'

'But, Alexander, this is the way things are going. If we don't let Christina go, and I quite see there's no law saying she has to go, but if we say "no" now, then she'll be at school here and her peers will go to Lerwick.'

'What's "peers", Mother?'

'Peers, Christina, they're your friends – no, more than friends – those who are at the same stage as you.'

'Oh.' Christina subsided.

'Anyway,' Charlotte continued. 'Christina's peers will go to Lerwick, have a broader education and experience than a primary school can provide. She'll be here.'

'What's wrong with 'here'? Anyway, you stayed at primary school and look how well you got on.'

19

'Yes I know, but Alexander the world's changing. We have to change too and allow our children to change. The subjects they're teaching are widening all the time. There'll come a time when all the children will have to go to secondary school.'

'Hmph. I can see you want her to go.'

'I don't want to lose Christina. I'll miss her so much. But, yes, I think it would be good for her, in her best interests to go.'

'What's this woman like – this Mrs Anderson?'

'Well I haven't met her – but she *is* Mrs Blance's cousin and she was so kind to Magnus and Lowrie.'

He heaved a sigh. 'Well I don't know. I never thought I'd see the day when I'd be letting my own twelve year old daughter into the hands of strangers. I don't know what Margery would think.'

'I think Margery would have been happy to allow Christina to take advantage of such an opportunity.'

'Oh Father, please.' Christina went over to him and held his hand tightly. 'I'll make you so proud of me. Please ...'

'Let me think lassie – now, you'd be home every weekend, and in the holidays. It's a pity we don't have one of these telephones that are coming in down south to make instant contact if need be. But we can make sure that Mrs Anderson can send an immediate letter if there was a problem. I'm not having problems stored up till the weekend like we did with Magnus.' He turned to Charlotte.

'Could you go and talk to Mrs Manson? Find out who else is going, see what she thinks, and then we'll see. I'm not promising mind. I still need to be convinced that this is the best way of getting you educated. I would really rather have you at home. But – well I'm prepared to consider it.'

'Oh Father, thank you.' Christina's eyes shone.

'Thank you Alexander,' Charlotte leaned over and touched him briefly. 'I'll go and see Ina tomorrow and see what she has to say.'

'Oh she'll be all for it.' he responded gloomily. 'Women always are. And,' he hesitated, 'I – I, suppose I can see the point, but she's my wee girl and it's very difficult...' He put his hand over his eyes. Charlotte caught Christina's eye and signalled to her to go to him.

'Father.' The arms went gently around his neck. 'Father, don't be upset. I love you so much.'

'I love you too. Now,' with a touch of asperity, 'what's the time? Goodness me, is it not time you were heading for bed? And, I think I can hear Hannah.'

Later that night when the house was quiet, they lay together.

'I was so proud of you this evening,' Charlotte said quietly.

'What do you mean?'

'Well you were big enough to move from one very strong stance to thinking about Christina's point of view. I think that was a very difficult thing for you to do, especially...'

'Especially? Especially what?'

'Well...'

'You mean because I'm a man?'

'Well, in this instance, yes, I think so. It must be very difficult for men who have been used to one idea of women, to see women asking for and even demanding change and more education.'

'Well it is. You should hear how some of the men speak to their wives.'

'So doesn't that make you see that change is necessary?'

'Yes of course, and anyway as I said earlier, I'm married to you. I'm being indoctrinated.' He held her closely. 'Mind you, I quite like being indoctrinated – let's do some more. It's a nice feeling.' She laughed and drew closer.

Chapter 4

Magnus was home for the holidays. Charlotte reached the door as he was getting down from the gig. He looked well, broader across the shoulders, swinging his bags down with gusto. He looked up and waved as she came down the steps.

'Charlotte, hello, I'm back.'

'So I see. Good to see you.' He looked at Hannah.

'Well baby sister, you've grown since Easter. Hasn't she?'

'She's a good wee soul.'

'So she should be, the amount of attention she gets.' Alexander came out on to the steps.

'Here.' He held his arms out for the baby. 'Papa's turn now.' He carried her tenderly back up the steps. Magnus's eyes met Charlotte. They smiled at the doting father behind the brusque exterior. Magnus picked up his bags.

'It's good to be home. You've no idea.' He stopped. 'Well I suppose you have, having left home in Towie to go to Aberdeen – but you know what I mean.'

'Yes I do.' Charlotte understood. It was quite a step to leave home when travelling was such an event that some folk in West Aberdeenshire had never left home in their whole lives. What would they want to go away for?

They walked up the steps to the front door of the house Alexander and Charlotte had planned together before their marriage in 1898. Magnus was sixteen then, a schoolboy with sore memories of his mother dying, and rows and anger with what he saw as a stubborn unsympathetic father.

Now he was grown up. Charlotte noticed it more each time he came home. His head was up, he was more confident, he approached Alexander more as an equal but retained the deference that a son accorded his father. There was still a guard there, but Magnus coped better now with his father's authoritative ways.

Charlotte preceded him into the house. It was good to see him. They had shared so much since she arrived in Shetland, Charlotte a young teacher of twenty and Magnus a boy of twelve. Through that difficult time when Margery, his mother, was very ill with consumption before she died, Charlotte supported him in his anger and despair. They came to know each other very well. There was a further difficult time coping with local gossip, a time of quite considerable unhappiness. Now he was on his way: his third year at medical school over with the summer holidays heralding entry into year four if all had gone according to plan.

'How did the exams go, Magnus?'

'Passed,' he said with a big smile. 'Isn't that great?'

'Oh, well done. Now you can relax for a few weeks.'

'Well I will for a wee while anyway.'

'Alexander hear this. Go on Magnus, tell him.' Alexander, on his knees where he was depositing Hannah on the sofa, looked up.

'Father, we just heard on the last day of term. The results were posted, and I passed all the year exams.'

'Oh, very good.' Alexander, ever formal, shook his son's hand warmly. 'I'm so glad.' Rare praise indeed – positive feedback was not one of Alexander's strong points. Charlotte moved to his side to join in.

'That's excellent Magnus. Now it's time for some fresh air.'

'Yes, but you should keep up your book reading Magnus. Don't let go, my boy. I agree you've done well but it's all too easy to slip back.'

Charlotte could feel rather than see Magnus withdrawing before he said carefully, 'Yes Father, of course,' before turning the subject. 'And how are you all?'

Charlotte sighed inwardly. Couldn't Alexander have sounded a bit more enthusiastic? Relationships between father and son, always fragile, had shown signs of easing, but this giving out didactic directions rather than encouragement was sometimes difficult to swallow. After all Magnus was twenty-two.

'Oh we're all fine,' she said. 'Magnus,' she hurried on, anxious to lift the sudden tension, 'let's get your things upstairs. 'Oh, and here's Christina.' Magnus turned as Christina came through the door.

'Christina, my best friend.' He crossed the room in a couple of bounds and held her in a bear hug.

'Ooh, watch my hair.' She broke free, flushed and laughing and patted her disarranged hair. 'I spent ages this morning getting it right.'

Hannah shouted from the sofa.

'Oh the poor wee thing, she's feeling forgotten.' Charlotte picked her up. 'Come on my girl, feeding time. I'll leave you to get organised.'

As Charlotte sat upstairs feeding the baby, the house resounded with feet running up and downstairs, high-decibel voices as Magnus and Christina called to one another, and the Alexander's quieter voice as he retired to his study for fifteen minutes with the newspaper before lunch. She smiled to the baby then took a deep breath and relaxed. But a niggling doubt in her mind remained. Every nuance of the delicate father-son relationship showed her that any goodwill lay on the surface only.

So, Magnus's holiday began. He was maturing fast and was more independent. He loved medicine and that evening after tea he said he was sure that this was for him. He was firm in his reasoning.

'The thing is, I remember what it was like when Mother was so ill. It was devastating. And there was nothing we could do. Oh I know, you pretended, or tried' – he modified his words as Alexander looked up in protest – 'to make her better. But eventually even Mother said it was no good. I think Dr Taylor knew from the time he diagnosed consumption. That was long before I knew, remember?' He looked at his father.

'Yes, I know,' said Alexander, 'but we didn't tell you for all the best reasons. Best for you, I mean.'

'Ay, well. Maybe you thought they were best but you'll never know how I felt knowing something was going on but not knowing what. Anyway,' he spread out his hands expressively. 'It's all in the past. But what I want to emphasise is that we could do nothing for her but keep her comfortable until she died. There *was* nothing else. I want to

23

be a doctor so that I can do that, yes, because the care and all that goes with it is important, but I also want to help more, find cures for these awful diseases, help folk not to die before their time. That's all.' He sat back and looked at them.

'Right. Well.' Alexander's eyes met Charlotte's. He cleared his throat. 'Quite a speech.'

'Yes,' Charlotte said. 'Well said, Magnus. You just carry on. We're proud of you.'

'So am I.' Christina gazed at him with adoring eyes. 'I think I'll be a nurse. I've been saying it haven't I Mother? And,' she turned to Magnus. 'I'm going to school in Lerwick after the holidays. It's all arranged.'

'Is this true?' Magnus, diverted from his personal passion, squeezed her hand. 'That's really good. How did you manage that?' His eyes full of mischief laughed at them as he said, 'Come on Charlotte, I'm sure you've been up to your persuasive tricks. Father would never have agreed alone.'

'Magnus…' Charlotte began but Alexander interrupted.

'No, no Charlotte, it's all right. Yes, Magnus,' he continued. 'I admit I was not too keen to begin with but Charlotte has convinced me and Mrs Manson has been telling us about the new arrangements in Lerwick at Mrs Anderson's house. (Mrs Blance's cousin, you understand).'

'Oh I remember her. Lowrie and I used to go round and see her. She's a great baker. She was always dishing out scones and cakes with homemade jam. You'll like her Christina. Hope you don't get too fat.'

'Magnus,' she cried, 'I'm not fat.'

'I never said you were, but you better watch out on Mrs Anderson's baking. Anyway you'll be able to work it off on the playing field. I hear they are getting a physical drill mistress for girls – yes,' as Christina gasped with excitement. 'It's good isn't it? After all why shouldn't girls keep fit as well as the boys?'

'How do you know this?'

'Oh well, Lowrie was telling me the latest news. Anyway,' he smiled at her. 'That's good. I'm glad.' Inwardly he said, and let her to spread her wings a little, away from Father's eyes.

Alexander's eyes were widening at every word.

'Physical drill?' he said. 'You mean gymnastic exercises?'

'Oh yes, Father. In fact I think some people are even beginning to call it gym.'

'For girls?'

'Yes, Father. Is there a problem?' Magnus's voice was innocent but Charlotte was watching and smelt trouble.

'That's all right Alexander,' she put in. 'I don't see a problem there. It will be very good for them. After all, part of my teaching course at Aberdeen included physical drill or exercises – this is just an extension of that idea. It'll be good to have a dedicated drill teacher for girls. How forward-thinking.'

'But is it good for them?'

'Yes.' Charlotte stuck to her point. 'After all, to be physically healthy is as important for girls as boys. You're always taking Christina out for walks.'

'Well, but, that's different. I really don't know if she should go now…'

24

'Now Alexander,' Charlotte said, as Christina gasped. 'You have said she can go. We've discussed the details. This is one little detail that we didn't know about but what's the problem? I taught drill to all my little ones ...'

'That's exactly it,' he interrupted. 'They were little. You're talking about big girls here. Supposing someone saw them.'

'Who would see them? And does it matter? Oh Alexander, they'll be much better keeping fit like this than tied up in whalebone corsets. That may come soon enough.'

'Anyway, Father,' Magnus said. 'They'll be in classes by themselves. They won't be doing it with the boys.'

'I should think not.' Alexander took a deep breath. 'Look, I don't want to be an old fashioned father here but this is my daughter we are talking about.' He looked over at Christina who was sitting, eyes popping, listening to the debate.

'Anyway, it will be part of the curriculum. Christina will be expected to do it.' Charlotte was outwardly calm. Inwardly she fervently wished that Magnus had kept quiet about drill or 'gym' or whatever the latest term for it was.

'Well, I suppose we'll have to go along with it.' Alexander was still doubtful. 'But just you take care – do you hear?'

'Yes Father,' Christina's voice was meek. Long experience had taught her when compliance was necessary.

Magnus went out early next morning. It was broad daylight. The early morning hours of the simmer-dim were long past and the sun was well up. He breathed in the air, revelling in its freshness.

'Halloo, Magnus.' He looked, waved. It was Lowrie, his long-time friend and confidant. Lowrie, who had talked to Magnus about illness and death, when his mother was ill. The two boys had cried together as Lowrie had revealed his personal understanding of illness in the family. It was Lowrie who had moved to the Anderson Educational Institute in Lerwick with Magnus and progressed through the school with him. It was Lowrie with whom Magnus had kept going on countless physical exercises and games. It was Lowrie who had picked up the pieces when Magnus was involved in a fight with Alfred Twatt over gossip surrounding Charlotte and Alexander. It was Lowrie's astuteness that had guessed that Magnus might be just a little in love with Charlotte himself, thus making doubly difficult any feelings he might have about his father's re-marriage.

Lowrie, too, was home for the holidays. He had chosen to go to Edinburgh for his Law course. The holidays were times of comparing notes, telling stories, walking the hills and roads of Shetland, going out in boats, fishing for piltocks, trout and other line-caught fish, and, talking, always talking.

He came up, panting.

'How did you do?'

'Passed. You?'

'Me too.' This was almost a ritual now.

'What was the worst?'

'Oh I don't know. Looking back, I think anatomy has been very difficult – it's so detailed. There's so much of it. But we passed that last year. But we have to keep remembering it. And now diagnosing diseases is hard. It's so easy to trip up. And don't the consultants know it. We really feel they're out to catch us. How about you? Seen any good court cases lately?'

'Oh yes, listen to this one. There was this man and he had been apprehended for…' The voices disappeared as the two young men walked away up the hill in the sunshine.

'So how are things at Birkenshaw?' Lowrie asked as they stopped to draw breath.

'All right, I think. Father's as usual, telling me to work and I'm saying, "Yes Father". Hannah is growing. Christina's fine, she's going to Lerwick after the holidays. Charlotte has worked hard on that idea to get Father to agree. Then I threw a spanner in the works by mentioning that the girls would be getting physical drill. Father nearly had an apoplectic fit.'

'Now you're showing off with your medical terms. Why don't you say "stroke" and be done with it? Anyway, did you take it *ad avizandum*?' The competition for the latest new words was an on-going thing.

'Well,' Magnus conceded. 'It *was* nearly enough to change father's mind. Charlotte again came to the rescue.'

'How *is* Charlotte?' Lowrie looked sideways at Magnus.

'She's fine.' Magnus started walking again. 'She's very busy with Hannah of course. But, she seems in good health and copes very well with Father.' He pointed out to sea, changing the subject. 'Look at Foula today – clear isn't she. Do you think we'll get a chance to go out these holidays.'

'I'd like to.' Lowrie, diverted, looked at 'the edge of the world' in the distance. 'We could maybe get a lift on the mail-boat one day. But let's go down now and look at the boats. I think they'll need a bit of attention before we go out.'

'I know,' Magnus interrupted, 'let's go in past Birkenshaw first for a fly cup. It seems ages since breakfast. I'm starving.'

Summer slipped past. One fine afternoon Magnus came round the corner of the house, back from one of his endless walks with Lowrie and spotted Charlotte weeding a bit of the garden she particularly liked. She was alone. Edie had taken Hannah off in her pram to wheel her down to the harbour and chat with her friends and indulge in some vicarious admiration as the young ladies cooed over the baby.

'It's warm,' he said, flinging himself down on the grass beside her. She looked up from her task.

'Yes, but how often do we say that in Shetland? It's a lovely day.' She wiped the back of her hand across her hot forehead. 'Here, have a drink. I always carry water out with me. It's behind the seat, in the shade.'

He poured a glass. 'Want some?'

'I'll have some in a minute. You go first.' He drank deeply. 'That's good. The old supply is still keeping up then.'

26

'Yes, we seem to have plenty of water and it's very good.' She sat down on the bench beside him and drew off her gardening gloves. 'Yes, please'. She nodded in response to the proffered glass. 'That's better.'

'Where's Christina?'

'Away seeing Jeanie and Mamie. They're having a meeting, she says, to talk about going to Lerwick. They're very excited about it.'

'How did the visit to Mrs Anderson go?'

'Oh, it was fine. Christina looked as though butter wouldn't melt in her mouth, was extremely polite, Mrs Anderson told your Father and me what a nice girl she was and he asked a lot of questions about house rules.'

'And are there? A lot of house rules I mean?'

'Well, nothing we wouldn't expect, all to do with meal times and light-out times and not shouting and ladylike behaviour – all that sort of thing. Alexander seemed quite happy.'

'And were you happy?' Magnus knew how close Charlotte and Christina were.

'Well, yes,' Charlotte spoke slowly. 'I think so. I shall miss her so much, but I truly believe that this is the best course of action to take. And this is the only way we can do it. Now that Peter Middleton has started regular runs with his motor bus to Jarlshavn from Lerwick, and on a Friday at the right time, it will make life that bit easier.'

'You mean you're not going to make her walk?' Magnus teased. 'I had to walk. It's not fair.'

'Magnus. You know we couldn't let her walk the six miles unescorted.' As Charlotte rose to the bait, Magnus held out his hands laughing, 'All right all right, only joking. I know she couldn't do that. In fact,' he went on, 'I'm amazed Father is even allowing her to come with Peter Middleton.'

'Well, of course that was another discussion,' Charlotte admitted. 'But seeing the others will be there, and we know Peter so well, he gave in. So, it's all arranged. She starts next week.'

'That's good.'

Magnus fell silent. He sat twiddling a piece of grass. He sometimes found it difficult to be alone with Charlotte. She officially was his stepmother. But how could he feel like a stepson when he was so near her in age? After all there were only eight years between them. Long ago, when he was only fifteen he had realised with something akin to horror that what he was feeling for Charlotte was love. It had to be love. Why else should he have been so angry when the very idea of marriage between his father and Charlotte was mentioned? It was anathema to him. To him, it was disgusting: his father, an old man, and the young, fresh, beautiful Charlotte.

Deep down, he knew there was no reason to think this. Many older men married younger women. But Magnus soon realised that his anger was because he loved Charlotte himself and there was nothing he could do about it. He told no-one, not even Lowrie. On the other hand, he was pretty sure that perspicacious Lowrie had suspected something. But he had refused to admit anything and now the subject was buried.

Chapter 5

On the Monday evening of the following week the Birkenshaw gig pulled up in front of the house and Alexander and Charlotte stepped down. Magnus ran down the steps to them.

'Is everything all right?'

'Yes,' said Charlotte. 'Stressful on our part I think. Christina is so pleased with being in Lerwick that I don't think she realises what a big step she has taken, going off to school like this.'

'I don't think she realises anything.' Alexander looked tired.

'Come on.' Charlotte tucked her hand into his arm. 'Let's go in. Magnus, please would you – ?' she looked at the horse standing patiently waiting for his next move.

'Of course.' Magnus went to the horse's head and started leading him away.

'I hope we're not going to regret this.' Alexander began as soon as he sat down.

'Why should we?' Charlotte sat beside him. 'She'll love it once she settles down.'

'Yes, that's as may be, but don't you think we've abrogated our responsibility? We've handed her over.'

'Oh Alexander, it's not like that.'

'Yes it is. I don't know what Margery would be saying if she could see what we're doing.' He shuddered. 'That's the awful thing. She probably can. She's probably thinking what a mess I've made, sending our daughter into the hands of strangers. It's my fault. I gave in and let her do it.'

Charlotte looked at him in dismay. 'Is that what you think?'

'Yes. Christina's my daughter and I should never have given in to this crazy idea. She's only a wee girl and I'm responsible for her.'

'Alexander, *we're* responsible for her.'

'It's not the same. You're not her real mother, never can be. You are Hannah's mother because you gave her life, but you can never be Christina's mother. *She* was Margery. Now she's gone, I'm responsible for Christina, not you.'

'Well, now I know where I stand.' Charlotte got to her feet and faced him. 'Just who has tried to be Mother to Christina all these years? Me. Who got up at night to her when she was crying? Me. Who helped her when she was upset? Who helped her with her homework? Me.' Her voice broke. 'And, I will continue to do so whether you like it or not. I am offended by what you have just said.'

'So would I be.' The voice at the door made them both jump. Magnus entered. 'I couldn't help overhearing. Father what a thing to say to Charlotte.'

'Be quiet, boy. How dare you eavesdrop on a private conversation.'

'I was not eavesdropping. I could hear you miles away, you were speaking so loudly. No wonder Charlotte's offended. How dare you imply that Charlotte is somehow second-best for Christina. Have you no conception how much Charlotte has done for Christina? Have you no idea how much Charlotte means to Christina herself? Christina can't even

28

remember Mother. Charlotte has been a mother to her. And now you're trying to take that away from her. From both of them. Father, I'm ashamed.'

'Be quiet.' Alexander shouted. 'I will not have you speak to me like that.'

'And I will not have you bully Charlotte –' Magnus stopped.

Alexander's face was puce. 'I beg your pardon. What did you say?'

'You heard.' Magnus looked stubbornly at his father. 'Go on, hit me,' he said as his father raised his fist. 'You know you want to. You've been wanting to for ages.'

'No, stop.' Charlotte stepped between them. 'Please stop. I – I can't stand it.' Alexander and Magnus stood glaring at each other.

Magnus turned to her. 'I'm sorry Charlotte. I'll be out at the front if you need me. I won't be far away.' He turned on his heel and walked out. Charlotte and Alexander stood in the sudden silence. Alexander put his hand to his head and backed into his chair.

'Are you all right?'

'Yes… no … I don't know. How could he have said that to me? I'm his father. He'll have to be punished.'

'Alexander, he's twenty two. He's grown up. He's not a wee laddie anymore.'

'Well as long as I am keeping him, he'll watch his manners and mind his tongue.' He groaned. 'All this over a wee lassie going to school. We should have kept her at home. Then none of this would have happened.'

'You think so?'

'What do you mean?'

'Well, don't you think that you and Magnus would have had a big row sooner or later? Don't you think that what you have just said to me about my ability to be a mother to Christina would have come out sooner or later?'

'Oh don't pay any attention to that.' He waved his hand dismissively. 'I shouldn't have said it.'

'No you shouldn't. But the fact remains that you did say it. What can I take from that? That you feel that I am only second-best?'

'Oh that's rubbish.'

'Well. You're implying that. What's going on? What's the problem?'

'The problem is,' he responded, 'that I have, against my better principles allowed my daughter to go into the hands of strangers.'

'Yes, you've said that.' Charlotte kept her voice low. 'But why are you saying this now? Why did you say that about me? No wonder Magnus came in and shouted.'

'Magnus had no right to listen.'

'He couldn't help it. Probably Meg and Edie heard as well. It's just as well we can trust their discretion or this would be all over the village.' Charlotte took a deep breath. 'I'm not happy about what you said to me. In fact I'm very unhappy. I'm going upstairs to see to Hannah. At least I feel I'm her real mother.' Quietly she went away, leaving Alexander alone with his thoughts.

As she crossed the hall to the stairs Magnus came inside. 'Charlotte, are you all right?'

'Yes Magnus, I'll be fine. I must go to Hannah.'

Nursing the baby gave her some comfort. At six months Hannah was growing fast, healthy, smiling and responsive. She still tended to wake later in the evening. Charlotte was not sure if she needed feeding then or if it was habit. Whatever the reason, tending to the baby at this peaceful time gave her such happiness that she had no problems prolonging the habit. She picked up the baby in her long nightgown.

'Oh you are beautiful,' she whispered. 'You could make any sore feelings better.' She sat with the baby at her breast, gazing out into the slowly darkening sky. What do I do next? I know I can never be Christina's birth mother but I feel motherly towards her. I've done my best – and she has responded. I love her and she loves me. It's as simple as that. So that's not the problem. The problem is what Alexander has just said. Is that what he's been thinking all this time? If so then he really has not accepted me. I'm going over the same argument that we had before, after Margery died. It hasn't gone away. How do I cope with it?

Charlotte

I sat there with my baby thinking back to the time of Margery's illness when Margery was so adamant that on her death I should be a replacement mother for Christina and wife to Alexander. I didn't dwell on this so much now. I'd thought we were well past that difficult time. But it seemed as though Alexander deep down felt he should be the decision-making parent for Christina – perhaps the only real parent. But I had been mother to her in every way, other than through birth, for the past nine years. Did this not count for something? Hannah hiccupped and I took her from the breast and sat her up. She dribbled milk sleepily down her chin.

A gentle knock on the door. 'Come in,' I called. It was Magnus.

'Charlotte, I'm going to my room now. I think I'll read my book for a while. Can I get you anything?' He sat on the window seat with his back to the window, looking at me anxiously.

'Magnus, I'm all right. A wee while up here with this little one is very calming. Where's your Father?'

'He's still in the parlour. I could hear the paper rustling as I came past. Charlotte,' he hesitated before continuing. 'What are you going to do?'

'What do you mean?'

'Well, what he said to you was really offensive. You shouldn't let him get away with it. You should…'

'Magnus, I need to think through carefully what was said before I think of doing anything. Sometimes the best thing is to do nothing.'

'But Charlotte, you can't just do nothing. He shouldn't have said those things to you.'

'And, Magnus, he's your father, and I'm his wife and this'll sort itself out. But you need to distance yourself from what you heard your father say to me. Now, I don't want to discuss it any more just now.' I got up and carried Hannah over to her cot, hoping he would take the hint.'

'But Charlotte…'

'Magnus, could you go now please? I need to settle Hannah. Go on, read your book.'
As I reached the cot I turned and looked at him. I smiled to him but he just looked at me.

30

There was such sadness there – I wanted so much to speak further, to comfort him, to tell him that I was there for him but I had to be loyal to Alexander too. I turned away and bent over the cot. As I tucked the baby in I heard the door click as he closed it and went away.

Another tap at the door. After a pause it opened very slowly. Alexander entered. I stood, waiting.

'Charlotte?'

'Yes?' I didn't feel like making it easy for him.

'Charlotte.' He stood at the threshold. 'Can I come in?'

'You are in.'

'Charlotte, it's bed time. Is Hannah asleep?'

'Yes, she's just sleeping now.' I hesitated then made up my mind. 'Alexander, I think I'll sleep here with Hannah tonight.' There was a single bed in the room which I always kept made up in case Hannah was restless or teething.

'Charlotte, I'm not happy about that. You should be in your own bed with me.'

'Well I think that for tonight, I'll be here.'

'Oh Charlotte, come on, just because I said something that you didn't like. That's not fair.'

'Life isn't fair, Alexander. Perhaps you've noticed. Anyway, I didn't just *not like* what you said. You really hit me hard. Now I need to learn how to cope with it. So I'll be fine here for the night.'

'Charlotte, please…' Alexander took a step further into the room.

'Goodnight Alexander. Please don't argue. I'll see you in the morning.'

He turned and made for our bedroom – the room from which I had barred myself. I ran downstairs to check that all was well in the kitchen. This was a nightly ritual. Tonight was no different. Meg sat there, Edie long since away to her own home.

'I'm going to bed now Meg. Is all well?'

'Yes indeed. I'm just about to go myself.' Meg got up with her empty cup and placed it carefully in the sink. With her back to me she said, 'Are you all right?' So she had heard.

'Yes Meg, I'm fine. Hannah is a little restless so I'll sleep in her room with her in case she wakes.'

'That's a good idea. I hope the wee one settles down.' She faced me. 'You look tired. You need a good night's sleep too.' I knew she had not been taken in but we both had to keep up the pretence that all was well.

'Good night Mrs Sinclair.'

'Good night Meg. Sleep well.'

'You too.'

Mrs Sinclair. As I got into the bed in Hannah's room with a stone pig to take the chill off the sheets, I wondered for possibly the first time if I had done the right thing in becoming the second Mrs Sinclair. It had taken a great deal of thought, developing love for Alexander and the need to know that he loved me for myself and not as some sort of surrogate mother with ready-made children. It was only when I was sure, when I saw myself becoming more and more relaxed and comfortable with him that I allowed myself to love him and to contemplate the idea of marriage with him and of course the children. Not that one marries the children but in a situation like this their circumstances loomed large.

It seemed to have worked, till now. Magnus, so near me in age, always refused to call me Mother. This I understood and accepted. We were friends and very close. To Hannah, I was 'Mama' from the start, changing only recently to 'Mother' and engaged completely with me in a mother-daughter relationship. Or so I thought. Was it all going to be spoilt now? Had Alexander all along been thinking the sentiments he displayed this evening? I'd no idea. But the thought that he might not consider me mother enough to Christina to take part in deciding about her schooling or anything else for that matter, hurt me deeply.

Through in his lonely marital bed, Alexander lay unsleeping. His initial considerations were all about himself. After all, I am her father. I should make the decisions. It's my responsibility. He breathed deeply. She's my daughter and in the absence of Margery I have to do my best. But, he argued with himself, Charlotte's there too. She loves Christina. She has been a mother to her. But not really, he thought. She could never be that. She did not go through the pangs of birth for Christina. But does that totally matter in the long run? He was uncomfortably aware of how much Charlotte had done for Christina. How he could not have managed without her. How perhaps Christina might have had to go to live in Orkney with his sister if he had not been able to cope. She had been very keen to 'take her on' as she put it. He shuddered. Perish the thought. He and his sister did not see eye to eye on many things one of which was children's upbringing. Anyway, he thought, I love Charlotte. I was just feeling guilty and unsure about Christina in Lerwick with Mrs Anderson. And blamed Charlotte for it because she thinks it's the best thing to do. Unfortunately I put it the wrong way. I didn't mean to say what I did. I'll tell her in the morning.

But what to do about Magnus? Young puppy. How dare he speak to me like that. His manners are getting worse and worse. Ever since he went sooth. Him and his university ways. He's getting far too uppity. I've a good mind to stop his money. That would show him. Bring him back here. But in his heart he was proud of his boy who was doing so well. He knew that he would do no such thing.

In his room, Magnus was awake. His book, long since cast aside, lay on the floor. He was still angry. Angry at his father for what he had said to Charlotte – how dare that man speak to her like that. Angry at Charlotte for not letting him speak to his father about it and for saying she might do nothing. How could she just do nothing? He was also angry at himself for the way he felt towards Charlotte. He didn't mean this to happen. He thought he'd kept it separate, in a compartment in his brain for all these years. Now, anger was pushing the compartment door open. I can't let that happen. I can't. I must go away before I crack. I'll go on the next boat, back to Aberdeen. Term starts soon – it'll be better this way. He lay in the darkness planning what to do next.

Chapter 6

Lowrie knocked on the back door standing open to the morning sunshine.

''Morning, Meg.'

'Good morning, Lowrie.' Meg smiled at him. She liked Lowrie. 'How are you this fine day? You'll be looking for Magnus, I expect.'

'Is he about?'

'Well he was, but he ran back upstairs for his gansey. He looked as if he was heading for the hill. He needs breakfast first though. Come in yourself and have a cup of tea and a bite. Here he is.'

'Thanks.' Lowrie entered the kitchen as Magnus arrived pulling on his Fair Isle gansey as he came through the kitchen door.

'My, you're late this morning. Not like you.'

'Ach, away.' Magnus looked tired.

'Now, boys.' Meg set the teapot on the table. 'Just you set in, fill yourselves up for the morning.'

'But I've had breakfast.' Lowrie's token protest went unheard.

'If you're going up that hill you need to be fed.'

Magnus was silent. He needed to talk to Lowrie but not yet, not in front of Meg. The best thing to do was be quiet, eat and then get away.

Fifteen minutes and a lot of food later they called their thanks to Meg and set out.

'So, what's the problem.' As soon as they were out of earshot of Birkenshaw, Lowrie spoke.

'What do you mean? Problem? What problem?'

'Come on Magnus, anyone with half an eye could see you're not at your best. You look as though you have not slept all night and you've got the weight of the world on your shoulders. Well? Am I right?'

'It's true,' Magnus admitted. 'I didn't sleep well.'

'Come on then, what's happened?'

'Well, this is completely private family business,' Magnus began.

'So, do you want to tell me?'

'Yes I do, but I feel so bad about doing it. But if I don't I'll feel bad too. I must talk about it.'

'Magnus, I won't tell a soul. If you want to say what's on your mind then pretend you're thinking aloud. Is it your father? Or Christina? Of course she went to Lerwick yesterday. Is that it? But I thought that was all settled.'

'It was.' Magnus sighed. 'Or it seemed to be. But Father had a fit of remorse last night and indulged in some self-recrimination. We finished up at loggerheads.'

'But I don't see why that's making you look so bad.'

'Yes, well, I'll tell you what happened. Then you'll see…'

33

'... Well,' Lowrie looked at Magnus some time later. 'Did you really use the word "bully"?'

'Well, yes,' Magnus said. 'He was bullying her. Verbally. It was awful to hear him, the way he spoke to her. He really put her down. After all she's done. I was furious. I showed it too, I'm afraid.'

'Why do you think you were so angry?'

'Well, anyone would be,' Magnus began, 'It's only natural to defend someone smaller, weaker, you know…' His voice trailed off.

'Yes but, em, don't you think Charlotte can stand up for herself?'

'Well, yes but – here, whose side are you on? I thought you'd be on my side.'

'Of course I'm on your side. What your father said to Charlotte was despicable. But what about you? You leapt in there to Charlotte's defence. Why?'

'Lowrie. Mind your own business. I just did.' Magnus started walking rapidly away from him up the steepest part of the hill.

'Come on Magnus.' Lowrie climbed up beside him. 'Let's get to the bottom of this. What are you going to do now?'

'I'm going back to Aberdeen. On the boat. At the end of the week.'

'But Magnus, term doesn't begin for another month.'

'I know. But I have to go. If I don't, I'll…' he hesitated, breathing quickly, out of breath from climbing too fast, out of kilter from boiling emotions, out of patience with himself for being so uncontrolled, 'I'll…'

'Yes?'

'I'll – oh Lowrie, I don't know what to do.' He sat down on the grass and put his head on his knees. Lowrie looked on deeply troubled. He hadn't seen Magnus cry for many years. Here he was now completely undone. After a moment's consideration he sat down beside Magnus and offered a not too clean handkerchief.

'Mop up.'

'Thanks.' Magnus blew his nose loudly. 'What a mess I'm in.'

Lowrie gave him a few minutes and then said, 'There's more, isn't there?'

'What do you mean?' Magnus looked up, sniffing and blowing.

'Well, if it were only a row with your father, you wouldn't be in this state. What is it Magnus? Is it Charlotte?'

Magnus nodded miserably.

'And?'

'Oh Lowrie, I love her. What can I do? Think about it. I'm in love with my father's wife. Now you see why I have to go away.'

'But you can't stay away for ever.'

'Well I can for just now.'

'Are you sure?' This was unknown territory for Lowrie. He'd felt various sexual urges – what young blood of twenty-two hadn't – but nothing that could be constituted as that mysterious condition known as being 'in love'. He had suspected for many years that Magnus had an unduly soft spot for Charlotte. He knew about Magnus's schoolboy difficulties before Charlotte married Alexander. He had challenged Magnus and been

34

hotly refuted on his feelings for Charlotte. Unconvinced, Lowrie had let the matter drop. Since then the subject had not been mentioned.

'Does Charlotte have any idea?'

'No.' Magnus was aghast. 'And she mustn't find out.' He leaned over. 'Lowrie, listen, no one must know, but most of all, Charlotte. D'you hear me?'

'Yes, yes.' Lowrie knitted his brows. 'But I'm just trying to think how I can help.'

'I don't think you can. I don't think anyone can. I thought I was getting over it. I thought hard work and enjoying Aberdeen and so on was helping. But then I heard Father getting at her and I just boiled inside. I'll have to go but I'm glad I've told you – I think.'

'Well you know what they say about a trouble shared.' Lowrie pulled up some grass by his side and twiddled the stems. 'I won't tell anyone, I promise.' Never having experienced love himself he couldn't quite empathise with the angst that Magnus was enduring. But he could see that his usually happy and hardworking friend was in dire need of support.

'All right,' he said. 'You say you have to go sooth.' Magnus nodded.

'Have you thought about your arrangements?'

'Well I should contact my landlady Mrs Gibson first but I think I'll just go. Almost the last thing she said to me was to return when I liked.' He smiled as he remembered the small plump figure waving him off at the start of the holidays.

'Cheerie bye Magnus.' Mrs Gibson had come to the door to, as she put it, 'make sure he went'. 'Have a good holiday. See ye end of September or so, but dinna forget, your bed's aye here. Aa'm nae lettin it oot this summer, so you can come back fan ye like.'

'So you see,' Magnus explained, 'I think I can just turn up.'

'Have you enough money?'

'Yes, I think so. You know Father gives me a monthly allowance. It's the same every month, term and holidays and I have to budget with that. Help me to understand that money doesn't grow on trees *he* says.'

'Can you manage.'

'Yes I think so. I have enough for the boat and a bit over. If I get stuck before term begins I can always do some casual odd jobs – but keep that under your hat – if Father heard I was casualling, he would be even more angry. As it is I'm surprised he hasn't had me in and threatened to stop my allowance. After all it's the only hold he has over me. It's the only way he can get at me.'

'Yes but I don't think he would do that. After all how could he explain it out and about? If he took away your allowance, you'd have to leave Aberdeen and there is no rationale for that.'

Magnus brightened. 'That's true.'

'Right,' Lowrie turned organiser. 'You need to book your passage on the boat, tell your father and Charlotte, and pack your bags.'

'Put like that,' Magnus half-smiled, 'it seems relatively easy.'

'I see,' Alexander looked down at his desk. 'So you're going back because you feel you need to work?'

'Yes Father. I've had a very good break but I feel I need to get a head start before the term begins.'

It was two days later and Magnus's plans for the overnight journey to Aberdeen were underway. Alexander's communications with him had been brief to say the least, mealtimes quiet and strained.

'When do you think you'll go?'

'Saturday night. I've booked a passage.'

'Right then, well, there's nothing more to say. Except for one thing. Never ever, speak to me again as you did the other night. Do you understand?' Magnus gritted his teeth.

'Yes Father.'

'Right, I hope you have a successful term.' Alexander looked away from his son, down at the plans on his desk for the latest ship ordered for the links to the islands. As Harbourmaster he had to scrutinise these things. Magnus, dismissed, left him to it.

'But why?' Christina wailed. 'Why are you going?'

'Because, I need to revise all my work before the beginning of term.' That could be said to be true, Magnus thought. He was trying hard to be patient with Christina. She had come skipping in from her first week in Lerwick to be met with Magnus's bags in the hall, Charlotte looking troubled and her father closeted for much of the time in the study.

'But you can revise here.'

'But I'm better able to work in Aberdeen. I have access to the library. Also I feel too much on holiday here.'

'Oh Magnus,' she sighed. 'I don't want you to go.'

'I know, but I'll be back soon. Now tell me about your first week. How did the boarding house go? And who are your teachers? Anyone I know?'

'Oh yes, Mr Keay remembered you and oh, Magnus,' she whispered, 'the new drill mistress was there.'

'And did you do drill?'

'Yes, but the mistress said the name was gymnastic exercises, and sometimes she called it gym, just like you said.'

'Was it good?'

'It was wonderful. It was much more, em, energetic, than we had had before.'

'Energetic?'

'Yes that's what she, Miss Gray, said we had to be. That was the word she used. We really enjoyed it.'

Magnus thought for a moment. Father will translate the word 'energetic' into 'unladylike' and that will cause more trouble.

Carefully he said, 'Christina, you remember what father was like about gym and girls? Well,' as she nodded, 'I think you should watch what you say about it. Could you manage to talk more about the other things?'

'You mean because he didn't like the idea of gym for girls?'

'Exactly.'

36

'Well, all right but I do like talking about it. We're all talking about it. I know, I could write you and tell you all about it. Oh I don't want you to go away.'

'But that's an idea. We can write to each other and tell all the news…'

On the day of his leaving he sought out Charlotte, up in the baby's room.

'I wish you didn't have to go.'

'I know, but I must. He looked at her with the baby propped up over her shoulder and wished he could imprint the memory on his mind forever. 'I think, I hope what has happened between you and Father will settle down better without me. I know I should not have spoken to him the way I did.'

'Why don't you apologise to him then? Say sorry. Then he'll be all right again. You and he can be friends again.'

'It's not as simple as that. Although I shouldn't have said it, I meant it, and I still mean it and so I can't apologise. I'm just acknowledging to you that I shouldn't have said it to him. Anyway Father and I – we've been walking on a tight rope. We're better apart. I'm worried about you though. I don't like to see you so quiet.'

'Look Magnus, your father and I will be fine. Alexander hurt me very much that night but slowly, slowly, we'll work through it.'

'Don't you want to shout at him?'

Charlotte smiled faintly. 'I did – shout, I mean. I felt like it later too and the next day. But as the week has gone on, although we haven't discussed it again, the heat has gone out and we'll be able to talk about this problem again in a more reasonable manner.'

'You're so calm about it. How can you do it? Oh, I wish – 'Magnus stopped.

'Wish what?'

'Oh, I don't know,' he said lamely, 'just wish things could be different. I don't like being un-friends.'

'Well you're not un-friends with me.' She put out her hand and touched his arm. 'We'll always be friends.' Now,' she said, feeling tears stinging the back of her eyes, 'take hold of this sister of yours and look after her for a moment while I take the baby-wash down.' She dumped Hannah in his arms, picked up the laundry basket and left him. He sighed, sat down and held the baby facing him.

'What would you do, Hannah?' She gazed inscrutably back at him.

Chapter 7

NOVEMBER 1906

'Oh Mother, isn't he lovely? He's so small.' Christina, home for the weekend, hung over the bassinet by Charlotte's bed. Her new brother lay, wrapped in a Shetland shawl and so many other layers that only his face was visible. He was three days old.

'I've been wanting to come and see him since I got Father's note. I was so excited. I told everyone that I had a brother. Mercy Twatt said I'd live to rue the day when he got big enough to meddle with my things but how I could do that? Anyway, Jeanie and Mamie think it's great and want to come and visit. May they Mother? I do want to show them. What's his name? Have you decided?' She paused for breath.

Charlotte, still in the lying-in period, and still (she sometimes thought thankfully) on restricted visitors, smiled and listened.

'His name,' she said, 'is Angus, Angus Gordon Sinclair. Don't you think that's a fine grown-up sounding name for a wee boy?'

'Mm,'Christina tried it out. 'Yes, Angus Sinclair, yes, that's good. Hello, wee Angus.' She bent over him. 'Do you know your name yet?'

'I hardly think it. But he will, sooner than you think.'

'What does Hannah think of him?'

'Not a lot.' Charlotte smiled. 'So far.'

'Has Magnus been home?'

'He had a wee while off on Wednesday afternoon and came flying in to see how we were. He didn't stay long as he had to be back for evening rounds. What a busy place that is – the Gilbert Bain. I suppose it's with being the main hospital in Shetland – they seem to tackle so many different ailments. They work all hours. He's getting plenty of experience now he's graduated.'

'Did he like – Angus?' Christina tried out the name.

'Yes, of course. He picked him up and, doctor-like, checked him all over before pronouncing him perfect. Father's happy too.'

'Oh yes,' Christina nodded wisely. 'He wanted a boy.'

'Did he say that to you?'

'No, but well, women just know these things.'

Charlotte hid her smile behind her hand and said, 'Well we can be women together.'

Christina took her hand. 'I'm glad you're all right,' she said, slightly choked.

'Of course I'm all right. Did you think I might not be?'

'Well, some of the girls were saying that some mothers died when they were having babies and I was worried that might happen to you.'

Charlotte held her closely. 'All right, that does sometimes happen, and it's very sad. But look, I'm fine. You'll be able to tell the girls on Monday how well we are. Now, listen,' she turned her head. 'I hear feet. Here's Hannah.'

'Oh, Miss, I mean Mrs Sinclair, I'm sorry, she was away before I noticed.' Edie came running in behind Hannah.

'It's all right Edie, it's time we said hello to her anyway.'

Later, when they left her to wash their hands before tea, Charlotte lay back on her pillows with a sigh of relief. She breathed deeply as Maggie had taught her. She could feel herself relaxing. Now Angus, just stay quiet and let me have a few minutes' dwam to myself.

Much later Alexander came in from the Harbour.

'All well?' He leant over and kissed Charlotte. 'How are my wife and youngest son this evening?'

'We're fine, Alexander. Angus has been very good.'

He touched the baby cheek briefly. 'Nice little lad. Like me, I think. What do you think, Edie? Who do you think he's like?'

Edie hanging baby clothes around the fireguard turned and said, 'Oh Mr Sinclair, I don't know, but he's so very fair, I think he's maybe got your colouring, and his eyes are blue, but then all baby's eyes are blue, aren't they, Oh I really don't know.' She stopped, flustered. Mr Sinclair flustered her. She didn't know why. He was so very serious when he spoke to her. She loved Mrs Sinclair of course. She would have walked on hot coals for her. Not that that was likely but that was the way she felt. She was sure she'd endured every contraction with Charlotte when she was in labour. Now she just wanted to do everything she could for her and help her through this time that Maggie called 'lying-in'. She ventured nearer.

'Can I get you anything, Miss – Mrs Sinclair. Some tea, or water.'

'No thank you Edie. But, is Hannah all right?'

'Yes, Meg's bathing her. She's in great form. Can't wait for her baby brother to play with her. I'll just go and see how your supper is getting on. Meg got some lovely fish.'

'That sounds good Edie,' Alexander said. 'I'm hungry.'

'That's fine Mr Sinclair. Where would you like it? Up here with Mrs Sinclair?'

'That's a good idea, if it's not too much trouble.'

'No trouble at all.' She slipped out and Alexander sat down beside Charlotte's bed.

'Have you been up today?'

'No not yet. I wish they would let me up but Maggie says bed for five days and only then if she says I'm able. I'm sure many women don't do that. What about those with no help? They would have to get up.'

'Well, yes, but you have help so you just do what they say. It'll do you good to have a rest. Christina – has she had a good week?'

'Yes she's fine, enjoying herself but I think she works very hard too.'

'She's a good girl. She's maturing very nicely.'

'Yes.' Charlotte thought of Christina's remark about 'women know these things' and smiled as she nodded. 'She's a lovely girl, very thoughtful.'

She loved this girl as though she were her own flesh and blood. The last incident about allowing Christina go to school in Lerwick, had revealed to Charlotte that Alexander saw himself as fully responsible for Christina. It seemed that Alexander didn't give credibility to her love for Christina and her part in her upbringing. The bruise to her spirit was almost tangible. It had taken a long time for Alexander to undo the barrier between them, raised by that day's heedless remarks. Slowly the hurt had lessened and as Christina thrived in the wider environment and her semi-independence Charlotte felt that her stance in choice of school at least, was vindicated. As if he could read her thoughts he spoke.

'You're quiet. Are you tired?'

'No, I'm fine, just thinking.'

'I've been thinking too.'

'Mm? What?'

'Well, I often think back to that day,' he hesitated, 'that day when we argued about Christina. You remember, when she went to Lerwick. I was a bit hard on you then. You know, about not being Christina's mother and, all that about Margery. You remember?'

Charlotte remembered. 'But, Alexander that's all in the past.'

'Yes I know, but I can't forget what I said.' He sighed. 'I just want to say I'm sorry. Charlotte, I didn't mean it. You have been and are a wonderful mother to Christina and I wanted you to know I felt like that.'

He held out his hand to her. 'I'm sorry about that day. I don't know what came over me. I just needed to get at someone – I was worried and felt guilty about sending her and then the business about drill and Magnus needling me. I just boiled over.'

'But it was two years ago.'

'I know.'

'Why did you not say all this before?'

'I couldn't.'

'Oh, Alexander. But why now?'

'Well, I just suddenly felt able to.' He held her hand between his. 'I'm just a cross, mixed up old man, but I love you very much.'

'You don't need to be cross or mixed up and I don't think of you as old.'

'Well,' he said, 'we'll let that flee stick to the wa,' as they say. But you do believe that I think you are doing a great job with Christina?'

'Yes, Alexander.'

'Sure?' He looked at her anxiously.

'Yes Alexander, really. That's all over. It's gone. I was hurt at the time but, time rolls on and these things heal.'

He gripped her hand tightly. 'I'm so glad.' He leant over and rested his nearly white head on her shoulder for a moment. 'What would I do without you?'

In the spring, Angus was allowed outside to lie in his perambulator, or pram as Christina was quick to say. Another winter baby, he had been kept inside until then, away from the biting winds. Some Shetland mothers when needs must, took them out wrapped tightly and held closely bundled in large shawls around both baby and mother and then tucked in, keeping the whole bundle of baby and shawl intact and close and warm.

However, Alexander's wife was not to be a shawlie-mother. The Birkenshaw babies would have a perambulator. This came from the sooth, transported from Aberdeen by boat, unloaded at Lerwick harbour, collected by Leask's Emporium there to await Alexander's instructions. All dealt with before Hannah's birth. You never took a pram into the house before a baby had been safely born. That would be tempting Providence. A few days after Hannah's birth, Alexander went to Leask's Emporium to inform the manager that the pram was now required and would he arrange for it to be sent to Birkenshaw.

'Yes, certainly, Mr Sinclair. Of course, Sir. And how is Mrs Sinclair? And the new little one?' The manager gazed at Alexander with big round eyes. 'I do hope they are both well? Such a business, women's troubles.'

'Yes, well, they're both fine, thank you.' Alexander disliked discussing anything to do with birth or the like. He stayed away in the farthest reaches of the house each time Charlotte had given birth and only approached the bedside when every vestige of the whole business had been cleared away and he could manage not to think about the messy, painful details. He couldn't help being like this – many men of the day were. It was just the way he was, possibly to do with his upbringing, his maleness in a prudish era, and the idea that birthing was a woman's matter. Let him organise equipment, like the latest pram, and see to the refurbishing of the wee room off their bedroom for the latest baby. And of course the important decision on naming of the baby. Those were within his remit and control. Anything else was for the women to deal with.

Naming of babies required careful thought. Traditionally, in Scotland, the first male child was named after his paternal grandfather and the first female child after her maternal grandmother, thus perpetuating 'family' names. Charlotte was keen to follow this old Scots custom and they planned to call their first baby, if a boy, Alexander John after his paternal and maternal grandfathers. Later, wee Alexander lay in the Tingwall Kirkyard beside Frances, Ingrid and Kenneth from Alexander's first marriage with Margery. They gave Hannah her great-grandmother's name Margaret which pleased her greatly. They chose Angus because they liked the name and gave him Gordon, Charlotte's maiden name as a second name, and kept family tradition going.

Naming babies in Scotland often went along with baptising. People said things like 'when's he going to get his name' meaning 'baptised' or 'christened'. Some parents took this connection further by refusing to tell anyone the name before the baptism. Fortunately Charlotte and Alexander had no problem telling folk their babies' names. However, Charlotte knew of one mother whose baby's name remained a close secret until the baptismal day. Even the minister did not know.

'How are you naming the child?'

The mother whispered in the minister's ear.

'I beg your pardon?'

The mother whispered again. 'Spindona'. The minister looked at her.

'Are you sure?' The mother nodded. The minister gulped, took a deep breath, and said, 'I baptise thee, Spi –'

'Na, na,' the mother interrupted. 'I'm telling ye –' she pulled at the baby's shawl and revealed a crumpled piece of paper pinned at an angle.

'There, A telt ye,' ''s *pinned on hur. There's* her name'.

Charlotte smiled when she thought of this story. No such confusion was allowed at Birkenshaw. Everything was planned with military precision. As was current custom in Scotland, both Hannah and Angus were baptised at Birkenshaw, that is, 'at home'. In place of the Godparent seen in some religious denominations, Charlotte asked Maggie the Jarlshavn midwife to sponsor Hannah at her baptism. And, in a further custom, Charlotte invited Maggie to dress the baby for baptism in the handmade and embroidered fine lawn Sinclair baptismal gown.

Then the time came for Angus's baptism to be arranged.

'Well, I think that's it.' Alexander surveyed his lists, of guests, food, sherry, notes of timings and whom to contact. 'What a lot of organising for one small baby.'

'Well, he's worth it. And you know you like arranging those things. There's just one thing, though.'

'What have we forgotten?'

'We haven't talked about who's going to carry him in.'

'Carry whom in where?'

'You know, carry Angus into the parlour to be baptised. Maggie did it for Hannah.'

'Well, can't Maggie do it for Angus?'

'It should be a man, as Angus is a wee boy.'

'Do we know any men whom we want to do this?' Alexander looked at Charlotte.

'Well, Alexander – 'she hesitated.

'Yes?'

'What about Magnus?'

'Magnus – but how could he? He's his brother.'

'All the more reason that he should do it. He's family, old enough to be aware of the responsibilities and loves Angus. I would like him to do it.'

'Have you spoken to him about this?'

'No, I thought you and I should discuss it first. But Alexander,' Charlotte said, 'it would be a good thing to do, from all points of view.'

'Except that he and I have a barrier between us…'

'Yes, but Alexander, this could help. Break the barrier down. Please, let me talk to him.'

'Ach, woman. Well, all right. Go and ask him and see what he says.'

Magnus also had misgivings.

'Are you sure Father's happy about this?'

'Yes. Magnus, he doesn't want to be at odds with you. I think he'd really like this. He just needs a bit of help to see it.'

So peace broke out in Birkenshaw for a January celebration. Father and eldest son lowered their barriers, looked each other in the eye, clapped each other on the back and toasted each other's health along with that of the reason for the gathering who hiccuped at the minister, protested at being shown off to the guests, and, in accordance with custom, slept the party time away in his fancy gown.

Chapter 8

A few months later, gentler breezes blew over Birkenshaw and the pram was parked in the usual place when Magnus came walking up the driveway.

He walked forward quietly. He wouldn't be popular if he woke a sleeping baby before his time. He looked in. Angus lay on his back with his hands encased in hummel doddies raised up next to his ears. He was fast asleep. A little dribble of milk ran out of the corner of his mouth. Magnus smiled to himself and walked on and up the steps.

'Anyone here?'

'Hello, Magnus, I didn't hear you.' Charlotte came round the side of the house. 'Come ben into the kitchen. How are things? Are you busy?'

'Yes, very. We just don't have enough beds most of the time.'

Meg was rolling pastry.

'Hello, Meg.' He stood beside her at the floury table. 'How are you?'

'Fine thanks Magnus. How's the toon.'

'Oh Lerwick's all right. Hospital's busy though. All Shetland seems to meet there.'

'I hear there was an accident on the cliff near the point.' Meg turned her pastry forty-five degrees and rolled again.

'No, really?' Charlotte hadn't heard. 'What happened?'

'Oh,' said Magnus, 'this poor chap went too near the edge, out beyond the point, slipped and fell. Fortunately he hit a ledge or he would have gone right down.'

'How is he?' Meg stopped rolling to listen.

'He's going to be all right, I think but it was a wee while before he was found and then they had to climb down the cliff and decide what to do when they got there.'

'So what did they do?' Charlotte asked.

'The men at the top lowered a stretcher and ropes. The lifeboat went out from the harbour and waited at the bottom. Then they tied him on to the stretcher and lowered him down to the boat.'

Magnus's account was brisk, but he was remembering that day, with the man lying on the ledge, the wind blowing, the men going down to him, and he as the youngest, fittest doctor available, also having to climb down to assess the man's condition.

'There must be more to it than that,' Charlotte said. 'How did they get the man on to the stretcher? And how did they know if they could lift him? They must have had a doctor. Did they – oh Magnus,' she stopped and looked at him. 'Magnus what really happened? Magnus, did *you* have to go down the cliff?'

He nodded.

'Ay,' said Meg. 'That's what they're saying in the village. You're name's on everybody's lips. How you saved the man because you went down and did the first aid on the cliff edge. I'm proud of you, laddie.'

'Ach, Meg, I was only another pair of hands.'

'All the other pairs of hands were used to the cliffs. If I remember rightly you have never gone down a cliff like that before.'

'Oh Magnus,' Charlotte repeated, 'you could've been killed. How could you?'

'But I was only doing my job.'

'But surely someone else could've done it.'

'Charlotte,' he said, 'I'm a doctor. The man needed a doctor. And there were others there. We were all roped up. It was nothing.' Inwardly he shuddered as he recalled the picture of the man lying at an awkward angle on the ledge, the wind and rain coming horizontally at him as he climbed down toe by toe and his fear that his freezing, wet fingers would slip.

'What happened when you got to the man?'

'Well, by that time there were three of us, two with the stretcher and me. I had a look at the man, who is Lowrie's cousin by the way – you know – Alfie Williamson. I examined him, only quickly mind. It was very windy and he was in a lot of pain. Then we bound him round and on to the stretcher.'

'Then –' Meg said, pastry forgotten.

'Then we lowered him to the lifeboat waiting below. It couldn't wait long either because of the wind and the waves. We couldn't hang about. Then I went down after Alfie into the boat.'

'You went down into the boat?'

'Well, yes.' Magnus looked at Charlotte's face.

'But you couldn't have been roped by then.'

'Well, no,' he admitted, 'but I had to do it. I had to see that he was all right.'

'What did the other two rescuers do?'

'Well, once they knew that we were all in the boat, they climbed up to the top again.'

'With their safety ropes?'

'Yes.'

'But you went down without them. Magnus, you could have been killed on the rocks.' Charlotte put her face into her hands and burst into tears.

'But Charlotte I wasn't – killed I mean. I'm all right. Charlotte, come here, it's all right.' He stepped over to her and put his arm around her shaking shoulders. As she turned towards him he brought his other arm up and around her. She leant into his chest and he held her as she wept. As they drew closer, a feeling of protective yearning welled up inside Magnus. He tightened his arms around her and with a little sobbing sigh Charlotte responded by resting her head on the wool of his jacket.

Only for a moment. Within seconds Charlotte regained control and pulled sharply away.

'Magnus – I'm sorry, I didn't mean... oh heavens, what can you think?' She turned away horrified.

'Here.' Meg briskly came to her rescue. She dug into her apron pocket and pulled out a bundle of hankies. 'Here, Mrs Sinclair. It's a good job I carry spares around with me. I must say I feel like having a good greet myself.' She dabbed her eyes and handed Charlotte the spare hanky. Charlotte took a deep breath, wiped her eyes and blew her nose.

'Sorry about that. You just took me unaware.'

Magnus regarded her steadily and did his best to act normally although inwardly his heart was pounding.

'All right now?'

'Yes, yes, I'm all right. But so proud of you, and angry with you at the same time. It's a funny feeling.' She turned to Meg. 'So you knew?'

'Yes, I heard in the village. I'm just back. I was just about to come and tell you when this,' she nodded to Magnus, 'blew in. Mr Sinclair will no doubt have heard. I'm sure he'll be full of it at lunch time. Which reminds me, the pastry. There'll be no lunch at this rate.' She turned back to her rolling and quarter turns.

'I can hear Edie and Hannah coming. Thank you, Meg.' Charlotte put the sodden hanky into her pocket and went away.

Her mind was racing. How could that have happened? I finished up leaning on Magnus and crying on his shoulder. For a moment I forgot what I was doing. It was Magnus. My step-son. And Meg saw. What can I say to her?

There was no escaping the subject of Magnus and the cliff rescue. Edie and Hannah had also been to the village. They came back agog with the news and delighted to see the hero of the hour there in their midst. Magnus began to wish that he could get away from the subject. I'd like to go and do an ordinary ward round where no one knows about any cliff rescue. But surely Father will play it down.

But no, as soon as Alexander came in and saw Magnus was there he went up to him and clasped him warmly by the hand.

'Well done, my boy. I always knew you'd do something brave. It's all over the village. Folk have been in and out of the Office all morning congratulating me on my son and what you did for Alfie Williamson. I must say, I think this deserves a glass of sherry. What do you say Charlotte?'

'Yes, indeed.'

'Are you able to stay the night, Magnus?' Alexander busied himself pouring sherry into the best crystal glasses.

'Yes, I think so. I was on duty all last night and tonight is my scheduled night off. I could do with a good night's sleep. The sherry will help.' He accepted his glass and took a sip.

'It's only lunchtime.'

'Well perhaps I'll have an hour this afternoon.' He smiled at them. 'Then I'll go out and have a look at how the trees are coming along.'

'That's a good idea. Maybe I'll come back early and join you. I want to ask your opinion about the condition of the rowans down in that wee hollow.'

Magnus lay on his bed supposedly sleeping but his mind was too busy. What can I do? I love her. I love her. I can't go on like this. My feelings nearly got the better of me there. But, and his heart leapt, she felt as though she wanted to be close to me. But oh, he sighed, it's no use, she's married to Father. But supposing she does care. We could run away. But no, he contradicted, she would never leave the children. How can I speak to her? We

45

could arrange a meeting. And then he remembered that Meg had seen what happened in the kitchen. He groaned as he remembered his arms around Charlotte and his needing her and Charlotte pulling away and all being seen by Meg.

Charlotte was also thinking about Meg. She was up in the wee bedroom giving Angus his afternoon feed. I need to speak to Meg. That was purely an accident. Just the upset of the occasion bringing us together like that. I'll tell Meg it's nothing more.

Meg was in the kitchen resting her legs for half an hour. Oh dear. She uncrossed her legs again. Do I smell trouble in the wind? It's none of my business, but if this got out the village would have a field day. Then she thought, if what got out? Mrs Sinclair was crying because of the emotion of the occasion and Magnus comforted her and I supplied a hanky. That's all. Nothing more, nothing less. End of story. She uncrossed and re-crossed her legs on the footstool which the doctor had told her never to do because doing that would not help her varicose veins, folded her arms across her chest and shut her eyes. But she knew in her bones that the way Magnus had looked at Charlotte as she stood in his arms was not only a look of comfort. It had been a look of tenderness, of passion, that only a man who loved a woman very much would give..

'Meg, are you there?' Charlotte entered the kitchen, Angus lying sleepily in her arms, Hannah trotting behind like a little dog. She had been playing with Edie during Angus's feed but now that was over. Who knew, perhaps Mama would be going to the kitchen and that meant biscuits.

'I'll bring you a biscuit, Edie,' she promised.

'Right, I'll tidy up before I come to get on with the ironing.' One of Edie's main tasks at Birkenshaw was the ironing. It was usually done in the kitchen so that the irons could heat on the range and be used in turn until the job was done for the day. As everything had to be ironed, the task was endless and there was always washing left rolled up damp for another day. Edie knew all the tricks of ironing – after all, her mother had taught her – and she was also an expert at the goffering iron which was brought out for all the little pleats and tucks on Hannah's frocks. Edie was, in short, a perfectionist. She liked working in the kitchen too. There was Meg to talk to as she did her baking and cooking and people going in and out and things happening.

Edie had missed the happening in the kitchen that morning and Charlotte was glad she was still upstairs when she entered looking for Meg that afternoon.

'Meg? Oh you're there.'

'Yes, Mrs Sinclair.' Meg sat up in her chair. 'I was just sitting with my eyes closed for a wee minute.'

'Yes, of course.' Charlotte sat down at the table with the baby on her lap. Hannah stood beside her. They make a lovely picture, Meg thought. I hope nothing happens to spoil it.

'Meg,' Charlotte hesitated, 'I just came down to mention about this morning.' Meg looked at her.

'Mama, can I have a biscuit?' Hannah's voice broke in. 'You said I could have a biscuit.'

'Yes, in a minute, Hannah. Meg, I just wanted to say, I was just, em, very upset, and ...'

Meg interrupted. 'Mrs Sinclair, we were all upset.' She looked Charlotte straight in the eyes. 'Think no more about it. It's all over and,' she smiled and said with an air of finality, 'we can all be proud of our doctor-laddie. Now, who wants a biscuit, then? Let's go and find the tin.' She took Hannah by the hand just as Edie came through the door with a bundle of rolled up washing in her arms.

'Right, well, I'll go and put this boy down to sleep.' Charlotte, feeling strangely guilty and yet relieved at the same time, carried Angus out to the waiting pram.

Chapter 9

Magnus's ward round was taking a long time. Everything was conspiring against him this morning. The nurses were exceptionally busy, rushed off their feet, and new patients were being admitted – some from a waiting-list and some, emergencies.

Alfie Williamson, who fell down the cliff and was one of the previous week's emergencies, was still on the ward. At a lull in admitting and clerking new patients Magnus took time to say 'hello' to him. Alfie's face looked pale and anxious below his windblown tan. His fractured femur was encased in a long Thomas's splint which was attached to the bed with a complicated looking arrangement of pulleys and weights. These hung at the bed-end to keep his leg extended – a hazard for passing staff. If they knocked the contraption they could upset the weights, set them swinging and cause extreme pain for the patient.

'Morning, Alfie.' Magnus stopped by the bed. 'How are things?' He thought Alfie looked tired.

'Ach, I'm all right – thanks. I can't move though. They say I've cracked my pelvis as well as broken my leg. How long do you think it'll all take?'

'It's difficult to say.' It would take weeks to get Alfie on his feet again but Magnus felt this was not the time to say it. After all it was only a few days since the accident. He was just beginning to say, 'I think it'll take a wee while,' and to try and work from there, when Alfie interrupted.

'Magnus, or I suppose I should call you "doctor" here…'

'That's all right.' He had known Alfie for years through Lowrie, Alfie's cousin. 'I don't mind. What was it you wanted to say?'

'I just wanted to thank you for well, you know, saving my life.'

'Ach away, man, you'd have been fine anyway.'

'Well, I don't know. You were the one who did what I needed and came with me on the boat. And, I hear, to do that you had to come down without ropes.' He held out his hand. 'Please accept my thanks.'

Magnus took the proffered hand. 'Alfie, I was only doing my job. Now, we need to get you on your feet again. How's the pain?'

'Oh they're taking good care of me. They're doing their best. Sometimes it's better than others. Sometimes, well, I just never imagined pain like it. Like when they're trying to move me.'

Magnus nodded. He had been there when Alfie's fractured femur was extended and his whole leg put into the Thomas's splint. Fortunately, for that procedure, another doctor had come and anaesthetised Archie with chloroform. Magnus looked at the way the leg was rigged up. Thank goodness for chloroform. It must have been awful in the old days.

'Is that the worst time?'

'When?'

'When the nurses are trying to move you?'

'Yes. I know they've to do it but my heart sinks when I see them coming. When they've to do anything to me the pain in my backside and down my leg is just – just, well unbearable.' His eyes filled with tears.

'Magnus, I cry. I'm ashamed to admit it but I cry. I'm like a baby. They are so good to me. But, it's awful.'

'You could have a little nitrous oxide when they're doing that, for a day or two, till things heal a bit further.'

'What's that?'

'A kind of gas that you breathe in. It'll make you a wee bit woozy while they are doing it.'

'Would it help?'

'It's worth a try. I'll see what I can do. See you later.'

'Thanks, Magnus.'

Magnus made a note and moved on.

'Morning, how are you feeling today?'

'Oh Doctor, I'm that pleased to see you.' This old man was keen to blether. It was good to be doing his round by himself. This was an exception. Usually the ward round was done with a flagship consultant in the lead followed by an ordered flotilla of lesser medical beings and the busy tugs of the ward sister and her staff taking their place in the line where necessary. Today the hospital was so busy that this ritual had not yet taken place and Mr Sanderson the consultant had detailed Magnus to go round on his own.

Magnus was enjoying himself, the responsibility, and the chance to speak to his patients without everyone hearing. He was also unconsciously glad of the busyness. This took his mind off his personal thoughts and problems and what to do about them. Suddenly he found that a whole morning had gone and he had not thought of Birkenshaw once. He smiled ruefully at himself. That's what I keep saying, hard work keeps the difficult thoughts at bay.

But there came a time when the hard work stopped and at night in the doctors' residence he lay, trying to sleep, knowing that he needed to sleep to be able to function, yet his thought patterns were crowded with pictures of Charlotte: Charlotte at Birkenshaw; Charlotte with Hannah and Angus; Charlotte talking with Christina; Charlotte and his father, walking in the garden, sitting by the fire, at the dining table, in bed –

Magnus sat up sharply. Just don't go there, he said to himself. Don't think about it. He sat on the edge of his bed and stretched. He heard feet. They stopped at his door. A tap.

'Just a minute, I'm coming.' He struggled into his dressing-gown.

A nurse stood there. 'Doctor, I'm sorry to wake you up. Sister sent me. There's an emergency coming in. Could you come right away please?'

'Yes, of course. I'll be there in five minutes.'

'Thank you.' She rushed off.

Sorry she woke me up. He sighed. If she only knew. He looked on this interruption to his night as a welcome relief from the restlessness demonstrated by the messed up bed he was abandoning and of course his need for sleep.

That afternoon, he had a few hours off. It had been another very busy morning. The night's emergency turned out to be a woman with pneumonia exacerbated by living in permanently cold, damp conditions with a diet less than adequate in both quality and quantity. Not many folks' immune systems would stand up to such conditions without something going wrong and the woman admitted that there had been something 'wrang wi her kist' for a long time. Now, what had undoubtedly been a chest infection had deteriorated into pneumonia and the woman was very ill. Magnus had been with her for a long time in the early morning, had not felt it worthwhile returning to his bed, with so much else to do, and anyway in bed he would once again be prey to these treacherous thoughts over which he seemed to have so little control. So, he had spent time writing up yesterday's admissions, checking on the woman with pneumonia, snatching a quick breakfast in the doctors' dining-room.

'Would you like two eggs Doctor Sinclair. You look as though you need them.'

'Yes please.'

'Coming up.' The cook turned the bacon deftly. 'Go and sit down. See you in a minute.'

Then he'd had to catch up with the consultant's ward round and amongst other things ask Alfie how he was. He knew the nurses had been giving him nitrous oxide as he had prescribed. They had been very positive about it. Magnus wanted to hear what the patient had to say.

''Morning Alfie. How are things?'

''Morning Doctor.' Alfie looked and sounded happier. 'That's great stuff you said I could have.'

'What, the nitrous oxide?'

'Aye, whatever you call it. A few whiffs and they can do what they like. I was laughing my head off. It's amazing. Mind you,' he added, 'it doesn't last long. As soon as you stop taking it, the effect begins to go away.'

'Probably that's all to the good,' Magnus said, laughing himself. 'What did the nurses say?'

'Oh, they were very professional, but I think they had a good laugh too. It certainly made all our lives much easier. Can we keep using it?'

'Yes, I think so, for a while anyway, until things have healed a bit.' Magnus had managed to find time to discuss this with the consultant.

'Well done, my boy. Well thought out. It's a bit unconventional – usually used for dentistry and childbirth – but I see no reason why Mr Williamson shouldn't use nitrous oxide *pro re nata* for the time being.' Mr Sanderson liked to use the Latin phrases in all their fullness.

It was Mr Sanderson who had insisted that he take time off.

'Go away Dr Sinclair,' he'd said sternly. 'You've been here too long. I know,' he said as Magnus protested, 'that you have things to do. But I also know that you've been up most of the night, that you're up for many hours lots of nights and if you go on without a break in the day you'll be no use to man nor beast. Go for a walk.'

Thus ordered, Magnus had given in and headed for the cliff-top. Gulls wheeled overhead, crying endlessly as they swooped and sailed on thermal currents known only to them. Magnus watched for a few moments their apparently carefree progress. A few flew out to sea. There were fishing boats to investigate. Fishing boats meant food for gulls and were usually accompanied by a trail of winged scavengers ready to pick up whatever came over the side. Free as a gull – that would do me fine. I thought I was coping with this, could go to Birkenshaw and visit and not mind. But I can't. I can't do it. If I go there, at some point I'll give myself away. I want to hold her, touch her, feel her, make her love me as I love her. It's no use. I'll have to stay away. He took a deep breath. It's the only thing I can do.

Along the cliff path Magnus saw a group of people approaching. Ach – people. He stuffed his hands in his pockets. I don't want people today. I just want myself. He hoped they would turn but the group continued on. He was, after all, standing in the path and the cliff top was a favourite walk. He resigned himself to making the usual civilities. That was the least one could do.

As they approached, he saw that this was not an informal cliff top saunter. The dozen or so young women walked in an upright manner, in twos, in what had become known comparatively recently as a 'crocodile'. The crocodile was headed by a woman – probably Magnus thought, I should call her a lady – a figure of authority. Tall, erect, arms usually by her side, she sometimes gesticulated as she talked, at times pointed out some item of interest, at which the crocodile obediently looked. Not to look would be observed and commented upon.

Magnus watched them. Girls, from the school. I wonder if they let Christina out in a crocodile like this. He looked more closely. Was that her? They all looked alike in those clothes. But, yes, there she was in the middle. He half put up his hand to wave but then thought I can't do that. It's not etiquette. What *is* the etiquette for a brother who sees his sister in a school crocodile and wants to say hello? The crocodile was fast approaching. Magnus could hear the teacher's voice now.

'Don't go too near the edge girls. Now, these cliffs are the nesting places of many birds – who can give examples? Yes Jean?'

'Seagulls, Miss Cunningham.'

'Yes, Jean, but can anyone think of something a little more unusual than just the basic seagull.'

'Black backed gull?' ventured one.

'Herring gull?'

The answers came now as one idea led to another. The group had stopped walking and some of the girls were identifying birds in flight. They talked about the guillemots sitting drying themselves on a small skerry not far out to sea. Someone mentioned puffins and the discussion turned to them.

'Where do they nest?'

'In burrows, Miss Cunningham.' They'd all seen them. Most of their fathers had caught them for the pot. This is an easy nature walk for these Shetland girls, Magnus thought. Now I'm going to interrupt it to see if I can say 'hello' to my wee sister. He straightened himself up, took his gaze away from the horizon, pulled his hands out of his pockets and turned in their direction. By this time the crocodile had re-formed.

'Right girls. March on Daphne please.' Magnus walked along to meet them. As he approached he realised that convention would expect him to step aside and give way to the crocodile. Miss Cunningham who he could see had observed him would be expecting this. He approached and said, 'Miss Cunningham, I hope you won't mind if I introduce myself.' She stopped (as her way was now effectively barred she had no option) and looked at him.

'I'm Magnus Sinclair. I'm Christina's brother, and I see Christina is with you today.' He held out his hand.

'Ah,' she said, taking his hand. 'I wondered who the brigand was. But,' she continued gravely, 'how do I know you are whom you say you are?'

'Well,' he said, in keeping with her tone. 'You could ask Christina to identify me. I don't know of any rules of etiquette to cover this situation but I would like to speak with my sister for a few minutes. I couldn't pass her on the path and say nothing.'

As he spoke, Christina broke crocodile ranks and ran to him.

'Magnus, what are you doing here?'

'Christina.' Miss Cunningham turned. 'You must not speak with young men. You know that's the rule.'

'But Miss Cunningham he's not a – I mean he's my *brother*. We're surely allowed to speak to our brothers.' Miss Cunningham allowed herself a faint smile.

'Yes, well, I suppose your identity is established Mr Sinclair. It is difficult is it not, when chaperoning rules have to be observed?'

'Yes, indeed,' agreed Magnus. 'Well, now, would it be possible, please? To speak to Christina?' He smiled at the teacher. 'Just for a few minutes? I don't want to hold you up but Christina and I don't see each other very often because of my work.'

'Your work?'

'Yes. I'm a doctor at the Gilbert Bain and I seem to work most weekends when Christina is at home.'

'Oh well, in that case, I'm sure we can manage something. I know this is not in the rules but – are you walking back into Lerwick?'

'I can do, yes.'

'Well, why don't we all walk the same way? The crocodile will walk in front and you may escort Christina behind us as far as the school. Would that be all right?'

'Yes, thank you very much. Christina?' He turned to her.

'Yes, I'm so glad to see you. What a coincidence. Thank you Miss Cunningham.'

'Right girls. Back en croc.' The girls fell in to their positions again and walked off chattering. For once Miss Cunningham let them.

'Magnus,' said Christina as soon as they were as near alone as they were going to get. 'What are you doing here?'

'It's quite simple. I've a few hours off and I came out for a walk. Now, how are you, Christina? How are you getting on?'

'Oh fine. School is, well, I really enjoy it. Can you believe that I have been here three years now? And Father has agreed to my staying on as a senior.'

'I should hope so.'

'Yes, but you know how he is. He wouldn't have been so ready to agree without Mother. She's been so good to me. What do you think Magnus?' she said earnestly. 'Don't you think my life would've been much more – curtailed – if she had not been there? I wouldn't have been here in Lerwick for a start.'

'No, you're right, or been allowed to do physical exercises.'

'Or an awful lot of other things. But Father's so helpful in his own way. Just think how he has helped with my Latin. And to begin with he pooh-poohed the whole idea of girls taking Latin. Anyway, we only have a few minutes and I want to know how you are Magnus. I hardly ever see you.'

'No, I know. We're so busy at the hospital.' Well, it's the truth, he defended his 'work excuse' to himself. 'I work most weekends.'

'I heard you say that to Miss Cunningham. I miss seeing you when I come home.'

'I miss you too. But that's the way it is for the moment, I'm afraid.'

'But you do still want to come home don't you?' Heavens he thought, can she tell?

'Yes, of course. It's just that it's difficult just now for the weekends at least. I was home last week for a night.'

'Well I won't nag any more. But you will try won't you – to come when I'm there, I mean?' She changed the subject. 'Isn't Angus growing? And Hannah ...'

'Hannah's very like you when you were that age. She's beginning to shriek just the same as you used to.'

'I don't shriek.'

'Ssh. They'll hear you.' Magnus nodded towards the crocodile. 'You're supposed to be being a young lady. They don't shriek like that. I thought you had stopped.'

'I have, really. Oh, Magnus,' she grabbed his hand and swung it. 'I'm so glad to see you. Could we meet again do you think? Here's the school. I'll have to go. I'm coming, Miss Cunningham,' she called politely. Magnus stepped forward.

'Miss Cunningham, thank you very much for allowing Christina to walk with me. I wonder, have you any way in which a brother could meet again with his sister, perhaps on an arranged basis?'

'In theory, Dr Sinclair, I don't see why not. In practice, I'd have to consult with my colleagues. Today's was just an informal snap decision.'

'I understand that and I'm very grateful. But another meeting would be good – for both of us, I think.'

'Oh yes, please,' Christina added.

'Well, I'll do my best.'

'Thank you so much. Well good bye, Miss Cunningham, Christina, young ladies.' Magnus tipped his cap and with a special smile for Christina, walked on his way.

A burst of chatter broke out.

'Christina, you never told us you had such a nice brother.'

'Where did you hide him?'

'When can we go a walk on the cliff again, please, Miss Cunningham?'

'Girls, please compose yourselves. Dr Sinclair is a very busy man. He may be given permission to walk with Christina because he is her brother, but no decision has been made. Now, please, en croc, round to the side door.'

Chapter 10

The SS *St Clair* lay at her pier-side berth in Lerwick harbour. Two gangways were in use. Men, weighed down with their burdens, toiled up and down loading the ship to be ready for the evening's journey to Aberdeen. A large crane operated busily and noisily, carrying carts, trailers, Shore Porter's house-removal crates, a covered wagon of frightened sounding sheep, all for transport to the wider world. Earlier the crane had deposited upon Shetland soil, household goods, supplies for the shops, sacks of coal (even in peat-rich Shetland they needed coal), and wood for building, fencing, joinery. The list was endless.

Charlotte stood at the harbour wall watching the comings and goings of the men. Some of them didn't look that old – probably just left school, their first jobs, being shown the ropes. The older men were shouting, haranguing a bit, in a hurry to get the job done. The crane operator swivelled back and forth. It's a long time since I've been on the *St Clair*, she thought. I'd quite like a trip sooth.

She felt strangely free. Here she was in the middle of Lerwick, standing by herself, watching the boats at the harbour. Not usual, not planned, but enjoyable, perhaps better for not being planned. She and Ina Manson, old friends and colleagues had decided to take the motor bus into Lerwick, for a day of shopping. Leask's Emporium beckoned, they didn't go shopping in this way very often, Edie and Meg would look after the children and give Alexander his lunch. Ina was on school holidays and her husband was happy to co-operate. The plan was set in motion and here they were. Only, outside Leask's, Ina had bumped into a very old friend whom she had not seen for a long time. Charlotte could see at once that here was an occasion when she had to do the decent thing.

After introductions and a few minutes of 'What a coincidence', and 'How long are you in Lerwick for?' Charlotte made a suggestion.

'Ina,' she said, 'Why don't you and Cathy go off by yourselves. I'll meet up with you later. No, it's no problem,' she said, as Ina started to protest that she couldn't possibly leave her on her own. 'I don't mind. You and Cathy must have so much catching up to do.'

'Well,' Ina was obviously very tempted. 'A wee while, maybe.'

'Go on,' said Charlotte. 'What do you think, Cathy?'

'Well, if you're sure you don't mind.'

'No, honestly. You need time to talk. I'll be fine.'

'I don't know what Alexander will say.'

'Alexander's not deciding this. He's not here. When shall we meet? Back here in a couple of hours? How would that do?' Charlotte took out her fob watch that Alexander had given her when Hannah was born. 'That takes us to about 1 o'clock.'

'All right. I'll meet you here, for lunch.'

Charlotte suddenly found herself with two hours to do with what she liked. She should have been shopping but the temptation of just walking by herself and taking in the sights and sounds around her was such an unusual treat that after a moment's hesitation she walked off towards the harbour.

She loved the sea. There was of course nothing like the hills and glens of her own Glenbuchat and Strathdon but perhaps it was the contrast that made her feel so attracted to the sea, whether crashing on the cliffs, rolling on to the beaches or ebbing and flowing in a busy harbour. She strolled along, enjoying herself. Then she saw Magnus.

Magnus's day off had begun at 8am after being up all night. He yawned. There was something distinctly unfair about working all night before a day off. I should go to bed, but then I'll never sleep tonight. I'll go for a walk again. Clear my head. I'm getting to know parts of Lerwick I've never known before. It's the Aberdeen run tonight. I'll go and have a look at them loading the *St Clair*. He left the residency and made for the harbour. The air felt fresh and salty; he raised his head and breathed deeply. Maybe he wasn't so tired after all.

He strolled along the side of the harbour. The smell here was more than salty, fishy too, mixed in with tar and oil and a seaweedy dulse smell which was particularly pungent when the tide was low and the wind in the right direction for the smell to enter the open windows of the houses. Gulls screamed as usual above. Fishwives offered their newly gutted fish, freshly caught and brought to harbour that morning. The ships' chandler was doing a roaring trade in all things for all sizes of boats as well as sea-going equipment and clothes for men and boys. Further along the harbour some old seamen sat mending nets, puffing on their pipes, swapping stories, throwing out remarks to passers-by. Magnus watched them for a few minutes before walking in the direction of the *St Clair*.

He was about fifty yards away from Charlotte when he noticed her, a quiet small figure in the midst of the activity, long skirted coat blowing a little in the breeze, gloved hand holding on to her bag. That looks like Charlotte. It can't be. She'd never come alone. He looked again. It is. What will I do? I can't speak to her. I mustn't. But I want to. What's she doing here? He lingered, looking at her standing there unaware. As she made a slight move as if to turn, he ducked into a shop doorway. She'll maybe go away. Then I won't have to walk away deliberately. He looked out. She was still there. He hesitated. Suddenly she did turn, she looked right round and straight at him. I'm stuck now, he thought. If I move she'll see me; if I don't move, she's bound to notice me anyway. This is ridiculous. What a stupid position to get myself into. I'll have to talk to her. Thus persuaded, he moved. At the same time he heard her voice.

'Magnus. Hello. Are you thinking of buying some new boots?' He realised then that the shop where he had taken cover was Goodlad's, Lerwick's renowned purveyor of Wellington boots. He smiled sheepishly and held his hand out.

'Just looking. But Charlotte, what brings *you* here? And, all alone?'

'Oh, I'm here with Ina Manson really.' Charlotte started to explain but she broke off. 'Oh here's Mr Goodlad.' The owner of the shop hearing the voices and hoping for a sale had come forward. 'Good morning, Mr Goodlad. How are you? And how are Peter and all the family?'

'We're all just fine thank you Mrs Sinclair.' Mr Goodlad shook her heartily by the hand. 'My, but you're looking well.'

'Oh, I'm fine thanks. This is,' Charlotte remembered Magnus, 'this is Magnus, my husband's eldest son.'

'Pleased to meet you.' The two men shook hands.

'I can't interest you in a pair of boots?'

'Well, I'll know where to come. What a good selection you have. Come to think of that, I think my father got his last pair from you.'

'Indeed he did. I well remember his coming in for them. A customer slipped past them into the dimness of the shop, 'I'd better be getting on. Good day. See you again sometime.'

'Good bye Mr Goodlad. My regards to Peter.'

'How did you know him?' Magnus said when they were alone?

'Easy really. His grandson, Peter, started school the day I started teaching at Jarlshavn.'

'Well, you must know everyone in the place.'

'Not quite,' Charlotte said, 'but it's funny how you keep bumping into people.'

'Anyway,' Magnus went on, 'what are you doing here? You were going to say something about Mrs Manson.'

'Yes, we came shopping and Ina met an old friend and I left them to chat for a while.'

'But –' he started to protest.

'I don't mind at all. It's rather nice to be away from folk for a wee while. I don't mean you,' she added hastily. 'But you know what I mean?'

'Yes, of course, but are you sure you should be alone, down here? Shouldn't you have an escort?'

'I don't think so, Magnus. What could go wrong?'

'Well, it's hardly the done thing for a young lady to go about alone at a harbour.'

'Magnus.' She laughed at him. 'I came to Shetland alone. Anyway, I wasn't brought up to be conventional.'

'No,' he looked at her admiringly, 'I don't think you were. But coming alone on a boat isn't the same as being in a harbour all alone. Anyway, don't let's argue about it now. What are we going to do?'

'What do you mean?

'Well, now we're here, we could walk somewhere? Take tea? Lunch?'

'But I've to meet Ina at one o'clock.'

'Oh,' his face fell. 'Well, what about a cup of tea. I know somewhere nice and quiet.'

His mind was racing as they walked away from the harbour up on to the High street to the little café he had in mind. What're you doing? This is the woman you shouldn't be with, who you're supposed to be avoiding. But she's my father's wife – I've every right to walk with her – why shouldn't I? But all his self-justification fell short. He knew he couldn't trust himself to keep cool and coherent.

The café was quiet. They found a little table in a corner. He watched her. Even the way she drew her gloves off, finger by finger, was a delight. She undid her coat and he solicitously pulled out a chair for her to put her bag on.

'So, how are things at Birkenshaw? How are my babies?' He often called the little children his babies. Hannah loved him – she couldn't quite understand the relationship. To her he was an adult yet he played with her, seemed to her more like a conspirator as he showed her how to play games that the others might have left until she was older.

'They're fine. Growing.' Charlotte talked of her beloved babies, how much she was enjoying being a mother. Then she said, 'but you could come out to Birkenshaw more to see them. Hannah would love that. She often says, "where's Magnus?" Couldn't you Magnus?'

'But you see, I have so much to do at the hospital,' Magnus demurred. 'I never know when I'm going to be called in. This last couple of days alone, we had I don't know how many emergencies during the night, then I'd to go to the maternity ward to help the midwife with a particularly awkward birth and I have all these ward rounds with Mr Sanderson.'

'But you must get away sometimes.'

'Oh yes,' he said, 'sometimes, but often for short periods at a time. Did you hear,' changing the subject, 'did you hear about my meeting Christina's crocodile last week.'

'Yes, Christina said she'd seen you. She was very excited. I think she's going to get to meet you again.'

'Oh that's fine. I asked if that could be arranged.'

'Yes, she says her teacher is going to write to you to explain how it could be done. I think it's a lovely idea that you two should meet here sometimes.'

He looked at her, so earnest, her hand lying on the table. He felt an urge to cover the hand with his own. I wish that we two could also meet sometimes. His mind said it. He almost said it aloud. Instead, he pulled out his watch and said, 'Charlotte, it's a quarter to one. When are you meeting Mrs Manson?'

'Oh, I'd better go. Oh, dear, I'd rather stay and talk.' She reluctantly got up. Magnus silently handed her handbag.

'Thank you, Magnus, very much for the tea.'

'Charlotte,' he held the door for her.

'Yes?' They were out on the street now. I must say something he thought. She'll be gone. He looked at her.

'Magnus,' said Charlotte. 'What is it?'

'I just wondered, could we do this again?'

'You mean, have a cup of tea? Here?'

'Yes, why not?'

'I don't know why not. I don't see any reason why not.'

He nearly said, 'Don't you?' Instead he said, 'Well, next time you're planning a shopping trip would you like to write me a note at the Doctor's Residency and give me a date and time and we could have tea again?'

'Yes, I'd like that. But you also could come and see us all at home. Please, will you try?'

'All right, I'll try.'

'Now I must go. Ina will be waiting.'

In the homeward-bound bus Ina, full of her encounter with her old friend, didn't ask how Charlotte had spent her morning. She just said she had gone for a walk and looked at a few shops and enjoyed her time doing that. They spent the afternoon together in Leask's Emporium shopping for their respective families.

Charlotte didn't mention her meeting with Magnus. Neither did she say she'd been to the harbour. Perhaps that was better left unsaid. But why not mention Magnus? Too much explaining Charlotte thought. But that didn't stop her thinking about him and planning her note to announce her next trip to Lerwick.

A week later found Charlotte making her way along the cobbled stones of Lerwick High Street. Alexander had looked at her in surprise at first when she said that she was going to Lerwick again.

'But I thought you didn't like shopping.'

'Well I didn't but the shops have improved and anyway I want to take back that coat I took out on appro for Hannah. It's just on the small side and won't last her any time. I'm going to get the bigger size.'

'That's fine then. Will Meg be here?'

'Yes, she'll have your lunch all ready. Edie will look after the little ones.'

She looked up and down the street. She didn't want to be waiting in a teashop doorway. If I'm there first, I'll just go in and order. I've never done this by myself before. I hope he comes. Don't be stupid. Where's the girl who came all the way to Shetland by herself? Yes, but as Magnus pointed out, a boat's different from a harbour, or street for that matter. Here's the place. She looked around. No sign, and then he was there.

'Hello, I'm here,' he was panting as though he had been running. 'I just didn't want to be late.' He shook her hand. 'I'm so glad to see you. I was scared you wouldn't come. Come on in.' He held the door open for her.

'Where's Mrs Manson?'

'Oh she's busy today. I came on the bus by myself.'

'By yourself?'

'Magnus, this is 1907. We're not in the dark ages.'

'We-ll, you be careful.'

'Magnus, you'll turn into your father if you're not careful.' She laughed at his horrified face. 'I'm only joking. The bus is fine though. There's no problem going on it.' She turned to the hovering waitress. 'Yes, tea would be very nice thank you, and some scones, please.'

Miss Cunningham was as good as her word. The day after the cliff top meeting, in a staff meeting they all agreed that although it was a school rule that the young ladies of the Anderson Educational Institute should not meet young men, there was no rule forbidding meeting with one's brother.

'And after all,' sighed Miss Cunningham, who wasn't that old herself and felt quite smitten with the handsome Magnus, 'He's such a personable young man'.

A few days later saw Magnus walking up to Mrs Anderson's house by personal arrangement. School was over for the day and it was that time between school and tea when the girls relaxed a little. Some sat and read a useful book, some read not so useful books but Mrs Anderson was not supposed to know that. However with her knowledge of girls' behaviour she was quite sure that they were not always reading improving books. Mrs Anderson was of the twentieth century though and felt that girls' minds needed to be opened to a wide choice of reading.

'How else,' she argued, 'could the girls make informed choices when they were grown up if they didn't know what to choose?'

So Mrs Anderson was waiting to greet Magnus as he came to meet Christina.

'Dr Sinclair. I'm so glad to see you again.'

'Oh, Mrs Anderson, I think you may dispense with the "Doctor" bit as you've known me since I was a wee boy. How are you?'

'I'm just fine thank you. And you've come to take Christina out for a walk, I hear.'

'If that's all right?'

'Of course. Miss Cunningham has it all arranged and I have been told an hour out before tea and if we are all happy then the exercise can be repeated about once a week as we arrange it. Is that all right?'

'Perfectly. Christina, happy with that.'

'Oh yes,' Christina was just coming out of the door drawing on her gloves. 'Thank you Mrs Anderson. I'll just be a wee while.'

'Ay, don't be late or I'll have Miss Cunningham to reckon with and she herself might get into trouble.'

'Now,' said Magnus as they walked off down the road at a smart pace. 'Where to?'

'Cliff again?'

'Right, we should just make it and back in the time. Come on.' An hour later, they were back, breathless but happy.

'That was good.' Christina turned to Magnus. 'Can we do it again?'

For the next few weeks they fell into this routine. Their after school walks became a weekly fixture. It was good for both of them. Magnus became an untouchable girls' idol. When he arrived to collect Christina there was the invariable peeping behind windows, the need to cross the hall while he shook hands with Mrs Anderson, the dropped book at a strategic moment. Magnus took it all in his stride. After all it was nice for a young man to have admirers, even from afar.

Christina thought it very funny to think that they should gawp at him in this way.

'Not that there's anything wrong with you Magnus,' she said one day as they were returning from a steep climb up the back of the town. 'But you're my *brother*.'

'Well,' he argued back, 'what's wrong with that?'

'Nothing,' she admitted. 'You're really nice looking.' He gave her a mock bow. 'But I've to cope with all the girls sighing over you. Now, here we are. When are you coming out to Birkenshaw.'

'Oh I don't know.' he said. 'I'll see what I can do.'

'Magnus you always say that. The little ones are looking for you. And I know Meg and Edie were saying that they hadn't seen you for ages.'

'I'll try soon,' he said, feeling the net closing round him.

'Well mind and see you do. Here's the house. I'd better go in. See, the heads are at the window again.' Suddenly the heads disappeared. 'Mrs Anderson will have found them. She's always doing the rounds. We're not supposed to look out of the windows.'

'You're not?'

'No,' she said. 'It's not done, Mrs Anderson says.'

Even Alexander came to see him. The once tense relationship seemed to have softened. Angus's baptismal day had eased the tensions. But now, Alexander missed his son's visits home and their arboreal walks and talks. Trees in twentieth century Shetland were curiosities, experimental, and they were always trying out some new variety.

'Magnus, how are you, my boy?'

'Father, how good to see you. But what are you doing here? How did you know I was off duty?'

'Oh, I was in Lerwick the other day and came and asked when you'd be off duty.'

'And they knew?'

'Yes, I spoke to that rather charming Dr Sanderson. He said he was sure you would be off by 3 pm today and so I thought I would come up and wait a while and see if you came out.' Magnus stole a look at him. He looked slightly complacent, as though he'd just engineered something successful.

'So that's why Dr Sanderson was so keen to get me off duty today. It's not the first time he's told me to go away for a walk.'

'It's pretty obvious that he cares a lot about you. He thinks you work too hard. Mind you pay attention to him.'

'Yes, Father. Anyway,' Magnus hesitated, 'it's good to see you. Is everything all right?' Magnus suddenly felt anxious. 'The children, Charlotte…?'

'No, no, everything's fine, but Magnus, it would be good to see you. At Jarlshavn, I mean. You haven't been home for a couple of months.'

Magnus swallowed. 'The hospital is very busy.'

'Yes, but not so busy that you can't have a day off. You'll be unwell yourself if you carry on like this. Come home for a week-end. Christina is always looking for you.'

'Well, I'll try and arrange my off-duty.' Magnus felt himself giving in under the persuasion and the sharp gaze of the bright blue eyes. What would he say if he knew the truth? It didn't bear thinking about.

They headed for the Lerwick Hotel for a 'refreshment' in the lounge there. This was not a public house – Alexander would not want that – but a lounge where gentlemen could go and have a quiet drink and a chat – rather like a club, leather armchairs, peaceful atmosphere, rustle of newspapers, murmur of voices, discreet service. A good place for father and son to sit and converse. Once again Alexander returned to the subject of a home visit from Magnus before they parted.

Magnus's problem had driven him to consider leaving the Islands and obtaining a post in Scotland. He knew he'd have no problem getting work; good Scottish-qualified doctors were always in demand everywhere. But, he loved these Islands. He was born into them. He'd enjoyed his time at Aberdeen University, but he'd been there for the specific purpose of getting his degrees, becoming a doctor with every intention of returning to the Islands. His time in Aberdeen was a means to an end. Now he wanted to stay in Shetland. But the woman he loved, this unobtainable woman was living there six miles away from him. He had to keep away. But, he argued with himself, he had already met her twice in Lerwick and, he thought, I coped very well. So I might manage at Birkenshaw. Who are you trying to convince? It would be too easy to be alone with her at Birkenshaw. You couldn't do it.

'So,' said Alexander rising to his feet. 'You think you'll be able to arrange your time off and come out to Birkenshaw?'

'Yes, I think so,' Magnus could see no way around this.

'Have you any idea when?' his father pressed. Magnus bit his lip.

'I'll speak to Dr Sanderson tomorrow and let you know as soon as I can.'

'Right you are. Can't say fairer than that. We want to see you there – it's your rightful place. We thought when you came back to Shetland you would be in and out all the time – but never mind. We'll maybe see more of you now that Dr Sanderson knows...' he stopped.

'Dr Sanderson knows what?'

'Why, that we want to see more of you.'

'You didn't say that to him, did you?'

'Well, it may have slipped out in the course of our conversation. He said a lot of good things about you. And he's happy for you to take some time off to come home.'

Magnus took a deep silent breath. Don't say a word. You've just been manipulated into a corner. Go with it for now or you'll have a row.

'Anyway,' resumed Alexander briskly, 'I'd better be off. The bus leaves soon from the Market Cross.'

'Thanks for coming up.' Magnus heard himself saying. They shook hands.

'Good lad.' His father patted him on the shoulder. 'See you soon.'

'So,' Alexander related later that evening. 'We had a long talk and Magnus is going to take a weekend off soon.'

'Oh that's good.' Charlotte sat in the window letting down one of Hannah's frocks. 'I wonder if that will do,' she said. 'She's growing so fast I can't keep up with her.'

'Charlotte,' he said. 'Are you listening? Aren't you pleased? I thought you'd be pleased to see him?'

'Of course I am. He does work so hard and such long hours.'

'Yes, well I hope he's going to be home oftener now. I'm pretty sure he will be.'

'Are you? How are you so sure?'

'Well, I had a chat with Magnus's boss, Dr Sanderson. Nice chap. Able man I think. Well anyway I just put a little pressure on about Magnus and home visits.'

'Alexander, you didn't, did you?'

'Yes, why not? I am his father after all.'

'Did you tell Magnus this?'

'Well, I mentioned it.'

'What did he say?'

'Nothing really. Said he'd come. He was a bit quiet but he seemed happy enough.'

Magnus must have been biting his tongue, thought Charlotte. Aloud she said, 'So, have you any date fixed?'

'No, he said he was going to sort out his duty times and let us know.'

'That's fine.' Charlotte rolled up Hannah's frock and got up from the window seat. 'It'll be good to see him.'

He picked up the newspaper. 'Yes, you haven't seen him for ages.' Charlotte looked at him.

'But I...' She stopped.

'Mmm?' Alexander, attention diverted by the paper, looked up briefly.

'Oh nothing, I was just going to say I must get something nice in for him.'

'That's the thing, a fatted calf will do. You women always think of food first.'

'I must go and check Angus.' She left the parlour and ran upstairs. Why did I not say I had seen him? Twice. That looks deceitful. It's one thing not to mention it but the way I've avoided it, it looks as though I'm hiding something.

Angus was fast asleep in his cot. She pulled his covers up over him and held his little hand for a moment. Why do lives get so complicated? Suddenly I've as good as told my husband a lie. Well, just not the whole truth. And why? There's not a problem really, it's just that he wants to know everything I'm doing, and now I've done something, twice, that I haven't told him and he'll wonder why and there'll be an atmosphere.

'Dr Sinclair.' Dr Sanderson entered the doctors' ward office where Magnus was writing up some patients' notes. 'Good morning.'

'Good morning Sir.' Magnus got to his feet.

'No, no, don't get up. I'll sit here.' The older man sat down with a sigh. 'That's better. These late nights take it out of you.' He and Magnus had been up very late the previous evening with a little girl with a acutely inflamed appendix. 'I'm glad we got to that wee lassie in time. Thank you for your help. You did well.'

'Thank you, Sir.'

'I was speaking to your father recently.'

'Yes, Sir.'

'Oh, you know do you?'

'Yes, Sir. He came to meet me.' Dr Sanderson laughed.

'Yes, he seemed quite anxious to see you. And, that you should have some time off. Enough to go home in, I mean.'

'Sir, my father ...' Magnus began, embarrassed at Alexander's taking on the role of unwanted off duty organiser.

'Ach, Dr Sinclair, don't worry, he seems a very caring man. And he's probably right. You should go and visit your family.'

'But, but...'

'You do want to, don't you? There's no reason why you don't want to go is there?'

'No, no.' Magnus thought of Charlotte. She is the one reason I can't give.

'Right then, that's settled. I'll leave you to work out the duty roster. I'm sure you're due time. The others all have their weekends.'

'Thank you, Sir.'

'No problem.' Dr Sanderson stood up and stretched. He picked up the little girl's notes. 'Right, let's go and see our little appendix.'

The following weekend saw Magnus away on foot to walk the six miles between Jarlshavn and Birkenshaw. He could have gone by the bus, now a thriving enterprise compared with its small beginnings. But Magnus was so used to his schoolday walks back to Jarlshavn on a Friday evening that he put his rucksack on his back and set out. I wish Lowrie were here. He would tell me what to do. But Lowrie was in far-off Edinburgh.

He met a few people on the road. Some in gigs, heading for Lerwick, some like himself heading homewards. He knew many. Eventually in the distance he could just make out in the dusk of the autumn evening, the shapes of the trees at Birkenshaw. Our trees. They seem to have grown a bit during this summer. I must have a look at them.

Christina was at the gate.

'You shouldn't have waited outside for me.'

'Oh I just wanted to see you walking up the road.' She held his arm tightly. 'It's good to see you.'

Inside all was warm and bright with the glow of the newly lit gas lamps.

'Father's talking about getting that new thing – electricity.'

'Is he? Well, well. That'll be something different.'

'Magnus.' Charlotte came to the door. 'Welcome.'

'Charlotte.' Magnus felt strangely formal. He held out his hand.

'Oh, Magnus surely you can give your old stepmother a kiss on the cheek.' She took him by the shoulders and kissed him lightly. 'There, how was that?'

The moment passed. They went in and he escaped to his room with his rucksack. Soon there was a hammering at the door.

'My want Magnus. My want Magnus.'

'Heavens, what a racket. Yes, just a minute,' he called. He opened the door, just as Hannah upraised her hand for another thump. She fell into the room. 'Magnus,' she howled, 'you felled me over.'

He picked her up. 'No I didn't. You felled yourself over. Let me see you.' He dusted her down. 'See you're all right.'

'My give you a kiss?' she considered, 'or should it be shake hands. Mama says shake hands with people but she kisses me. Can you kiss me?'

'I think that would be allowed?' They kissed.

'Mmm. Nice,' she said. 'Magnus coming now?'

'Yes all right.' He allowed himself to be towed downstairs.

'Ah. There you are my boy. Just in time for a sherry. It's Friday night. A celebration.' Alexander busied himself with the decanter and glasses. Charlotte came in.

'Sherry, my dear?'

'Thank you.' She sat back. 'Your health Magnus.'

Chapter 11

That weekend was the first of a few visits to Birkenshaw. Magnus was glad when Sunday evening arrived and he could set off on foot again for Lerwick with his rucksack, now laden with baking.

Meg had insisted. 'I'm sure you're not fed properly at yon hospital. You look real peaky to me. Give me your bag and I'll put some real food into it.'

Magnus had meekly complied. He spent the whole week-end complying. It seemed easier that way. He walked with his sisters (Hannah's turning into a bossy wee thing, he decided), pushed Angus in his pram. Fortunately Angus did not cry but looked quizzically at this latest pram-pusher and welcomed them all as long as the pram kept moving. He discussed the trees and their growth with his father.

'I'm concerned about the rabbits,' Alexander confided. 'This fencing is good but there are one or two getting in somewhere and getting at the bark. I don't want any of these trees to be ringed.'

'Are any of them gone?'

'Not totally, but a few are quite badly damaged. If the damage goes right round the bark, we'll lose the tree.'

'I'll take a walk round the perimeter fence and see if I can find where they are coming in.'

'Are you sure? You're supposed to be having time off.'

'No, no.' Magnus was glad of the chance to go out by himself. 'I'll get my boots.'

Later he reported. 'There are one or two weaker bits at the bottom of the fence. I think they may be getting through there. I'll take some more fencing down and see if I can try and strengthen it. They might just burrow deeper, though.' He went out again. Alexander sat down gratefully. I'm not getting any younger he thought. I wonder if I've taken on too much with this. He dozed lightly.

Midsummer came and went. Christina started her school holidays and looked forward to Magnus's visits home which became more flexible. Magnus and Christina were very close, walking around Jarlshavn, over the cliff paths and hills. Lowrie joined them when he arrived for his summer break.

One day the two young men were out alone. Christina had gone away to Lerwick with Charlotte.

'How are things?' Lowrie panted as they neared the top of the hill at the back of Jarlshavn. He sat down to get his breath back. 'I'm not fit.'

'It's too much sitting in a lawyer's office that does it.'

'You're right. I should get out more. Anyway, you haven't answered my question. How are things?'

'With whom?'

'Magnus, you don't make it easy. With Charlotte. With your father.'

'Well, I'm only here because I have been painted into a corner. I wrote and told you about what happened in the kitchen after Charlotte heard about going down the cliff.'

'Yes. You said you were going to stay away.'

'Yes, well, then I met Charlotte in Lerwick.'

'You what?'

'Yes, well, it was an accident, not planned. But, then we met again. And Charlotte wanted me to come out here. Then Christina put the pressure on. And then my father came to the hospital and spoke directly to Dr Sanderson. So I had no excuse like too much work, for not coming. So that's it. I'm here. I make a point of coming every so often, and stay overnight and everyone's happy.'

'And you? How about you?'

'Me? I do my best not to be alone with Charlotte. But,' he looked down, 'it's very difficult.'

'And your father?'

'Well,' Magnus said. 'I was quite annoyed with him for speaking to Dr Sanderson like that.'

'I'm not surprised. Did you say anything?'

'No I couldn't. It would have caused another row. So for the moment, I'm doing what he wants, what they all want. Father and I talk about the trees and how they're growing and what he could plant next. But I don't know how long I can keep it going. The more I see her the more I feel I should clear out and the more I don't want to leave her.'

'I'm just going out to feel the air.' Alexander got to his feet and went to the parlour door. 'It's a fine evening.'

'It might be a bit nippy.' Charlotte sat by the fire. Even though it was still officially summer the evenings were chilly as the days grew a little shorter and the long light of June and July was becoming less.

'Yes, I'll get my jacket. See you in a wee while.' He went out.

Charlotte sat on in the fading light.

'All alone?' Magnus came in. 'What a quiet, still evening. Where's Father?'

'He's just gone out to feel the air as he says. Christina's gone upstairs. Did you have a good walk?'

'Yes. Met Lowrie and went round the harbour, up the back hill, along the cliff and back.' He smiled. 'Lowrie feels a bit fitter now than he did a couple of weeks ago. I told him he was sitting in his office too much.'

'Poor lad. You give him no peace.'

'Nonsense. Do him good.' Magnus hesitated then sat down next to her. 'What have you been doing? Mending again?'

'Oh, just getting some of Christina's things ready for school. They go back so soon. The holiday's just flown. There's a point, Magnus. Are you having a holiday this year?'

'Well, we have leave from the hospital but…'

65

'Yes I know, but you haven't had any for ages.'

'Och, I might take a week or so later on. I'll see. Anyway,' he added, 'what about you?'

'Me, oh I can't remember when I last left Shetland. Just living here is fine.'

'But it's not a holiday. Perhaps you need one.'

'Oh Magnus, I don't need a holiday. Think of the upheaval. Getting the babies organised. It's more relaxing to stay at home.'

'It would be good,' he said, 'to go, on holiday, just with you.'

'Magnus,' she said. 'What an idea.'

'Well. Just think what we could do? No cares, no worries. Just holiday. For a few days. Just you and me. Oh I know it's a dream,' he added. 'But, there you are. Dreams...'

'And dreams they're going to stay.' Charlotte said firmly. 'Dream away. Now, I'm going up. 'Night, Magnus.'

'Good night, Charlotte.' He sighed, and picked up the latest copy of *The Shetland Times*. He heard his father locking the door as he came in.

Magnus didn't stop dreaming. All the past constraints seemed to be welling up and boiling over. The holiday suggestion, lightly and spontaneously made which Charlotte took as a joke was an off-the-cuff remark about an event which both realised would not happen.

But a couple of weeks later, after Christina was back to school, Magnus paid his first weekend visit to Birkenshaw. She was delighted. Somehow weekends were special. Magnus walked in the back door on Saturday morning.

'Hello, Magnus,' she called. 'How was your week?'

'Busy.' He sat down at the table. Meg fussed round him with the teapot.

'Thanks Meg.'

'Did you have any sleep at all?'

'Some,' he said. 'Probably not enough. Where's everybody?'

'Oh here and there. Your father's gone down to the harbour office for the morning. Mrs Sinclair is upstairs with the children. I can hear them coming now.'

'Magnus.' Hannah burst in and hugged his knees.

'Hello.' He heaved her up on to his lap. 'Morning, Charlotte. How are you?'

'Fine, thanks Magnus. You? Been busy?'

'Always busy,' broke in Meg. 'I don't know what that hospital's coming to.'

'Would you like to go for a walk in a little while to clear your head?' Charlotte suggested. 'We could all go – provided it's somewhere we could push the pram. Meg will be glad of the peace won't you Meg.'

'Well, I'll get on with the lunch anyway.' Meg was as diplomatic as ever. Lately Hannah had taken to 'helping' her in the kitchen which slowed up the cooking process considerably.

'Right.' Magnus drained his cup and stood up.

'My want a carry.' Hannah, deposited on the floor, stood with her arms up.

'No, no, not just now. Later maybe. I'll just take my rucksack upstairs.' A walk he thought. With Charlotte and no Father. Suddenly his tiredness lifted. He ran upstairs, dumped his rucksack on his bed and ran down again.

Charlotte and Edie bumped the big pram down the steps at the front door. Christina stood at the top, holding Angus.

'Come on my wee man.' Edie ran back up the steps and collected him. 'In you go.'

'I'll push,' volunteered Christina.

'My help.' Hannah held on to the handle.

'That's fine.' Charlotte walked behind the pram with Magnus. 'If they want to do the work I don't mind. So how's *your* work?' she continued. 'And, that reminds me, how's Alfie?'

'He's much improved. He's getting up now and walking for short distances and doing leg exercises. I think he'll soon get home.'

'What about the future?'

Well, he'll never be quite the same, but he's done very well. He'll be able to do most things that he wants to, without going daft. I wouldn't like to see him at the fishing again. But there's a lot he'll be able to do.'

'Poor lad. He'll need to think of something to do other than fishing.'

'Yes. Has his father said anything?'

'Well, of course his father expected him to take over the boat. He was very competent. Now they'll have to think again. But anyway, they're just thankful he's alive. Thanks to you.'

'And the others,' Magnus reminded her.

Charlotte was silent. She knew now from all the stories that Alfie's survival owed much to Magnus's presence on the cliff and subsequently on the lifeboat.

They had reached a point where the path became steeper. Charlotte hastened her footsteps.

'We should give Christina a hand with the pram up this hill.' She hurried in front, turned her ankle on a stone, missed her footing and fell.

Everything came to a halt. The pram pushers stopped in their tracks and turned round to see, to their consternation, Charlotte on the ground, Magnus running towards her.

'Mama,' screamed Hannah.

'Mother, are you all right?' Christina, torn between looking after the pram and the precious Angus and the sight of Charlotte on the ground, hopped from one leg to the other.

'Yes, yes, I'm all right. Don't let go of the pram, Christina.'

'Charlotte.' Magnus was beside her, kneeling down, helping her to sit up. 'Are you in any pain? No, don't get up yet –' as Charlotte made to get to her feet – 'just wait until I have a look. Do you mind?' He felt her ankle carefully. 'Is that sore? That? This way?' He tested it carefully. 'Stop crying, Hannah. Mama's all right.'

'Yes, I'm fine,' Charlotte protested. 'What a stupid thing to do. Please let me get up. I just tripped. Thanks Magnus.' She accepted his hand and got gingerly to her feet.

'See,' she tapped her foot. 'See, it's fine.' Magnus still held her arm.

'Oh Charlotte,' he said. 'I'm so glad, nothing's wrong. I couldn't bear it if you hurt yourself.' He put his arm around her. 'Are you sure you can walk?'

'Magnus, I'm all right. Look, you're worrying the girls.' Sure enough, not only was Hannah clinging to her skirts but Christina had manoeuvred the pram round and was returning down the path to them.

'Are you all right, Mother?'

'Yes, of course, just a trip. Sorry for all the fuss. There.' She dusted off her skirt. Shall we go on, or have you had enough?'

'I think we should work our way back,' said Magnus, 'and not put any more strain on that ankle than you need to.' He held her carefully. She gave him a quick glance. Surely this concern was a bit excessive?

'Come on then everybody,' she called cheerfully. 'Down the hill, quick march.'

'Carry now.' Hannah stood at Magnus's legs again with her arms up. 'You said.'

'All right then.' He hoisted her up. 'Are you sure you can manage, Charlotte.'

'Of course, Magnus. Let's go.'

Back at Birkenshaw, Christina and Hannah made straight for the kitchen. Hannah made straight for Edie.

'Mama fall.'

'Oh dear, is she all right. Can she walk?'

'It's all right,' Christina reported. 'Mother tripped and turned her ankle but she's fine, no damage, Magnus says and – oh here she is.'

'Here, Mrs Sinclair.' Meg pushed a chair forward. 'Sit down. How's the ankle? What happened?'

'So silly, I missed my footing and went over on the path. I'm fine.'

'Where's Angus?'

'He's asleep.' Magnus came in. 'I've left him outside. May I look at your foot again.'

'Yes, of course, but it feels fine.'

'Yes, Mrs Sinclair,' Edie said. 'You should let Magnus examine it. Here rest it on this stool. I'll help you off with your shoe.'

Charlotte gave in and submitted to their ministrations. When her foot had been displayed to all, examined in detail by Magnus who at the same time gave a treatise on the anatomy of the foot and ankle to his delighted audience and pronounced both to be in good health, she said, 'now thank you all very much for your care and attention. May I go and put on my other shoes now please? No, no, I'll get them myself,' as Edie leapt to her feet and made to run for them.

Upstairs, she pondered. Had she imagined it or had Magnus used the opportunity to hold her, put his arm around her? Don't be silly she told herself. Don't even think such things.

But at other times when Magnus walked in she knew she wasn't imagining the looks he gave her, the way he brushed her arm with his as he passed her, the meaningful glances. Never when Alexander was around. Then Charlotte started to notice that he sometimes appeared when he must have known that his father would be at the Harbour Office. When once he was 'too busy' to come to Birkenshaw, now, he seemed to throw caution to the winds and appeared at any time.

Meg was worried. She could say nothing, but did her best to divert Magnus with cups of tea in the kitchen, bringing in logs, engaging him in conversation. She couldn't keep it up for ever though and sooner or later he found Charlotte, usually with the children. They noticed nothing. To them Magnus was just a delightful adult who had come to play with them.

'When are you coming into Lerwick again?' he asked one day. The weather had turned windy and wet and he stood at the window looking out at the grey clouds flying past.

'Magnus, I don't think so.' Charlotte looked up from the dolls' house where Hannah and she were rearranging the furniture. 'What about trying the sofa in there, Hannah?' Magnus bent down to help.

'Please come, he said quietly. It means so much to me. And it's difficult to see you alone here.'

'But we don't need to be alone. My place is with the children.'

'But we need time for each other too.'

'Magnus, we are not for "each other". My "other" is Alexander, your father. I can't come to Lerwick to meet you again. It's not right.'

'Well, you were happy enough to come before.'

'I did come before,' Charlotte conceded, 'but I felt after that it wasn't the thing I should be doing.'

'What shouldn't you be doing Mama?'

'Nothing, Hannah. Come, I think I hear Angus waking. Let's go and see.' They went off leaving Magnus at the dolls' house. He slammed its little front door.

'I won't give up,' he muttered. 'I will see her.'

One day Alexander found them. Magnus was standing very close to Charlotte.

'Charlotte, we must talk. Please meet me, in Lerwick.'

'Magnus, I've said I can't. We've already met twice and I avoided telling your father. I feel really devious about that. I'm not doing it again.'

'But Charlotte, I must see you.'

'You do see me.'

'Yes, but we can't talk here with the children around. Charlotte –' he grasped her arm...

'Charlotte, I love you.' She looked at him bleakly.

'Magnus, you musn't.'

'How can I not. I have loved you since I was a boy. I realised it years ago. But, could say nothing.'

'Magnus, don't say these things. I'm married to your father. Please, please...'

'But don't you feel it too?'

'What's going on?' Alexander's voice at the doorway. They sprang apart.

'Alexander.' Charlotte walked swiftly across to him. 'You're home early. Is everything all right?'

'Everything is all right at work. But what about here? I come back and find you two in very close conversation. What was it about?'

'Nothing at all. Have a seat Alexander. What can I get you? Some cordial?'

'I don't want a seat. I want an explanation. Magnus.' he barked. 'What are you doing here?'

'I'm doing what you asked. I'm home for my day off. It's what you wanted, remember.'

'I didn't want you home to stand whispering to my wife. She's almost your mother, boy…'

'But she's not my mother.'

'…and she deserves a mother's respect,' his father carried on without pausing to draw breath. 'Not whispered, hole in the corner conversations.'

'It's not hole in the corner. It's all right, Charlotte,' Magnus said to her as she laid a quiet hand on his arm. He turned to his father.

'You see, I love her. Really love her. More than you could possibly imagine. I want…'He stopped, horrified at what he had just said.

'Magnus,' said Charlotte. 'Don't…'

'Don't what?' said Alexander. 'Say any more? Go on Magnus. What were you going to say? What do you want?'

'I want to take Charlotte away from here. I want to be with her.'

'It's not Charlotte who will be leaving here. It's you. I am deciding here and now that you are going to go to Canada, away from this family, away from Charlotte, away from Shetland. I do not want you here again.' Magnus stood, white, fists clenching.

'I won't go. You can't make me.'

'Oh can't I? Right my boy. I'll show you 'make'. If you refuse to go, I'll cut you out of my Will. Not a penny of my money will you get.'

'I'm not interested in your money. Do you think I'm to be bought just like that?'

'Right, if you still refuse, then I shall report this to Dr Sanderson, your boss. You won't keep your job at the Gilbert Bain and you certainly won't get a reference for any other job once he knows what has been going on.'

'You wouldn't do that.'

'Watch me. I'll wager that not only would you lose your job and have no reference, you will probably be struck off the Medical Register as well. And then where will you be? No job, no reference and no prospects. Well, well.'

'Now Charlotte,' he turned to her. 'You will go to Towie for one month to visit your grandparents with the children until this is over. Please will you go now to your room and write a letter to them saying you will be on the boat on Wednesday. That should give you time to pack and make the necessary arrangements. You may take Edie with you to help with the children and to be your maid.'

'But what if she doesn't want to go? I…'

'I'll make it worth her while.' His voice was grim. 'Now please leave us. Go and write your letter. Magnus and I have things to discuss.'

'Charlotte.' Magnus held out his hand. 'Charlotte, you don't have to do what he says.'

'This time,' said Alexander, 'there is no room for discussion. 'Charlotte, please…'

'But Alexander, you can't just send him away like that. He's your eldest child. He belongs here.'

'Well he's forfeited that with his behaviour. Now please go and attend to your arrangements.' Charlotte raised her head and, without looking at the two men watching her, left the room.

'Now, Magnus,' his father turned to him with distaste. 'I thought I had brought you up to behave in a more gentlemanly way. However,' he sniffed, 'it seems that I was mistaken. Propositioning my wife behind my back. How dare you?'

'But we love each other. We want to be together – and we would be if it were not for you.'

'How dare you. You may think you love Charlotte. But believe me you haven't a clue what love means. You only want to gratify your desires. And as for Charlotte, she is my wife. No one else's, and especially, not yours. I should have known you would make trouble. I blame myself for not seeing it coming all those years ago.'

'Now go back to your hospital. Hand in your notice. Tell them you're leaving immediately. I don't care if you're breaking your contract,' he said, as Magnus tried to interrupt. 'You've just made a big effort to break Charlotte's marriage contract with me. You shouldn't be bothered about your contract with Dr Sanderson. Come back in one week's time and I'll have your papers for you. And, make no attempt, none, mind you, to see Charlotte, or the children.' He marched out leaving Magnus standing ashen faced in the middle of the floor.

Chapter 12

At half past two on an early October afternoon the train steamed into Alford station.

'Here we are.' Charlotte held Angus firmly. 'It's all right, Hannah, hold Edie's hand. Step down carefully.' A porter came forward to help. 'Thank you very much. Please could you get the luggage? There's a box in the guard's van. Thank you.'

'Oh Miss … Mrs Sinclair, what a size, I've never seen the like.' Edie looked up at the train from which she had disembarked. This had been yet another new experience to add to those she had encountered on the *St Clair*. Edie had never been sooth before and had been impressed by the novelty of the four berthed cabin, and a stewardess.

'Now ladies, if there is anything you need just tell me.' Edie had been about to say she was the maid here and she would get anything they needed, but Charlotte smiled at her and stayed the words.

'And would you like tea in the morning?'

'Thank you.'

'Dinner is upstairs in the dining room. You can go early if you like because of the little ones. I'll maybe see you later.' She bent down and patted Hannah's head, said, 'Must get on,' and rushed off.

Then there was the train. Edie had never seen a train before. She was horrified at the sight and sound of the great snorting, steaming engines, the rumble and crash of coal sliding into the tender. The size of them.

'Oh Miss, Mrs Sinclair. Will it be all right?'

'Yes, of course, Edie. Come on, I think ours is on platform 4.' The porter carried their bags and saw them on to the train.

Edie clasped Angus to her. Whatever happened, she would save him. She didn't understand why they were taking this journey so suddenly. Hadn't Mrs Sinclair been saying that she didn't want to go on holiday as it was too much of an upheaval? And now here they were. All she knew was that Mrs Sinclair had come through to the kitchen and said she had to go to Towie to her grandparents for a short holiday, and would Edie come with her for company and to help with the children? Then Mr Sinclair had appeared and given her extra pay. She had protested of course, but he had insisted. Said he was very grateful to her. And that was all. It was all arranged very quickly. Magnus disappeared back to the hospital and as for Mr Sinclair, apart from that one time in the kitchen, well, he wasn't speaking to anybody. Apart from the usual politenesses, that was. Edie couldn't understand it at all. She asked Meg if she knew what was going on but Meg just tapped the side of her nose and said, 'Least said, soonest mended,' which Edie thought was a really silly phrase and not helpful.

'That's fine Edie.' Charlotte's voice was firm. 'It's all right. We're here now. And here's young Jock with the gig.' 'Young Jock' came forward touching his cap respectfully.

'Good afternoon Mrs Sinclair, Miss,' he nodded to Edie. 'I'll get the box and bags.'

'Thank you Jock. How's your father.'

'Oh he's not so bad, a bit sair-made with the arthritis but he copes. Ye'll need to go down and see him.'

Later, when the bustle of arriving had died down and the children had gone out for a walk with Edie pushing an ancient pram, found in the loft, for Angus, Charlotte sat down with her grandparents in the parlour at Trancie House. She looked at them. They were getting old. She hadn't seen them since before the children were born and her grandfather in particular looked what he was, an old man. Weathering well, but nevertheless eighty-seven years old, Granny at eighty-three seemed as brisk as ever – the hair a bit whiter, the face a little more lined but still the active figure that she had been.

Charlotte looked around her with pleasure. 'It hasn't changed a bit.'

'Oh don't say that,' protested her grandmother. 'Please notice the new wallpaper.''

'Yes, you told me about that. It's really lovely. Did Jimmy Allardyce come and do it?'

'Yes, well, young Jimmy – his father's too old now to do big painting jobs. But young Jimmy is good, trained by his father and right into the business. It's a while now since he took over as the main man. Some folk don't like to give up.'

'Now, who are you getting at?' Granpa looked up and smiled. Granny and Charlotte looked at each other and laughed. Granpa had found it very difficult to let go of the reins of the Towie medical practice and hand them over to a younger man.

'Never mind, Granpa, I'm sure the folk like seeing you around just the same.'

'Ay, ay. I take a walk down to the village and have a craic now and again. Some of the old boys are still there. But we're all getting on now. I go and see Jock. He can't get up here so easily now so I go and see him.'

'How is he?' Charlotte had a soft spot for her old friend and mentor, Jock, Granpa's horseman for many years. It was Jock who'd taken her from her home at Glenbuchat when she was six, to her new home with her grandparents in Towie; who'd sensed her grieving, her need for comfort on that first momentous change in her life; who'd been there for her whenever she needed a listening ear. Now, he was an old man, in his eighties, like Granpa but stiffened with arthritis.

'He's fine really,' said Granpa. 'A bit stiff. It takes him a while to get moving in the morning and he gets cold as he can't walk quickly enough. He kens you're coming. He'll be looking for you.'

'I'll go and see him tomorrow. Would he like to meet the bairns, do you think?'

'Of course he would,' said Granny. 'He was saying that to me only recently. He wanted to see them before they got past the baby stage. Charlotte, it's lovely for us to see you here again. I can't remember when last you were here. Before Hannah, certainly. Anyway, here you are with your two precious little ones.'

'Doubly precious, I'm thinking after all the problems you've had,' Granpa said. 'You've had quite a time of it.'

'Yes, I know, but I'm fine now. I'll never forget the other babies, neither will Alexander. They will always be remembered, and little Alexander is buried in the Kirkyard. Hannah even says, "My go and give flowers to Alexander".' She smiled. 'She's a joy. Mind you she can be a wee besom too.'

'Well, we're delighted to see you,' Granny said. 'Quite sudden though. We only got your letter the other day. Is everything all right, Charlotte?'

When Charlotte did not reply immediately her grandparents looked at each other and then at her.

'Charlotte,' Granny said. 'What is it?'

She looked at them, their dear trusted faces regarding her so anxiously.

'Well,' she hesitated. 'It's difficult.'

'What's difficult, Charlotte?'

'Telling you.'

'Is anybody ill, Charlotte?' Granpa leaned forward and touched her knee. 'What's happened?'

Charlotte took a deep breath. 'It's Magnus – oh, I didn't mean to start like that. I knew I'd have to tell you, but I wanted it all to be so, you know, sensible.'

'Stories of problems rarely come out sensibly,' Granny commented. 'But, come on, it's Magnus. What about Magnus? He's working as a doctor in Lerwick, isn't he?'

'Yes, but, Alexander is sending him to Canada for ever. That's why I'm here – to be away until he's gone – then I'll go back with Edie and the children.'

'But why?'

Charlotte looked at them in despair. 'Because, he says – he says, he's in love – with me. Alexander's furious.'

Gradually the whole story came out, beginning with the accidental meeting in Lerwick, building to her gradual awareness that Magnus was engineering time to be alone, ending with his declaration of love.

Once she got started the telling Charlotte found it difficult to stop and the whole story came out. Her grandparents sat silently, listening. Once or twice, Granny drew breath as though to ask a question. Granpa put up a restraining hand and she was silent to let Charlotte carry on.

'That's all,' she said finally. 'He'll be gone on the boat very soon. Alexander is booking him a passage on a ship from Glasgow – I don't know, whichever one is going. Anyway, by the time I get home to Shetland, he'll be gone and I'll never see him again.' Her voice trembled. She took a deep breath to control herself before continuing.

'No-one else knows about this – I think. Meg may know something. She's very observant, but very discreet.'

'The children?' Granny asked. 'Are they all right? Hannah? Angus is too small to pick up anything.'

'Yes, and Hannah sees Magnus as a favourite person who flits in and out and plays with her. Christina is more difficult. After all she's nearly sixteen and very quick. Magnus has been meeting her in Lerwick for weekly walks. Yes,' as Granny exclaimed – 'yes they've been allowed to do that. Magnus used to laugh at the Band of Hope standing at the windows of the boarding-house as he arrived. But,' she said sadly, 'there'll be no more of that now and Christina'll want to know why he's gone away so suddenly.'

'What will you tell her?'

'Oh, Alexander will have thought up a story. He'd never tell her the truth about this.'

'And you,' Granpa said. 'What about you?'

74

'Oh Granpa, I don't know what to do. I'll just have to carry on, I suppose. There's naethin else fur it.' They acknowledged her resignation, but he said, 'Do you love him?'

'Who? Magnus?' He nodded.

I'm not sure. Oh, I love him, but then I've always loved him even when he was a boy and Margery was dying, and we used to spend hours talking about it. I loved him then. I've loved him through the years.'

'And now?' Granpa insisted.

'And now?' Charlotte twined her handkerchief between her hands. 'And now, I don't know. I love him, yes, but,' she faltered, 'only recently I've felt I could, yes I could love him as one adult loves another. But I'm married to Alexander. He's my husband, the father of my children – I love him too. But…'she paused. 'But it's different. I think there's a spark between Magnus and me which is not there with Alexander.'

'What are you going to do?'

'Oh, I'm not going to run off to Canada too, if that's what you're worried about. No, no, if it's all right with you, I'll stay here with Edie and the children for the month and then go back to Shetland and be with Alexander. That's…' her voice wobbled, 'that's my duty, and I'll do it. Smiling.' She looked up with a smile on her face belied by the unshed tears in her eyes.

'Oh, Charlotte.' Granny got up and sat on the sofa beside her. She put her arms around the still, upright form and held her closely. Gradually she could feel the tension leave Charlotte's body as she leant into the embrace and at last the tears fell.

It didn't last long, the weeping for what had happened, for what might have been, for a marriage so suddenly on rocky ground. After a few minutes, Charlotte sat up. 'I'm all right, Granny, Granpa. Just give me a moment.' She wiped her eyes and held her grandmother's hand tightly. 'I'm glad I've told you. You needed to know, and I needed to tell you. But now I've offloaded my burden on to you too.'

'Don't worry about that lassie.' Granpa's voice was gruff with emotion. 'Who else would you unburden to but us and we're always here for you.'

'Thanks, Granpa. You always were the recipients of all my troubles.'

'How does Magnus propose to keep in touch?'

'Well, I don't know. You see, I never had any time alone with him after that awful day. He went back to Lerwick and then Edie and I packed up our things and the children's, for a month. We only had a few days. I hope he'll write – but he may be too angry to begin with.'

The month at Towie flew past. Neither of the children had been 'sooth' before and Hannah was amazed at the height of the trees, the size of the hills, the different voices of the children. She had little cousins now up at the Kirkton of Glenbuchat, children of Lizzie, Charlotte's sister and they were happy to take her in tow when they visited.

Another excitement was Granpa's latest acquisition. Motor cars were the latest up and coming mode of transport and Granpa and Young Jock had put their heads together and acquired the latest *Albion Tourer* which Granpa would own and use and Young Jock would maintain and drive. Young Jock was delighted and spent many hours polishing lamps, bonnet and bumpers which hitherto he would have spent tending his horses and the gig. Not that these were neglected. Young Jock loved his old friends but at the same time you had to move with the times.

He was good with the children too. He took them out in the gig and even saddled up the old pony for Hannah and gave her riding lessons which Edie and Charlotte watched with not a little misgiving – Edie because she was frightened of horses but Charlotte because she feared that once the horse-riding bug had bitten Hannah, there'd be no peace until she had a horse of her own.

Hannah and Angus became great favourites with the Glenbuchat cousins. Lizzie, Charlotte's younger sister, greeted her with cries of joy and what seemed to be armfuls of children. In fact there were only three, but the whole house at the Kirkton of Glenbuchat was such a busy place that Charlotte declared it felt like far more. Lizzie had more than fulfilled her ambitions to be a nurse. She had also done midwifery training at Aberdeen although at the time in Scotland there was still no legal requirement for midwifery registration. However, Lizzie was determined.

'I ken it's coming,' she said. 'It's jist these fowk in Edinburgh and Westminster that are haudin the hale thing back. An the doctors oot and aboot. I think they're a bit feart o midwives comin in an stealin their patients.' She herself had been given the post of midwife in the area and she was on call day and night. Tom her husband, an incomer from over the hill at Tomintoul was grieve at the Kirkton.

'He's a saint,' said Lizzie as she sat at the kitchen table talking to Charlotte. 'He nivver complains. He jist lets me get on wi'it. As lang as he has maet on the table, claes on his back an the bairns are aa richt, he's happy.'

They were a happy family, backed up by a housekeeper and a lassie who seemed to do everything else, and outside stalwarts for the beasts and the land. They were a big contented happy family coming in and out to be fed, watered, cleaned, clothed and loved. Noisy but cheerful, they opened their arms to their Shetland visitors and Hannah and Angus disappeared into the children's vigorous circle.

Charlotte's father was still at the Milton with Cathy his second wife whom he had married the year after Charlotte's mother died. Charlotte was glad to see him quietly happy, at peace with himself and with her (at one time he had wanted her to come back and become his housekeeper). Cathy welcomed her too – very much the farmer's wife greeting the long-away eldest daughter.

One day they all returned to Trancie House from a day at Glenbuchat. Granpa and Granny had stayed at home and Young Jock had helped Charlotte put the horse into the gig. Lizzie knew they were coming but even so, with two babies expected, Charlotte was not sure she would be there. But she was, and with the children kept well occupied under Edie's supervision, the two had spent a special day free from chores, cares and worries. Charlotte felt relaxed and happy as she turned the gig into the Trancie House gate. How she loved this place. She raised her hand in greeting to Young Jock who came out of the stable at the noise of the wheels and took the horse's head.

'All well, Jock?'

'Aa thin's fine. Miss. Here, A'll tak him noo.'

'Thanks. Right, Edie.' Edie held on tightly to Angus as she got down. He wound his arms around her neck.

'Cuddle, cuddle, cuddle,' she whispered into his neck.

'Da, da, da,' he shouted.

'No no, he's not here. Only Edie and Mama.'

'Ma, Ma, Ma.'

'Here I am.' Charlotte on the ground held out her arms. Edie handed him down. 'Now Hannah.'

'I can manage.' Hannah carefully negotiated the step to the ground. 'See, I'm big now. Not like that little baby.'

'Come on.' Edie took her hand.

'Did you have a good day?' Granny stood at the top of the steps.

'Yes. Lovely, thanks.'

'I played with kittlins,' Hannah said. 'There are four.'

'That's nice. They always seem to have kittens on the go. What are these ones like?'

Hannah thought for a moment. 'Two ginger and two black. I like the black ones best. They're all sooty and one has white feet like socks. I'll call him Socks. That's his name.' She skipped into the house.

Granny followed with Charlotte.

'There's a letter for you.'

'Oh?' Charlotte looked at her. 'From...?'

'Yes, Shetland. I think it's Alexander's writing. It's on the hall table – here.' Charlotte looked at it, recognised the careful copperplate handwriting. Was this her order to go home? She had been away for nearly four weeks. Four weeks in which her recent troubles had, not gone away exactly, but had receded into the background. The letter was brief.

23 October 1907

My dear Charlotte,

I have to inform you that Magnus left for Canada via Aberdeen and Glasgow on the *St Clair* on Wednesday last.

I have therefore booked passage for you, the children and Edie. You should join the *St Clair* on Thursday afternoon, 31 October, in readiness for the trip north. I enclose tickets and cabin bookings for you all. I plan to be at the pier when she docks to convey you to Birkenshaw. Your luggage will be carried separately.

It is my resolve to make no further mention of the reason why Magnus has left us and gone to Canada and it would be appropriate for you to adopt the same approach. We will not refer to this unfortunate episode again. You may inform Edie and Hannah that he has gone (I do not think that Angus will notice particularly) but of course give them no reason except for the possibility of work in Canada. I have also informed Christina.

I remain,
Your loving husband,
Alexander Sinclair.

77

Chapter 13

Clyde Avenue
Glasgow
31 October 1907

Dear Lowrie,

You probably won't get a surprise when you get this letter from me as no doubt you'll have heard from your mother that I've left Shetland and am *en route* to Canada. Whatever else you have heard, this is the real story.

What we discussed in the summertime about my feelings for Charlotte came to a head a few weeks ago. They all nagged me to visit Birkenshaw and as you know I finally gave in. I expect I overdid the visiting. One thing led to another and I suppose I got a bit too close to Charlotte on one or two occasions. To be fair to her, she gave me no encouragement apart from that day she agreed to meet me in Lerwick. But I love her so much – I just couldn't resist any chance to get near her. Anyway, one day Father came in and found me whispering to her. Hannah was there too. Father demanded to know what was going on and I lost control of my tongue completely and told him how much I love Charlotte and that I wanted to take her away from there. He went into a colossal rage and to cut a long story short, he has ordered me away to Canada. If I don't go he will cut me out of his Will. When I challenged that, he said he'd tell Mr Sanderson, my boss, and then I would not only get the sack (instead of the more respectable resigning which I have had to do) but I'd probably be put off the Medical Register because of 'behaviour unbecoming to a member of the medical profession'. I can tell you, I was so angry. I still am.

Anyway, I'd to give in. Father sent Charlotte and the children with Edie to her grandparents for a month and I was ordered back to Lerwick to resign and keep away from Birkenshaw until Charlotte had gone. I haven't spoken to her since that day.

When I got back to Lerwick, the next thing I'd to do was speak to Mr Sanderson. That was not easy. Can you imagine? Here I am, doing fine at my work, getting on well (I think) with my boss and then, out of the blue, I've to go to him and say, 'Sir, I've come to hand in my resignation'.

He said, 'Sit down, Dr Sinclair.' Then he said, 'What's going on?' I said that there was nothing going on and that I'd considered my position and felt I needed a change.

'Where are you changing to?' he said

'Canada, Sir.'

'I see. Why Canada? Do you have any particular area in mind?'

I did not know what to say. If I said 'it's Canada because my father has said so,' he would immediately realize that Father had something to do with this. If I said that I had always wanted to go to Canada, he would know that wasn't true as I had only recently told him how important Shetland was to me. And, I didn't have a particular area in mind. I don't know Canada – at least no more than we learned at school.

In the end, he said, 'Come on Magnus' – he actually called me Magnus – 'there's more to this than meets the eye. Why do you really want to go?'

'I don't want to go.' By this time I was beginning to feel quite upset.

'Then why?'

Eventually I said, 'Because my father has ordered me to, Sir.'

'Ah, your father.' He nodded in such a perceptive way you'd have thought he had inner knowledge of the whole thing. I can see him yet, sitting there, leaning on his desk with his elbows, twirling his spectacles round and round.

Then he said, 'I have, as you know, met your father. I don't know him well. However, I get the feeling that if your father is ordering you to Canada, then that is a done deed.'

I was about to speak, tell him a little more, I don't know, you never know what you might say. But he raised his hand up to stop me and said, 'I don't need to know any more about anything that may or may not have happened at your home. I am truly sorry to lose you and this hospital will be a lesser place when you have gone.' He spoke so kindly I nearly cried. Then, he told me he was friends with a consultant in the Calgary General Hospital. Calgary is in Alberta, quite far west. Would I like him to contact this doctor on my behalf and see if he had an opening for me? He also said he would give me a very good reference. What could I say but 'thank you very much'?

Well, the next thing was, he called me in one day and said he'd had a telegram from his friend in Calgary who said he had an opening for me, a job is available and to go to the hospital in Calgary and let him know my estimated date of arrival. So this I have done and I'm on my way. I go to Liverpool tomorrow and sail on the *Empress of Ireland* the day after.

I'm still very angry with Father. At the moment, I feel I never want to speak to him again. But, then there's Charlotte. I want to contact her and yet I won't be able to – not by herself anyway. Do you think I should write to them all together and that way be writing to her? I don't feel like writing to my father but maybe this is the only way to keep in touch with Charlotte.

I can't tell you how sorry I am not to see you before I go. Please, keep in touch and let me know how you are getting on and what is happening in Jarlshavn. If you write to the Doctors' Residence, Calgary General Hospital, Calgary, Alberta, Canada, that should get me.

Thanks for all the good times we've had together and for listening to all my problems over the years.

Your good friend,
Magnus.

14 November 1907

Dear Magnus,

Thank you for your letter. As you say, I was not surprised by your news that you had left Shetland. My mother wrote me at my rooms in Edinburgh in not a little excitement to say that you were away although she seemed to have no idea of the real reason. She seems to think that you have had some sort of idea of travelling the world. I expect that's the story being put about. Anyway, better that than the truth.

By the time you get this I hope you are in Calgary and settling into the new job. Setting everything else aside, it should be quite an interesting experience, new country, new faces and all that. Who knows, I may come and join you.

Regarding your problem about writing to Charlotte, I think the best way to do it would be to get on with it and write a letter to the whole family. Then it is totally open. My feeling is that you should not mention the problem which sent you to Canada in the first place. Make it newsy, tell about your journey, your new job, the hospital and what you think of Canada and Calgary.

I must rush as I am due in Court shortly. I just wanted to let you know I had received your letter. I'll write again soon.

Your friend, Lowrie.

> Doctors Residence,
> Calgary General Hospital,
> Calgary,
> Alberta,
> Canada.
> 25 November 1907

Dear Father, Charlotte, Christina, Hannah and Angus,

I arrived here about ten days ago. As you will know the *Empress of Ireland* left Liverpool on 3 November. The crossing took about a week. It was very stormy and I felt sorry for some people who didn't have much space. In a strange way I quite enjoyed the stormy weather. It was exhilarating to be on deck watching the waves and seeing as well as feeling the movement of that big ship. It was also an exciting feeling to see land at last (even though it really hadn't been that long since we had left Liverpool) and eventually steamed past Newfoundland on our right (sorry, starboard) side and Nova Scotia on the port. We could even see Prince Edward Island and I thought of *Anne of Green Gables*, Charlotte. So that was us well into the Gulf of St Lawrence and when we docked at Quebec City I felt a long way from Shetland.

I didn't stay long in Quebec – only overnight and not long enough to find out much about this city which I must revisit sometime. I had to use my school French to order dinner that night. Fortunately, I managed – and the dinner was very good.

The next morning was an early start as I had to get a train on the Canadian Pacific Railway for my journey west to Alberta and Calgary. It's a long way. Apparently this railway has been and still is very important to Canada's history and has played a major role in it. My knowledge of Canada is being added to as I go along. Everyone I've spoken to is very helpful and keen to tell their story. The areas of the west only agreed to enter the Dominion of Canada when they were promised a rail connection and most European settlers have used the line to get them across the country. Just as I have done. It's a vast railway company.

Then, into Alberta and eventually Calgary. Alberta only became a fully-fledged Province of Canada in 1905. It was called after, not Prince Albert as you might think, but

Princess Louise, whose full name is Louise Caroline Alberta. I never knew that before. The folk here seem to know so much about what they call the home country.

Calgary is the second town in Alberta. I like the name – I'm told it means 'clear running water' in Gaelic and is named after Calgary Bay on Mull. You can see the buildings for miles as the surrounding plains are so flat. There are lots of farms around and you are just beginning to think, is it all as flat as this? when you look west and in the distance you can see the Rocky Mountains. It's not as cold as I thought it would be. I expected it to be very cold, and it was in Quebec. But here what they call the Chinook winds blow sometimes off the mountains and help to raise the temperatures.

When I arrived I headed for the hospital. They were expecting me in the Residence, although not completely sure when. It's not a big Residence but room for each doctor to have a room to himself. The nurses stay in another building quite near. We usually eat in the hospital dining room.

I got unpacked and went for lunch with Gavin MacKenzie who is another young doctor here. He's been here for a couple of years, comes from Oban and trained in Glasgow. He's been showing me the ropes. He introduced me to my new boss Dr Alan Ramsay, another Scot – the place is full of Scots. I had a very good interview with Dr Ramsay and then Gavin showed me round.

The current Calgary General Hospital has beds for 35 patients. Gavin told me this particular building has been on the go since 1895 when it took over from the original CGH which started five years before with only eight beds. He showed me some of the old annual reports – they must have worked on a shoe string. There are lists of donations like sheets, jars of marmalade, eggs and even live hens – to mention only a few. This was when Calgary was really very much a Frontier town and the CGH was very much a Frontier institution. How they managed, I don't know. As the town grew, I think they quickly realized that they required something more substantial and this present hospital even though it is small, has had running water and electric light right from the start. It even has some private wards. However it's still too small and plans are already underway to build another CGH on a different site near Bow River to the north of Calgary. I haven't seen this site yet but the staff seem quite pleased at the idea of a larger modern hospital. It is due to open in about three years' time. This time, Gavin says, the hospital Board is thinking of something much bigger. They are certainly crowded out here.

Life is very busy. We deal with everything from birth to death, casualties, medical conditions, surgery and so on. Everyone who comes through the doors. Many are admitted if we have space. Some are walking wounded. This is Indian country: the big local groups were the Blackfoot, the Sarcee and the Stoney. At the same time there were a lot of European trappers and traders and the two sides as we all know from history books did not get on, to say the least. Now we have the well-established Northwest Mounted Police to keep things in order, with a headquarters currently at Fort Calgary and of course the Canadian Pacific Railway which brought me here. It also brought loads of settlers twenty or thirty years ago as well as cattle herders from the USA looking for good grazing. So Calgary is very much a cattle centre and this leads to a significant number of related injuries as the cowboys are forever getting into trouble with their horses, cattle and rodeos. I haven't been to a rodeo yet but Gavin has given me a graphic account.

I must go now and get this away to the post before I go on duty. I hope you're all well. A belated happy first birthday to Angus. I hope the day went well.

Yours affly.,

Magnus.

Birkenshaw
14 December 1907

Dear Magnus,

Thank you for your letter of 25th Nov. It was good to hear from you and to hear that you are getting on all right and seem to have settled down.

Everything is fine here. Christina tells me to say that she will write to you soon and that she would like a letter for herself please. The small children are well. Angus's birthday passed without anything untoward happening.

The weather has been cold with a few gales and one particularly bad northerly where we had to send out the lifeboat to the *Mary Adie* which got into trouble. All were fine however and the vessel towed into harbour.

The hours of daylight are very short now. I'll be glad to see the shortest day pass next week and then we can begin the long pull towards the lighter nights.

Take care. Work hard and do your best.

I remain,

Your affectionate father,
Alexander Sinclair.

Birkenshaw,
Jarlshavn.
14 December, 1907

Dear Magnus,

Your Father said he was writing to you in response to your letter and agreed that I could also write and we would put my letter in with his.

Thank you very much for your fine newsy letter. It was very good to hear from you and know that you are all right after your long journey. You sound as though you have landed in a very interesting place with many challenges.

We are all fine here. Christina is missing you and your walks in Lerwick very much. She is very busy with schoolwork though, and doesn't have much time to do what they now call 'extra-curricular activities'. She says she is going to write to you when she has time and give you all her news.

Hannah and Angus are well too. As you know we went to Towie for a month. Edie was a tower of strength and Hannah and Angus were, on the whole, very good. They took the long journey from Shetland to Towie in their stride. I was amazed at Hannah and the grown up way she behaved on the boat. In the dining room she sat up straight and was forever 'sorting' Angus – wiping food off his face and that kind of thing. When it came to going on the train, she was not bothered at all but Edie thought it was a monster and was quite scared to begin with.

Granny and Granpa seemed very pleased to see us and not at all put out at our sudden visit. They send you their love and best wishes for your new venture. So do the Glenbuchat folk. They were very interested to hear about where you were going.

Granpa has invested in a car. He's very forward thinking for his age. Do you remember my telling you about the water-closet at Trancie House? They got that before anyone else in Towie or the surrounding area. Now he has achieved another first in the area with his car, or more specifically, an *Albion Tourer* – one of the latest models. It's very grand looking and seats four people. So of course we've all been in it and at the moment Granpa records every journey it does with the mileage and how it performed and so on. It's going to be quite a record. Of course, he doesn't drive it himself. Young Jock who's really there for horses is now the car man or *chauffeur*, I suppose we should call him. He's delighted with his new role and spends a long time under the bonnet cleaning the innards as well as polishing the outside. Granpa takes a great interest and does some polishing too and gives lots of advice as he reads through the instruction manual.

Now we're home again and Christina will soon be home at the end of term with the New Year almost upon us. Everyone sends you lots of love and best wishes. Meg says, 'Make sure and eat plenty'.

Yours affly,
Charlotte.

Calgary
7 January 1908

Dear Christina,
Happy New Year. I hope 1908 is a good one for you.

I have been thinking it was high time I wrote to you. I know you're included in my family letters but sometimes it's nice to get a letter to yourself so here goes. I can hardly believe it's such a long time since I saw you. The end of the year just rushed in especially with my move to Calgary and having to learn all about the new job as well as a new country and customs.

The job is fine and my boss Dr Ramsay is very helpful as well as Gavin, my immediate senior on the team. Dr Ramsay is really a surgeon but in a place like this you have to be able to turn your hand to anything. I can tell already that it's going to be good experience. I've also been into the maternity ward. The labour ward is busy sometimes but most babies are born at home. Still, when they have problems they come to us, from quite far afield.

We, that is Gavin and I, have also acquired bicycles. Gavin's had his for a while but when I arrived, he said, 'I'll show you where to buy a bike'. So we went down town to a bicycle shop and there were quite a few to choose from. I bought my bike – black with an oil-bath chain guard – very up to the minute and then we had to cycle back to the hospital. No, before you ask, I did not fall off. I can ride a bike, remember. But there are more vehicles on the road in the middle of Calgary than there are in Shetland, and I don't think the folk are so careful. We have to watch where we are going.

Anyway, having the bicycle has widened my horizons as I can now get out of Calgary more easily when I am off-duty and explore the countryside around. Also it is quite flat for a long way on the prairies – you'll have learnt about them in Geography and they are used for wheat growing and so on. In the distance I can see the Rocky Mountains. One day I may get there. Flat countryside gets a bit boring after a while. Not that there is time to be bored – we don't have much off time.

Tell Meg that the food is fine – she keeps sending messages to keep eating. Save the stamps for your collection. If you like I'll collect more here and send them to you.

I'm missing our walks and your smile. Please write me a letter when you've time.

Your loving brother.

Magnus.

Anderson Institute Girls'
Boarding House,
Also known as Mrs Anderson's House,
Lerwick.
Thursday 30 January, 1908

Dear Brother Magnus,

I was so happy when your letter came through the post all for me. Thank you <u>very</u> much. It was good of you to send it here. It made me feel really special. Do take care on that bicycle won't you. I was telling Mother about it and then let her read the letter. I hope you don't mind but I think she liked reading it. She smiled when she came to the bike bit. She said she could just see you on it.

We are very busy here. The teachers keep telling us the examinations are not far off and we have to keep working. We try but there's a lot to do. We have English, Mathematics and that as you know includes Algebra and Geometry. Then there's Science, French, Latin, Geography, History. The light relief is Physical exercises or gym. Miss Gray is still here and she is so popular. So many of the girls have crushes on her. I don't, because Mother said you could like somebody without having a crush on her. So, I like and admire her. I really enjoy gym and do my best to take exercise at other times too.

I miss our walks very much. I wish you hadn't had to go away. I still don't know why you went. The girls keep asking me where you are – they were so excited when you came to the house to collect me. Mrs Anderson was like a sheep-dog trying to herd them into the back room. I think they had a crush on you!

Up Helly Aa was on Tuesday of this week. Lerwick was in a great stir about it and we even had a day off on Wednesday as all the grown-ups had been up all night. The men were going from hall to hall in their guising costumes and doing their performances and the women were in the halls supplying food and drink. We went out *en croc* to watch the procession and the lighting of the galley. It was spectacular. The rain stayed away for once and there was enough wind to make the flames jump but not enough to be dangerous. Then we had to go back to Mrs Anderson's. She was very kind and gave us extra cocoa and biscuits, as it was a special night. It was lovely not to have to get up so early for school the next morning. And we were allowed out for a walk – not alone of course but in twos and threes. The only thing was Lerwick was so quiet because so many people were asleep.

Hannah and Angus are fine. I see them at the weekends. Angus is walking now although he gets to where he wants to be faster when he crawls. He's got hair now but Mother hasn't allowed it to be cut yet. One day I tied a ribbon in it – it was only a joke but Father didn't think it was funny. He said Angus wasn't a girl.

Anyway, I must go and get my homework finished. I'll post this on my way to school tomorrow morning. I think the post office will be open.

Take care, my brother, so far away.

From your loving sister,
Christina.

Three years later

Birkenshaw
13 May 1911

Dear Magnus,

Thank you for your last letter to us. We are pleased to hear that you are doing well and that it appears that you have gained advancement. That is very good news indeed. You have obviously gained the approbation of your fellow doctors and we are glad for you. It's a pity that it could not have been here where medical expertise is so greatly valued and needed. However it was not to be.

All is well at Birkenshaw. Charlotte had a cold two weeks ago but she is much improved especially with the advent at last, after a particularly long cold winter, of some very good spring weather. Now I hope we can look forward to the growing season and light evenings.

Christina has settled into her nursing course at Aberdeen Royal Infirmary. She seems happy although works very hard. Sometimes she has to do night duty. I do not like the idea of her being on duty all night. However, there is nothing I can do about it and she does not complain. I have written to the Matron regarding certain aspects of the nurses' living quarters, for example, making sure the outside door is locked and when they have to be in their rooms in the evenings. She wrote back, quite abruptly, I thought, saying that all the young ladies in the Home were well cared for and supervised and that the Rules were there and followed. She did not mention Christina by name. I had expected a more personal letter.

The country is getting very excited about the Coronation of the new King. It is over a year now since Edward VII died and the people are getting used to not having him. There was quite a lot of talk about him and his rather unkingly behaviour. King George V and Queen Mary will be crowned on 22 June. The schools are having a holiday. London seems a long way from Shetland but even here they are getting flags out.

I don't know if you will have heard about the great new liner that White Star Line is building. They say this is going to be a totally new concept in liners. This one – they say – will not sink. It's something to do with the hull being in separate compartments. Quite revolutionary. I get quite a bit of the news because of being Harbour Master and there is quite a buzz going on. It will be launched at the end of this month and when it goes into service I think it will be the biggest liner yet. Of course, there was great excitement when Cunard Line launched the *Lusitania* in September 1907, but this one is bigger and, I have to say, promises great things. These shipping lines are getting more and more competitive.

85

On another subject, do you get any word about what is going on in Europe? We are all paying close attention to what is happening. It seems that the Kaiser is rattling his sabre rather loudly. I would not like to see a war but I think we will if things go on like this. Some of the young men are already saying that they are going to enlist if it comes to war.

Hannah and Angus are fine and doing well at school. Hannah's reading is very good. Charlotte is adding a note in with this letter.

I hope everything continues to go well with you.

Your affectionate father,

Alexander Sinclair.

13 May, 1911

Dear Magnus,

Just a note along with your Father's. Everything's fine on the whole although it's been a long winter and we're glad to have some warmth.

Hannah and Angus are very well and growing like weeds, which means letting down clothes and so on. Meg is being so helpful. Unfortunately her ankles are quite swollen and she's been told to sit with her feet up. So when she sits, she alters clothes. Edie, as usual, is another tower of strength.

I have been watching the press with great interest about the doings of what have become known as suffragettes. The whole idea of women having political and social inclusiveness has been going on for a long time. For women to be able to go out to work and take part in the world on a similar footing to men has always been part of my thinking – that was all part of why I wanted to train and work as a teacher and keep going after marriage. It was and still is very important to me. Now across the country women are campaigning for women's rights and have formed themselves into a sort of Union. I've copied it out of the paper for you – the National Union of Women's Suffrage Societies (NUWSS) and a more militant branch called the Women's Social and Political Union. I feel very sympathetic towards these women and although I can't do anything active for them, I think about them a lot and thought you would be interested to hear what's going on. Of course, these big unions started in England and get all the publicity. But they're alive in Scotland too.

It was good to see Lowrie home for a short while at Easter. He's looking very well and said to tell you that he is missing your dragging him out for walks but is trying to keep fit. His parents have got a Shetland collie now and he has been all over your usual walks with her. He says he'll write to you soon.

I had a letter from Granny and Granpa the other day. They seem to be fine although quite slow now. I noticed quite a difference in Granpa especially when I was in Towie last autumn. Mind you, he's 91 and I think he's pretty good for that. He's still very pleased with the car and goes out in it as often as he can. Leslie keeps him up to date with medical matters. They are always so interested to hear about you and what is happening in the CGH. They were delighted to get your letter at Christmas.

All news from Christina is good. She's very keen on her work and makes no complaints about anything. Your father worries about her doing night duty but she's fine. It's all part of the hospital scene as you will know only too well. She seems to like

Aberdeen and has managed once or twice to get out to Towie to see Granny and Granpa. Needless to say they welcomed her with open arms.

And don't worry about me either – I've only had a cold. I just need to sneeze and your father wants to wrap me in cotton wool. He is quite fit. He's gradually allowing others to take over some of the work at the Harbour Office but wants to continue in his post for a while yet. He's very interested in the shipping of the wider world, not just our own area and of course he gets news first-hand at the Office. The building of this big new steam ship is fascinating to him. Imagine! They say the likelihood of its sinking is practically negligible. She won't be ready for her maiden voyage until next year of course but what a to-do there will be. The preparation for the launching is causing enough stir in the papers.

I'll close now. Take care.

Yours affly.,

Charlotte.

Alexander to Magnus

1 June 1911

Just to let you know that the new liner was launched yesterday – called the *Titanic*. She's quite amazing. The White Star Line should be proud of her. The photos will be out soon. Watch for them. I'm sure they will be in your Canadian papers. She'll now have to be fitted and I think they're planning her maiden voyage next spring.

Nurses' Home
Royal Infirmary
Woolmanhill
Aberdeen
19 July 1911

Dear Magnus,

I am so sorry I have not written to you for a while but I feel that if anyone understands the pressures of hospitals and the work that goes on inside them, you will, and I beg for some patience from you. Thank you for your last letter to me. I was delighted to get it even though your writing is not getting any easier to read (only joking).

Your work at the CGH sounds excellent. I'm glad you like the new hospital. It must be good to work in up-to date conditions. Here at Woolmanhill [Aberdeen] things are rather cramped and old fashioned. This, I think is made doubly difficult when doctors with their new knowledge are wanting to try out new treatments and there's not the equipment to do some of these with. But there's good news here too. They, that is the doctors and committees and councils who organise such things, are as I write, building no less than three new operating theatres and a Casualty and Out-Patient Block. The place is growing before our eyes. It should all be completed by next year. Evidently a man from Dufftown went to Canada, made his fortune and donated a large amount of money for this. Now you see what is expected when you go off to Canada!

I'm enjoying the work and training here – most of it. Some days we're very tired and just want lie down when we get off duty. We think of all the poor souls and the misery and the unhappiness and could get quite down ourselves. Then we start talking everything through, about the day and what has happened and after a while we seem to be able to get it into perspective, see it all in a slightly different light and feel a bit better. The Sisters are interesting. Some are so helpful, take time to teach us and show what has to be done and are wonderful with the patients. But one or two are quite hard – I don't know why. (Please don't mention any of this to Father. It would just worry him).

Talking of Sisters, I sometimes see Aunt Lizzie. She was very helpful when I started and came in from Towie especially to show me around lots of places in Aberdeen where I and my friends in the class can go and have a cup of tea and it's not too expensive. That kind of thing. She was so kind. It's a pity in a way that she's not working here now but I know that she's happy doing what she is doing and it's nice to go and see her at Glenbuchat. She did say I might go and see a birth with her one day if it happened when I was at Towie. That would be wonderful. Maybe I'll be a midwife.

I have an anatomy lecture in the morning so I must go and prepare for it.

Enjoy the Canadian summer.

From your affectionate sister, Christina.

Magnus to Alexander, Charlotte and children:

1 October 1911

All is well here. It is the 'Fall' and the autumn colours are magnificent. How I wish I could paint, but I don't think even the best painting could reproduce this. Gavin and I have been out on our bikes and are now in the doctors' sitting room awaiting the summons to dinner. It's usually very good but not the same as good home cooking though. Then he's going out again – to visit his young lady and her parents. They live reasonably near. I am on call tonight so will be around.

Work is interesting and a challenge as always. There is talk, though, about War in Europe. There is quite a lot about it in the papers. I'm thinking about joining the local Militia which meets every week to have some military training just in case.

Alexander to Magnus

4 November 1911

I note what you say about joining the Militia. Please be careful. Remember your first calling of Medicine.

Charlotte to Magnus

4 November 1911

Just a note in with your Father's. It's always good to hear from you…do take care. Militia to me means guns and bayonets and I don't like to think of anyone using these. But while there's a struggle for power some men will see a need for these instruments of war and others will have to defend themselves and their families.

Magnus to Father, Charlotte and children

5 March 1912

Sorry I haven't written for a while. Work is very busy and now I have joined the Militia much of our spare time is taken up with that. Gavin has joined too and we work a lot together. They are taking the threat of War very seriously.

Charlotte to Magnus   16th April 1912

Dear Magnus,
You will be surprised to see a letter from me without one from your Father. I'm sorry be the sender of bad news. Your Father had a stroke yesterday – he's in bed at home. He was adamant that he did not want to go to the hospital and so Dr Taylor agreed that he could stay at home and we are nursing him here.

It happened quite suddenly. He was at work. Apparently news came through to the Office that the Titanic had struck an iceberg on her maiden voyage just before midnight on the 14th April (two days ago) and had sunk at approximately 2.20am on the 15th. Alexander was deeply affected by this. You know how he watched the Titanic's progress from start to finish – right from the time when she was up on the stocks at Harland and Wolff's shipyards in Belfast until she was launched last year. Only recently he saw photos of her sea trials in Belfast Lough and then out to sea before heading from Belfast to Southampton for her maiden voyage. I can't tell you how much he lived and breathed this. In effect, he was there. And that made his reaction all the more acute when the news came that the Titanic had gone.

The first I knew was when I saw him walking up to the house. His head was down, his shoulders were drooping – he suddenly looked old. I went out and said, 'Alexander, you're home early. Is everything all right?' Angus was with me – he's had a bit of a cold and I kept him off school. He shouted, 'hello, Father,' and couldn't understand when Alexander just looked at him and didn't respond. He walked past us and into the parlour. Then he turned and said, 'the Titanic has gone. Struck an iceberg.' He sat down and then – flopped sideways in the chair. His right arm hung over the side quite limply and I knew, I just knew he'd had a stroke. I don't think he was unconscious. He just looked at me.

Meg and Edie were great as usual. We called Dr Taylor and he came as quickly as he could. He was very reassuring but confirmed a stroke but seems very hopeful of a good recovery. He wanted Alexander to go to the hospital but if there's one word he can say clearly it is, 'No', so we did not want to upset him any further and he is here at home. We've made the back bedroom into a room for him until he can get up and move under his own steam again. He seems quite happy with that. His right side is paralysed but Dr Taylor feels this may improve with quiet and rest. His speech is affected a bit but even today it seems to be clearer. And he is taking some soup and other soft food. So you are not to worry. He's going to be all right.

Angus was a bit upset too especially as he was there when it happened but is coping. He is very busy helping and running errands.

I hope you're well. I'll write soon and let you know how things are.

Yours affly,
Charlotte.

Charlotte also wrote to Granny and Granpa with the news of Alexander's illness. Always regular correspondents, Granny's reply came sooner than expected.

Trancie House,
Towie.

My dear Charlotte,

I thought I'd write a quick note right away to say how sorry we are to hear of Alexander's stroke. Granpa says 'if he's able, get him moving, even in bed, as quickly as you can'. I'm sure you're doing this already but I needed to pass on the message. Let's hope that he is up and about soon.

We were interested to hear of Magnus in the Militia and although we 'guess and fear' we hope that any military intervention from ourselves and our allies will not be required. Magnus seems to be taking life in both hands – well done.

We are not too bad here. I'm a bit worried about Granpa. He's slowed down a lot recently and seems very tired. Leslie is keeping a medical man's eye on him. Do not worry – I'm sure he'll be fine. Just the weather.

Tell Alexander to get well soon.

Love to all,

Granny.

That letter arrived on 24 April. Charlotte sat on the steps and looked at it. Granpa. Granny worried. She wouldn't say she was worried without reason. I wonder how he is.

Later that day the telegram boy came peching up the hill on his bike. The telegram was brief.

Regret to inform Granpa died this morning stop Heart attack stop Granny writing stop love Lizzie stop.

Meg heard her as she passed the parlour door.

'Mrs Sinclair are you all right? What's happened?' Charlotte wordlessly held out the telegram and Granny's letter.

'This came earlier this morning', she said. 'Then the telegram. The boy has just been. Meg, he's gone. Granny's alone.'

'I'm sorry,' Meg said. 'I know how much you loved him. Edie will be sorry too. She liked him very much. So good with the children.'

'I'd better go and tell Alexander.' Charlotte got up and went up to him.

22nd April 1912

Magnus to Alexander

I was so sorry to hear the news of your illness, Father. I hope very much that you'll be up and about soon, and writing to tell me about what's going on. I have seen quite a few people who have had strokes and they have done very well.

90

Everything is fine here. We are busy with a great many admissions and of course the Militia.

Charlotte to Magnus: 30th April 1912

I'm happy to tell you that your Father is much improved and doing very well. Even from the day after his stroke we could see signs of improvement. And his speech is so much better.

I am deeply sorry to tell you that Granpa has died of a heart attack. I had a wee inkling that all was not well when I had a letter from Granny saying she was a bit worried about him. Then the telegram came. I feel sorry for myself but more sorry for Granny – she will miss him very much. They were a great partnership. Sorry this is a letter with bad news.

Charlotte to Magnus   30th May 1912

We are sitting here together in the sunshine. Suddenly things are better. Alexander has improved so much this last week. We have spent a lot of time exercising his 'bad' side, first in bed, then Dr Taylor said he could try his legs out over the side of the bed, and then standing holding on to the back of a chair. Then up to sit and then a few steps and so on. It's taken him a lot of work but you know how determined he is. So now we have reached the outside and the sun has come out in welcome. It's really warm.

He sends his love and thank you for your letters.

I have written to Granny and had a letter from her too. She is missing Granpa very much but is thankful that for him, his passing was quick. She has a lot of support from family and all her friends in Towie. She's very strong. I've also had a letter from Lizzie and she reports that Granny is bearing up very well and coped well at Granpa's funeral. He's buried in Towie.

Please take care. Will write soon.

Yours affly.,

Charlotte.

4th August 1912

Dear Magnus,

This is my first letter to you since I took ill. As I have been paralysed down my right side it has of course affected my hand-writing and I fear it is not very good. However I can but try and hope you will be able to read it.

I have just managed my longest walk yet and have had a look at the trees which are in good fettle. I am now sitting in the parlour and writing this to you before lunch. Christina says she will post it for me.

The children are still on summer holidays. Hannah will read the paper to me later. I can read it myself but get tired. Hannah reads well – just like all of you. It must be in the blood.

My boy, take care, do not work too hard. Remember there are other things in life.

I remain,

Your affectionate Father,

Alexander Sinclair.

Chapter 14

Magnus stood in the middle of his room in the Residence. His bags and boxes lay packed on the floor. With his room stripped of pictures, books, and other things collected over his time in Canada, it looked forlorn, bare, impersonal. Just as it had looked the day he arrived.

Now he was on the move again. He had been happy here. From a start which had come so out of the blue, Magnus had progressed, flourished, done well, gained promotion. But the coming of the war in Europe had changed Magnus's direction just as it played a part in changing so many other lives. From a part-time start in the Militia, Canada's home army, Magnus's commitment had grown. Alongside this there was the day-to-day news of Britain's impending part in the growing conflict that became World War 1. On 4 August 1914, war was declared. The Canadian Government was not long in offering help which the British Government accepted, in the shape of an expeditionary force. On 14 October the first contingent of the Canadian Expeditionary Force – the CEF – sailed for England. There were over 31,000 men, many of them British.

Magnus and Gavin MacKenzie were not on that first contingent. Home hospitals had to be kept running.

'I fully understand that,' Magnus said to Gavin. 'The folk here have to be considered too. But there must be some doctors who can't go to France and who could take over here. I feel it's so important that we should go and do our bit. I feel quite guilty not being in the first group.'

'I bet your father's not saying that,' said Gavin. 'I know mine is saying things like "I'm glad you're safe in Canada". As if he didn't realise that folk from all over the Empire will be hot-footing it to the Front. He maybe hasn't taken that in. He maybe thinks it's just the British at home who are going.'

'Well, my Father realises it,' Magnus said. 'He watches the newspapers like a hawk There was something in the paper a wee while ago about the fact the Government had accepted Canada's offer of help. Of course he was pleased – about the help I mean. But I can tell he doesn't want me to go. Oh, he hasn't said it outright. But then he said something in a letter about "of course you'll be staying at the hospital. I have reassured Charlotte about this as she is very worried". That's really like blackmail.'

'Has Charlotte said anything?'

'Not directly. She leans on the other aspect. I mean, she says things in her letters like, "I'm so glad you are happy at CGH, and what a good job you seem to be doing". Things like that. Then she says how sorry she is for the families of all the men at home who are going away. You know, all very round about.'

It wasn't long however, before help arrived at the hospital in the shape of two doctors who had lived in the area all their lives, who had trained and worked for a time in the old CGH and who were now too old to volunteer for active service.

'Well, we can be active here at home,' Harry Mack said when he came to talk to Allan Ramsay, Chief Medical Officer at CGH. 'I would give a lot to get over there and take the Hun on. But I guess my fighting days are over.'

'Me too,' agreed Willie Smout, there on the same errand. 'But we can be here and free someone else to go. What do you say, Allan.'

Allan Ramsay looked at his two volunteers. They were old friends, golfing buddies, knew each other well.

'Well, I do have two young members of the medical staff who have come to me and stated their wish to go to the Front. I told them I couldn't let them go because I had no replacement for them – but of course this changes things.'

'Of course it does.' Harry Mack looked at the other two. 'What do you think, Willie? Aren't you just dying to see the inside of a ward again? And not from a bed?'

'Talking of which,' Allan said, 'how are you both? Fit enough I hope?'

'No bother,' said Willie. 'I know my old ticker was a bit erratic but that's all OK now.'

'Me too.' Harry jumped up and flexed his arms. 'I'm fine.'

'You won't have so much time on the golf course,' warned Allan. 'Or your private patients.'

'So what?' said Willie. 'There's a war on.'

That meeting took place in the third week of October 1914. By the following week Magnus and Gavin had handed in their resignation and been granted a special waiver of their contracted full notice of one month. This, 14th November, was their leaving date.

There was a knock at the door followed immediately by Gavin.

'Ready?'

'Yes,' said Magnus. 'Just, well, just looking around. He walked over to the window. I'll miss that view. The Rockies in every season.'

'Ay, but you'll be back.' Gavin put a hand on his shoulder.

'Well, we'll see. Come on.' Magnus turned away. 'Let's get on with it. At least we don't have to go through the recruiting office. I hear it's a mad house at the moment.'

The Barracks which they knew so well from their time in the Militia was also very busy. Men from the Militia now volunteering to become regular soldiers were joined by men straight from the recruiting station where they had been through the process of volunteering to fight in the European war: the initial interview and taking of personal details, the medical, the acceptance or in some cases rejection. Non-commissioned officers (NCO) from the Militia used their experience to shout, order and marshall men, some of whom looked too young to be away from their mothers, into orderly lines for identification and classification, accommodation, uniform and other kit allocation.

'I'm glad they don't get guns yet.' Magnus spoke through the noise.

'What a thought. Some of them don't look a day over fifteen. How did they get through the medical?'

'Good morning,' a voice spoke briskly behind them. They turned. The owner of the voice, the Militia Sergeant, saluted smartly. As they returned his salute he addressed them. 'Right Sirs, I have you on my list here. We're expecting you. Welcome to this – a bit busier than you're used to. The CO is waiting for you. Everything is being speeded up. Follow me please.'

'He called us "Sir"'. Gavin made to follow the Sergeant.

'Yes, I think there's no going back now.'

'Do you want to go back?'

'No. Do you?'

'No.'

'Well then, what are we waiting for?'

The Commanding Officer's door was ajar. At the 'Come in' the Sergeant ushered them in, introduced them as Drs Sinclair and MacKenzie. They stepped forward, saluted and the CO said 'Right, thank you Sergeant.'

Within minutes, Drs Sinclair and MacKenzie were commissioned as Medical Officers (MO) with the rank of Captain into Canada's contribution to the war effort, the Canadian Expeditionary Force.

'Thank you very much.' The CO, himself a Militia man, looked at them. 'I understand what has transpired at the hospital in order to release you both. I appreciate what you are doing.'

'Thank you Sir.'

'Now, there's a lot to be done before we go. I know you've both done your basic training but you need to go a bit further in the next week or two to be as ready as you can be. In addition as Medical Officers you need to test and possibly upgrade your skills in certain areas. Sergeant here will take you to our Chief Medical Officer, Major Adrian Blackwell who will be in charge of your further training until you go.'

'Thank you Sir.' They acknowledged his salute and followed the Sergeant from the room.

That was in November 1914. It was six full months before Magnus found himself on board the SS *Carpathia* bound for England with the rest of his battalion now officially known as the 31st Canadian Infantry Battalion, CEF. Six months of training, military as well as further intensive medical training to learn to deal with the specific injuries that would surely emerge in the war situation. While he and Gavin chafed at the initial time spent in preparation, they saw the reasoning for it. Never before in the Militia had they had to soldier so intensively: parading, keeping fit – if Magnus thought he was fit before he had never been like this. And the shooting practice, the bayoneting, responding to the cry, 'Fix Bayonets: Charge,' learning to scream while they ran at full tilt towards supposedly human-like sacks of straw to tear them open with razor sharp bayonets. To blot their minds to the idea that these were *in loco humanis* and that someday soon they could be doing this for real. But they were doctors. Surely they did not have to do this, they pondered.

'Yes, that is true,' conceded Sergeant Morrison, from Inverness, when they asked. 'But Sirs, ye need to know what the other men are going through. You must be able to do and understand what they have to do. You must be credible in their eyes. And, forbye, ye never know when you might have to do it for some reason, either to save yourselves or some other body.'

These wise words went for shooting as well. They practised on the Ranges nearly every day. They became crack shots.

They learned how to pack their kit, so that it could go into the smallest space possible. They had to be able to carry it all. A carefully thought-out list of necessary items. This was frequently checked at specific parades and after a couple of weeks of practice every man was expected to come on parade correctly kitted out. This included all the necessities that a soldier had to carry or wear, either worn or carried in pouches, belt, haversack and valise with supporting straps. Of particular importance were identity discs, basic rations, water bottle and personal field dressing.

Once they were through their training they set sail for Europe and the War.

Magnus was at the Casualty Clearing Station (CCS). For days he had worked amongst the parody of a parade – an endless queue of wounded, walking, carried, pushed, limping, brought by ambulance or whatever vehicle could be mustered from an ADS.

There were few doctors. A few more nurses, not formally trained, VADs who moved from bed to bed extending their limited experience day by day amongst sights and situations totally out of their experience. The trained nurses, Sisters, although also few in number did the acute work, dressings, splints, patching the people up, teaching the VADs what to do. They moved quietly, surely, with authority, compassion. They never seemed to go off duty, Magnus felt, although he knew they did. They had to sometimes. The sisters were particularly watchful of the VADs. With little previous experience they had to be taught the discipline of caring for themselves too.

'But Sister,' he heard one VAD saying. 'I can't go, I'm needed here.'

'Yes,' the Sister replied. 'But you'll be needed here tomorrow, and tomorrow and tomorrow. You won't be able to do that if you don't take time off. Now go, please.'

The girl had gone but as she went, she looked back on the carnage and her eyes were full of tears. She was back after her six hours sleep and understood then.

Chapter 15

LATE SEPTEMBER 1916

The doorbell rang in the kitchen. Edie was there doing the daily ironing when she heard the tingle. She looked up at the row of bells, each one linked with the origin of the sound. 'Front door,' she sighed putting the goffering iron carefully back on its stand. 'I wonder who that could be.'

The boy stood there, envelope in his hands, breathing heavily from his rushed cycle ride from the Jarlshavn Post Office. He looked at the small yellow envelope in his hands as though it might explode and thrust it at her.

'Telegram Edie,' he said. 'For Mr Sinclair.'

'Oh dear.' Edie stood, hands at her mouth. Telegrams could only mean one thing – news of the Front and in particular, news of the family member at or near the Front.

'Go on.' The telegram boy held the little envelope out. So harmless looking and yet potentially so life changing. 'Take it. I have to get on.'

'What is it Edie?' Charlotte heard the voices.

'It's a telegram Mrs Sinclair.' Edie took the telegram from the boy and passed it to Charlotte.

'Thank you Geordie,' called Charlotte.

'Will there be an answer?'

'I don't know,' said Charlotte. 'If there is, we'll bring it down.' She returned to the parlour.

'Alexander…'

'Yes?' he looked up from his reading. 'Anything in the post?'

'It wasn't the postie, Alexander. It's a telegram. Addressed to you.'

'Oh.'

He turned the envelope over, examined the back, checked the name and address on the front.

'Alexander,' Charlotte said. 'Open it. It can only be about one person. Here's a paper knife.' She stood, watched and hardly breathed. So precisely he slit the envelope along the top. So carefully he pulled out the single sheet of paper. He looked.

Charlotte waited.

'It's Magnus,' he said. 'He's missing. Missing in action.'

'Oh, Alexander.' Charlotte sat down beside him and held his hand. 'The poor boy. Does it say anything else?'

'No, just "details to follow". When was it sent?' He looked. 'Yesterday, 29 September.'

The details followed two and a half weeks later with Saturday's lunch-time post: a letter from the CO of the ADS just behind the Front line.

Dear Mr Sinclair,

It is my sad duty to inform you that your son, Captain Magnus Sinclair has been posted as 'Missing in Action'.

'A' Company of the 31st Battalion the Calgary Highlanders to whom he was attached as Medical Officer was in action at Thiepval Ridge on 27 September last. The Company, along with others came under enemy fire. His name, along with the names of other missing personnel has been posted to the appropriate authorities. Every effort will be made, firstly to locate him and secondly, to keep you, as Next of Kin, informed. I have waited for a fortnight before writing in the hope that we would be able to find Magnus. So far this has not been possible.

On a more personal note, I have known and worked with Magnus for two years and have found him able, trustworthy and brave. In this latest incident he showed the highest order of courage.

I remain,

Your respectful servant,

Archibald Oliphant (Major, R.A.M.C.)

Alexander passed the letter across the dining-table to Charlotte. 'He could be anywhere. Nice letter though.' His voice shook.

'May I see, Mother?' Charlotte silently handed over the letter to Hannah and watched her read it.

'It can't be true. He's got to be all right.' Hannah's eyes filled. 'Say he'll be all right, Mother. Please say it.'

'I can't say it.' Charlotte reached out her hand. 'We can hope though. Magnus is very strong. I'm sure he has a good chance.'

'I don't want him there.' Angus burst out. 'I want him here now. He's my brother and I don't know him. I want to know him. You've never let me know my brother.'

'Angus...' Charlotte began. He stood up from the table, banging his chair back. Evading his mother's outstretched hand and ignoring his father's, 'Sit down at once, Angus,' he rushed out of the dining room. His feet thumped up the stairs, his noisy crying lingered on the air before they heard a distant door slam and then, silence.

Charlotte bit her lip, half made to follow him, checked herself, read the letter again. Hannah sat twisting her napkin into a crumpled rope. Tears ran down her face. She didn't really know her brother either. Her memories of him were those of a three year old.

Alexander sat very still. Then, as Charlotte looked across the table at him, he slumped sideways over the arm of his chair. His eyes looked startled, shocked yet curiously glazed. He stared at her. He attempted to speak but distorted sounds emerged from the misshapen mouth.

'Mother,' shrieked Hannah. 'Father. What's happening?'

Charlotte rushed to Alexander's side. 'Hannah, get Meg and Edie. Your father's ill. It's all right Alexander, I'm here.' He looked at her imploringly. His right arm hung limply. She supported him in the chair to prevent his slipping further. 'Here are Edie and Meg now. We'll get the doctor.'

Charlotte

Later, much later, I sat in the parlour with Hannah and Angus. They were subdued, quiet, wondering.

Hannah spoke. 'Mother?'

'Yes dear?'

'What happened? What happened to Father. Why did he do… you know… what happened?'

'He had something called a stroke.'

'What's a stroke?' Angus hiccupped. I could hear the sob in his voice.

'Come here,' I said. 'Come and sit with me and I'll try and explain.'

When they were both settled on the sofa with me, one on either side, I said, 'It's when something like, an accident, happens in the brain, and a bit of it stops working.'

'What *kind* of an accident?' Angus persisted. 'How can you have an accident inside your head?'

'Well, it can happen sometimes.' I was at a loss for explanation, at least an explanation that wouldn't frighten him more than he had been already. 'You see, you know we're full of blood vessels – look, if you look at your wrist you can see them just under the surface of the skin.' Angus and Hannah looked. 'Yes, these little blue things. These are blood vessels called veins and arteries. Hannah you'll have learned about them in biology. She nodded.

Well, we have veins and arteries all over our bodies, even in our heads. They are like little roads and carry the blood around our bodies.'

'All over?'

'Yes, there are big ones and little ones and even tiny ones. Like one little road leading off another. But, if, say, the side of one of the roads breaks down for any reason then the blood running along that bit of the road, of the blood vessel I should say, escapes. When it escapes in the brain, then it causes a problem to the brain. Now, as you know, it's the brain which helps us move and speak and do things as well as think about things.'

'So that's why,' Hannah began, 'that's why Father can't lift his arm, and why he can't speak. He's had an accident to his brain.'

'Yes, that's it, really,' I said.

'And moving?'

'Yes, sometimes.'

'But he'll be all right tomorrow, won't he?' Angus sounded uncertain.

'Well it won't be quite as quick as tomorrow. Maybe, in a few days.'

'But will he get better? Will he be able to speak and move again?'

'Well, as you maybe saw, it's his right side that is affected. I should think that we'll see a big improvement over the next few days and with his speech too. We just need to keep him warm and quiet. But remember he had a stroke before – remember after the Titanic went down?' Hannah nodded. 'About four years ago. You were much smaller then, but that was a stroke then and he was fine afterwards. He just needs some rest and quiet and then he'll be fine.'

I tried to keep positive in front of the children but in truth Alexander's stroke this time seemed worse than the last one. His speech on that first day was non-existent, the right side of his face drooped and he had a marked paralysis of the right side. Dr Taylor prescribed complete rest.

'Can we see him now?' Angus pulled my arm.

'Well, I think he's sleeping now. Dr Taylor gave him something to help him sleep and give his brain a rest. Meg is sitting with him. But if we went up very quietly and just tip-toed in for a quick peep, I think it would be all right.'

Alexander was sound asleep propped comfortably on a mound of pillows. His face looked less florid than it was a few hours previously. His arm lay outside the covers. Meg sat beside him, knitting as ever, stopping every so often to wipe the brow, check the pulse. I was so glad to have her. I was reluctant to leave him in these first hours after the doctor left. I was so frightened that he would have another stroke when I was not with him.

'You *must* get a break, Mrs Sinclair,' Dr Taylor said when he called back later. 'Meg is willing to sit with him. Allow her to give you some time with the children – they're quite upset, and,' he half-smiled, 'be kind to yourself as well. I was sorry to hear about Magnus,' he continued. 'It's too early to hear any more news, I suppose?'

'We don't know any more. Do you think it's this that has brought on Alexander's stroke?'

'It's more than likely. But you know, he's had one previously. Any bad news or upset could have caused another. His blood pressure is quite high.'

'Do you think...?' I found it difficult to frame the question, but he seemed to understand.

'Absolute quiet for the next few days, no worries, and then we'll see,' he said, closing his bag with a snap. 'Is Christina away just now?'

'Yes, she's in Edinburgh now.'

'Perhaps it might be a good idea to let her know what's going on. She'll probably get some compassionate leave. They're very good at that kind of thing at the Royal in Edinburgh, and she could come up. I'm sure you'd all be glad to see her.' He checked his watch. 'I must go. I'll see you tomorrow. Call me if you need me.' With that he was away.

After the children had seen Alexander asleep and looking so peaceful, they seemed happier.

'I'm hungry.' Angus reached the bottom of the stairs and headed for the kitchen. 'Edie, are you there?'

'Yes, I am Angus. What are you after this time.'

'Oh Edie, thank you for staying so late.' I followed Angus into the kitchen.

'Oh, Miss, how is he?'

'Sleeping. Meg is with him. We've just been up to have a peep and he's sound.'

'Will he be all right?' Edie's voice shook.

'I'm sure he'll be a lot better after a long sleep. Then, we'll see.'

'And Magnus, what are we to do about him?'

'Well, at the moment, we can only wait for news.'

'Oh Miss, how can you manage with all this going on?'

I looked at her. I could feel the tears at the back of my eyes. She put out a hand and smoothed it protectively up and down my arm. 'We're in this together,' she said. 'Now,' she turned to the children. 'Did I hear the word "hungry"?'

'Yes,' cried Angus.

'All right, something to eat and then bed.'

'Bed?'

'It's long past bed-time,' Edie stated. 'But this evening you must go up very quietly and let your father sleep. No high jinks mind.'

'All right, Edie.' They were meeker than usual. Quieter. Not my usual enthusiastic bairns. But then it had not been a usual day. Two major incidents don't come often into one day and the children were not alone in finding it difficult to cope with.

Meg and I had agreed that she would sit with Alexander until midnight. She promised to call me if there was any change. Then I could take over and be with him for the night. I sat quietly in the late evening, resting, waiting for the night to come. I did not sleep although I probably should have. My mind was too busy for that.

Edie came with a hot drink at half past eleven.

'Edie, you should be in bed.' She'd insisted on spending the next few days at Birkenshaw instead of going to her own home at night.

'No, no, Mrs Sinclair. I'm fine. But how are you? This has been a difficult day for you, I'm thinking.'

I looked at her, so concerned, and was thankful for such care. Both she and Meg – what would we have done without them?

I said something of this to her and when she brushed it off, I said, 'Well, you go and get your cocoa too and sit and keep me company for a wee while before you go to bed'.

So, we sat in the firelight speaking of things happening, things in the past, when I had just arrived in Jarlshavn as the young, new junior school teacher and she was the appointed maid at Da Peerie Skulehoose. What a lot had happened over the years.

'Did you never want to get married Edie?' I asked.

'No, no, Mrs Sinclair.' She hesitated for a moment then went on, 'Well, there was a boy, he lived in Lerwick, that I thought I might one time have married, but he went sooth and I never saw him again.'

'Wouldn't you have gone sooth too.'

'He never asked me. We never got to that stage. But,' Edie shook her head, 'I wouldn't want to leave Shetland. And besides, there's Mam. She's alone now. And working here, and watching Hannah and Angus and Christina grow up. I'm so proud of her. And Magnus'– her face changed and her eyes filled. 'Magnus, that lovely young man. Where is he now? Miss, do you think he'll be all right?'

'I cannot tell,' I said. 'I can only hope and pray. Now, Edie,' I stood up. 'It's ten to midnight. I think you should go to bed now, and I'll go upstairs to Mr Sinclair.' She was already gathering the cocoa cups and smooring the fire.

Alexander lay more or less as he had before. Together, Meg and I freshened the bed, made him as comfortable as we could for the night. He was drowsy but able to take some sips of water. His eyes knew me. He raised his good hand in greeting. Meg slipped away. I turned to the bed.

'Alexander, can you hear me?' The good hand rose in response.

'I'll be here with you. Don't worry. Just try and sleep.' I gave him his medication that the doctor had left. It was liquid. Even so I had to put it into his mouth for him with a teaspoon and then hold his mouth closed and chin up a little to make sure he swallowed.

'Well done. Do you think you can sleep a little?' My hand was holding his at this point and I could feel his response as he tightened his fingers against mine.

'That's good. Sleep well, my dear. I love you.' Again the response. The faint gleam in the tired eyes.

The next few days saw a gradual improvement in Alexander's condition and we moved into a routine. Meg and I took turns in the sick room during the day. We set up a folding bed for me to sleep in at night with the knowledge that Meg was not too far away should I need to waken her.

Edie stayed, cooked, washed, ironed, cleaned, supervised Hannah and Angus, kept Birkenshaw ticking over. Hannah and Angus tried to carry on as normal although Hannah wasn't so sure about heading for Lerwick for school on the Sunday after Alexander's stroke.

'Mother, I can't go,' she pleaded that afternoon. 'Please don't make me go when Father is so ill.'

I had great sympathy with her. I remembered long ago when Magnus's mother Margery was very ill and Magnus had been very upset at the thought of going away to Lerwick under these circumstances. During that sad time, Magnus was allowed to stay at home and return to the Jarlshavn school. Although this situation was different I could see that sending Hannah back to Lerwick with the double burden of a very ill father and a much-loved brother missing at the Front was too much to ask.

'It's all right,' I said. 'You can stay at home for a wee while. But,' I reminded her, 'this is not a holiday. You must work at your schoolwork every morning at least and take some exercise every afternoon. Is that understood?'

'Yes, Mother. Thank you Mother.'

'Very well. I'll need to write a couple of notes. Could you be ready to take them round to Elizabeth and ask her to deliver one to Mrs Anderson and the other to your class-teacher? What's her name again?'

'Mrs Laing.'

'Yes, Mrs Laing. Once she gets the letter, then she'll know what to do next.'

'But why can't I stay at home too?' It was Monday morning and Angus was getting ready for school.

'Angus, Hannah's not staying at home for a holiday. Look, she's getting out her books on the table just like you will be doing when you get to school.'

'But I want to do it at home too.'

'Angus,' I began, but Edie broke in.

'Excuse me, Mrs Sinclair. I could walk along with Angus, if he would like to. Then I'll come back and get on here. Come on, Angus,' she wheedled, 'let's time ourselves. Do you still do 'walk a hundred steps and run a hundred steps'?'

'Yes, sometimes.'

'Come on then, let's see if I can do it too.'

'You?' said Angus. 'But you can't do it. You're a lady.'

'Some lady,' said Edie. She picked up her skirts and ran out of the door. 'Race you.'

''Bye mother.' Angus kissed the air somewhere near my face and ran after her.

'Good for Edie,' said Hannah. Then, 'did Father have a good night.'

'Well, he slept most of the night, thanks I think to Dr Taylor's medicine. He's awake now. We've washed him and Meg is sitting with him for a while. Then we'll see what the doctor says about him when he comes.'

'Has he had any breakfast?'

'He's had some tea. Meg unearthed an old cup with a spout from the back of a cupboard somewhere.' I suddenly remembered that that cup was surely last used for Margery. 'He drank some of it. He's swallowing well which is good.'

'And Mother, what can we do about Magnus.' She reached out.

'Hannah.' I held her. 'Hannah, as I said yesterday, there is nothing we can do at the moment but hope and pray that he will be found.' I did not add, by members of our own side. I did not dare think of the consequences should he be found alive by the enemy.

Christina came, a ray of busy sunshine into our rather grey world.

'Hello, anyone at home?' Feet bounded up the steps, the front door opened and I heard a voice saying, 'That's grand, thank you. I can manage now,' and the sound of bags being dragged into the hall.

'Christina, it's Christina.' I turned to Alexander. He had just awakened from a light sleep. He looked better, more relaxed, less red in the face, eyes more alert. We were practising between us lifting his paralysed hand off the bed and he was just beginning to raise it himself unaided. We were also doing bed-exercises with the paralysed leg and foot to get them moving along with maintenance exercises for the other side. Even his speech was beginning to improve a little. Now to keep us all on the hop was Christina, now working as a Staff Nurse in the Royal Infirmary of Edinburgh (RIE).

I had written Christina and told her our two lots of bad news but had been pre-empted by Dr Taylor who had telephoned the Matron at the Royal Infirmary of Edinburgh and told her of the situation.

Alexander smiled. I looked at him. Even this was improving. True, it was still lopsided, but the smile was there.

'Father, Mother, it's me.' Christina opened the door and entered unceremoniously. She sat on the edge of the bed – 'I know this is against the rules but I'll do it anyway,' and looked at him critically.

'Well, you've had a fair shake up and no mistake, I'd say,' she said. 'But you're going to be fine, aren't you?' She held both our hands.

'I'm so glad to be here. When Matron called me in and told me about Father and then about Magnus, I didn't know what to say. But I didn't need to say anything. She just said, "Now, Staff Nurse Sinclair, just you go and pack your things and get the train to Aberdeen". So I did, and then the boat – fortunately there was a berth or I would have had to sit up all night, and here I am. I've got a week's compassionate leave. Not a lot, but we're very busy with casualties and so on. Now what can I do for you? That's what I'm here for. Pillows, drinks, anything at all.'

'Christina.' I smiled at her. 'Let's just be happy that you're here, first.'

She sat still then, pleating the edge of Alexander's sheet with her fingers.

'Magnus?' She said. 'Any news?'

'None. It's too soon. It's only a week since we received the official letter from Major Oliphant.' The October sunshine slanted in through the window lighting up tiny dust particles in the air. She got up from the bed and looked out.

'It's so beautiful,' she said. 'I couldn't bear it if I thought Magnus would never see…' her voice faltered and she stopped.

'Christina,' I said. 'We're not thinking like that. We're hoping and believing that Magnus will be found, possibly in a hospital somewhere and that he'll be all right. That, in time he'll get home to us.' Alexander squeezed my hand in affirmation and support.

Later, when we were alone in the parlour, she said, 'Do you really believe that?'

'Believe what?'

'That Magnus will be home all right.'

'But we must believe it. We must keep going with positive thoughts. Otherwise it's so easy to let negative ideas slip in and then that would be even worse.'

'But Mother,' she persisted, 'between you and me. What do you really think?'

I hesitated. 'I don't know,' I said at last. 'I just don't know what to think.'

'Someone I know in Edinburgh,' she said. 'One of my friends. Her parents got word too, that their son was missing, a while ago. Anyway, they waited and waited. The contacted the Red Cross who really worked to try and locate him. Anyway it took six months, *six months*, before they found him, or rather, his things. He'd been killed and all that was left of him were his identity tags and a few bits and pieces. I don't know the whole story. That's the problem. Neither do they. It's this business of not knowing. But six months… and I'm sure many people have to wait longer. We have them coming into the wards in Edinburgh. They've been through such a lot.' She stopped and looked into the fire.

'Why does it happen, Mother? War is so needless. Why can't people just leave others alone? Why can't people just *be*?'

'It's always been this way, Christina. Men or, some men, strive after power, after bigger and better empires. They stamp underfoot anyone who gets in their way.'

'Like we're getting in their way now? But we won't be underfoot for long. We've maybe lost a bit of ground now but I bet we've learnt a lot of hard lessons from the Somme. We won't be making the same mistakes twice.'

'Well, I hope not.'

'Mother,' she continued. 'There's something else I wanted to ask. Why did Father send Magnus away to Canada in the first place? It all happened so quickly and I missed a lot of it as I was at school. But all was well, or seemed to be well and then suddenly, you and the little ones and Edie were off to Towie and Magnus was packed up and on a boat to Canada. Nobody saw fit to tell me anything. I felt very out of it.'

'What did Magnus say to you?'

'Nothing. The last time I saw him before he went away, he was so sad.' Christina looked into the fire again as she remembered. We went for a walk and he said, "You know I'm going?" "Yes Magnus," I said. He said, "I don't want to leave you, Christina, but my life lies elsewhere in Canada, for the moment". I asked him why. "Why, Magnus, Why must you go? You came back to Shetland to work. You have a good job. You get on well with people. We love you. Why must you go?"'

'"I cannot tell you. I'm bound not to tell you. One thing little sister, I will love you forever. I'll think of you when we are in faraway places and one day we will see each other again." Then,' she said, 'the next day he was away. Father was so quiet. So was Meg. We really missed you. What really happened, Mother? Why did he go?'

This was the question from Christina that I had been dreading. The temptation to tell her everything, to unburden myself to her who knew Magnus so well was very great. She was so grown-up and serious and, in a way, inviting. It would have been so easy to drop my guard and tell her. But I drew back from the brink. I had thought many times about this situation and how I would respond to what must inevitably be questioning from an adult as opposed to a child or girl in her mid-teens as she was when Magnus went away. But I had to remind myself that however mother-like I felt towards her, Christina was not my daughter. We were very close in a happy mother-daughter way and were great friends. Perhaps the fact that we were such friends lulled me into a false sense of security that she would understand. But Alexander was her father and Magnus her brother. I was the wife of one and the – what? – of the other. I wasn't sure, and I decided, however difficult, that I wasn't able to discuss the story with Christina who was so close to the main protagonists.

So I didn't tell her. I didn't even make up a story. Eventually she looked at me and stopped her questions. We sat for a while in the firelight thinking of Magnus, wondering where he was, hoping for news soon but aware that news could be not what we wanted to hear.

Chapter 16

Major James MacLeod (AChD) walked up the steps of the Abbey at Royaumont twenty five miles north of Paris. It was 1916, a slightly misty late October day, and two years since the thirty three members of the Scottish Women's Hospitals (SWH) had taken over the most of the abbey buildings as a hospital for War casualties. In that time they had transformed it from a place, beautiful, but partly derelict, very dirty, with no electricity or running water to a functioning, hygienically-equipped hospital with full services, wards and operating theatres with doctors, nurses, orderlies, administrators and drivers. At the start, in the abbey, only five real beds existed for the advance party. The rest of the staff had to carry in newly-bought straw mattresses. By May 1915 the hospital had beds for 178 patients with beds for more as they arrived and the French inspector of military hospitals was glad to give his approval for its use for the care and treatment of wounded French soldiers.

James had heard a little of Royaumont and its story. Representatives of the British Government rejected the offer from Dr Elsie Inglis and her SWH team to establish a hospital for War casualties because they were women. The more enlightened French Red Cross with a greater appreciation of their skills and an acute shortage of doctors and nurses gladly accepted the offer of medical and nursing care of the *blessés* and offered the Abbey at Royaumont as the first French SWH site.

James stopped at the top of the steps and surveyed the scene. This was his first visit and he looked around in appreciation. Set in the midst of ancient forests, the Abbey and its garden had an old almost other-worldly air. With its cloisters and air of peacefulness James felt he could almost forget the War until, in the stillness he was brought back to reality by the sound of distant guns. To make him even more aware, he could see walking round the cloisters, men, some limping, some strolling, some in chairs and covered in rugs against the late autumn air and pushed by others. Men from the battlefield.

Battles. James sighed. He had had a fair share of battles and battlefields one way or another. Where and when would it all end? He had felt duty-bound to volunteer and his congregation in St Fillans had been sad but proud at his going. 'Aa the ither men are awa,'said one old veteran of the Boer War. 'He needs to go – and anyway the Padre is needed out there noo.'

So James had gone. He was commissioned as Captain in the AChD and posted directly to Otterpool Camp in the south of England to do four months training for the Front. However, no training could prepare them for what was ahead. He did weeks of chaplain's duties in all areas of his Division during the Somme battles which started on 1 July until they were eventually ground to a halt in November 1916. Some of this time had been in the muddy, filthy, rat-infested trenches with the men. Watching through the night as men, due to go over the top the following day, tried to get a night's rest; talking with those who could not sleep; helping others write a letter home before they went into action; promising to see that letters were sent; listening as men told in the darkness of the night their private

105

thoughts and feelings; comforting as men unburdened themselves to him of their faults and misdeeds; and trying to comfort again and again men who knew that the likelihood was very great of their being killed or severely injured on the morrow; then, watching with heavy heart as they scrambled up the ladders towards the tangled barbed wire set ready for them, the guns and the maelstrom of battle.

Other times he was on duty in the tented Casualty Clearing Stations (CCS). Here was where the bulk of emergency interventions and lifesaving surgery was carried out. But here also was where many men, waiting on the grass for surgery, waited too long in the never-ending queues of wounded, closed their eyes and quietly died. Some, overcome by the anguish and pain of their suffering did not die so quietly.

There was little the medical and nursing staff could do. The tents were full to overflowing. More wounded from the Front line arrived every day at the CCS from the RAPs, Field Ambulances, Dressing Stations, which in their turn were all full. Stretcher bearers were at a premium. Their members were increased early on in the Somme offensive. Many became casualties as well as the Front line soldiers and were replaced by men not directly involved in the fighting: labour corps, engineers, artillery men. Lack of stretchers proved to be another problem leading to improvisation with anything available.

As a chaplain, James found an open door to most areas. In addition, although he originally anticipated being attached to one battalion, in this war situation he was posted to a Division comprising many battalions. This meant that he could go anywhere he was required within the Division – a daunting prospect but one which, after initial trepidation, he looked on as a challenge and an opportunity to use his skills to the full in all directions. Now, after months of interchanging from the trenches of the Front line, RAPs, ADSs and CCSs, taking his turn as stretcher bearer with the occasional week's respite behind the lines, James had seen more than a lifetime's worth of suffering. How could he comfort a young man with most of his face torn off, his abdomen gaping and deep shrapnel wounds in his legs by telling him he was going to be all right? How could he give water to a man with no mouth? How did you tell someone with his life in front of him, that he was going to die, that nothing could be done for him?

He felt for the medical and nursing staff who had to hurry past the cries of wounded men whom they had no hope of saving to tend to those whom they felt able to help. He sat with the dying until they died. He closed their eyes, removed an identity tag from each, noted the spot where the body lay for official records, said a quiet, necessarily brief prayer, and moved on.

Time and time again.

Some of the dead were collected or found later and given a more formal funeral and burial. James found these to be, on the one hand, of necessity brief and even perfunctory. On the other hand, he felt and he knew from their comments, that many of the men felt the same, that men who were buried with even a little ceremony were acknowledged there and then by their peers, their graves (sometimes multiple) marked often with a cross, and if available, a spare ID tag.

It was all desperately sad and an appalling waste of life. Through it all James was constantly amazed by the spirits and courage of the men: those who crawled out from the trenches under fire armed with a pair of wire-cutters, to try and free a wounded comrade hanging on uncut wire; the men who brewed up tea in the trenches for others; the singers who led the choruses of songs whose verses developed on a daily basis as the soldiers kept their spirits going by poking fun at what they saw as the less attractive characteristics of the enemy.

James had not been present at the unofficial break in the hostilities in Christmas 1914 when the soldiers of both sides had put down their arms, sang *'Still the Night'* or *'Stille Nacht'* across no man's land, climbed out of the trenches, smoked each other's cigarettes, looked at photos, spoke of home, became brothers. Perhaps hope was present in that brief encounter but hope was dashed when the order from on high came to resume hostilities. Within a short time the newly acquired brothers were at each other's throats again.

Through his busyness James, like all the rest, thought of home and those whom he loved. Thoughts of his boyhood home in Perth where his mother and father still lived were coupled with dreams of his beloved Perthshire. Often and often his thoughts returned to his lovely county, his boyhood bicycle runs in all seasons along the Perthshire roads and tracks, his beloved parents, so proud of their minister son, so anxious to see him happily settled. To them, especially his mother, 'happily settled' meant setting roots and you couldn't set proper roots unless you were married. How happy they had been when they heard about James and Charlotte's secret engagement. Their excited hopes were dashed to hear the news that James was called to St Fillans, so near when you compared it with Shetland. But no, for some inexplicable reason, Charlotte would not be with him. The wedding was off and James's entry into the St Fillan's Manse was not as an excited bridegroom with a wife in the wings, but as a bachelor.

Effie MacLeod found it difficult to understand. Who could reject her boy, and with such prospects. She felt almost offended, even angry, sure that it couldn't be James's fault. She also found James strangely unwilling to discuss the whole affair and finally, on the counsel of her husband, Ewan, her questions subsided.

'Leave the boy,' he'd said. 'It's his business. Something's gone wrong certainly, but we can't do anything about it. He's got to work it out by himself.' So Effie had stopped her sighs, her anxious looks and her pointed questions. James had moved into his new manse and was inducted by the Presbytery of Perth to the charge of St Fillans.

That was ten years ago. The good folk of St Fillans had accepted his ministry well, despite being in want of a wife (and a president for the Woman's Guild) and no one there knew about Charlotte. To them he was a confirmed bachelor.

But James often thought of his only love. In the beginning he went over and over in his head the last scene in Da Peerie Skulehoose and his telling Charlotte of his call to St Fillans. Initially he felt inclined to blame Charlotte for what he saw as her stubborn behaviour and couldn't admit even to himself that he might be in any way at fault. It was only much later as anger and denial subsided that he began to look in a more moderate way at Charlotte's point of view. After all, she had only voiced opinions and beliefs about teaching and women's role in the world and her part in it that she had spoken of before. She had just come from the traumatic situation of her mother's sudden death and the subsequent being taken for granted by both her father (who wanted a housekeeper) and a farmworker (who wanted a place in the farmhouse, favour with his immediate superior, a warm bed and a wife into the bargain). Could he have been a little too precipitate? Had he taken her for granted? And now, it was too late. Charlotte was married, happily he presumed, to Alexander.

And here am I he mused, standing on the steps of an old abbey turned hospital waiting to be let in. He'd seen a few of these temporary hospitals by this time. Some were, like this one, peacefully set in the countryside or villages. Some were right in the middle of busy thoroughfares. One in particular that he had come to know very well had been hurriedly created from a public recreation hall for the care of up to eight hundred wounded.

The front area of this temporary hospital was littered with the detritus of war. Inside the gates lay rejected rubber tyres, a broken-down ambulance stood to one side, rubbish lifted and shifted with the slight breeze. Outside on the street, soldiers squatted around fireplaces built of discarded stones and bricks. The smell of their cooking hung on the air. Local folk went about their business apparently unfazed by this intrusion of the *poilus* into their usually well-ordered space.

'Can I help you?' The voice coming from within was polite, professional. James turned from his scrutiny of the outside of the Abbey to see a tall slim figure in Sister's uniform coming towards him. He saluted and held out his hand.

'I'm James MacLeod, one of the Chaplains.'

'How do you do.' The Sister took his extended hand and gave it a firm shake. 'I'm Alison Forbes. I'm one of the Nursing Sisters here at Royaumont. It's good to see you. Up until now we haven't had that many British Chaplains here as of course Royaumont was initially established by the French for French casualties. But since the Somme...' she raised her shoulders in a bleak gesture '...since the Somme, with the number of wounded, well, we've had a great many more men from elsewhere too. So, you're doubly welcome.'

'Thank you. Where are your patients from?'

'From all over, really. Canadians, English, Scots, and so on. Even some Germans. We are expecting another consignment today or tomorrow from one of the CCSs. They are still full up and very busy. What a good job they do.'

'How long have you been here?'

'Well, the hospital was set up about two years ago. I arrived in May last year.'

'You'll have seen some sad sights.'

'Too many. Sometimes it's terrible...the poor souls. But you,' she changed the subject, 'are you going round all the hospitals?'

'Yes,' he said. 'I've been at the Front, in the trenches, and in the RAPs. From there to ADSs and CCSs. We just have to go where we're needed most. We get posted to a Division but in this kind of situation it all becomes much more mixed up and we can be called to anything or anywhere. I've been working in these areas for a year now – except for a week's leave last May when I went home.' He smiled, remembering. 'It seems a long time ago now.'

'Where's home?'

'Perth.'

'Oh, I'm from a bit further north,' she said. 'Just outside Aberdeen.'

'I thought I recognised the accent. I used to know someone from Aberdeenshire. Anyway,' he continued. 'I've been ordered to give chaplaincy cover to hospitals in this area and I'm trying to visit as many as I can. Would it be all right, do you think, for me to speak to anyone who feels up to it and, of course, who wants to speak to a Church of Scotland chaplain. I realise that you will have many Roman Catholics here but …'

'Don't worry about that. We have priests visiting sometimes but – I think War brings down a lot of barriers. The men are looking for comfort and don't seem to mind what kind of priest or minister is offering it. I think they'll be glad to see you. And the staff – a lot of us are Scots. Come through.'

She preceded him into the cool reception hall. Doors led off.

'This is our receiving ward today.' The beds lay white, quiet and still, ready for new occupants. 'It won't be like this for long. It'll be full to over-flowing by night and we'll have extra mattresses between the beds. But, come, there's another ward through here.'

In the ward opposite, all was activity. The men lay in two rows of beds along the long walls of a large room, like a hall or possibly the Refectory. Some had their eyes closed. A few looked up as they entered. Some moved restlessly in bed. Fractured limbs hung on pulleys, bed cages protected amputated stumps from the weight of bed clothes. The dressings-round was well underway. Men groaned as they underwent the ordeal of being touched, handled, dressings removed, wounds probed and cleaned. Sometimes it became too much and a scream of pain sounded through the ward.

'Excuse me a moment.' Alison Forbes went over to where a nurse was trying to cope with the dressing of a young man obviously in great pain. She looked with compassion at the man.

'Hold on there, Jim, won't be too long.' She looked at the nurse, 'Just a moment and I'll come back and help you.' She returned to where James was waiting and looking around the ward.

'I have to go and help Nurse. Can you go round on your own?'

'Yes of course – if that's all right.'

'Yes, that should be quite acceptable. We're on to the second side of the dressing-round. If you'd like to start at that end I think most of the men will be awake and glad to talk to you. We can meet up later and see how things are going.' She went off to help where she had promised. James turned his attention to the start of his own ward round.

His first patient lay neatly in the bed. No disturbance here of bed-cage or pulley but clean tidy lines indicating, James knew, a patient either too ill to move around in bed, or perhaps with too little will to take much notice of his surroundings. The man turned his head at his approach. The arms lying outside the counterpane did not move. The left was heavily bandaged from hand to shoulder. His head was swathed in a heavy capelline bandage. His open eyes watched James's approach warily. James picked up the right hand and shook it gently.

'Hello, I'm the Padre. How are you getting along?'

The man bit his lip, did not speak. James pulled a chair into a comfortable position. 'All right if I sit a while? I don't want to disturb you if you're too tired.'

The man looked at him, non-reacting at first then he slowly moved his head as if to nod, but immediately winced and was still.

'Bad, is it?'

'Yes,' the man said, so quietly that James had to bend his head to hear him. 'Every time I move. I got caught in the push last week.'

'Want to talk about it?'

There was a long pause. The young man – more of a boy than a man – looked away, back again, hesitated, then said, 'My best pal died.' His eyes filled with tears, and he stopped. James sat still.

Eventually the soldier gave a sigh and said, 'I think that's even worse than being wounded yourself, seeing your friends go, I mean. My best mate comes from the same village as me. How can I face his parents?'

'I'm sure they will be very glad to see you though. And to hear what happened.'

'Surely not.' The soldier raised his eyes. 'Why should they want to know? Surely they will hate the very sight of me, because I'm alive and Bill's dead.'

'Well,' said James. 'I've found that the folks at home who've lost a son or a husband or anyone, want to know about their last hours, what they were doing, how they were, who they spoke to, what they said and so on. And particularly what happened to them. They really want to know.'

'But why should they want to even *see* me? I'm here and he's not.'

'They don't seem to bear any ill-will towards a friend who comes back alive.'

'I feel so bad that he is dead.'

'What happened to him?'

'Well,' the soldier looked at him again. 'It was like this. We were waiting to get the order to go over. We were all ready – if you can call it that. The word came along the line, Captain Smith blew his whistle, and before we knew what we were doing we were up the ladders and over and into it.'

'The noise was terrible. The guns were going the whole time. We were running forward, running forward, shouting, someone was shouting, "Come on, come on." And we did. All of us. Until we started to fall. It was all so quick. Bill was just saying "we're nearly at them" when he fell. I stopped with him, he was pouring with blood and he just said, "I'm gone, Joe. Give my love to Mary and my Mum and Dad." His voice got slower and slower and his head just dropped back. It was awful. I've never had to do that before – be with someone dying, I mean. We've all seen them lying around dead. But actually to be with someone when he goes – well that's something else.' He stopped, bit his lip again, blew his nose. James waited. The young man gathered himself and went on.

'Then, when I was – was, sure that he was dead …' he looked piteously at James … 'it's difficult isn't it? You know they've gone but you don't want it to be like that so you keep hoping that you're wrong. D'you understand?'

'Yes, I do,' James said. 'It's not an easy thing to do, to be with someone who is dying.'

'No, not easy,' Joe agreed. 'But I had to do it. I had to stay with him. I couldn't have left him.'

'No, you needed to stay.'

'Well anyway, when it was – over – I took off one of his dog-tags as we had been told. We've all been told what to do.' James nodded. 'I got the dog-tag and then I went into his pockets and took out some things. His letters, and photos and, well, personal things. I thought Mary and his Mum and Dad might want something as a minding.'

'Yes, of course. Who is Mary?'

'His girl. He went on and on about her. There was no one like her for him. No-one else. Even at base-camp when the some of the others went with the local girls, he never did, never. He must have loved her an awful lot.'

'That will be something you can tell Mary when you go back. That he was faithful to her. That would be important for her to hear. How old is she?'

'Oh, just about eighteen. He was only twenty. Same as I am. We were at school together.'

'Well, Joe, when you get home you be sure and tell Mary about him. And his Mum and Dad.'

'Yes, I will.' Joe gave a long sigh. 'If you're sure it's all right, that they'll want to see me.'

'They'll want to see you. You see, you are their link with Bill's last moments. You were there. That's important.'

'Thanks Padre. I think I might sleep now.' His eyelids relaxed their anxious opening. James could see the tension creases in his forehead smoothing as he drifted. He walked slowly to the next bed.

Carefully he worked his way up the ward. Some of the men were too ill to speak; some were asleep. One clutched his hand wildly.

'I can't do it again. I can't.' James had seen this anxious restless man from down the ward, watching his movements as he moved from bed to bed.

Many heads turned wistfully at his approach looking for the visitor to stop and talk. And in talking, each like Joe, unfolded his own horror of war even through discussing his injuries. A man here had his leg fractured in three places – would he, could he, ever walk properly again? The next was lying with his right arm gone. He still felt its agony though.

The next man's right eye was completely destroyed and the other so badly injured that it was unlikely he'd ever see out of that one either.

'This eye's going to be fine though Padre. Isn't that great? I'll be able to see all right out of this one. My girl will still want me because I won't be a blind cripple. Once they get the bandages off, I'll be able to see.'

James looked up at the nurse hovering. She shook her head. Nobody as yet had had the heart to tell the man the truth.

Further up the ward, a man was sitting up looking very well. James approached him, wondering why he was there. The man looked friendly, shook hands, acknowledged the greeting, waited.

James sat down. 'How are you?' The man didn't speak. Instead he pointed to his mouth and shook his head. He waved a newly written letter at James.

'What do you want me to do with it?' The man pointed to James, then the letter. 'Shall I read it?' The man nodded.

'Sure?' The man nodded even more emphatically and thrust the letter at James who took the paper and read:

Dear Mother,

This is to let you know that I am in hospital. I was stricken dumb a few days ago and made deaf in one ear by a shell exploding beside me. Some of the lads were killed by the shell. I am all right but can't speak. I might get home soon. I hope so. I hope you and the little ones are well

Love from Tommy

James put down the letter.

'Thanks for letting me see this,' he said. 'How are you otherwise?' Tommy nodded again and raised his right thumb.

'Your speech may well come back. I hope so.' Tommy nodded. He pointed to his affected ear.

'Do they think your hearing will come back?' He gave a down turned face and shook his head but brightened as he indicated his other ear.

'It's well?' Tommy nodded.

'That's good. Would you like me to post your letter to your mother?'

A while later he moved on, letter in pocket, admiring Tommy for his strength and coping strategies. He was already writing messages with notebook and pencil supplied by a nurse and devising a series of communication hand signals which he explained by drawing to all who would stop, look and listen.

Some of the men had many wounds and most of them when James asked how they were, said that they were 'All right'. One of the most severely wounded – James finally found out that he had eleven wounds – was keener to ask how the War was going than go on about how badly wounded he was. He was one of the many who had saved a piece of shell from the depths of his wound. 'A souvenir', he called the jagged piece of metal held up for James's scrutiny. He also showed off his bent buckle as proof of his narrow escape.

'Padre,' he said, 'I've never been so thankful before.'

In a corner lay a wounded German prisoner. He was very ill and kept up a succession of cries and groans. James went to his side and held his hand for a moment. The cries stopped.

'He's always like that.' A nurse came up. 'It's very sad. He cries out all the time unless we sedate him. If someone goes to him he stops. Even though he is hardly aware, somewhere inside himself he must be so lonely. And,' she added, 'we just can't be with him the whole time.'

Towards the end of the morning James saw Alison Forbes at the ward door. He went over.

'I think I've spoken to just about everyone who is able.'

'Thank you so much,' she said. 'The men really appreciated your visit. They've been telling the nurses.'

'Is there anyone else I should see today? Can I come back and meet some of the other men?'

'Oh yes please. It does their morale no end of good. There is one man you haven't seen, just off this ward. He's unconscious – most of the time. Every now and again he begins to mutter, and then he goes back again. Come,' she indicated, 'let's go and see him.'

'What's his name?'

'Well that's the other problem. His ID tags are missing. They must somehow have been lost. We've no means of identifying him. The only thing is he was wearing a Canadian uniform. He's in here.'

They went into the side-ward and James looked at the still figure lying under the bed-clothes.

Chapter 17

Christina was walking. Walking the paths and cliffs she used to walk with Magnus as a schoolgirl on their weekly outings which she'd enjoyed so much before he had gone away.

She could hardly believe the changes that had happened. Her father very ill; her beloved brother missing; bad news from the Front; papers full of it. Even though the Somme Battles were officially past their peak and would she prayed soon be called 'over', battles were still going on elsewhere. Men and boys, and women too were being killed every day. She sighed. And I have to go back to Edinburgh in a couple of days' time she thought and I want to get back to my work but it's difficult. She stared out to sea. A mist hung over Foula. She couldn't see the peaks today. She carried on along the path.

'Christina,' a voice called behind her. 'Christina. Hang on.' She turned. A figure was running along the path behind her. A figure in uniform.

'Lowrie, it's Lowrie.' She smiled suddenly, a broad, happy welcoming smile and started back towards him.

'Lowrie, where did you spring from?' They shook hands but then Lowrie put both his hands out and held her shoulders and kissed her lightly on each cheek.

'I think that would be allowed considering the times.' He looked down at her, smiling.

'But why are you here?'

'I'm home on leave. Simple as that. I arrived yesterday, heard what was going on at Birkenshaw, came to say hello, spoke to Mr and Mrs Sinclair, heard that you were away along the cliff for a walk and came to catch you up. You do walk quickly,' he reproached. 'I'm all out of breath.'

'Well, I'm a nurse,' she protested. 'We all walk like that. It becomes ingrained. But anyway, never mind that. It's so good to see you. It must be years. You… you've changed,' she added more soberly. 'Lowrie, are you well?' She looked up at the face of her brother's best friend, so well-known once, now with little lines which had not been there before, handsome yes, he had always been a good looking boy but now there was a difference, a maturity of a kind. The little moustache he sported was one thing, but this was different. The War had taken its toll and the boy would never return.

'Yes, I'm fine. A bit tired, that's all. This is my first leave for a while.'

'How long have you got?'

'A week.'

'Just a week? And then?'

'Back to France. But that's all I'm allowed to say. Christina…' he stopped walking, turned to face her. 'Christina, I'm heart sorry for your troubles, your father and…and Magnus.' He stopped. 'He was – *is*,' he said fiercely, 'he *is* my best friend. He is somewhere, I know it.'

'Oh Lowrie. It's so good to see you.' Christina could feel the prickling at the back of her eyes. 'You, of all people, know Magnus so well.' Tears rolled down her cheeks.

'Here.' Lowrie pulled out a handkerchief and handed it to her. 'Here, he'll be back. He'll be in a hospital somewhere or got into the wrong battalion by accident – you've no idea what it's like. There are literally thousands of men all over the place and in the battles they get all mixed up. Then they just have to take cover wherever they can and whichever group they can attach themselves on to. He'll be out there somewhere.'

'Do you really think that?' She sounded very doubtful.

'I have to think that. It's happening all the time. Mind you,' he hesitated. 'I wish I knew. I would feel better if I really knew.'

Charlotte took a step towards him. 'Me too,' she said. 'Me too.'

He looked at her. 'I've never seen you as a grown up person before.'

'Well, I *am* grown up.'

'Perhaps I just haven't looked. I have always thought of you as Magnus's wee sister. And it's been a while. Now it's different.' He shook his head sadly. 'And it takes a War for us to realise that we're not wee lads and lasses any more. May I take your arm as we walk along?'

'Please do.' The reply was as formal as the question but the warmth in the voices was unmistakeable. They walked in silence for a few minutes. Then Lowrie said.

'When do you have to go back?'

'Day after tomorrow.'

'What? So soon?'

'I'm afraid so. I only got a week and really feel a bit guilty about that. They're so busy. But Father will make good progress now I think. He's even out of bed for a while each day and Mother's managing with the help of Meg and Edie. Dr Taylor comes in and out. He's still here – he's too old to be called up. Hannah will go back to school in a week or so I expect. Mind you, I'm glad she's had some time at home. She'd have felt very cut off in Lerwick all week. But even so – she still has the worry of Magnus. As do we all,' she added quietly. 'But I need to get back.'

'Yes, you do, but, could you spend some time with me tomorrow, do you think. I know you're here to be with your folk, but you will need to be going for a walk again, won't you?'

'Well, I'm encouraged to get myself out every day.' Their eyes met, and they smiled.

'That's settled then,' Lowrie said. 'Nothing like a bit of exercise. You should hear Magnus on the subject.'

'I have. And, been made to suffer. But, we'd better walk back now. I've been away for ages.'

'Oh, it'll be all right,'Lowrie said airily. 'They knew I was going to catch you up.'

'How did you find Lowrie?' Charlotte asked. She and Christina were sitting by the fire in the soft gas lighting of the sitting-room.

'He seemed quite well, but I thought he was tired. It must be awful in France just now.'

'Yes, I think so. I don't think we know anything like what's going on. I'm sure much of the news is being suppressed.'

'I think so too.'

'Did he say when he is going back?'

'Yes, he has a week, and then he's going back – to France – but he couldn't tell me where.' Christina looked over at Charlotte. 'Mother, he asked if we could go walking tomorrow. I said I would. Is that all right do you think?'

'I don't see why not.' Charlotte thought a moment. 'Let's not formalise it though – keep it casual.'

'Yes, Father worries so.' Christina was well aware of her father's anxieties. 'That's fine then.' She got up and yawned. 'I think I'll go up.'

'Sleep well. It's good to have you here. I'm coming in a minute.'

Once in bed, Christina lay quietly thinking over the day. She felt much happier about her father now. What a difference the last week had made. The immediate post-stroke paralysis was improving day by day. He could now get out of bed and walk to his chair with help. True, he was not able to get down stairs yet but he practised a few steps each day and each day saw him going a little further. He was not the best of patients but they all felt that their patient who could argue and grumble a bit was making better headway than the poor soul of the first twenty-four hours of his illness.

Now he was asleep. She looked quietly in on him before going to her room, nurse-like straightened the bed-clothes, felt the brow. He was so much better. Christina felt she could go back to Edinburgh with a happier mind and wrote to Matron to confirm her return on the arranged day. She also made a point of thanking her for the privilege of compassionate leave. It was a privilege granted to all the staff in times of acute family difficulty – a frequent occurrence in these troubled times. Nevertheless Christina thought, you can't take it for granted.

Her thoughts shifted to Magnus. Still no word. How long would they have to wait? The worst thing is, not knowing. Or, is it? I don't know whether I would rather not know or know definitely that he has been killed. Oh. Magnus, if you're out there, feel me thinking about you. Remember our happy times, our walks, the Band of Hope at the boarding house. Somehow, somehow, let us know. She blew her nose.

A tap at the door, quietly opening.

'Mother?'

'Yes, are you still awake?' Charlotte walked over and sat on the edge of the bed.

'Yes, I was just thinking – about Magnus, you know. I wish we could hear.'

'I know. Just keep hoping and praying. Think on the bright side.'

'That's like what Lowrie said.'

'What did he say?'

'He seemed to think that Magnus was either in a hospital somewhere or mixed up with a different battalion or group. It seems this happens in a big battle.'

'Yes, I've heard about that sort of thing – sometimes reported in the papers. It's all very difficult to imagine when we've never been through it or seen it. In either of these situations though, he'll surface one way or another.'

Charlotte sounded more confident than she felt. She was beginning to lose hope of ever seeing Magnus again. Her misgivings had been made worse by the news in Jarlshavn that another local man had been posted missing and then his belongings and identity tags had been found a few months later. She couldn't help thinking that they would finish up with the same news.

'I hope so…'Christina blew her nose…'but it's difficult to keep positive Mother.'

'I know, but we must, for the sake of your father and the children. And ourselves. It's much easier to keep going if we speak about "when" and not "if".'

'You're right, I know. I'll tell Lowrie tomorrow that we're positive thinkers too.'

Charlotte looked at Alexander before she got into the other bed. He seemed to be asleep and comfortable. She lay back. However much she tried to relax, her brain kept whirling. Night-time was possibly the worst when she wasn't actively occupied. Time to think, worry, reflect on the past, Magnus, where was he, how was he, was he even alive? She didn't know what she felt about him. She cared deeply about him and what happened to him. It was years now since she had seen him. Their correspondence, shared with Alexander and the children, had been family letters. Any feelings she possibly had for him were blanketed over, shut out, not allowed.

Always in the background was the lingering shape of James MacLeod. What would life have been like if she had gone with him, if she had given up her ideals of teaching, or, if he had caught her at a different moment, instead of a time when she had felt very taken for granted and not improved by what she saw as his thoughtlessness. Anyway, stop this, it's all past. James is in Perthshire – or, she paused, or is he? He might just have gone to War. I just hope he's safe – that's the main thing.

Contrary to what Christina and Charlotte thought, Alexander was not asleep. He looked asleep, had kept his eyes closed and breathing even, as they checked that he was all right, endured the 'sorting' of his bedclothes. But he lay, as he often did, thinking about Magnus and what he saw as his part in Magnus's current status of *missing in action*. If he hadn't sent Magnus away, he wouldn't be in this situation now. However much his brain said 'ridiculous' to this, he still came guiltily back to it. The once intransigent angry father was now faced with losing his eldest son, and he was hurting. That day when he had sent him away, how angry he, they both, had been. He had doubted Charlotte's part in the affair. Well you could hardly call it an affair, but there was something, even if it had been one-sided. But now Magnus was missing. The father mourned the son even as though his coffin were lying up in the Kirkyard with his other dead siblings. But Magnus wasn't dead – at least they didn't know if he was. That almost made it worse. If not dead then where was he? And who if anyone, was with him? Were they being kind to him? Or, and Alexander gave an involuntary shiver, was he in the hands of the enemy? He moved restlessly. How could he have sent him away as he had done?

'Alexander,' Charlotte, also unsleeping had heard the movements and was at his side. 'Are you in pain? Can I get you anything?'

'No, no, I'm all right. Just can't sleep.'

'Some water? Or tea? Can I make some for you?'

'Yes, tea would be good. What's the time?' She looked at her watch in the dim glow.

'Just after one. I'll be back in a minute.'

'Thanks.' She made as if to go but he put out his good arm and held her hand. 'I love you, you know.' She smoothed his forehead.

'I know. And I love you too. Why can't you sleep?

'Just…thinking.'

'About Magnus?'

'Yes, and … how it all went wrong. If – I hadn't sent him away then he wouldn't be missing now.'

'You can't say that, Alexander. You just don't know. And anyway you never intended this to happen.'

'No, I know, but even so, it has happened and I feel …'She waited, then, carefully,

'What do you feel?' she asked.

'I feel, so sorry,' he said. 'It's just been something that once it was set in train, there was no way back. I miss him so much and, and' – he swallowed – 'my pride has affected so many lives.'

'Oh Alexander,' she was on her knees at the bedside now, holding him tightly. 'It was a bad time – there's no denying that. But we can't go back.'

'I know,' he said. 'But I'd like to be able to tell him I'm sorry. What a waste of time.'

'No, you mustn't say that. It's a pity, certainly and we can all look back and wish we had done things differently. But not a waste of time – no experience is wasted – and Magnus will, in his own way have benefited from different countries, people, experiences and so on. Now,' she said, unable to say more, 'I'll get your tea.'

She made her way carefully down to the kitchen in the half-light of the tilly-lamp burning very low on the window-sill half-way down the stairs. She stood for a moment waiting for the kettle to boil on the range. Poor Alexander, what it must have cost him to admit that he feels sorry.

She made the tea and returned to the bedroom.

'Here's you tea.'

'Thanks.' She helped him sit up and gave him the cup. They sat in silence.

'Do you think he would come back?' Alexander's voice broke the silence. 'He could take up his work at the hospital again. We could go on as we were.'

'Alexander, we can't make plans. We can't think that far ahead. We don't know whether or not Magnus is alive or …'She hesitated.

'Or dead,' he supplied bitterly. 'Dead – and if he is, I sent him to his death.'

Two days later Christina kissed them farewell and went off to Lerwick to get the boat for Aberdeen and from there the train to Edinburgh. Lowrie insisted on accompanying her to the boat.

'Yes, of course I will,' he insisted when she protested. 'You must have someone to wave you off and your mother finds it difficult to leave your father just now. Now just do as I say. I'll bring my father's gig round just after lunch.'

So Christina had given in – not that she needed much persuasion. She had not been looking forward to seeing herself on to the boat with no-one to wave to. Lowrie's insistence on accompanying her was very pleasant. Indeed, she thought, any time with him is very pleasant. Their second walk had been in all ways a breath of fresh air. Not only was the weather breezy and sunny but Lowrie was a delightful companion, funny, serious, joking, thoughtful. Christina had never been treated in quite this way before.

As they were walking homewards, he said, 'I wish we could have had more time.' Christina looked at him.

'You know,' he said, 'time to get to know each other.'

'But we do know each other.'

'Yes, but really know each other – as you and me.' He looked at her. 'Time is so short. Would you write to me, d'you think? And I'd write to you.'

'Yes. I think I'd like to do that.' Some of Christina's friends wrote to men in the Forces away from home. 'But,' she said anxiously, 'I won't know where to write to.'

'Don't worry about that. You give me your Edinburgh address and I'll write to you first and tell you where to write to.'

'You'll forget – you'll forget all about writing once you're away.'

'I won't, I won't, I promise,' he said earnestly. 'Please let me write to you. I would so much like to hear from you.' He stopped and looked down at her. 'I really want to keep in touch. Please.'

'I'd like to keep in touch too but…' she was affected by his urgency. 'Wait a minute. I'll give you the address.' She hunted in her bag for a pencil.

'Here's my diary.' he held it out. 'Write in there.'

'Now,' he said satisfied as he stowed the diary away. 'I will not lose that, and I will write, every da…'

'Lowrie,' she said laughing, 'don't make promises you can't keep.'

'Well, as often as I can. And,' he said grandly, 'I'll think of you every day.'

Even though Christina felt things were running along more quickly than she might have anticipated she did concur, 'And I'll think of you.'

Down at the dockside the *St Clair* was loading. In a few minutes passengers would be allowed to go on board. Lowrie and Christina stood back from the crowd, in their own space. The time for joking was over. In a few days Lowrie would be heading back to the Front, quite where, he knew not. Christina shivered.

'Cold?'

'No, not really, just wondering – what will happen next?'

'Come,' he put his arms around her. 'We don't know what the future will bring. One thing I do know, though, we've seen each other for two days after a long, long time and now I never want to let you go. I think… I hope, that you have this feeling too.' She nodded, too full for words. 'So, little Christina, whatever happens, remember that.' She gave a deep sigh, comforted.

'Now,' he said, 'I hate to say it but I think they've opened the gangway. Have you got your boarding pass? I'll put it with mine.' He pulled out his non-travelling boarding pass and waved it. 'Now, let's go and find your cabin.'

Two weeks later, on a fine sunny November afternoon, Charlotte put on her old coat and went quietly through to the kitchen.

'Is that you away out?' Edie was at the ironing.

'Yes Edie. I won't be long. Just a little fresh air. Mr Sinclair's asleep.'

119

'Have a nice walk.' She went out into the cold winter afternoon. Even though it was only two o'clock she was aware of the afternoon light changing as the sun dipped lower. It would become even darker in the next few weeks. She pulled her hat firmly down and stepped out. In the distance she could see the telegram boy peching up the hill from the village on his bicycle. I wonder who's having a telegram this time, she thought. Poor souls.

The boy came nearer. Charlotte watched his progress and gasped as he turned in at the Birkenshaw gate. Oh, mercy, he's coming here. She ran across the grass towards him.

'Hello, Geordie, I'm here.'

The bike stopped. Geordie put a foot on the ground and searched in his bag propped on the metal basket in front of him.

'Telegram Mrs Sinclair.' He waved it as she came up. 'I hope it's better news this time.'

'Thank you Geordie. I'll have to take it in. I'll be down if there's an answer. Wait a moment.' She searched in her pocket for a tip.

'No, no, Mrs Sinclair, don't you worry about that. I'll be on my way. I've another one to deliver.'

'Take care.' She called to his retreating back. He waved. She turned and looked down at the envelope, addressed to Mr Alexander Sinclair. The temptation to open it was very great. However, mindful of Alexander's ideas about others – even his wife – opening even a telegram addressed to him, she picked up her skirts and ran to the house, through the back door, past Meg darning by the kitchen fire, and Edie ironing on the table, up the stairs and came to a sudden halt outside the door where Alexander was napping.

She took a deep breath, opened the door quietly and stepped in. He slept. Telegram in hand, she walked over to the window, and looked out at the cold landscape. Long pale shadows fell across the grass from the bare trees. The winter sun was going down through layers of clouds. It was going to be another frosty night. Even when she was out she could feel its crunch beneath her feet. She held the telegram tightly. What are you telling me? If only you could speak.

The voice came from the bed. 'What is it, Charlotte?' She turned.

'I thought you were asleep.'

'I was. But I'm awake now. I've slept for a good while. What's that?' his voice grew anxious. 'Another telegram? Oh, God, my boy, my Magnus? Is he…is he dead?'

Charlotte went over. 'Alexander, I haven't opened it – I don't know.'

'Open it, please. Tell me.'

She slit the envelope, pulled out the harmless enough looking paper and read it. She sat in silence, holding the telegram, tears coursing down her face.

'Charlotte? Charlotte, tell me. He's dead isn't he?'

Chapter 18

Royaumont

EARLY NOVEMBER 1916

The man in the bed was very pale and so still that James could hardly see the rise and fall of his chest as he breathed. He and the Sister stood watching.

'He's had a very bad head wound,' she said. 'Apart from other shrapnel wounds in his limbs and abdomen. He lost a lot of blood. We nearly lost him. He must be quite a strong man to withstand this level of wounding. I've seen many another with less, not able to live through it.'

'Our main problem now,' she continued, 'is the fact that he's unconscious – sometimes deeply so. We've noticed though,' she added, 'that his levels of unconsciousness are changing. As I said, sometimes he seems more aware. He's beginning to mutter occasionally.'

'Can you tell what he is saying?'

'No, it's still too vague, but hopefully that will improve. But what's also strange is that he doesn't sound Canadian – he was in Canadian uniform.'

'Yes, of course. Was there anything in his pockets?'

'Nothing significant. If he'd had anything, it's gone.'

'Was he brought in from the Somme?'

'Yes, from that massive offensive at Thiepval Ridge at the end of September in which the Canadians were so much involved.' James nodded. He'd been part of that battle scene too: the particular phase which ended on 28 September by the 51st Highland Division capturing Thiepval Ridge. This had been one of the German's most powerful positions, much of it underground but strategically and tactically vital as it topped the highest ground for a long way. Small wonder then, that the British Expeditionary Forces and the Germans fought so hard for its possession during that long weary summer of 1916: the summer of the Somme which started on 1 July and finally ground to a halt in November.

'A lot of men came in just after that time,' Alison Forbes said, 'from all over that area, from the CCSs and so on. This poor soul was in one of the batches. It's amazing he's alive. Would you like to sit a while with him?' she continued. 'Have you time? You see, we're wondering what we're missing by not being with him continually – but we can't because we are so short staffed.'

'Yes, I'll sit and watch for a while. I can do my notes here as well as anywhere else.' James pulled out his records book which went everywhere with him.

'There's always admin isn't there?'

'Yes, and if I miss it, it just backs up and I finish up with too much to do.' He sat down on a chair by the man on the bed.

'All right, I'll send you some tea. Could you let us know if you see any change please?'

Left alone, James looked around. The cubicle didn't hold that much: just the bed and its occupant; a small bedside cabinet; a trolley at the other side with the accoutrements necessary for nursing a seriously ill patient. The man, his head swathed in bandages, leaving not much more than his closed eyes, nose and mouth visible, looked peaceful enough and James opened his Records Book and found his indelible pencil. In truth, James preferred to use pen and ink for writing up his records but in his current transient situation his pen and ink were too easily damaged, bottles of ink could get split, and even the now-popular fountain pen was easily broken. James got out his pen-knife and proceeded to sharpen his indelible pencil into the waste paper basket.

He settled down. A VAD came in with some tea and some dark-looking bread with cheese.

'Sorry this is all we have,' she said, 'but it's local cheese and it's very good. We eat a lot of it.'

James suddenly realised he was hungry. It was 1 o'clock and many hours since morning réveille. He ate his hospital rations (the cheese *was* very good, he noted) and started catching up with his Records. The man on the bed lay still, breathing quietly. James stopped writing every now and again and watched him. There was something very vulnerable about the unconscious. It's more than sleeping. When you're asleep you can usually waken right away even though a jump into wakefulness may not be pleasant, or good for you. Much nicer to come to gradually. But if you have to, you can. This is different. This is something you can't just poke awake.

'Who are you,' he wondered aloud? 'Where are you from? What are your hopes, dreams, aspirations?' There was, as James expected, no response.

He sighed, returning to his work. A nurse came in to attend to the patient for a few moments, checked the bandages for bleeding, went out again taking away his cup.

Then the man sighed. James stopped, waited, watched. His breathing had changed. It was faster, more noticeable. James took hold of the nearest wrist, checked the pulse. It was rising as well.

As he sat there, the man's hand in his, he felt the fingers twitch. And again.

'Hello.' James spoke quietly. 'Can you hear me?'

No response.

Then, the twitch of the fingers.

'Hello.'

The man's lips moved. They looked dry. There was cotton-wool and water on the locker. James wet some cotton-wool and moistened the man's lips. They immediately responded, almost a lick. James wet the lips again. This time the lick was unmistakeable.

He mumbled something that James couldn't catch.

'What was that? I'll help you if I can.'

The man mumbled, 'Mo-o…'

'Would you like some more water? Is that what it is?' This time the fingers lifted off the bed. James moistened his lips again, and again. The man licked eagerly.

'More,' he whispered. The word was clearer now.

'Wait a minute until I ask someone.' James went to the cubicle door and looked down the ward. At the far end he could see Alison Forbes with some nurses.

'Sister.' She looked up quickly.

'Sister, could you come please?'

'What's wrong?' She walked swiftly towards him. 'Is he all right?'

'He's, well, he's wanting water. Is it…?'

'He's what?'

'Well, I moistened his lips with some water and he licked them and wanted more. So I did it again and he said, "More". Clear as anything.'

By the bedside, Alison Forbes laid her hand on the man's forehead.

'Nice and cool anyway. Pulse is up, though.'

'Yes, and,' James added, 'He was twitching his fingers, moved his hand. Look, there it goes again.'

The man spoke. 'More,' he said.

'Would you like more water?' Alison Forbes was ready with the moist cotton wool. The fingers moved.

'Here you are then.' She put the wet cotton wool to his lips. He responded at once. She squeezed and he licked away the drops.

'We need to see if he's swallowing. Let's raise his head a little.' A few drops of water later she said with satisfaction, 'There he is. Look, he's swallowing. Now we know he can do that, we can give him a little more.'

A little while later, the man opened his eyes for a second.

James, watching, said, 'Could you try opening your eyes again?' But the man who seemed to have returned to the deep well of unconsciousness from which he was trying to drag himself, didn't respond this time. James was disappointed but Alison Forbes said, 'No, Padre, I think he's made good progress today. I think when you return tomorrow you'll find that he's even better. I hope so anyway. But now that he's come this far, we mustn't rush him.'

'Of course, you're quite right. I'll be back tomorrow. But in the meantime can I visit a few more of the men before I get back to Base?'

'Of course, that would be excellent. I know the men upstairs are hoping that you will go up and speak to them. They've heard about your morning visit. You can't visit one lot and not the other.'

'Right, show me where they are.'

The following morning Alison Forbes waved briskly as she saw James coming back up the Royaumont front steps.

'Good morning Padre. Are you well today?'

''Morning Sister. Yes I'm fine thanks. How are you? And all your charges?'

'We're …busy you could say. We had a large group of admissions late yesterday evening from one of the CCSs. Most of these men had had enough surgery or treatment to save their lives but not much more than that. Two died as they arrived. Poor souls, they were conscious to the end and in great pain. What a journey they must have had. The others were in a state one way or another – but we're attending to them.' She stood straight and determined but James could see the fatigue in her eyes.

'Have you slept?'

'A little. But I don't go off duty until they're all settled.' James looked at the busy scene.

'What can I do for you?'

'Well, have you time?'

'I go where I'm needed,' he said. 'If I'm needed here then I'll be an extra pair of hands or whatever you feel I can do.'

'Well, could you go into the ward you were in yesterday, in the morning and just go round all the men and see that they're all right? That would be so helpful. They haven't had much attention today although they've had breakfast. A very good VAD nurse is there but it's a lot for her to do on her own.'

'That's fine. How's our friend in the cubicle.'

'He's had more water. And he's opened his eyes a couple of times. I think he's much nearer the surface than he was yesterday. You could look in on him too, if you would.'

'Of course.'

James put a lot into that morning. He started it as a routine ward round but it soon turned out to be a round with many turns and deviations as one man after another requested beds and bedding pulled straight, asked questions, wanted to talk, asked for water, could he do a dressing (a job for the VAD), help them with a letter home, say a prayer. Physical, mental, spiritual requests came rolling in and James finished with his jacket off, his sleeves rolled up and moving swiftly around as he answered the calls.

'Think I could get a job?' he asked the VAD nurse.

'I'm sure you could,' she said. 'It'll calm down a bit now that we've caught up with the things we needed to do. Thank you so much.'

'Not at all,' he said. 'I'll just go and visit the chap in the cubicle.'

He had looked in on the man in the cubicle a couple of times during the morning and each time he seemed to be unresponsive. This time, James walked in and touched his hand lightly. Immediately the hand lifted as if to say, 'I know you're there.'

'Hello,' said James. 'It's me again. Came to see you yesterday. Would you like some water?' He put some on the man's lips.

'M mm…'

'I don't know if you're saying, "Mmm that's good," or "Mmm that you want some more",' said James.

'Mmm – more.'

'Ah, that's better.' James lifted the feeding cup he found on the locker. 'Now just let me raise you up a little.' He put his arm around his patient's back and raised his head.

'Now,' he said. 'Here you are.' He held the spout of the cup to the man's lips and dribbled a little into his mouth.

'That's good,' he exclaimed as the man swallowed.

'Thanks.'

'What was that you said?'

'Thanks,' the man repeated.

'You're welcome. Would you like some more?'

'Yes, please.'

They were right. He's certainly not Canadian, James thought as he helped the man to more water. This time he could see the man's hand almost involuntarily trying to rise up to take the cup.

'How does that feel.'

'Good. Fine.'

'Can you open your eyes do you think?'

'Too tired.'

'Right. Water?'

'A peerie bit more, please.' The man's voice was low, but there was no mistaking the 'peerie'.

James helped him to water and then said, 'Do you know what happened to you?'

'Battle... noise...' the man's gaunt face contorted in remembered horror. 'O-oh, what a noise.' His lips trembled. James put his hand on his arm.

'It's all right. It's over.'

With difficulty the man turned his head to James. Slowly he lifted his eyelids and James found himself looking into blue, tear-filled eyes.

'It's over,' James repeated. 'You're here, in hospital, in France.'

'When did I come?'

'A while ago.' Softly, softly, James thought. Don't rush this.

'You were knocked out,' he said aloud, 'but you're going to be all right now.' The man pondered for a moment.

'Is there anybody else here?'

'You mean from your battalion?'

'Yes, the boys from Calgary, where I live. Are they here?'

'I think,' James spoke carefully. 'I think you might have been separated from your mates. You see, you don't have your dog-tags on. Were you with the Canadians?'

'Yes, we came over on the boat.'

'But, I don't think you're Canadian are you?' James was sure that was a Shetland voice that he was hearing.

'Am I not? But that's where I came from. But,' the man stopped. 'Who are you?'

'I'm the Padre. I've been visiting and trying to help.' The man looked at him.

'But I've seen you before...somewhere. Where was it now?' His face furrowed in thought.

'I suppose padres get around,' reassured James. 'We've maybe bumped into each other at some point.'

'No, I ken the voice. Where...where...?' he slumped back. 'It's no use. I can't remember. Can't you think?'

'Could we have met before the War?' James was intrigued by the man's Shetland voice, the very blue eyes. Where had he seen eyes like that before? The only person he remembered with such piercing blue eyes was Alexander Sinclair. He tightened his lips as he thought of him and then thought, Magnus, how old would Magnus be now? Could this poor, thin, wounded man somehow be the boy whom James had known, liked and helped all those years ago, the boy whose father had married James's one and only true love, Charlotte Gordon?

He took a deep breath and sat down at the bedside. Careful, he thought. Go easily on him. You don't want to set him back.

'Where were you before the War?' The man's voice was weak but unmistakable.

'Scotland, in Perthshire. What about you?'

'In Canada, Calgary. I went there on a train …' he paused '…I remember now – the Canadian Pacific Railway. Amazing experience. Then we came back and got on a boat.'

'What did you do in between?'

'Worked in a hospital in Calgary.' The man looked up in surprise.

'That's it,' he said, 'I worked in a hospital. I'm a doctor.' He made as if to push the bedclothes aside. 'Oh,' he gasped as the pain of moving hit him. 'What's the matter with me? I'm a doctor. I should be working, not lying about in bed.' He sank back. 'What happened? Who am I? What's my name?'

'Look,' said James, 'take it slowly. You were very badly wounded. Being knocked out is only one of the things. I think you're going to be bedded for a wee while yet.'

'Bedded for a wee while yet,' the man repeated. 'You sound just like the folks at home.'

'So where is home?' asked James. 'Where do folk speak like that? Can you remember your father and mother?' The man's face clouded. The blue eyes filled again.

'My mother's dead,' he said.

'Are you sure?'

'Yes. She died. I missed her so much. But there was someone there helping me. A lady. She was beautiful.' His face fell. 'I haven't seen her for a long time. I had to go away.'

'Can you remember her name?'

'It's Charlotte. Yes, it's Charlotte. I remember because I refused to call her Mother. She wasn't my mother. My mother died.' Tears rolled down his cheeks. 'My mother died,' he repeated. 'I loved her so much. But then – but then Charlotte was there.'

James swallowed. Here was Magnus but Magnus didn't realise it yet. He held out a handkerchief and Magnus wiped his eyes.

'What about your own name?' The man shook his head.

'Do *you* know?'

'I'm trying to help you. What about the place where you grew up? Could it be a village with houses round the harbour, with stormy seas and wild winds and sometimes blue skies and cliff top walks.'

'Cliff top walks, cliff top walks. I used to go cliff top walks – with Lowrie and, and Christina.' James smiled.

'I think you're getting there. Do you know who Christina is?'

'She's my sister.' The answer was immediate. He looked pleased with himself. 'Yes, she's my sister. She was at school.'

'Well,' James said, quietly. 'If Christina is your sister, do you know who you are?'

'So, I must be – I must be, Magnus.'

'What makes you say that?'

'Well –' with a hint of impatience –'Christina's brother is Magnus and she's my sister, then I'm Magnus. Right?'

'Yes I think so. There's no faulting your logic. I'm sorry I didn't recognise you straight away. It was your very blue eyes that I noticed when you opened them.'

'But who are you? Do you know me then?'

'Well, I think I know now who you are. I'm James MacLeod. I knew you when you were a boy. We – used to talk.'

'James… James MacLeod,' Magnus wondered aloud.

'Minister,' James prompted.

'Oh, yes,' Magnus said, a look of relief on his face. 'I remember now, Church of Scotland, and we went to the Cong. But I saw you at school and,' his face fell, 'at Charlotte's.'

'Yes, at Charlotte's.' There was silence for a moment. Magnus slumped back on his pillow and closed his eyes. James looked at him.

'I think you've had enough for today. You need to sleep now.'

'But you haven't told me about the battle, or why you're here.'

'Later,' James promised. 'I'll come back later and we'll talk again.'

That evening he returned. The Duty Sister smiled.

'Come to work another miracle?'

'Is Magnus all right?'

'He's much better. After you left, he slept for a couple of hours, real sleep this time. Then he was able to have some soup, and we were able to do his dressings. I think he's looking forward to talking to you again.'

'How much does he know?'

'Well, he wanted to know how long he'd been in a coma so we told him. He asked about his family but of course we don't have details – but you…'

'Yes, I've got the details here. I've also found out he was posted missing in action on 29 September 1916 and his father was informed by telegram followed by a letter two weeks later. If it's all right with you, I'll arrange for another telegram to go after I've spoken to him again. And, of course,' he added, 'I can do the official informing as well.'

'Yes, thank you very much. We thought that sort of thing would be best, especially as you know the family.'

Magnus was looking better. His eyes were clearer, brow less anxious.

'Hello, Sir,' he began.

'You don't need to 'Sir' me,' James said. 'We're old friends.' He held out his hand and Magnus grasped it.

'Thank you,' he said. 'I'm here again, thanks to you.'

'You would have found yourself eventually.'

'We-ll maybe, but you were there and you were able to put two and two together.'

'How are you feeling now?'

'Better, thanks, but still thinking.'

'Don't think too much. You might get a headache. How is your head, by the way?'

'I'm just being careful with it.' Magnus looked down at his bandages ruefully. 'I think I've a lot of mending to do.'

'Yes, you're going to be quite a while before we get you out of here.'

'What happened? Do you know?'

'Well, as I understand it, the Canadians were at Thiepval Ridge. They did a great job. You were there with them, giving medical aid to the wounded and in the middle of it you were badly wounded yourself and somehow became separated from the rest. It must have been right at the peak of the battle because the very next day the 51st Highland Division who were there as well, captured the Ridge.'

'Oh, I'm so glad.' Magnus's eyes lit up. 'What happened next?'

'Well, the 'Somme' as they call it has continued but, it could stop in the not too distant future. But of course, the War goes on.'

'How long?'

'Who knows? It's a ghastly business. But,' James said, 'at least you're alive, and now that you've come this far you'll be fine.'

'Yes, but,' Magnus hesitated. 'What about my Division, can you tell them. What will they say?'

'Well now we know who you are,' James said, 'we'll inform them and then all the official wheels will start turning – with their usual speed – and what *you* have to do is get yourself fit again. I seem to remember you were quite keen on being fit at one time – you and Lowrie.'

'Yes, I wonder where he is.'

'Did he go to the Front?'

'Yes, but I don't know where he ended up. I'll need to find out what's happened to him.'

'All in good time, said James. 'You've only just come round, you're wounded. Give yourself time. How have you been today anyway?'

'It's been quite a day so far,' Magnus admitted. 'I've had my dressings done.'

'How was that?'

'Not very nice, but they say I've healed a lot since it happened. James, it's been five weeks. I've lost *five weeks*. I can hardly believe it.' His voice shook. 'I'll never get it back.'

'No, that's true,' said James. 'But just think. You might have been killed. You nearly were. And you're here.'

'Yes, but look at me. Oh, I'm glad to be alive, I think – but what a mess I'm in. Do you think I'll ever practise again?'

'I don't know,' said James. 'The first thing is to get you well again and up and about. Then you can think about the future. Just take one day at a time. This last couple of days have been momentous for you. It's all a lot to take in.'

'It was good of you to come back.'

'Well, I wanted to see how you are. And also,' James said, 'I have a duty to let your father know by telegram of your whereabouts and that you're alive. And, of course the Red Cross and any other official bodies who've been looking for you.'

'My father?' said Magnus.

'Yes, he's your next of kin. He's among the first to be told.'

'He won't care,' said Magnus.

'Why do you say that?' asked James. 'I'm sure he cares deeply about the fact that to him you are missing. And Charlotte too. They'll want to get you home as soon as you're able.'

'I can't do that. I can't go home to Jarlshavn.'

'But why not, Magnus?'

'I just can't. I can't tell you. I can't tell anybody.' His blue eyes filled with tears again. 'It's impossible, I tell you.'

'Let's leave it there for just now,' said James. 'But one thing I'm required to do – that is, inform your father where you are and that you're alive. You know that Magnus. I have to do that. Any other decisions can be left for another day.'

He watched silently as Magnus wiped his eyes, gave a deep sigh and finally said, 'All right. I know you've to do that. When will you send it?'

'Tonight, when I get back. I'll follow it up with a letter in a few days. Is that all right? Will you agree to that?'

'Yes. Thank you.' Magnus looked very tired.

'I think you've had enough for one day.' James touched his shoulder lightly, made his farewells and left, not before informing Sister Alison Forbes that he was sure there was something on the patient's mind and he would be back on the morrow. In the meantime would they see that he got something to ensure a good night's sleep?

Chapter 19

The following morning, when James walked in after his tour of the upstairs ward of Royaumont, Magnus was sitting up and looking better.

''Morning,' he said. 'Do you know they gave me porridge – not quite home porridge but it was good. It's part of the staple diet here I'm told.'

'Feel better.'

'Well, I certainly feel more myself. I'm still not quite sure what to make of the new me but I feel more like attempting to cope.'

'I sent the telegram.'

'Any reply?' Magnus's hands anxiously plucking the sheet belied the casual question.

'No, not yet. I wouldn't've expected it yet. I've been speaking to the doctor and sister. They think you'll be here for a while yet. It's either here or transferring you to a hospital in the South East of England. Seems the feeling is, given where you come from, that you'd be better here for the time being. How do you feel about that?'

'All right, I suppose. They're very kind here. And friendly.'

'And then we'll maybe get you to a convalescent hospital in Scotland for a while. How would you like that? They're opening up a few now that there is such a need for them from the military.'

'Where are they?'

'Well the War Commission is requisitioning large houses and castles as hospitals offering different levels of care. I was thinking of Glamis Castle for you. The Bowes Lyon family have agreed that most of it should be used, and of course the grounds. I haven't seen them but I hear that it's all beautiful.'

'Glamis. And is the Lady Elizabeth in attendance?'

'I think she probably is.' James laughed. 'The men are probably all head over heels in love with her.' He paused, 'And then when you're better you could think about coming home.'

'I told you yesterday. I can't go home. Shetland is over for me.'

'But why, Magnus. Why? Your life was there.'

'*Was*,' said Magnus bitterly. '*Was* is the word. But if you'd been ordered away, told not to come back, threatened with your livelihood, would you go back?'

'But who did that to you?' There was a pause.

'My father,' muttered Magnus.

'Your *father*? But why?'

Magnus looked stubborn. 'Just leave it at that. I had a row with him and he ordered me out. I went to Canada. That's it.' His mouth folded in a tight line.

The door opened. A VAD stood there.

'Tea,' she said. James was glad of the interruption.

'Thank you.' He took the two mugs and handed one to Magnus.

'Can you manage?'

'Yes, thanks. I'm holding things better today and as long as it's not too hot I can manage to drink it.' He sipped cautiously. 'It's fine.' They sat for a moment. James broke the silence.

'Would you like to talk about it?'

'I don't know. It's all so long ago and yet I can remember it as though it were yesterday.' He hesitated. 'Of course it was all my fault, mostly, but he was so autocratic and nasty.'

'Have you spoken to him since you left?'

'Oh we correspond, even he writes until he had that stroke in April 1912 – after the Titanic went down. That was a blow. He lived and breathed the Titanic. Anyway he couldn't write for a while after that. But I don't write to him alone. I write to the family. Then I can let myself write more naturally.'

'How did you know about the stroke?'

'Charlotte wrote and told me. She often writes a separate letter from my father – gives the news from a different perspective. They come together. She doesn't usually write alone.'

'Charlotte, how is she?' James couldn't resist the question.

'She's fine, the last time I heard, worried about the War, like everybody. There may be mail waiting for me somewhere, or maybe it's lost too.'

'Well you're not lost now.'

'I feel a bit lost,' Magnus admitted.

'Magnus, why won't you go home? You could go to Glamis after you're able to leave here and then on to Shetland for a bit. They'd be so pleased to see you.'

Magnus shook his head. 'Even if I felt I could go back after I've been ordered out, I don't think my father would have me in the house as long as…' he stopped.

'As long as what, Magnus, or, who? Is it somebody?'

'It's Charlotte.'

'What about Charlotte? Don't you like her? But I thought you got on so well.'

'We do get on well – did, I mean,' Magnus said, desperation in his voice. 'That's the point. Too well.' He looked down at his cooling tea. James turned.

'Charlotte?' he said. 'You mean, you and Charlotte…?'

'Oh it wasn't Charlotte's fault. Not really. But if she'd been free, I could have made her care. I wanted to take her away. I love her so much.' He wept.

James sat stunned. He hadn't expected this. Charlotte, the only woman I'll ever love, loved by Magnus and married and loyal to Alexander. He put his head in his hands.

Magnus wiped his eyes, looked over.

'James, I'm sorry,' he said. 'I shouldn't be burdening you with my troubles.'

James, pulling himself together, waved away the apology. 'That's what I'm here for,' he said. He could see Magnus had no idea of his past involvement with Charlotte.

'Does anyone else know?'

'Only Lowrie.'

'Lowrie?'

'Yes, he knew for a long time what was happening to me. When I left for Canada, I didn't have a chance to say good-bye to him as he was in Edinburgh. I wrote from Calgary and told him – that my father had found out, was very angry and had ordered me out. Threatened me with losing me my job and my credibility with the GMC – yes it's true –' as James raised his eyebrows. 'He threatened to report me to my boss and so on. I had to go.' He continued, 'I told Lowrie and he was very helpful.'

'What did he say?'

'Well of course knowing a bit about the background, he wasn't all that surprised. But apart from that, I wanted to write to Charlotte and of course I couldn't. Lowrie advised writing to the whole family and therefore including Charlotte. It's worked fine until now.'

James swallowed. Whatever happened, Magnus must not get to know about him and Charlotte.

'Magnus, I'm so sorry…'

'Not half as sorry as I am. Sometimes I wish that I'd never been born, or died as a baby like the wee ones. My brothers and sister,' he added by way of explanation. 'And, look at me now. A complete wreck, no job, can't work, no home, got to be looked after…'

'But it won't always be like that. Look, you've only just come out of a coma. Look at you today – so much better than yesterday. Give yourself time, man.' Magnus sat silent.

'Now,' James said. 'You need to rest. I've brought you something to read. He put two books on the table. And I have to write in my professional capacity to your father and Charlotte that you're making progress and taking nourishment and so on. I'll keep it brief but they need to know how and where you are. Any other decisions can be left until another day. Is that all right?'

'Yes…yes thank you.' Magnus hesitated. 'Please … say, love to all and I'll write when I'm able.'

'Right I'll do that and…'

'James…'

'Yes?'

'Don't say anything about, well, you know…'

'I'm not daft.' If Magnus only knew, James thought, that's the last thing I'd mention. 'You relax now and stop worrying. Probably see you tomorrow.'

'Thanks for coming.'

Chapter 20

Charlotte wiped her streaming eyes. Alexander looked at her.

'He's dead isn't he? Magnus is dead, and I sent him away.'

'No.' Charlotte's response was quick. 'No, Alexander, he's alive. They've found him. See,' she held out the telegram. 'He's in hospital in a place called Royaumont. He's going to be all right.' She made another effort to stem the tears, looked at Alexander and gave a watery smile.

'Thank God,' breathed Alexander. 'How is he?'

'It says, "Making progress. Writing".'

'Who sent it?'

'I haven't even looked.' She scanned the telegram. 'A chaplain, I think … someone called James MacLeod. One of the military chaplains I expect … Oh.' She clapped her hand over her mouth as realisation dawned. 'James MacLeod, chaplain. Of course, it must be James MacLeod who was here.'

'Ah, well, it could be,' Alexander said cautiously. 'But it's not so very unusual a surname. But, well, I suppose that's a reasonable conclusion.'

'What a coincidence,' he continued. 'I wonder if he was the one who recognised Magnus. It's a long time since he was here. They must have changed quite a bit.'

'Right, my dear,' he carried on, not noticing that Charlotte had gone silent. 'Is there an address on that telegram?'

'Well, a sort of central address.'

'Well, could you write a short note on our behalf to this Mr MacLeod …'

'It says Major…'

'Well, whatever he is, and thank him and ask him for any further details. We must arrange for his homecoming as soon as he is able.'

'But, Alexander…' Charlotte hesitated.

'Yes?' said Alexander. 'Of course he must come home. He'll want to come home. He'll have got over all that silly nonsense about you by now.'

Charlotte couldn't argue, couldn't open all the old sores, couldn't deal with the Alexander so sure that his boy would be eager to return.

'I'll go and tell Edie and Meg the news. I'll bring you back a cup of tea.' She hurried downstairs.

'Edie, Meg, are you there? He's alive. Magnus is alive.' Edie and Meg met her at the kitchen door and they stood for a moment, arms round each other, tears running down their faces.

'Mother, why are you crying?' Angus stood there watching them. Girls he thought. Always crying.

'Angus,' Charlotte, smiled through her tears. 'Angus, Magnus is alive, he's in hospital but he's alive.'

'O-oh,' he said. 'That's good, isn't it? Will he come home now?'

'Well, I don't know yet what will be happening. We've only had a very short telegram. See.' He studied it.

'Is there a letter?' he said. 'Says a letter.'

'Yes but the telegram comes quickly to give the news. Then the letter will tell us what's happening.'

'He's my brother.'

'Yes.' Charlotte smiled at him. 'He's your brother and he's alive.'

'I don't know him.'

'No I know, but now I hope you'll have a chance.'

'I must tell the boys when I get back to school,' said Angus, pleased. 'My brother.' Then, in an abrupt change of subject: 'Is lunch ready?'

'Angus, I'm sorry, you must be hungry. Lunch is ready, we just sort of – forgot about food for a moment.'

Angus slipped past the excited atmosphere. 'I'll just wash my hands.'

Charlotte looked at Edie and laughed. 'Nothing will keep him from his food for long.'

'Och well, Miss, I mean Mrs Sinclair,' said Edie. 'He's a growing boy. But I think he'll be bragging about his brother in school this afternoon.'

That afternoon Charlotte settled to compose her letter to James MacLeod.

Birkenshaw etc,

Dear Mr MacLeod,

Thank you very much for your telegram which arrived this morning. I am writing on behalf of my husband Alexander Sinclair who is recovering from a stroke which he suffered a few weeks ago.

It has indeed given us great pleasure to have the happy news about Magnus and that he is making progress. We have been greatly worried about him and your telegram has eased our minds considerably. We look forward to any further news that you can give us. We would also be grateful if you could include an address for Magnus to which we can write.

We hope that you, yourself are well.

Please give our love and best regards to Magnus if you are still in the area where he is hospitalised.

Thank you.

Yours sincerely,

Charlotte Sinclair.

There, she read it over. That's it, keep it pleasant but formal.

The letters crossed in the post. On leaving Magnus, James wrote and posted his letter to the Sinclairs regarding Magnus's address at Royaumont, his state of health, a brief comment on where and how he had been injured and that he had been unconscious and minus his identity tags for five weeks, hence the delay in finding and identifying him. He finished by saying:

It remains for me to say that Magnus sends love to you all and that he will write when he is able. This, I am sure will be reasonably soon. He seems to be making very good progress on a daily basis. I am sure that he is looking forward to hearing from you.

If there is anything that I can do to help you please feel enabled to ask.

I hope that you will accept my very best wishes. I remember my Shetland days with great pleasure.

Yours sincerely,
James MacLeod (AChD).

Charlotte read the letter slowly. The past was very near. She allowed her mind to drift back to happy, younger days, on the cliff top, amongst the books of her own Peerie Skulehoose where James MacLeod had been such a regular visitor, in the Manse garden, the smell of the flowers was so strong, so evocative – she stood up quickly. No, she told herself. Keep out of there. She walked briskly to the stairs and hurried up.

'Here,' she said, 'Alexander, here's a bit more news about Magnus. I'm sure we'll hear from him himself soon.'

He took the letter, read it, looked out of the window. In his mind Margery, his first love and Magnus's mother, walked past. She looked at him and smiled encouragingly. Then she was gone, but Alexander was comforted by the notion that she might be keeping a watching brief over their boy.

'Alexander?' Charlotte took his hand. 'Are you all right?'

'What,' he looked up at her. 'Oh, yes, I'm fine, just thinking. Yes, it's good news, good to hear. We'll need to get writing to him. Tell him his bed's here, waiting – that sort of stuff.'

Birkenshaw

Dear Magnus,

We've just received a letter from Mr James MacLeod giving us your address and telling us a little bit about what has happened to you. We're all so happy and thankful that you're alive and although injured, Mr MacLeod seems to think that all will be well. This is wonderful news. It is difficult to put into words how we feel. Suffice it to say that we've been so worried and now we feel as though a burden has been lifted from our shoulders. Your father has asked me to tell you that he has not been very well recently. He had another stroke from which he is recovering and he hopes soon to be able to write to you himself. He says that you're not to worry about him. He's getting on fine. I've to add he has shown great improvement especially since we received the telegram saying that you were all right. Today's good news letter will set him up even further.

The rest of us are fine. Christina was home for a week's leave recently. She was very helpful and it was very good to see her. They are very busy at the Royal Infirmary of Edinburgh with casualties from the Front and we're grateful that they spared her to us for a week. I'll send her your address.

Hannah and Angus are well too. Hannah had some time at home after your Father took ill but has now gone back to Lerwick during the week. Angus is growing – he's a real boy, always out and about and needing his clothes mended although I don't think he would bother if they were not.

I'll write again soon. In the meantime I hope that your health keeps improving and that you'll soon be up and about. Your father says to tell you that your bed is here. He would like to see you. It would make him very happy.

With love from us all, including Meg and Edie who are asking very much after you.

Yours affly.,

Charlotte.

PS What a coincidence hearing from Mr MacLeod. It is a small world.

Magnus recognised the writing as soon as the VAD nurse handed the letter to him. Charlotte, he thought. She's written. His hands trembled slightly as he clumsily tore the envelope open. He read the letter and then leant back on his pillows holding it in his hand. Charlotte, her writing, her – he sniffed. A light fragrance lingered – her perfume. What am I to do he thought? I'm like a school boy. He read it through again. Not a sign of anything. But Charlotte wouldn't, she wouldn't show by the slightest comma in a letter that she was writing on behalf of Father that she had any feelings for me. She's too honourable. So Father's had another stroke. Poor old boy – no, he chided himself for the unkind thought – I wouldn't wish him ill. But – there you go, he has her and I don't. I must try and write them a letter. Later.

Later. The ward was quieter that day. Some of the more able men had been evacuated to the French coast with a view to getting them across the English Channel or, *La Manche*. From there they would be sent on to yet more hospitals, convalescent homes or rehabilitation centres. Some even hoped that they might be allowed to go home.

Magnus sat in his chair and thought about writing. Sitting in a chair was the latest big step in his recovery and it had taken all the persuasive powers of doctors, sisters and VAD nurses to coerce him out of his bed.

'You're getting too comfortable there, Magnus,' Alison Forbes had said. 'What about getting up for a while?'

'No, I'm fine. Honestly.'

'It'll do you good.' The doctor chimed in.

'I'm tired.'

'Yes, but just for a wee while. Let's see how your legs are.'

He'd felt very dizzy sitting there on the side of his bed swinging his legs.

'See, I told you I was better in bed.'

But they persisted. Slowly, slowly they moved him to the edge, then like tugs round a liner, they brought him to his feet.

'I'm falling,' he gasped.

'No, you're not. We've got you. Put your arms around my neck,' Alison Forbes commanded. 'Now birl, just a half-turn. Now down. There you are.' They lowered him into the waiting chair and triumphantly stood back, admiring their handiwork.

136

That had been two days ago. Now, Magnus was getting used to the experience and he had to admit felt the better of the change from bed to chair.

But writing. That was another thing. And also, what could he say about the War? He could just say nothing about it. They wouldn't understand. It was one thing to talk to the other men about it – and the staff. But folk at home? How did you go explaining to them. All too difficult. Best say nothing.

James had left him one of his beloved indelible pencils and some notepaper and envelopes the day before. He had no excuse. I haven't written anything for weeks, he thought. I've forgotten how to. No you haven't, a little voice nagged in his brain. Get on with it. Remember, you told James to tell them that you would write when you were able. But I'm not able. But he knew he was.

Dear Father and Charlotte and everybody,

Thank you for your letter. It was good to hear from you. I am making good progress and everyone is very good to me. I am getting up to sit in a chair every day now so that's a step in the right direction. Some of my bandages are off now and my head is improving too.

Sorry to hear of your illness Father. I hope that you're soon going about again.

I'll write again soon but will close this now and hope to get the courier tonight.

Yours affly.,

Magnus.

There he thought, it's done. The writing's awful though. Worse than it was before. And, I can't mention going – anywhere.

He addressed the envelope, sealed it and dropped it on the table with a sigh.

Charlotte went up to Alexander, letter in hand.

'What do you think? she asked as he finished reading and handed it silently to her.

'Well, he's obviously been very ill, the letter is much more basic than he would usually write and the writing – well it's quite shaky don't you think?'

Charlotte nodded. 'Yes, he must have been very bad. Poor soul. This is not the Magnus we know – but he will improve.'

Chapter 21

Captain Lowrie Harcus sat in his 'Captain's Dugout' at eight o'clock one Wednesday evening writing dispatches. The chill December air crept even below ground. Heating of any kind was non-existent. Lowrie was in as much clothing as he could wear complete with a scarf knitted by his mother in the colours of the Anderson Educational Institute of Lerwick. She and her friends knitted socks, scarves and fingerless gloves on a non-stop basis for the men away at the Front. Lighting in the dug-out was supplied by a poor quality candle stuck into the neck of a wine-bottle. The smoke from this combined with the reek from Lowrie's pipe and that of his companion Lieutenant Harry White to create an atmosphere as thick as any London pea-souper. Lowrie's eyes watered. He rubbed them irritably.

'I can hardly see to write,' he said. 'But I'm nearly finished. I've done all the official lot. Just a note to Christina now.'

'Who's Christina?' Harry looked up from his paper. It was a week-old copy of *The Glasgow Herald* going the rounds of the trenches in the vicinity. There was even an official *Herald* reading queue which became depleted when names were scored off as their owners were killed.

'Is she your young lady?' Harry asked again.

'What?' Lowrie looked up. 'Sorry, I was writing.'

'Christina,' Harry repeated. 'Who is she, your girl?'

'Well,' Lowrie hesitated. 'She's a nurse in Edinburgh. We promised to write. Here, this is her.' He fished in his inner pocket and drew out a small photo of Christina and Magnus.

'Very nice,' said Harry, impressed. 'Who's she with?'

'That's Magnus, her brother. He's, missing, missing in action.'

'Oh, I'm so sorry.' Harry was sympathetic. 'How did you find out?'

'When I was last on leave.' Lowrie sighed. 'He's my friend. We were at school together.'

The courier arrived. He saluted smartly.

'Attending for dispatches, Sir.'

'Thank you.' Lowrie looked up. 'You're new aren't you? I haven't seen you before.'

'Yes Sir. I've just come back from sick leave. I'm Corporal Crozier, Sir.'

'How do you do, Corporal. I'm Captain Harcus. Have you been off sick long? Were you wounded?'

'Yes Sir. Shrapnel in the right shoulder, Sir. I was in hospital for two weeks and then one week behind the lines. Now here, Sir.'

'Well, take care, won't you. Where is your home?'

'London, Sir.'

Lowrie sealed his dispatches and handed them over.

'Thank you Corporal. By the way, where were you in hospital?'

'Royaumont, Sir.'

'All right, was it?'

'All very good, doctors, nurses and so on. Worked off their feet of course, Sir. But,' he shrugged. 'What can you expect? The casualties arrive in great batches.'

'They were a good bunch of men there too. All mixed in well, when they could. Officers, men, all helping each other. One chap, Sir…' in a rush of confidence… 'this chap, he'd been very ill, and once he was a bit better, he used to come and talk. I think he was a doctor but he was just like anyone else. In fact, Sir, he talked a bit like you – Scotch-like but with a bit more. Begging your pardon for being personal, Sir.'

'No that's all right, Corporal. That's very interesting. A doctor, you think?'

'Yes, Sir. Not that he ever said that to me, but I overheard him one day speaking to the Padre. He was quite fed up. Said he should be out there in the CCSs rather than in hospital being a patient. I think, Sir, he was worried he'd have to stop, you know, doctoring.'

Lowrie was all attention.

'Did you get his name, Corporal?'

'That's a funny one Sir. I did hear something but it was a name I'd never heard before and so I didn't know if it was a name or what it was, Sir. It was the Padre that said it.'

'And…?' Lowrie prompted.

'Well, it was something like – em, Mag-us, Magis or something like that.'

'Magnus?'

'That's it, Sir. That was the word. Is it a name?'

'Yes Corporal. It is. And it comes from where I come from.'

'Do you know him Sir?'

'I think I might. Thank you very much for the information, Corporal. Well observed.'

'Thank you Sir. Will that be all, Sir?' The Corporal took the dispatch bag.

'Yes, thank you. Take care on your rounds. The enemy seems quiet at the moment, but you can't trust him.'

'No Sir. Thank you Sir.' Corporal Crozier saluted and left the dugout.

A week later, Lowrie and his Company were behind the lines. This was a rotational move. Men spent weeks in the trenches, then every so often they were sent back and were replaced by those who came forward. Being behind the lines was not a holiday. A strict routine ensured that discipline was enforced with the men turning out for training, marching, target practice and attack practice. At the same time they had a chance to wash themselves and their kit, de-louse as far as possible, eat at reasonably regular times and have a break from the seemingly interminable barrage of gunfire. True, they could still hear the thunder of the guns, but it was further away, not quite so all-encompassing. For a short time, they could set aside the dread of having to leave the comparative safety of the trench, go up the ladders and over the top.

Lowrie was very glad of the break. During that last spell on the Front line, he had lost a significant number of men, some killed, some badly wounded. He himself had had a near-miss when a bullet sang past his head just missing him.

'Someone looking after you, then?' His shaken Sergeant had said.

'Too close for comfort.' Lowrie's casual comment belied his inner feelings.

A few days into their time behind the lines, Lowrie set out for Royaumont. He had been planning this since Corporal Crozier had told him about the patient with an unfamiliar name and with an accent 'Scotch but more so'. Since then, Lowrie had done some investigation and confirmed that a certain Captain Magnus Sinclair RAMC, posted as missing, was now located, seriously wounded in Royaumont.

Lowrie didn't know what to think. Date of being posted missing was 27 October 1916. It was now late December in the week between Christmas and New Year. True, the days all seemed to merge into one another. Christmas Day was their second-last day in the trench. There had been no amnesty that Christmas. Quiet for a time, then the firing had started again. But the date meant that Magnus, if this were he, had been there for two months. Lowrie pondered. How was he? Would he be able for visitors? But Corporal Crozier had said he had been speaking to the other men so he surely would be able to see visitors. Lowrie decided to go and see for himself.

He went to see his Commanding Officer, Lt Col Jonathan Fairhead. His billet was a room in a deserted farmhouse. He was sitting at a big table writing up his Records.

'Good morning, Sir.' Lowrie saluted.

''Morning, Lowrie. How are you?'

'Fine thank you, Sir.'

'And the men?'

'All fine, thanks. Better now than they were a few days ago. Morale is improving.

'So what can I do for you?'

'Sir, I was wondering...' Lowrie hesitated.

'Yes?'

'I was wondering if you could allow me a Pass for the day and lend me your horse for the day if you're not requiring him.'

'My horse? Thinking of going riding?'

'Well, Sir, it's like this.' Lowrie had known that an explanation would be necessary.

'I've reason to believe that a friend of mine, Captain Magnus Sinclair RAMC is lying wounded in hospital at Royaumont.' Lowrie then proceeded to elaborate on his story with what he had found out.

'So you see Sir, I'd like to go and see him. Lieutenant White is on duty and has offered to stand in for me here, but to get there and back in good time, I really need a horse. Please.'

The CO was a reasonable man. He knew and trusted Lowrie and that however far-fetched, the story would be true.

'Right, Lowrie, take Dobbin. Here.' He scribbled on a pass-sheet. 'Show this to the horse Corporal and he will saddle him up for you. Be back by tonight please.'

'Yes, Sir. Thank you very much Sir.'

'I hope you find your friend improving and can do something to help him.'

'Thank you Sir.' Lowrie saluted again.

'Take care.' The CO returned to his Report and Lowrie to organise Dobbin and hand over to Harry White for the day.

140

It wasn't that far to Royaumont, a matter of fifteen miles. As Lowrie approached the Abbey he looked around in appreciation. Amazing that such peace can exist with mayhem just a few miles up the road.

He jumped down at the gate and made to open it.

'Here, let me help you.' A pale-looking man limped forward. 'I'll do the gate.' He swung the latch and the heavy gate swung back. Lowrie led Dobbin through.

'Thank you. Is there anywhere I can put my horse for a while, do you know?'

'Yes, Sir.' The man turned and pointed. 'Over there Sir, round to the right. I'd do it for you Sir, but as you can see, I'm a bit handicapped at the moment.' He raised his crutch slightly.

'Yes, I see. At the Somme, was it?'

'Yes, Sir. Just at the end Sir. Got me in the leg Sir. Can't see me able to get back Sir.' Lowrie smiled. He doesn't appear too regretful about it. Aloud, he said, 'They're busy here?'

'Yes, a lot of the time Sir. Some days it's pandemonium then gets quieter as they sort folk out. Some stay, some go back home earlier, across to hospital in the South of England.'

'How about you?'

'I think I'll get home in a couple of weeks. Here, Sir,' the soldier added, 'here's the stable.' They had rounded the side of the Abbey and were approaching buildings which now constituted stabling for around half a dozen horses.

'There's sure to be a space. They're never all used at the same time.'

'Thank you very much.'

'You're welcome, Sir. If you go back round the front and up the steps, the main entrance is there.' He turned and limped away. Lowrie watched him go for a moment before turning his attention on stabling Dobbin and going in search of Magnus.

Chapter 22

He walked into Royaumont's entrance hall taking off his glengarry at the door. It was still, quiet, quite cold, not with the heavy chill of winter that lay outside like a freezing blanket but cold as if a room just awaited a fire to be lit to throw it into life. Lowrie looked around. Sure enough, there was the wide empty fireplace awaiting a spark.

'We don't light it until 2 pm.' A voice broke the silence. Lowrie stepped forward. 'Then we know it will last the rest of the day. Otherwise we run out of fuel. Mind you, the men – the fitter ones, that is – are very good at scavenging for wood. They bring in all sorts.'

The owner of the voice stepped towards him. She was small, erect, grey hair worn back off her face. She held out her hand. 'I should have introduced myself. I'm Dr Edith Strachan, the Superintendent of this hospital at Royaumont for the moment. I saw you lead your horse round to the stable. You are…?'

Lowrie shook hands. 'Captain Lowrie Harcus.'

'And what can I do for you, Captain Harcus?'

'I'm looking for a friend of mine. I have heard that he is here. Captain Magnus Sinclair.'

'Ah, Magnus.' Dr Strachan smiled. 'Yes, Magnus is one of our successes, I think. But how do you know Magnus?'

'How do you mean?'

'Well,' she responded. 'I must be sure that a visit would be in my patient's best interests. He's been very ill and I can't take the slightest risk of doing anything to set him back.'

'I'm sorry to hear that he has been so ill,' Lowrie said gravely. 'I only heard by chance that he was here and my enquiries have only been able to confirm that and supply the barest of details.'

'As for my credentials, I can tell you that Magnus is my oldest friend. Here,' he pulled out his wallet. 'Here is his last letter to me, written a while ago now, I fear.' He proffered the letter to Dr Strachan who scanned it briefly before handing it back.

'He volunteered from Canada and I from Edinburgh where I was working. And then, well, things went a bit haywire and we lost touch over the last two years. But, we were boys together, went to school, walked the cliffs of our homeland, shared each other's joys, sorrows and pain. Now, please, how is he?'

Dr Strachan observed him as he talked. Here's someone who knows Magnus very well. Perhaps he can help to bring Magnus into the next stage of recovery.

'Well,' she said. 'As I said, Magnus has been very ill. He was unconscious for five weeks. A head injury like that alone, leaves its mark. He's lost – time out of his life, in a way. Added to that he's had multiple wounds from which he has to recover. Now, he gets up, visits other patients, talks to them sometimes but this last week he hasn't moved forward in the way that we might have expected.'

'What would you have expected?'

142

'Well, once he was up and about, the natural step would have been to join in for meals and also want to get outside. But Magnus seems reluctant to do these things. He may be getting a little low. You may be just the tonic he requires.' She smiled at Lowrie. 'Let's go and see how he is.'

She led the way to where Magnus was, still in the little room off the main ward. Lowrie had frequently visited CCSs, military hospitals and the like so was unfazed by the proliferation of injuries, bed-cradles, Thomas's splints, bandaged heads and eye-patches that met his gaze. Most of the men raised a hand in greeting. A few were, he supposed asleep. Eyes closed anyway. They stopped at a door.

'Wait a wee moment.' Edith Strachan smiled at him. 'Let me have a word first.' She knocked.

'Come in.'

'Good morning, Magnus. Sorry I haven't been in earlier. I've been rushing around. How are you today?'

''Morning, Doctor. I'm all right, thanks.'

'How did you sleep?'

'Not too badly, thanks.'

'I've brought you a visitor.'

'Who? James?'

'No, he's not here today. No, someone you haven't seen for a while.' She held the door wide and Lowrie stepped forward into the tiny room.

Magnus looked up from his chair. His brow furrowed in anxiety and exasperation as he looked at the features of the man standing before him.

'Who are you? I...I know the face...'

'Take it slowly Magnus.' Lowrie himself was taken aback by the gaunt pale appearance of his friend and probably would not have known him if he'd not had prior knowledge.

'That voice – the voice. Reminds me of home.'

Lowrie pulled up a chair and sat down. 'Yes, Magnus. Reminds you of home, just as your voice reminds me. Now we can remember together. Remember the walks around Jarlshavn, going to school, all the fun we had training, how you beat me at putting the shot, or, boulder, I should say.'

'I remember these things,' said Magnus. 'But I used to do them with Lowrie. I, I haven't seen Lowrie ... I can't remember how long for. Not since before ... before ...' He stopped.

'Before what, Magnus?'

'Before I had to go. Leave, Shetland. Lowrie was in Edinburgh. I wrote and told him I'd had to go. Told him about – about ...' he stopped again.

'About what, Magnus?' Lowrie leaned forward.

'Something that only he knew about until then. He understood what I was talking about in the letter. We did write after that but since the war we've somehow lost touch. He could be dead and I haven't heard. The only friend who really knows me. I haven't seen him for years and I don't know where he is or how he is.' He turned away. 'I sometimes feel I can't go on.'

Lowrie couldn't bear to see his friend in such a state. 'Magnus,' he said. 'Magnus. Look at me. Look.'

Magnus turned back, and looked at his visitor. His eyes narrowed as he squinted up. He looked harder. Recognition flared as his exhausted brain registered the identity of the man in front of him.

'Lowrie. Can it be you? Lowrie. Lowrie, where have you been?' He got unsteadily out of his chair and walked towards him. 'It is you, isn't it?'

'Yes, it's me. Come to find you.'

The two men clasped each other in an embrace that covered so much time of separation and fear for each other. Dr Strachan gave a satisfied smile and slipped away quietly. Perhaps we'll get somewhere now, she said to herself.

Left alone, Magnus and Lowrie stood and looked at each other.

'Well, I've seen you looking better,' said Lowrie, light words concealing the concern he felt at the sight of the man standing there.

'You're not such an oil painting yourself.' Magnus, feeling his balance going, grabbed the end of the bed.

'Here,' Lowrie took his arm. 'Sit down, for goodness sake before you fall down.' He helped Magnus back to his seat.

'Now,' he said, 'how are things? You've had a bad time I understand.'

'Oh Lowrie,' Magnus's voice shook. 'The Somme, it was terrible. It went on and on. The casualties kept pouring in. I can see them yet.' He hesitated, head lowered, biting his lip. Then he continued, 'and in the end, well I got it. I don't know what happened but one minute I was going from man to man trying with the orderly to do what we could to patch them up before shipping them out. Then there was yet another almighty bang and then I remembered nothing more until – until, they say, five weeks, five weeks I was unconscious, Lowrie.' He held out a thin hand. Lowrie took it.

'And, I'm so weak,' Magnus went on. 'I can only walk round the ward. I'm full of shrapnel. That Henry Shrapnel who invented these bombs to maim and kill – well they certainly work.' He added bitterly, 'Especially when they're used against your own side. Doctor doesn't think they got it all out. There's still some in my right side somewhere and I don't know where else. Lowrie, I'm a doctor. I must get back to it. They need me and I'm wasting time here and I can hardly move.' His eyes filled with tears again.

Lowrie said, 'Look Magnus, Magnus, look at me.' Magnus reluctantly raised his eyes.

'Oh, I'm so glad to see you,' he said. 'I've missed seeing you so much.'

'I'm glad to see you too,' said Lowrie. 'Now, we need to help you move to the next step. Have you had any other visitors?'

'Yes, there's been James. It's been good to have James visiting but …'

'James?'

'Yes, James, you know,' as Lowrie looked at him. 'James MacLeod, who was the minister in Jarlshavn for a while.'

'Oh, yes, I remember now. Seems ages ago. How did he find you?'

'Well, I was in a coma the day he came first, but I heard about it after. Apparently he'd been going round hospitals in the area, doing what he could. What a job it must be dealing with all these wounded men all the time. Anyway,' Magnus continued. 'He came here, visited the folk in the ward and then Sister let him in to see me. I didn't know he was there, of course. He stayed a while, saw signs of life. Eventually over a day or two I came back properly'. He looked down at himself. 'If you can call this "properly".'

'It's properly enough for the moment,' said Lowrie. 'Go on.'

Magnus sighed. 'Well,' he said. 'He was very good. Stayed a long time, helping and so on. He brought me a pencil and paper to write a letter. He's come, and well, listened. He's good at that. He's a good man. I remember him when my mother was so ill – he was at Charlotte's one day when I was there and I was very angry at first. I felt he was encroaching on our private family affairs. But he wasn't. He was a great help. I saw him quite a bit at school after that – you remember he used to come to the school while he was at Jalrshavn?'

Lowrie nodded.

'The way he came to the school meant you could speak to him even if you didn't go to his Kirk. He was very easy to talk to – better than Mr Jamieson of the Cong. He was OK but you couldn't speak to him the way you could to James. My parents didn't go to his Kirk but Charlotte did before,' he hesitated, 'before she married Father. But by that time James had left. Charlotte married Father, and I, I wouldn't call her Mother, because – because I love her. And now I can't go home because Father threw me out. Oh it's all such a mess. I wish I were dead…' The flow of words stopped and he put his head in his hands.

'No, you don't,' said Lowrie. 'What you need is to get better. Then you'll cope better with the problems. Now firstly, how are things between you and the family? Are you in touch?'

'Yes, Charlotte wrote on Father's behalf. He's had another stroke.'

'Ah, yes, I called in in October when I was home on leave. I saw Christina too.'

'Oh yes, she was home for a wee while. Charlotte said in her letter. It was good to hear from her.' Magnus stopped. 'But, but, she was quite formal, you know, in the way she wrote.'

'Well.' Lowrie was gentle. 'You wouldn't expect anything else would you?'

'No,' Magnus admitted. 'I wouldn't but, I wish … I wish,' his voice broke. The head went down. His voice was muffled. 'I want to see her so much. I miss her so much.'

Lowrie sat down beside the thin shaking frame and held him.

'It's just as bad, then?'

'I'll never forget her. I think it's worse now than it was before.'

'But you know it…'

'It's hopeless. Lowrie, have you seen her? Did you see her when you were home?' Magnus looked at him, eagerly, searching for news.

'Yes,' said Lowrie, 'I was home and saw her. My mother told me in a letter that you were missing so I went up to see your folk. It hasn't been easy for them. In fact, it must be awful for folk at home not knowing what was happening. My mother would hardly let me out of her sight to begin with, after I arrived home. Anyway, the day I visited Birkenshaw your father was in bed. I just popped my head round the door and said "hello" to him but didn't stay.'

'And, and Charlotte? How was she?' Magnus looked down. 'Was she well?'

145

'She was all right I think, given the circumstances,' said Lowrie.

'How did she look?'

'She actually looked as if she's bearing up remarkably well. I think she's tired and, when I saw her she was very anxious about you. However,' he added quickly. 'Now that they know that you're still with us and being properly looked after, that will be a great boost to them. And then, she has Meg and Edie – they're a great support for her and Christina was home on a week's compassionate leave and that was good for them all.'

'How was Christina?'

'She's fine, worried about you but she'll be better now that she knows the good news.' He laughed. 'The day I called, Charlotte said she was out a walk on the cliff-top so I set out to catch her up. What a speed that lassie walks at. Anyway I eventually found her away along the cliff. It was good to see her.'

'Did she know you?'

'I think she did.' Lowrie smiled at the memory of their meeting on the cliff top.

'How did she know you under that "mouser"?'

'Oh she just did.' Lowrie stroked his precious moustache self-consciously. 'Anyway we went for a walk and caught up with the news. It's a pity our leave only overlapped by a couple of days. But,' he added, 'we're keeping in touch. By letter, you know,' as if letters were newly invented.

'By *letter*,' said Magnus. 'You mean writing to her?'

'Well, yes.'

'But why?' said Magnus. 'Why should you be wanting to write to each other? She's only a lassie. She was at school last time I saw her. We used to go for these long walks on the cliff top,' he said. 'We were allowed an hour.' Lowrie raised his eye brows.

'Yes,' Magnus insisted. 'It was touch and go whether or not I could go out with her at all, even though I'm her brother. Especially, unchaperoned. We were allowed once a week and the girls were always around, you know, accidentally on purpose. Anyway,' his voice dropped. 'That all had to stop when my father put me out. I bet they never told Christina why. Anyway,' he carried on, 'why do you want to write to her?'

'Magnus.' Lowrie felt he was in a minefield as he explained. 'When I was in Jarlshavn on leave about six weeks ago I caught up with Christina on the cliff top as I said. We met again for a walk the following day. She needed to get some fresh air, and then soon she had to go back to Edinburgh as her leave was up. We said good bye when she left and agreed to write to each other sometimes.'

'Oh. I see. But she's still just a lassie.'

'But Magnus, she's moved on – she's not the school lassie any more. She's a really lovely young woman. She's a qualified nurse. She's in Edinburgh working with men wounded here in France. She's a young woman now. She's grown up.'

'Oo-h,' Magnus put his head in his hands. 'I hadn't thought. Of course, she's grown up. She won't need me anymore.'

'Of course she'll need you, said Lowrie. 'You're her brother. You know her better than anyone. Look what you've been through together. Yes, I know there's an age gap but look what you've been to each other, what you mean to each other. Of course she'll need you. Why shouldn't she?'

'Well, look at me, for one thing.'

'Don't be daft, man, you'll be all right once you're properly on your feet again.'

'And then,' Magnus continued. 'If she's grown up she won't want a brother to look after her. She'll be getting boy-friends and looking everywhere but at her crock of a brother.'

Lowrie looked at him. He really is feeling sorry for himself. What can I do to get him out of this?

Aloud he said, 'Magnus, firstly, you may be feeling like a crock just now but remember how you egged me on to raise my fitness levels? Remember how you were the fittest boy of your year at school? Remember how you landed the punch of the year on that Alfie Twatt? You maybe got the belt for fighting but that was a day to go down in the annals of the history of the Anderson. Now for goodness sake stop thinking about being a crock or you will turn into one.'

'Those were the days.' Magnus smiled a little ruefully. 'Remember the bruises – and then facing my father and the row.'

'That's better.'

'Lowrie, you said 'firstly'. What was secondly?'

'You were going on about Christina and boyfriends. But what if there was only one?'

'Only one what?'

'You know.' Lowrie felt a little self-conscious. 'If she had only one, em, particular male friend.'

'What? Why are you putting it like that? Lowrie you've gone all red. Lowrie,' as the penny dropped, 'Lowrie do you mean that you, you and Christina…?'

'Well,' said Lowrie, 'we've agreed to write to each other. And we do hit it off rather well. What do you think?'

'What do I think?' Magnus shook his head. 'It's great. Do Charlotte and Father know?'

'For Heaven's sake, Magnus. No. Please don't say anything. This is just the beginning – I hope. You won't say anything will you?'

'No, no, certainly not. But can I speak to Christina about it.'

'No,' said Lowrie desperately. 'You can't. It's too soon. Oh I shouldn't have told you. It just slipped out. You don't mind do you?'

'Mind? There's no-one I'd rather have for my sister than you,' said Magnus. 'Don't you worry, I won't interfere, and I'll keep quiet about it.' He looked at Lowrie and smiled. 'Well, that's a turn-up for the books. Who'd have thought it?'

'Well, why not?' Lowrie said. 'I mean,' he sat up straight. 'I'm not *that* bad looking.' Magnus, why are you laughing?'

'I'm just watching you trying to improve yourself – in front of me. Who knows you. Dinna bother laddie. It's impossible.' He laughed out loud at Lowrie's discomfiture and then sat back with a groan – 'Ouch, my laughing muscles are out of practice – ooh my chest.' He gasped as his ribs twinged with the unaccustomed movement.

'Are you all right?' Lowrie bent over him anxouusly. 'Shall I get the Sister?'

'Yes, no, it's all right, I'm fine,' said Magnus. 'I was just pulling your leg and it all got too much. Oh that was sore.'

'You need to laugh more,' said Lowrie.

'Yes, I know but I needed you there to kick start it. Lowrie what am I going to do?'

'Frankly, Magnus, at the moment, I don't know. You're steady here for a good few weeks I should think. They won't want to move you till you're much stronger. Has anyone said anything to you about future plans?

'Well, James did say that Glamis, you know the Castle in Angus has opened up for folk convalescing from the Front. He suggested that given where I come from, Glamis would be a good option.'

'What do you think?'

'Well, it's Scotland, but it's within striking distance of home. One thing sure,' he said, 'is that my father won't be able to come and visit me. He couldn't cope with the journey. So I'm safe from that anyway.'

'But what about him, Magnus?'

'Well he won't want to have me in the house.'

'Has he said as much?'

'Well, no, not really. In the letter from Charlotte she said that Father said my bed was there for me. But…'

'There you are,' said Lowrie. 'Couldn't you think about it?'

'Look Lowrie, if he's thinking at all about what happened, it'll be that it's all past, I'll have got over all that by now and so on. He'll be shoving it aside as some childish nonsense. I don't care, whatever he says, Charlotte and I had something going. I loved her, love her now, and I know she felt something for me. Oh, she never said, she's too loyal to Father for that, but if I could've persuaded her to go away with me she would've said it. So don't you see, I can't go to Birkenshaw and be there?'

Lowrie nodded slowly. 'Yes, I can see that.'

'It's obvious. What I need to do is, when I'm ready, go to Glamis if I can get a convalescence posting there, stay as long as I can building up my strength and go in front of a Canadian Army Board when I'm able and see where they want to post me.'

'It'll be a good while before you reach that stage I'm thinking.'

'Well,' Magnus shrugged then winced. 'Ouch, I see what you mean. No seriously, between you and me you're right. From a medical point of view I'm going to take a long time. I don't think they'll let me back to the Front.'

'How do you feel about that?'

'Do you really want to know?' Magnus said. 'I – I don't want to go back, but, well,' he paused, then said, 'but I feel very guilty at the thought of not going back when doctors are so badly needed. And even the knowledge that it's not my choice or fault that I probably won't go back doesn't help. I still feel awful about knowing what's going on there, that I feel I should be there and I'm not able to.'

Chapter 23

Birkenshaw
20 January 1917

Dear Magnus,

Here I am again. Thank you very much for your letter. It was very good to see your writing on the envelope and know it was really you who had written it. You sound as though you are making good progress.

You'll be glad to hear your father is also making progress. He's still upstairs but doing exercises with his legs and arms, especially the right side which is quite badly affected. However, he's getting on and his speech is returning most of the time except when he gets tired.

It was wonderful to have Christina for a week. Then who should walk in but Lowrie. It was very good to see him again. He looked tired but very smart in his uniform and moustache, which I suppose many of the men have now. He had a couple of walks with Christina and took her to the boat when she left – such a help. Christina says she'll write to you when she has a moment. I think they're run off their feet in that hospital with all the casualties.

Angus and Hannah are coping. Hannah has gone back to school now that your father is a bit better. It's hard on her but being at school and with her friends seems to help take her mind off things. She was very good when she was at home, really worked at her school subjects and I hope was able to keep up with her class work. Angus is being Angus – always hungry and wanting out to play. He was very upset about you but is delighted that you've been 'found' and on the day we heard, told everyone at school. Certainly knowing that you are all right has done wonders for family morale.

Your Father joins me in saying take care of yourself and get well soon. Is there any news of where you might be discharged to?

Yours affly.,
Charlotte.

Royal Infirmary of Edinburgh
25 January 1917

My Dear Brother Magnus,

How are you? I just thought I would drop you a line just now before I go on duty and I can catch the mail as it goes out. We've all been thinking so much about you and hope that you are just about to get up and dance a Quadrille with the nurses. And if they don't know how to dance a Quadrille then you'll have to show them! I know that Lowrie has been to see you as he wrote and told me and when he gets to see you again you could teach them between you. They can't do Quadrilles in Edinburgh but can do other dances when there's time. We sometimes do Scottish Country dancing in the evening if we're not too exhausted.

149

We're very busy. The trainloads of wounded men from the Front just keep coming – I know that you know all about it so I won't go on but it is heart-rending to see them.

I was very glad to get the chance to go to see Mother and Father. Father is improving – no doubt about that. I wish he could have some speech therapy – he gets very annoyed with himself when he can't get the words out when he knows what he wants to say. He is practising writing so sometimes tries to write it down. One day you'll get a letter from him.

Mother is great. Nothing too much trouble. And Edie and Meg. They are so strong.

Must fly and get my cap on straight. Take care dear brother – I told Hannah and Angus that I would send you love from them too when I write so

Love always, from the three of us.

Christina.

Royaumont

2 February 1917

Dear All at Birkenshaw,

Thank you for your last letter Charlotte. It was good to hear from you and hear how you are all getting on.

Yes, Lowrie has been here. He borrowed a horse when he was behind the lines as he had heard by chance that I was here and rode over. It was very good to see him. He's back at the Front now I suppose. He said he would write but I know that it's difficult.

I'm making good progress. I'm up and walking about now. The next thing is, where next for convalescence? James MacLeod told me that Glamis castle was handed over a while ago for convalescent soldiers so I have applied for a convalescence posting there. I await the response. Of course it'll be up to the doctors but it seems like a good idea. In the meantime I'm getting on here. Thank you for all letters and please thank Edie and Meg for the baking. We enjoyed the fruit cake.

I send love to you all.

Yours affly.,

Magnus.

Royaumont

3 February 1917

Dear Christina,

Thank you so very much for writing. You've no idea how much your letters mean to me. You sound very busy but believe me you're doing a very good, necessary job. I thought seeing you're 'in the trade' as it were, you'd like to hear a little about this place where I've ended up.

I've been here for so many weeks now and watch those wonderful nurses in action doing everything possible for the men in their care and sometimes very reluctant to go off duty as they see the amount of work still to be done especially when the ambulances are bringing men in from the CCSs. Sometimes it's so cold the ambulance drivers wear fur coats. The ambulances are very draughty – the men must be freezing. There don't seem to be many porters here – I suppose they are required at the Front where they're called 'orderlies'. Anyway the nurses do the carrying in of the wounded on stretchers. Four to each stretcher, one at each corner. They're washed, fed if possible and their general condition assessed and wounds examined. If the men need to be X-rayed they've to stretcher them out again to the X-ray car, get them in, the X-rays are done and then the patient is stretchered back to bed again. The staff work on and on.

You'd be amazed to see this place being used as a hospital. It's an old Abbey, with cloisters and church style high ceilings – not the warmest in winter – a lovely entrance hall with a fire that only goes on at 2pm because of the shortage of firewood. The men are mostly in long wards. I was put in a side room for quiet when I was here first. I'm still officially there but I get out and speak to the men now that I'm better on my feet. I've also been outside but it's still very cold and icy with some snow and I must be careful – I don't want to fall now. My shrapnel wounds are improving too. They used what they call German Creosote in the wounds as an antiseptic or 'flesh preserver' after they remove the shrapnel. It's horrible when they are putting it on or rather, in, the wounds. It stings like anything, but I think it works. I have quite a few bandages off now. I still have some shrapnel left in my side that they couldn't get at. I'll just have to live with it. They say the pain will ease in time. One good thing, my head wound is a lot better and my balance is improving.

My writing is still very poor – never good I know but I apologise for this hen's scratching. I think my hand gets tired. I wrote to Charlotte and Father yesterday but waited for today to write you. I told them that I'd applied to go to Glamis Castle to convalesce. That was yesterday – today I've heard that's going through. I don't have a date but at least I know where I'm going next.

I think I'll stop now – the writing's getting worse. It was good to see Lowrie recently. We had a long talk – I felt much better having seen him.

Take care, my wee sister. Write soon when you can.

With love from Magnus.

PS It will be a wee while before I'm ready for Quadrilles and Scottish Country dancing – but it's a nice thought and I can hear the tunes in my head. Love, M.

Royal Infirmary of Edinburgh
1 February 1917

Dear Lowrie,

Thank you so much for writing. I was very pleased to get your letter. Home Sister handed it over, looking over the top of her spectacles at me and said very severely, 'and one for you Staff Nurse Sinclair. From the Front, I see'. Then I noticed the twinkle in her eye and realised she was really quite sympathetic underneath.

I'm very pleased to hear you've been able to find Magnus and that he's going to be all right. What a great piece of detective work on your part. I had a good long letter from him telling me what Royaumont is like – a busy place. He also says he's being posted to Glamis to convalesce. I know you thought that this would happen – now it's definite. He just needs to have a date and I suppose a lot depends on how he is.

We also are very busy with soldiers coming back from France. The trains from the south keep coming. They say the ones who come back are the lucky ones but sometimes I wonder – some of them are very badly wounded. How can some of them ever recover? And what happens to them once they are discharged? However, we try and keep their morale up while they're here – we also help them by reading and writing letters for them if they can't see, or get too tired to write, sometimes reading, sometimes sitting with them if we can spare the time, and talking with them.

I'm glad to say that Father is improving in health. He now sits in his chair, still upstairs, most of the day. He practises walking on the landing but will need to be helped on the stairs. Mother wants him to start sleeping downstairs again and then he would be able to move outside more freely when he gets to that stage. We'll see.

I still think about meeting you again in Shetland. It was lovely to be home but you really brightened up my week. Thank you also for taking me to the *St Clair*. It made going away a much happier experience.

Take care Lowrie. Thinking of you.

Yours affly,

Christina.

In my dugout
Somewhere in the trenches
7 February 1917

Dear Magnus,

Sorry I have not been able to write sooner. It's been all go since I saw you at Royaumont. I'd a reasonable if chilly ride back on Dobbin to our camp behind the lines, handed him over, went and reported to the Colonel and thanked him for the loan of his horse. He asked very much after you, whether or not I had found you, how you are and so on. Nice man. I feel he cares about his officers and men and what's going on in their lives.

A few days later we were back to the trenches. Perhaps I should not speak of it but I know that you understand what is going on. It has been Bedlam. Going over the top does not get any easier. There are so many men killed or badly wounded. It's really bad. We can do nothing for the dead except give them a decent burial if we can. But it's the wounded – you know – we, the non-medical folk want to do so much and feel so useless and incapable in the face of such terrible wounds. All we can do is immediate first aid and get them to the nearest RAP. I know you feel bad about not being able to return to the Front. Please accept that you have done your bit and that a hopefully calmer posting awaits you eventually.

I had a letter from Christina. She seems very busy. She said your posting to Glamis has been confirmed. That's very good. Now all you've to do is get yourself to that stage when you can be discharged from Royaumont. Keep going.

If you want to write just send it to the central mailing point and it'll get to me. It would be good to hear how you are getting on. We mustn't lose touch again.

Take care.

Yours aye,

Lowrie.

Lowrie's Dugout
7 February 1917

Dear Christina,

Thank you very much for your letter. A courier brought it to me along with the dispatches in the middle of a very noisy night. The barrage about half a mile to our right went on for hours. I'm not allowed to say any more but we will all be very glad to see the back of this War. So your letter was doubly welcome – it brightened up a dreary trench-bound night and when I did get some sleep I put it in my jacket pocket so I could feel it now and then.

I still think about our happy walks on the cliff-top – only too short. I'm looking forward to the day when I can get back to you in Edinburgh and we can pick up the threads of our lives and move forward together. What do you think? I've never felt anything like this about anyone before.

Write soon.

With my love to you dear Christina,

Lowrie

Christina to Charlotte re Lowrie: 13 February 1917

... I have just received a letter from Lowrie in his Captain's Dugout. I really feel sorry and sad about what is going on. Lowrie said it was a very noisy night but I don't think our newspapers and wireless reports are telling us truthfully what is going on in France and Belgium. I know that if Lowrie said any more it would be censored anyway but as well as the official reports, I get the feeling that men don't want to talk about all the horrors and also that the Government does not want us to know the truth.

One thing that Lowrie did indicate and I want to tell you is I think he's getting very serious about 'us'. It's not been very long since we met again after all these years but Mother, I think I'm serious about 'us' as well. I am so looking forward to seeing him again. I just hope and pray that he lives through it.

Please don't tell Father yet what I have written to you. He gets so worried. I'm glad to get the chance to write to you alone....

Charlotte to Christina   17 February 1917

My dear Christina,

Thank you so much for your letter. This also is just from me to you. Rest assured that I won't tell your father you've written to me personally, or that I'm writing to you. I don't like keeping things from him and in a normal everyday situation, I wouldn't do this. However these are strange times and I feel it's better to keep what you say to me private between you and me for the moment. Lowrie has always been a friend of this family and just happens to be one of my favourite people. Just take it slowly. I remember long ago asking Granny, how do you know if you're in love? She said that you know when it happens. If it has happened to you two then you will know.

Having been through the worry about Magnus, I feel that I can empathise with you regarding your worries about Lowrie's safety...

…It was very good to get your letter. The postie practically waves it aloft when he appears – he's so pleased that you are all right. Then he hangs around for any news. We're getting on; making progress. Father's coming round to the idea of moving downstairs. He was quite reluctant at first. I think he saw it as a retrograde step – you remember when he had the last stroke – he was there for a while and I think he felt that to be in bed downstairs was seen as a very 'aald mannie' thing to be doing and he couldn't get back upstairs fast enough. However, this time the pull of getting outside is getting to him and he realises that to be up-and-down the stairs all the time wouldn't be feasible. I fancy one trip downstairs with all hands on deck will be his limit (and ours too). Don't get all worried about our getting him down – we have lots of willing strong helpers and once he's down he'll get more practice walking on the level and then, get outside. What a blessing we had the new water-closet put in downstairs a few years ago.

I saw Lowrie's mother the other day. She was asking very much after you so I was telling her that you're heading for Glamis, hopefully quite soon…

Alexander to Magnus   17 February 1917

…As you see I am more able to write now that my right hand is improving. We have been in the 'Wars' my boy, you, literally, I'm afraid. I hope that you, too, are progressing. I am very pleased that you are coming as far north as Glamis. I pray God that it will be soon and that you have a safe journey. As time passes then we hope to see you here where you belong…

Hannah to Magnus   17 February 1917

My dear brave big brother,
                    I am so happy that you are getting better. I give everyone at school progress reports. My friends are all very interested.

It's good to be back at school. Mother was wonderful when Father had the stroke and you were missing. She was so worried about everything but she arranged for me to stay at home and do school work at home so I could be with them. I'd've been very sad being away all week when you were lost and Father was so ill. Angus wanted to stay at home from school too but he was fine eventually. I spread all my things out on the table so that he could see that I was working and not playing. Edie sometimes walks him, or rather, races him to school.

Mother says that you are in a hospital in a big church. That sounds amazing. I hope that you're not cheeky to the nurses. I wish I could come and see you but seeing I can't, I send you a great deal of love.

From your wee (but growing) sister,
Hannah.

Dear Brother Magnus,

How are you? Mother says that you are making progress. I forgot to ask her what progress is so would you tell me please when you write. Why arc you making it? Anyway I hope that you are getting much better. Do you have any shrapnel? The boys at school were asking. We would like to see some shrapnel as we have never seen it and no-one seems to know what it is like. School is all right, I suppose. I am in the senior class at Jarlshavn primary School. I expect that you will know about it as you went there too but it was so long ago since you were there that you've probably forgotten. I think that I'm going to the Anderson Educational Institute after the summer holidays. Hannah likes it there. She comes home on a Friday teatime.

The best thing about school here is the soup. We pay for this. It used to be a penny but it is now two pennies. Mrs Isbister across the road from the school makes it. She's married to the other Mrs Isbister's son. The biggest boys get to carry it across. Mrs Manson our teacher said it had to be this way as they would be the strongest. But the other day two boys couped the soup a bit and she said what a waist and perhaps bigger didn't mean more careful so maybe the slightly smaller boys like me will get a turn at carrying the soup. I would like to do that. I would be very careful and I know that Mrs Isbister gives a sweetie to the boys when they go to get it. I asked Mrs Manson why it is two pennies now and she said that the price of food has gone up because there's a War on. Everyone says that – the minute you say anything that a grown-up does not like or can't answer properly, they say don't you know there's a War on?

This is a very long letter for me to write. I will stop now. Good bye.

Love from Angus.

Magnus to all at Birkenshaw

24 February 1917

…I am getting on fine. I'm on my feet and getting dressed. James MacLeod came in the other day with some uniform obtained from a Quartermaster. The staff at the hospital can write out a requisition form and the QM will supply it if he can. James has done this a few times for men who have been patients but are ready to move on and are reasonably mobile. Sometimes they have uniform or parts of their uniform but sometimes it's beyond any other use and has to be incinerated. Some of the men are issued with what they call 'hospital blues'. They are truly awful and do nothing for the morale. There are also armbands denoting 'wounded' to wear outside. Not sure what I feel about this. I'm supposed to be mobile but I feel very slow sometimes. However, now that I'm going to Glamis soon I would rather be up and dressed than be stretchered about.

Talking about James, he won't be around here much more. He's been ordered back to the trenches alternating with areas behind the lines. He's been a very good support to me here.

I've been in Royaumont so long now that I think I'm going to miss it in a funny sort of way. 'When the hurly-burly's done', you know, when there has been a lot of stramash with casualties coming in and folk hurrying about, and then eventually things are quieter, the place can take on quite an atmosphere – an aura almost – voices seem to become quieter and the very ill and stressed men seem to quieten and calm down. It's strange. I've noticed it a few times.

Anyway, I'll be away soon and who knows, my next letter to you might be from Glamis.

Take care all of you.

Yours affly.,
Magnus.

Chapter 24

Birkenshaw

1 MARCH 1917

It was the weekend. Hannah was home. Life sat back a little. Angus could play all day as long as he was not too rowdy within earshot of his father. 'That,' all the womenfolk of the house said, 'would not do.' So, Angus was mouse-like anywhere near his father but out of earshot, he ran about with his friends, delighted with the space they had for their games. They respected the sheep in the adjoining field and took care not to disturb them but when the sheep were moved the boys turned their attention to the rabbits. No one ever objected to their chasing the rabbits as long as they always closed the heavily rabbit-proofed gate into the Birkenshaw field and its precious young trees.

Sometimes they saw a black rabbit. Angus was desperate to lay hands on the black rabbit. He would be so good to it. It would be his pet and he would train it to do tricks. And, Edie and Meg would surely give him some leftovers for it. Charlotte had told him that on 1 March it was an old custom when you woke up to say, 'Rabbits, rabbits, rabbits.' Magnus had said this mantra diligently before breakfast that fine Saturday morning. To add to this, he, for once was alone. No other boys to chase and shout. He would be subtle, quiet and methodical. He would say 'Rabbits, rabbits, rabbits,' in his head. It was all part of a plan.

Putting the plan into practice by catching the black rabbit proved to be difficult. Time and again Angus crept up on the black rabbit, which, apparently unconscious of the looming danger, ate continually at the still-short grass. Every time he thought he was getting there, the black rabbit nipped down the nearest rabbit-hole. He waited five minutes and the rabbit popped up again and continued feeding. Angus felt it was laughing at him.

At length he became fed up trying and wandered back to the house. He saw two of his father's friends walking up to the door and ringing the bell before opening and calling. Edie was there to usher them in.

''Morning, gentlemen. How are you both today?'.

'Fighting fit, Edie.' The taller of the two, Mansie Halcrow, ex-army, flexed his muscles. Rarin to go.'

'How is Alexander?' The smaller, quieter man, Bertie Gear. wiped his feet carefully on the door-mat.

'He's coming along all right,' said Edie. 'He's ready for this move, I think. It's taken Mrs Sinclair and the Doctor a bit of persuading but he knows that to get outside, he needs to be downstairs and he can't get up and down easily.' She gave a half-laugh. 'That's why you're here.'

'Right.' Mansie made for the stairs.

'Wait a minute,' Edie stopped him. 'I'll go up first and tell him you're here.'

Angus appeared, out of breath. 'Hello, Mr Halcrow, Mr Gear. Are you going to visit my father.'

'Well, you could say that,' said Bertie. 'It'll be a working visit though.'

'What do you mean?'

'Well, we're going to get – I mean, help him downstairs today.'

'Wow.' Angus was impressed. 'I'm glad I came back in time. Can I help?'

Edie sighed. 'I hoped that we'd get this done while you were out in the fields. Why don't you go and get a piece from Meg while we get on with this.'

'But, I can help …'

'What were you doing in the fields?' asked Bertie.

Instantly diverted, Angus said, 'I was trying to catch a black rabbit.'

'Did you get it?'

'No, It kept going down a hole.'

'I remember chasing a black rabbit when I was a boy – never did get it. It's probably an ancestor of your one. Slick as they come, these black rabbits. But, we've got work to do. Come down to my house one day Angus and I'll show you our rabbits. If they have more babies before then you might even get one.'

Angus's eyes shone. 'D'you mean that Mr Gear?'

'Ay, nae bother. That is,' added Bertie, 'if you're allowed. You'll need to ask.' Angus nodded.

'Now,' said Edie. 'Go and get a piece – your father will be glad to see you when he's down in the other bedroom.'

Upstairs, Alexander stood unsteadily beside his chair. Charlotte hovered.

'I don't know if I want to do this,' he muttered.

'Alexander, we've been through this before. You're stuck in a rut up here. You need to get downstairs – I can hear them coming. Come on now. You'll be fine.' Edie's voice sounded on the stairs.

'This way gentlemen, Oh, of course you've been up before. Hello,' to the pair in the bedroom. Can we come in?'

'Yes, come on in.' Charlotte opened the door. 'Thanks for coming.' The men walked in, shook hands with Alexander.

''Morning, Alexander.'

'Good morning. Thanks for coming – but I'm really not sure …'

'Oh come on man,' said Mansie, I've been practising for this.' Alexander gave a half smile.

'You'll maybe get more than you bargained for.'

'Let's get on with it.'

Alexander had been walking in the bedroom and on the landing for over a month. He fended off the eager arms until they reached the top of the stairs where Edie had a small chair ready. He sat down carefully and looked doubtfully at the stairs. His two helpers gave him no time to think.

'All right, Alexander. Which is the best side?'

'Left.'

'Well,' said Mansie. 'It can do some work. We'll hold you by the oxters in a double grip, I'll take the right side, and help you manoeuvre your right leg, and you can help by stepping your left leg downwards when I shout, "left". Bertie will be at your left side supporting and making sure that you do it. Is that clear?'

'Well, I'll give it a try.'

'Good. Now ladies, keep out of the way please. This is men's work. Mrs Sinclair, could you lead the advance party please and show us the route once we get down. Please keep well away in case we should trip. Only joking,' he added as there was a united gasp of concern from Charlotte and Edie. Alexander closed his eyes in resignation. 'Of course we're not going to trip.'

They moved off, step by step. Mansie took up his position at Alexander's right side and manoeuvred himself so that Alexander's right arm was across his shoulders and he (Mansie) supported from underneath the arm. At the same time he lifted up the dragging right leg. Bertie, on the left, supported Alexander under the left oxter and helped him move his left leg step by step. Charlotte moved off first, a few steps in front of the group. She walked backwards, watching their progress with apprehensive eyes. Edie, brought up the rear, arms laden. Hannah came quietly out of her room where she had been doing her homework, to watch the action. They reached the half-landing. 'Need a breather?'

'No, no, let's get on with it now we've got this length.' Alexander shuffled to the top of the next flight of stairs.

'Right then. We're on the last lap. As you were everyone.'

Then, they were down. Hannah coming behind with the chair, rushed to put it under him.

'Sit down, Father. Have a rest.'

'Thanks.' He sat and puffed slightly. 'I wouldn't want to do that every day.' He looked about him. 'Nice flowers. From the garden?'

'Yes,' Charlotte said. 'They've done very well. You'll get out for a look if the rain holds off. Now, what about walking to your room?'

Meg, preparing lunch in the kitchen saw the postman coming. She went out to meet him.

''Morning Meg.'

''Morning. What do you have for us today?'

'Just the one. A military one though.' He scrutinised it carefully, squinting at it in the sun. 'Looks like Magnus's writing.' He handed it over. 'How are they all.'

'Not too bad, thank you. Mr Sinclair's just come downstairs for the first time since his illness so he'll get outside now. That's a great thing for him.'

'That's great. Better go. Tell him I was asking after him.'

'Bye Jimmy. Thanks.' Meg waved the letter and headed for Alexander's new room. Mansie and Bertie were just taking their leave.

'Right, Alexander, are you sure there's nothing else we can do for you at the moment.' Bertie pulled his side-table another inch nearer to him.

'Yes, yes, I'm fine thanks , and thank you both for all your help.'

'Right,' said Mansie. 'We'll be off and leave you in peace. If there's anything we can do, just give us a shout.'

'Thank you very much,' said Charlotte walking them to the door. 'You've been so kind and patient. Come back any time to see him. He enjoys your visits. They cheer him up.'

'We'll do that. We'll be marching him round the garden in no time.'

'Mother.' Hannah came through as she was closing the door. 'Here's a letter, from Magnus.'

'Oh, good. Has your Father seen it?'

'No, not yet. Here you are.' Hannah hovered.

'Come on then, let's get the envelope knife and take it in to him.'

'Letter from Magnus.' He looked up from his *Shetland Times*.

'Any news?'

'Yes, it's definite that he's going to Glamis.' She read rapidly. 'That seems to be going ahead quite soon. And – oh,' she checked herself. 'He mentions James MacLeod. You remember Alexander, the minister who was here, the Padre who identified Magnus when he was so ill. They're sending him back to the Front.' She looked up. 'That's not so good. I hope he'll be all right. Here,' she offered Alexander the letter. Then a half-hearted attempt at a joke. 'Read it for yourself – his writing's improving.'

'Thanks, now, where are my spectacles?'

'On top of your head, Father.' Angus giggled.

'What, where? Oh, of course.' He peered at the letter.

'I'll just see how lunch is getting on.' Once out of the room Charlotte stopped and gazed out of the window for a moment.

'James, she whispered. 'Take care.'

160

Chapter 25

3 APRIL 1917

It was time for Magnus to leave. To leave Royaumont and embark on the long journey to Glamis.

He lay in his bed that morning, eyes closed, acknowledging, accepting, fearing. After nearly five months in Royaumont, with just an occasional foray beyond the hospital grounds, Magnus was apprehensive of this next step. He knew he had to take it. He wanted to take it but going to Glamis, to Scotland, meant decisions, thinking about what he had to do next, encountering people he knew, relatives possibly, his Father? Charlotte. A tear squeezed out from within the closed lids.

A knock at the door.

''Morning, Magnus.' Barbara, one of the VADs entered. 'Are you going to waken up?'

'I'm awake,' Magnus opened his eyes. 'I'm hearing you.'

She looked at him. She saw the uncertainty in his eyes.

'What can I do for you Magnus. This is a kind of mixed up day for you. A double edged sword, I'm thinking.'

'How did you know? I should be longing to get out of hospital.'

'Magnus,' she sat down beside him. 'Here you are leaving the security of this place where I think, you've felt safe. Now you've to go into the unknown. It raises all sorts of questions for you. Am I right?' He nodded.

'Yes. I'm just wondering what's in front. I can't get excited. It's more like dreading. It's funny. You'd think I'd be happy to be leaving a hospital.'

'You're not alone with these feelings you know.'

'I suppose not.'

'What about making a start?'

He was at his porridge when Sister Alison Forbes came in accompanied by James.

'Here he is,' she said. 'Eating as usual.'

'Don't get up Magnus.' James sat down beside him. 'Yes please,' he nodded at the large teapot the VAD waved at him. 'I'd like some tea, please. How's the porridge today?'

'Very good. But what,' Magnus said, 'are you doing here? I thought you were off?'

'Yes, I am, but I wanted to come in here first and wish you all the best. It's a few days since I've seen you. How are you?'

'Oh, well, you know,' Magnus hesitated. He looked down, then met James's eyes. 'It's a bit, well, nerve-wracking you know. But,' he stopped. 'What am I saying? Here am I being jumpy when you're heading for the Front line. How do you feel about that?'

'Oh well,' James said, 'I'll just have to keep my head down now won't I?'

161

'Well, make sure you wear your helmet, at least.'

'Ay, ay.'

'You do have one?'

'Yes, of course,' James protested. 'It's with my kit. Anyway I didn't come to check on my helmet. I just came to wish you fair winds and all that.' He finished his tea, held out his hand.

'James.' Magnus swallowed. He stood, took the proffered hand. 'Thanks for coming,' he said. 'Thanks for everything. Take care.'

'I shall.' James looked at him soberly. 'See you soon, I hope. God bless you.' He saluted smartly, turned on his heel and walked quickly to the door, hoping that Magnus had not noticed the tears that lay unshed.

There were three of them leaving Royaumont that day. Magnus, a very young soldier on a stretcher called Robert Fletcher who was accompanied by Pete Long, one of the Royaumont orderlies, and Captain Iain Dawkins, who was heading for Craiglockhart Hospital in Edinburgh. He sat silently, his hands clenching and unclenching.

Magnus looked at him. He had heard about Iain Dawkins, spoken to him a few times on his perambulations around the ward. The whisper, 'shell-shock' came and went, but he did not need to hear the words to recognise it himself. How many officers and men had he treated with the terrible affliction before being wounded himself? For how many had he recommended evacuation back to England or Scotland or wherever they came from and to be looked after? He never recommended that they return to the Front either. To have shell-shock was as much a 'Blighty one' as any severe physical wound. The difference was that here there was no blood, no amputation, no shrapnel wounding. Nothing to see. Yet the damage to their mental processes was as damaging to their ability to live a whole healthy life as many physically crippling wounds. Magnus sighed. Would that others could see it.

He knew that there were some hard attitudes towards those with shell-shock. Where soldiers, after convalescence had to undergo vigorous examination and questioning regarding their fitness to return to the Front. With shell-shock they couldn't assess healing in the same way as with a physical wound. Many men still suffering were sent back to the Front. They suffered agonies. Many were killed in the next ghastly response to the whistle to go forward, the climb up the trench and into the mêlée of battle. Some came back, wounded physically this time. Some cooried in a corner of a dugout until it was time to go out again. Some went out but ran the other way to be shot in the back for cowardice. Some who ran the other way were picked up and faced a firing squad made up of men from their own side. Some faced court-martial. The problem lay, not just with the person with shell-shock, but also with some members of the Board. If they did not believe in the existence of shell-shock as a real illness then they were unlikely to support a shell-shocked soldier's desire for discharge on the grounds of illness.

At the same time in those 'Great War' days much of the public did not believe in it either and a man at home with shell-shock was likely to be an object of derision and even hatred, seen as a coward. Then, rather than risk being offered a white feather from some energetic woman or hear other verbal indignities, the suffering man would sometimes try to pass himself off as fit for return to the Front. Some committed suicide.

Magnus looked across at Iain Dawkins. He sat, in khaki, partly supplied by the Quartermaster, his own cap and cap-badge, eyes closed. Only the clenched hands betrayed his wakefulness, his tension.

Magnus had seen him in different aspects of his illness over the weeks since his admission to Royaumont. The nightmares, fear of sleeping, pacing the floor till all hours of the morning, rolling into a ball and physically turning away from human touch, shouting, crying, lack of eye-contact, flashbacks, waking visions of the horrors of war, corpses, trenches, rats, severed limbs. Magnus recognised them all, but he also recognised that with shell-shock or neurasthenia the patient's brain for whatever reason couldn't cope. It was only now that the Royaumont staff considered that Iain Dawkins was able to travel. It was better that he should travel in a small group, at least to begin with. The orderly with Robert Fletcher on the stretcher was also officially with him.

Dr Edith Strachan, the Royaumont Superintendent, had also observed Magnus talking with Iain and felt that here was some sort of rapport which could be tapped into. She went to see Magnus a few days previously.

'Hello,' Magnus was writing his diary. 'Have a seat. Have you had a busy day?'

'Yes.' She sat with a sigh of relief. 'Another convoy in today. Others moved on, heading for home. I hope their ship's able to leave Le Havre when they get there. Ambulances in and out all day. Theatre's been going like a fair and likely to go on for a while yet.'

'I wish I could help.'

'I know you do. There is one thing though.'

'Yes? What can I do?'

'Well, you know that young Lieutenamt, Iain Dawkins?'

'You mean the chap with – shell-shock?' Magnus hesitated over the word. He was not officially supposed to know the diagnoses of his fellow patients.

'Right, Magnus, you said it.' Edith Strachan leaned forward. 'Magnus, he's leaving here for Craiglockhart on the same transport as you. He's very aware of his problem although he might not say it out loud. I've seen you speaking to him sometimes. He'll be in the official care of the orderly, the ambulance driver to Creil station is a QA sister and then you'll all be on the hospital train from Creil to Le Havre with medical and nursing staff. If you have to wait for the train at Creil there's a small canteen at the station – I think it's currently run by the French Red Cross but later this year our own SWH may be taking over. I think the *Regulateur de la Gare* is quite keen that we do this.'

'Anyway,' she continued, 'that's beside the point. You'll be able to get food and a hot drink there. Then there's the train journey – that'll take, goodness knows how long. well, it's only about 169 kilometres from Creil to le Havre and you'd think it wouldn't take that long but you never know with these conditions. Once you're on the boat there will be other staff.'

'But,' she went on. 'The poor boy is very alone. Do you think you could be a bit of company for him? Keep an eye on him for us and alert the Sister-in-Charge if you notice anything amiss? Could you? Please?'

Magnus looked at her. Can I do this, he wondered? Am I able? I'm not that far away from shell-shock myself. But I'm more able than this poor lad. He took a deep breath. He looked at Edith Strachan, so worried.

'Of course I will,' he said. 'If you're sure that I can cope.'

'I'm sure,' she answered. 'You'll do. And, if anyone understands, has an inkling of what he is going through, you have.'

Magnus looked again at the young Lieutenant sitting huddled in his too-big greatcoat.

'Ready?' he said. 'We're about to leave. Here's the driver.'

Sister Mary Gillespie, driving that day came out briskly.

'Right, all aboard?' Magnus looked out. Edith Strachan stood with Sister Alison Forbes arms raised in farewell. Magnus lifted a hand in salute to them standing at Royaumont's front door, representatives of the work that went on day and night despite the War.

The ambulance in its white paint with red crosses on sides and roof moved off slowly on the pot-holed road. The injured boy on the stretcher groaned. The orderly leaned over him.

'All right, son. It'll be better when we get you on to the train. At least they won't have potholes on the rails.' The boy didn't answer. It was very slow and bumpy. He continued to groan with every lurch. Iain Dawkins trembled visibly.

From relative security into the unknown, a new chapter had begun for them. Magnus looked out of the window. It seemed quiet – the few trees just beginning to show tentative signs of spring after the long hard winter. Green showing in fields as winter gave way to new growth and the frost eased its way out of the ground. Perhaps there would still be snow in Scotland, he thought. There often was in March. What else would he find there? What else would the future bring?

The ambulance came to a grinding, shuddering stop.

'Sorry everyone,' Mary Gillespie called. 'There's a massive pot-hole ahead. It can't have been there long. Must have happened in that bombing last night. The ambulance inched forward. Down over the edge of the hole. Firm-ish underneath, forwards. Then the back-end going down with a bump just as the front wheels started to climb out. She revved slightly. The engine whined. Slowly the ambulance crept forward, up and out. The back wheels had just cleared the pothole edge when Magnus heard it.

'Stop,' he called. 'Please stop. I heard something.'

Sister Gillespie braked. 'What is it? Is everything all right?'

'I heard a voice, outside, calling. I could hardly hear for the noise of the engine. Listen.' The voice called again.

'Aidez-moi. Je suis ici.' They could hear quite clearly now.

'There is somebody,' the orderly said.

'I see him,' said Magnus. 'It's a man – this side. Lying at the side of the road. He needs help.' He looked at the orderly as the driver pulled on the hand-brake and opened her door.

'I'll go down. Sister Gillespie may need help.'

'But you can't. You're a patient.'

'I'm also a doctor. You stay with young Robert. He's your priority.' He turned to Iain. 'Are you all right?' He nodded.

Magnus moved to the back of the ambulance, opened the door and clambered down. Sister Gillespie approached from the front of the ambulance with a First Aid box.

'You shouldn't be here.'

'Never mind that now. Let's see what we've got here.'

The man lay on the verge, very still and pale. His eyes were open, dark and appealing. *'Merci, mille fois…'*

'That's all right.' Sister Gillespie bent over him. 'Let's see how you are.'

Magnus bent down beside her. His eyes, his hands, his whole self, so long kept from medical examinations, moved immediately into the caring professional that he was. He looked at the man who gazed back.

'We need to take him to Creil with us. We can't leave him here. You're the driver. Agreed?'

'Yes.' Sister Gillespie looked critically at the man. 'We'll need to make room.'

'He's a stretcher case. It's going to be tight. He's got a nasty head injury and I'm not happy about his legs and pelvis to say nothing of internal injuries.'

'There's a stretcher with poles in the back. I'll get them.'

'Just a minute, before you go, is there any morphine in your kit?'

'Yes.' She handed the box over.

'Thanks.' Magnus started to search the contents. 'I'll give him some pain relief now to try and help him when we have to lift him.' She nodded and hurried round to the back. Magnus heard her speaking to the orderly.

'You stay here please. We'll bring the patient round on the stretcher but can you create a bit of space please. Mr Dawkins, Iain, are you all right?'

'Yes, yes.' He looked anxious but in careful control of himself.

'Do you think you could sit in the front with me? That would give a bit more space in the back for the stretcher.'

'Yes, I'll do that.' He got to his feet.

'Just stay here until we come back. When you see us with the stretcher, come carefully down the back step and go round to the passenger side, please.'

She returned with the stretcher and poles to Magnus and his patient. Magnus was just putting away the syringe.

'Should help a bit,' he said, 'but, he's badly injured.'

However careful they were getting the injured man on to the stretcher he was still in great pain. Now semi-conscious, he groaned as they moved him, rolling him as gently as they could on to the base canvas of the stretcher. As they pushed the poles up the sides of the stretcher canvas Mary Gillespie looked at Magnus.

'How are you?'

'I'm all right, thanks. Not quite what we expected but I'm glad we found him.'

'Can you cope in the back?' Magnus nodded. 'I'll drive very carefully. At least we're past that awful hole. It must have been the same blast that injured our poor French friend here. Right,' she added. 'Let's go.'

165

Together they grasped the pole ends and lifted their patient round to the open back doors and with Pete helping from inside, they lifted the injured man on board. Magnus got in after him.

'Come on Iain,' Sister said. 'I just need to pick up this First Aid kit. Here Magnus,' she called. 'You have this – you might need it.'

'Thanks.'

She slammed the doors, saw Iain into the passenger seat then got in herself.

'How are you feeling?'

'All right. I wish I could help though. It keeps my mind off – things.'

'Here's the map. Could you keep an eye on it for me please, and also on the road? Keep a watch out for any more holes in the road and anything else that shouldn't be there. Two heads in front are better than one.'

'All right in the back?' she called.

'Yes Sister,' Pete returned. She let in the clutch and the ambulance rolled forward again dodging the potholes, pushing along at walking speed. After what seemed a long way and a long time later they reached the outskirts of Creil and stopped at the side of the road to look at the map.

'Here we are I think,' Iain pointed. 'There's the station. It's not that far, unless, that is, the bombing has closed the roads.'

'Which is quite possible.'

'How are we getting on?' Pete the orderly called. 'My patient's very tired.'

'We're just aiming for the station and there's a canteen here at Creil although I heard they're still operating out of a van. But there will be something and hopefully we can also get help for our new patient. How is he Magnus?'

'Much the same. His pulse is quite fast, he's very pale but I don't think he's any worse than he was. I'd just like to get him some help before the morphine wears off completely.'

'Right, we'll move on now and hope that there aren't too many hold-ups.'

It didn't take very long before they saw the signs: *'On ne pas passer. Cette une barrage'. 'Allez à droit'*.'

Mary swung the wheel to the right.

'Here goes, Are you following this on the map, Iain?'

'I'm doing my best,' he said, trying to hold the map steady. 'See if you can bend round to the left to aim in the general direction of the station.'

'It can be a reasonably straightforward drive too. Never mind. Keep going.'

There were another two diversions before they could see the station in front of them. All around were ruins, buildings in bits, some with side walls out and anyone who tried could look in and see other people's living spaces open to the world. A forlorn curtain flapped, a once-solid front door hung dejectedly on its hinges. A pall of dust lay over everything and came up in puffs as people walked. There were clouds on the roads where the few vehicles ground past in low gear as they negotiated the hazards of more potholes and fallen masonry and wood.

'Nearly there.' Magnus looked out. A few looked up as they passed. One or two raised a hand in salute to the red crosses on the ambulance.

166

'At last, twelve kilometres and three long hours after they left Royaumont the ambulance drew up a few yards from *La Gare de Creil*. Their way was blocked again.

'Here we are,' called Mary Gillespie.

'It's busy,' commented Magnus.

'I know, isn't it? Creil station is getting bigger, more important in the scheme of things. More troops going through, more trains, more people. And, the more noticeable it becomes, the more attention it attracts, the more vulnerable it'll be to bombing.' She cut the engine.

'I'll be as quick as I can. I'm going to get help to carry our stretcher cases in and then we'll work from there. Are you all happy with that? Magnus?'

'Yes.'

'Iain? Thanks for your map reading. Can you sit there please till I come back?'

'Yes,' he said, still holding the map.

'Pete, how are you coping?'

'All right I think. Robert –' he bent over the injured soldier. 'Can you hang on for a wee bit longer until we find out what's going on in the station?'

'Are we there?'

'Yes, we're at the station. Just need to get you organised.' He raised a hand to Mary. 'Right Sister, we're fine here for the moment.'

'See you all shortly.' She jumped down. They watched her disappear past the *barrage* into the station.

Magnus felt his patient's pulse yet again. Still too fast. His head moved. He opened his eyes. He whispered, *'J'ai soif.'*

He drank from Magnus's water-bottle and closed his eyes again. Magnus returned the bottle to his bag. I hope she won't be long. He needs help.

Mary wasn't long. She came out of the station accompanied by three orderlies. They went immediately to the back, swung wide the doors and clambered in.

'Is this the Frenchman? Poor soul, he looks a bit shocked.'

'Yes,' said Magnus. 'I'll come with you.'

'Right, Sir. We've another ambulance round here and we'll probably transfer him once our MO's had a look.'

The small group worked their way as gently as possible to the inside of the station. It was busy, with troops in transit waiting in groups, either for their next trains or instructions where to march next. Some wounded lay on stretchers lined up beside a wall. Others sat on the flagstones, backs to the wall, waiting. Perhaps, mused Magnus, perhaps for the same train as us.

The orderlies seemed to know where to go. They marched swiftly to a cordoned-off area with a large Red Cross flag beside it. Carefully they put their stretchered burden down on the flagstones.

'Here we are Sir,' one turned to Magnus. 'And here's our MO. Captain Drinkwater today.'

'Thank you very much.' Magnus shook hands with them. 'You've been a great help.'

'That's all right. All in the job. Hope he gets on all right.' They moved on swiftly.

'Good afternoon,' the receiving MO held out his hand. 'At least,' he said, 'I think it's afternoon, but I never seem to know. Time passes so quickly.'

Magnus shook his hand. 'Yes it does but I can assure you it is after noon. I'm Magnus Sinclair by the way. I've been attending to this gentleman since we picked him up.'

'What happened?'

'We were making our way here from Royaumont to catch the hospital train to Le Havre. We've taken a long time – three hours. The road's in an awful state. Just after a huge pothole we found him lying by the roadside. So, Sister who was driving and I got down for a looksee. He has a head injury, I'm pretty sure that there are problems to his legs and pelvis and possibly internal. Pulse pretty rapid, very pale. He was in a lot of pain. I gave him a quarter-grain of morphine prior to moving him. Ideally he should have been in more specialised transport but…'

'Were you in charge of the ambulance party, then? Where are you headed for?'

'No, to the first. Sister Mary Gillespie is in charge – she's also the driver. She's away now sorting out our other two patients with our orderly. We're supposed to be heading for Le Havre. I wonder, have we missed the hospital train?'

'Well, one went a while ago, but there'll be another one in today. But,' the MO said. 'Where do *you* come in all this? If you're not in charge what are you doing looking after this very ill man?'

'I'm,' Magnus hesitated. 'It's a bit difficult. I'm an MO really but wounded and on the way to Scotland for convalescence.'

'What? How are you? I thought you looked a bit pale. Did you have to take over the care of the Frenchman.'

'Yes. I'm pretty glad to get here I can tell you. I thought we were going to lose him at one point.'

'Do you know his name?'

'No. He says he's thirsty now and again and I've been giving him sips of water and keeping him as comfortable as possible. No obvious serious haemorrhage, a few outer light wounds except for the head injury but I do think the legs and pelvis will need a lot of attention as well and, of course, I'm worried about internal bleeding.'

'Of course,' the MO called to an orderly hurrying past. 'Jones, can you and one other take this French gentleman into the First Aid Station now please, and very gently, start attending to him.' He turned to Magnus. 'No ID I suppose?'

'No, none.'

'Pity, well never mind, we'll do what we can.'

Magnus bent over the man on the stretcher.

'Monsieur, pouvez-vous m'entendre?'

The old man opened his eyes.

'Oui. Je vous entend.'

'Maintenant il faut que je pars.'

The old man held out his hand. *'Monsieur, je vous dois ma vie. Merci pour tout. Sens vous, j'aurais été mort.'* He put up a trembling hand to brush away his tears. *'Merci. Donnez-moi votre main.'* Magnus held out his hand and a lifelong memory was sealed.

The orderlies came to carry him to the First Aid Station. *'Au revoir, mon ami. Bonne chance.'*

'Et à vous aussi.' Magnus raised his hand in salute as the old man was carried away.

'I wonder if he'll make it.'

'Well,' the MO said. 'I hope so. I wouldn't be surprised. These old country folk are hardy. Now,' he turned his attention to Magnus. 'How are you? That's been a big strain for you. How long have you been in hospital? Where were you?'

'I was in Royaumont. Admitted in October…'

'Oh, so you were in the …'

'The Somme, that's right. I got caught up in the shelling – head injuries, five weeks, they say, unconscious, but I can't remember.' He smiled at his feeble joke. 'Multiple wounds but thank God, I'm OK, for the moment.' He rocked on his feet slightly.

'Here,' the MO took him by the arm. 'Sit down. He lifted Magnus's wrist, took his pulse, looked critically at him. 'You need to rest now,' he said. 'That was too much for you all at once.'

Suddenly Mary Gillespie was with them.

'Magnus, is everything all right? Are you?' She looked at the MO. 'Hello,' she said. 'It's Captain Drinkwater isn't it? Where did you spring from?'

'Hello Mary, taken over the driving now? Wasn't nursing enough for you?'

'Well you know how it is, they allow us to take the wheel now and then. We just have to do what's necessary. We had quite a morning today, though.'

'So I'm gathering.'

'Which takes me back to Magnus. Are you all right?'

'Yes, yes,' Magnus began, when Mark Drinkwater cut in.

'No, he must rest now and be quiet for a while. Have you any other patients?'

'Yes, they're over here. One soldier, a stretcher case in the immediate care of an orderly, and one officer with shell shock, who has coped well with the journey but would be better of some quiet too.'

Later in the afternoon, after the cups of tea, the thick wonderful sandwiches, the smiles of the French Red Cross canteen workers, the hospital train for Le Havre came in. The orderly gave Robert Fletcher another sip of water, made sure that his water-bottle was full, checked his dressings for the last time. Made sure also that his name, rank, number and unit were all fixed to his uniform, ID discs on, and signalled to two VADs loading stretcher patients on to the train that his man was ready to go. Mary Gillespie held all the handover notes of her three patients. She moved forward with Magnus and Iain and handed them over officially as wounded personnel to the Sister-in-Charge of their coach. She gave a brief report on each, who they were, the nature of their wounds and state of health and their destination after Le Havre.

Iain got on the train, trembling a little but keeping himself tightly in check. There was a seating area for walking wounded. He sat down with relief.

Magnus stopped at the door of the train and turned and looked at Mary.

'You've been with us a long time,' she said. 'We've enjoyed having you, watching you come from the dark into the light, being with you. You did well today. Thank you for your help. The old man was right. He would have died without you. Now, go into your new chapter.'

'Thank you, Mary.' Magnus saluted. Then, feeling this was somehow appropriate, bent his head and kissed her on the cheek. He climbed into the hospital train. They waved.

With what seemed to be an enormous effort, the hospital train bound for Le Havre, clearly identifiable for what it was with its white livery and prominent red crosses on sides and roof, slowly pulled itself out of Creil station.

Chapter 26

Edinburgh

Christina had a day off. At least, it was time off after seven busy nights on duty and she was off duty now for the next two nights. Normally bed would beckon after a night on the receiving ward but today was different. Today, she was going to meet Lowrie.

She skipped up the steps of the Nurses' Home. Sister Ross, the Home Sister watched her from her office window, situated there so that she could see all who came in and out and when, how they looked, not just their tidiness or otherwise and, that was a very important aspect. Sister Ross was well known for stopping a nurse on the steps and inviting her to go back in and put her cap on straight or make sure her apron came down to the same length as her skirt. But that was only a part of Sister Ross's observations – and she was a very observant lady.

She also watched to see the demeanour of 'her' nurses. After all they were in her care – even the Staff Nurses. She watched to see if they looked happy or sad, shoulders back or head drooping, eyes laughing or possibly crying, skipping or walking briskly, or dragging their feet. Even if they were alone or in company, chatting or silent: each of these signs said something to Sister Ross and she occasionally took action if she perceived there to be a need.

Now, she watched Christina as she came up the steps with a quick light tread, even after the nights on duty. She remembered the military letters coming from the Front that she had placed in Christina's pigeon-hole and smiled. Something going on there, she thought.

'Good morning, Staff Nurse Sinclair.'

'Good morning, Sister Ross,' Christina stopped in her tracks by the call, turned towards the office and tapped on the door. They'd known each other for a long time.

'How are you? You look happy.'

'I'm very well, thank you Sister. It's a lovely day.'

'It is, indeed. And what are you going to do with it? Go to bed, I expect?'

'Well,' Christina hesitated. She knew that was expected, even at the beginning of nights off. 'Not quite yet, Sister … you see, well, I'm going down to the station.'

'The station? Meeting a train, are you?'

'Yes Sister.' Christina could bear it no longer. 'Yes Sister, I'm going to meet a friend on leave from the Front. He's coming in on the troop train this morning.'

'I see. And do your parents know about this friend?'

Christina smiled. 'Oh yes, they know Lowrie. He's a very old friend of the family. He's my brother Magnus's oldest friend. Lowrie's part of the family.'

'Does he come from Shetland too?'

'Yes, from Jarlshavn.'

'Well,' Sister Ross gave in. 'You go and have a happy day. But, don't get too tired. Make sure that you eat properly and be back here on time.'

'Yes, Sister, thank you.'

Christina went out and Sister Ross lent her elbows on her desk and thought a little of days gone by when she too had been young and energetic, in love and full of dreams of the lad who had gone to the Front at Bloemfontein and, in his case, had never come back. She liked Christina Sinclair. She hoped she would find happiness.

Christina walked down Princes Street and turned right to cross the Waverley Bridge. This was one of the two bridges crossing the railway to the station, also named Waverley after Sir Walter Scott's novels. It was popular with pedestrians as it led directly to the station. The other bridge, built in 1897, was windy with little shelter and passed high over Waverley station's eastern section.

She stopped for a minute and leaned on the parapet. Funny that it used to be three stations, she thought. It's not so very long ago. The building of this one only started in 1868, or so I've read. I like it. She walked on, turned left down the road into the bustle of the forecourt.

The train was not in but she could tell by the air of expectation that it wouldn't be long. Crowds behind the barrier thronged the entrance to the platform, early though it was. They said it was always like this when a troop train was due.

She could feel the mood of the crowd changing. The chattering grew louder. Children clamoured to be held up to see. Christina could feel the vibration of the train as it neared, slowing down as it came to the bend and then it was in sight. The crowd cheered. As the train approached she could see the carriages, many windows open with arm outstretched to grasp and turn the door-handle the second the train stopped.

Suddenly men were pouring off the train heaving kitbags behind them. The crowd surged past the now-open barrier. All was confusion.

Christina's first thought was one of panic. I can't see him. I'll never see him in this crowd. Then reason took over and she thought, don't be daft, just wait, he'll be there. I wonder if he'll recognise me – will I recognise him? I wonder if he'll still have his moustache. Oh, I wish he would come. She looked up and down the length of the train. Then suddenly, from behind her.

'Christina, Christina.'

She whirled round and there he was, running towards her, glengarry ribbons flying, arms outstretched.

'Oh, Lowrie, I thought you weren't there.'

'What and miss this, one of the best moments of my life. Not likely.' He held her in a close embrace, kissed her on the lips, ruffled her hair, hugged her again, held her away from her and looked at her and then hugged all over again.

'Oh, you've no idea how I've looked forward to this moment.'

'Oh Lowrie,' she held him tightly. 'Are you all right? All in one piece?'

'Yes, I'm fine, nothing that food and a bath won't fix. And,' he looked at her, 'seeing you, of course.' He replaced his glengarry which had slipped off his head with the hug and tucked her arm through his.

'Come on, I'm starving. Let's go for breakfast.'

'Breakfast? Have you not had any?'

'No, the train ran out of food miles back. They were very short all the way north. Everyone used up what little rations they had and there was only bully beef being served out. Bully beef. I never want to see the stuff again. We hoped to get some food at Preston but another troop-train had been in half an hour earlier and been issued with it.'

'Oh, you poor souls,' Christina said. 'That can't be good for you.'

'Well everyone will be ready for their breakfasts I can tell you.' He walked along at a great rate, out of the station and up towards Princes Street, Christina's arm tucked firmly in.

'Come on my darling. Let's eat.'

'Where are we heading?'

'Oh, I think the North British.'

'The North British? But Lowrie, that's terribly expensive.'

'Oh, didn't I tell you, we were paid. Paid at last. There was a sort of hold-up and then suddenly we were told that it had come through. So, let's go.' They turned along Princes Street.

They entered the North British Hotel by the front door. It was very grand, very modern, built as an hotel for the station and opened in 1902. Christina stepped inside and looked round. This was a first for her; impecunious nurses didn't usually go to such places. She hoped her hair was not too ruffled. Perhaps she should have worn a hat. She was glad she'd changed out of her uniform.

'Yes, please, a table for two, in the dining room, for breakfast.'

'Please come this way, Sir, Madam.' The elderly waiter, noting Lowrie's pips on his shoulder, bowed respectfully. He ushered them to a secluded table, held Christina's chair out for her and picked up their napkins with a flourish.

'Are you from the Front, Sir?'

'Yes, just home for a few days leave.'

'I'm sure you deserve it.' He draped their napkins over their knees. 'Now, here are your menus. And, would you like tea or coffee?'

When he had disappeared, they sat back and looked at each other.

'You haven't changed a bit,' he admired.

'Nor you.'

'Did you think I might have?'

'I, I wasn't sure. I'm glad you haven't. You look a bit tired, though. Was the train very bad?'

'Oh, it wasn't so bad. It was packed but, apart from the poor rations that is, conditions on this train were a better than the one we were on in France. There, one of the doors had broken off in the carriage next to ours and some of my colleagues felt driven to get out in the night and jog along by the side of the train to keep from freezing. Some of the men were in cattle trucks. It's very bad the way some of them are treated.'

173

'I never knew it was like that. It's bad enough being in a War without our own men being badly treated by their own side. We don't hear any of that.'

'There's a lot that's kept back from the press. Anyway, come on Christina, let's eat. What are you having – eggs Benedict? See, it's on the menu.'

'How exotic. I've never had that before.'

'Come on then. And coffee? She nodded. And toast?'

'What shall we do with our day? Let's see, it's ten o'clock now. I need to go back to my wee place to freshen up and then the rest of the day is ours to do what we like with. When do you have to be back?'

'About 10 pm at the latest.'

'Right, that gives us the rest of the day. Are you off tomorrow?'

'Yes, but aren't you heading north?'

'Yes, but not till the day after tomorrow. Would you like to spend tomorrow together or have you anything else planned?' He looked hopefully at her.

'Well now,' she said, 'I think I can squeeze a meeting with you in between all my appointments but I…'

'Christina, don't do that. I can't stand it. Are you free tomorrow? Yes or no.'

'Yes.'

'Right, may I have the honour of collecting you in the morning and we'll do something like … 'he hesitated. 'What would you like to do?'

'We could go for a walk? Round the Botanic gardens perhaps, or up Arthur's Seat.'

'At least you haven't suggested shopping.'

'Don't you like shopping?'

'Well, I don't like wandering around aimlessly. If I'm shopping it needs to be for something. Anyway we'll go walking. Let's wait and see what the weather's like. Let's go and see if Mrs Duns has the boiler on for hot water.'

'Who's Mrs Duns?'

'She's my landlady where I live at the Stockbridge Colonies. She's great. You'll like her. Her husband's a stonemason – a lot of them live there. She lets me have two rooms as my Edinburgh home. It suits me and it suits her to be able to let rooms. Helps their income, I suppose. Now,' as they left the hotel, 'let's get a – ah,' he waved his hand – Taxi.'

'Stockbridge Colonies please.' Lowrie opened the back door and ushered Christina in and gave the rest of his address.

'Yes, Sir.' Again the respect. Christina had noticed this before. Uniformed personnel home on leave were afforded great deference. It was the civilian way of showing appreciation for what they were doing.

Mrs Duns was watching for them.

'Oh, Captain Harcus. I'm delighted to see you again. Your bathwater's hot just as you asked and the kettle's on the boil, in case you want a cup of tea. And is this your young lady?'

'Hello Mrs Duns,' Lowrie turned from paying off the taxi-driver who had waited patiently for his tip and shook hands with her. 'Yes, it's good to be back. This,' he drew forward Christina, 'this is Miss Christina Sinclair.'

'Oh, Miss Sinclair, I'm so pleased to meet you. Please come in.'

At last, by themselves, in Lowrie's 'rooms with bathroom' they stood quietly. Then Lowrie stepped towards her and held her.

'Oh my dearest, I have missed you so much. I've thought about you night and day.' Suddenly it was all too much. Tears ran down his tired face.

'Lowrie, sit down, see, here with me.' She cradled him in her arms and said nothing for a moment.

'It's been the longest six months of my life, I think. I wouldn't have got through it without you to think about. You're what kept me going. It's awful out there. It's even worse for the men – I can say it to you because you see the damaged men coming back to lie in hospital. Thing is, we can't say it to anyone else. The mud, the blood, the stench, the bodies, the noise, the killing, the screaming and yelling. The public just doesn't understand.' He held her closely.

'Christina, I'm so tired. Suddenly all the fushen's gone out of me.'

'Just rest, then. Here on the sofa.'

'Can I really? Can I just stop for a minute?' He shut his eyes and leant against her. Silence fell. She could feel his breathing becoming slower, more relaxed. She looked up at his face. His eyes were closed. He seemed comfortable. She gave a sigh of contentment and leaned back on the sofa with him.

An hour later he stirred.

'Christina, we've been asleep. What must you think?' He looked around. 'I haven't even unpacked my kit. I really should have a bath.'

'What's the time?' Christina opened her eyes and stretched.

'It's after one. Do you feel like lunch?'

'After that breakfast?'

'Well, perhaps not. We can eat later.' He looked at her. 'This is not much of an entertaining day for you.'

'Lowrie.' She smiled at him. 'I'm not here to be entertained. I'm here to be with you. Doing nothing if that's what you want. I'm happy.'

'Right, I need to unpack and have a bath.'

'Would you like me to run it for you while you unpack some of the kit?'

'Would you? Righty-ho, thanks. It's through there. I won't be a minute.'

He came back through with his shaving kit.

'Look at that,' he said. 'Heated towels, dressing-gown hanging there and, a beautiful woman running my bath for me. What more could a man ask for?' His eyes said it all.

'I don't know, but I'm getting out of the way.' Christina skipped past him and closed the door. She smiled to herself and returned to the sitting room.

A good-feeling room, she reflected, not too fussy, but nice, light and furnishings. Was this Lowrie's choice? She wasn't sure, but liked what she saw. In the window was evidence of Lowrie's work as a lawyer with an Edinburgh firm. A small table which obviously served as a desk. A few papers lay in very tidy piles. Ready for him to attend to? One day after the War. What's through here? She went out into the small landing which served as a hall for Lowrie's rooms and across to the other room. Here was a bedroom with a sturdy double bed, ready made up, chest of drawers and wardrobe. An armchair sat in the window recess, while beside the open fire, set and ready to light, was a Shetland kishie filled with, not peats as it would be in Shetland, but, dry logs ready for the first burning. A couple of old upright chairs stood against the wall, a big square rug on the wooden boarded floor, a couple of pictures of Shetland scenes on the wall. Not a big room, but just fine. Or so Christina thought.

She sat down on the edge of the bed, her mind whirling. What am I to do, to say? This is going so fast. But, I love him. I know. Mother said I would know. I do know. She was right. But can it really happen so quickly? But, she told herself, you've known Lowrie for so many years. Yes, she argued back, but not in that way. This is new. Well she told herself, you've had seven months to think about it. Since last October. But we've been apart? Yes, and you still feel the same way. In fact, she told herself, if anything, it's more so.

She gave a sigh. I would love to lie down she thought. I'm so tired after last night on the receiving ward. Just for a wee while while Lowrie's in the bath. It can't do any harm. She kicked off her shoes, swung her legs up on to the bed and lay down. She stretched again and slowly relaxed every muscle in her body. In two minutes she was fast asleep.

Lowrie lay back in the bath – the first long soak for many a long day. I am so glad to be here. I must try and let things go and live for now, not in the past. Think of Christina, my Christina. I can't believe it. I think she loves me. An old man like me. Well, not so very old, but he conceded, developing a few grey hairs here and there. On the other hand, he breathed in and held his already lean abdominal muscles in under the water, quite fit. He leaned forward and turned on the hot tap again then off again as the water level headed for the overflow. I feel so much better. He ducked his head under and then scrubbed vigorously. I hope I don't have any wee beasties – that would never do. Although, he thought on, I bet Christina's seen a few sights in her time. But, I don't want them on me. He changed direction. Is it too soon to ask her to marry me after the war? Why not, he thought. I love her, oh I want her, to be my wife, my everything. Can I ask her? Should I? Should I ask her father first? No. I need to speak to her first. I can't bear the idea of asking a father before speaking to the one you love. It's a daft idea.

He stood up, water streaming, pulled out the plug, leaned over for a warm towel and began to dry himself briskly.

Dressing gown on, bath empty and rinsed, he looked in the sitting room for his intended. All was quiet. Not there, not on the sofa where he had expected her to be. Funny, could she have escaped? He crossed to his bedroom, saw to his relief that her coat was still on the chair in the hall and looked into the bedroom.

There you are my sleeping beauty. He tip-toed across and looked longingly at her. She lay so fast asleep he hadn't the heart to waken her. Well, he thought, there's only one thing for it. He picked up a woollen blanket off his armchair, very gently covered Christina, then lay down beside her and pulled the blanket round himself as well.

Chapter 27

The Front, near Arras

EARLY APRIL 1917

Padre James MacLeod was back at the Front.

Ever since his early student days James had envisaged himself somewhere in Scotland in a kirk with a manse, in a parish with a settled congregation. Jarlshavn beckoned. He loved it, the congregation, the sea, the Shetlanders, their customs, Scottish yet not Scottish in so many different ways with language and customs and genetic traits that came from another place, another time.

Then Charlotte Gordon had appeared on his scene. For James, Charlotte was the one he had been waiting for. They truly loved each other while mindful of watching eyes and claiking tongues. Then it had all gone wrong. James left Shetland, alone, without his (as he liked to put it) Charlotte, he still felt, the only woman he would ever love.

He liked life at St Fillans – his new parish. The folk were friendly, kind, attended the kirk, accepted his ministry, invited him into their social life. It was fine. It was what he had set out to do. But, something was missing; there was an empty space in the back of his mind.

After he left Jarlshavn Charlotte had married Alexander. James knew that part of the reason for his losing her lay with himself. He'd taken her for granted, that she would drop her beloved teaching post and go with him without question. He had implied that his work was more important than hers.

Life went on. The seasons, the years, came and went. James heard of the doings at Birkenshaw in a roundabout way from his mother who, a one-time frequent visitor, remained friends with some of the Jarlshavn ladies. He knew about the babies, heard a little about the bad times and the good. But he never asked. His mother just filtered the news through when she saw him.

Then came the War. To become a chaplain and see War in all its awfulness was a far cry from James's dream.

His latest move was, like many another, a return to the Front. All through March 1917 the Allied armies including British, Canadian, New Zealand, Newfoundland and Australian troops continued to gather in tunnels around Arras in north east France. In this build up to a major confrontation at Arras, a significant number of Scottish Divisions was included in the total. Amongst them were the 51st Highland Division and the 9th and 15th Scottish Divisions, with the 34th Division, containing many Scots, near at hand. James was glad to hear the Scots voices, be greeted as one of their own although he was there for anyone who needed him. By the time he arrived in mid-March 1917 preparations for a spring offensive were well advanced and troops were pouring into the area.

He was impressed by the amount of work going on underground. Trenches and tunnelling were vital to early twentieth century warfare but he had not seen tunnelling to this extent before. Hundreds of Royal Engineers, New Zealand Pioneers and Northern English Bantams formed Tunnel Companies (TC) and had been hard at it since October 1916. Already under Arras was a locally-created network of caverns, galleries, sewage tunnels and even quarries dug from the chalky rock and called locally the *boves*. The TC extended the original network of *boves* to enable troops to arrive at the battlefield in safety. They constructed assault tunnels near the German line, to be blown open on the first attack along with mines left under their Front line.

They worked round the clock, building twenty kilometres of underground tunnels to carry personnel on foot, trams, light trains, to get troops and ammunition to the Front line and remove casualties back. Areas underground equipped with electricity contained medical centres with operating facilities, kitchens, and latrines. It was a vast undertaking. By the end of March they expected to accommodate 24,000 men underground.

Everyone knew the enemy was doing the same thing. Underground had its own dangers. The Germans knew what the Allied tunnellers were doing. They excavated their own subways to assault and countermine the Allied tunnels and the men moving towards them, with sometimes tragic and disastrous results.

The big battle at Arras was planned for 9th April. All the time the troops were gathering the fighting went on. There was constant movement within the lines, incessant sniper-fire, shelling and the tension of waiting for shells coming over, bombardments by trench mortars, and trench raids. Then there was the dealing with the aftermath, the never-ending stream of dead and injured soldiers heading for first-aid posts and beyond.

Men handled the growing and sustained tension as best they could. Some coped quietly, got on with the job but became more sombre as time went on; some laughed and joked with each other and hoped for a 'Blighty wound'; some gave no sign of concern other than being without a 'fag'; many worried about their families worrying about them; many were afraid, but more afraid of showing their fear or, letting their fear prevent them from doing the job expected of them and being seen as a coward. Then, there were the ones who claimed to have no fear. You had to do the job, get on with it and if you were hit, then, well, it must have had your number on it. If it didn't have your number on it then you wouldn't be hit. At the other end of the scale were the men like Captain Iain Dawkins with shellshock, whose mental state was such that many were hospitalised, although with a view to making them 'better' and returning them to the Front.

In the early morning of 8 April, Easter day, James prepared to leave his dugout in the support trench, behind and more or less parallel to the Front line and connected to it by smaller communication trenches. The dugouts were used as shelter, for men coming from the Front line, as signallers' telephone positions or, Platoon or Company Headquarters. James's dugout was just large enough for three or four men, cut into the side of the support line. It was well-constructed by engineers, with heavy wooden planked walls and roof reinforced by sandbags. James looked around.

One young lieutenant about twenty years old from the Gordon Highlanders lay on his mattress in an exhausted sleep after a night in a listening post. This was situated at the end of an advance trench often called a 'sap' probing out from the Front line towards the enemy lines. Saps often went beyond the extensive protective areas of barbed wire, and stopped somewhere in 'no man's land' between the two opposing Front lines. The listening post at the end was usually manned by one or two soldiers. They were there to listen to the enemy, pick up first-hand information regarding the enemy's plans, write it down for immediate dispatch to the officer in charge for further action. It was a dangerous job. Men who returned from a shift on the listening post, if they returned, as enemy snipers were on the watch all the time, were exhausted, tense, irritable.

James took care not to wake up the sleeping man. He strapped on his steel helmet firmly, checked his ID tags, water bottle, pay book, his pockets and pouches for his Bible, book of prayers, notebook, a couple of indelible pencils, gas mask and his portable Communion set. He also carefully filled one of his pouches with a supply of cigarettes for any soldiers who had run out. He didn't smoke himself although strongly tempted sometimes. He had a lot of sympathy with those, many of whom had never smoked in their lives before, who had started smoking to help them get through being a soldier at the Front. In his haversack he carried his emergency rations and basic first aid kit as well as field dressings which they all carried.

His eyes swept the dugout in one last look. His main back-pack or valise, lay in a corner. He left it there – he would travel light today. The young officer slept on. James stepped out into the support line aiming for a RAP further along the line. It was a busy place. Soldiers came and went the whole time. Some going on or off sentry duty, some dispatch runners, some carrying stretchers of wounded coming from a raid and heading for the RAP, many preparing to go out on a raid. About fifty yards along the line he passed the turn-off at right angles to a communication trench leading to the Front line or main fire trench. He walked on, slightly stooping to make sure his head was below the top of the trench. All the time he watched and listened.

In a way, he was fortunate, he thought. Within the remit of his calling and rank he was relatively free to go where he liked. He felt privileged to have a sleeping space, even temporary, in a dugout in the support line. From there he could reach many spots, even the Front line and listening posts if he thought it was necessary. He felt sorry for the Padres whose COs would not allow risk their lives by Front line service. Most chaplains, if given the opportunity, seized it. The men with whom he spoke seemed to appreciate his being there. They enjoyed the craic, they were able to talk about life and death and what was it all about when they were apparently throwing their lives away and being a party to killing others. Then, here was the Padre sitting down beside them in the trench in the middle of it all, risking his life alongside them, offering out cigarettes. Somehow it helped. Somehow, for some, it brought God a little closer, even helped to make a little sense out of the War. On the other hand, James was very aware of the vulnerability of his situation. He, like all padres, was unarmed but even more important as far as he was concerned, because of this, he did not want to put any soldier into a dangerous position trying to protect him. So, he picked his times to go to the Front line. To go during the day did not help – he would be in the way and compromise others. Night-time was more appropriate; under cover of darkness men were ready to talk, to listen, to be comforted and James, too, felt strengthened by their comradeship.

As he hurried along that morning he remembered one other day, not long ago. It had been a long, bad day with shelling and sniping from daylight to dusk. The men in the trench had lost colleagues, some killed outright – some wounded. James worked in the RAP as men were brought in, some walking wounded, some borne by stretcher-bearers who were becoming fewer as they were picked off by enemy fire. He worked all day alongside the MO and his staff, assessing the state of men who came in, giving immediate emergency treatment, sending the walking wounded when able, back to the ADS and thence to the CCS behind the lines. Stretcher cases, once initially assessed, were transported to the ADS and CCS via ambulances waiting in line on the nearest access points. Some were dying of their wounds. Those men were spared the discomfort and pain of going any further and looked after where they were.

When dusk fell, it became quieter, both outside and in the RAP. They stopped, breathed a collective sigh, looked at each other, removed bloody rubber aprons to add to the pile that an orderly with a scrubbing brush had already started on, to be hung up ready for use again.

'Thanks for your help, Padre.' The young regimental MO, Captain Robert Duncan, not long arrived from his post-university house resident's year, looked very tired. 'I appreciate your help today. In fact,' he said, his face very sombre, 'I, personally, couldn't have done without you. If this is pre-battle, what on earth is it like when the real battle is on? How will we or, I, deal with all the tomorrows?'

'You'll manage,' said James. 'You'll manage because you must. You won't be alone. I know sometimes it seems like it, that you have all this responsibility but there'll be others there with you, coming and going. It'll seem overwhelming but, there's a job to be done and we'll do it, as and when it comes. And, I know it'll be to the best of your, our ability.'

'How, how do you cope with – with all those dead and dying young men? Just boys. How? I've never seen so many go like that before.'

'I do my best to cope because I must. These boys need help. If they're too badly wounded to be saved physically, then I need to give, if I can, the strength to move forwards spiritually.'

'How do you mean? They didn't teach us anything about this at medical school.'

'Well,' said James. 'Sometimes this involves speaking with them, praying if they want it, holding hands, listening to last requests, confessions of past deeds that they need to unburden themselves of before they die, writing messages for loved ones, even Holy Communion. The way a man dies is often totally different from his neighbour. Sometimes,' he hesitated, 'nothing I can say or do helps. The fear, the protests, go on until the last breath.' He sighed and momentarily put his hand over his eyes before continuing.

'These, I think are the most difficult for me personally. I'm left feeling that I've somehow failed. But then,' he added, 'that's very subjective and selfish of me and I try not to think like that. I try to be thankful that they're at peace even if I feel at times that I have not been able to help.'

'I don't know how you do it.'

'Just try,' James said. 'Even if you don't know what to say, just holding a dying man's hand will give him a contact. You never know where that will lead. Now,' he said. 'Time's getting on. You need a break from here. My medical advice to you –' they smiled

180

at each other – 'is to go and get some food, sit down, read your latest mail and put your mind somewhere else for a while.'

James was thinking about that other day as he moved along the trench, standing aside for soldiers coming the other way, those already in their places, or those in the shelter of small temporary dugouts having a brew-up. Sometimes I feel so helpless. It's difficult to put advice into practice sometimes, especially in this sort of situation.

''Morning Padre, want a brew?' A voice broke into his thoughts.

'Thanks, but I won't today, I need to get to the RAP. How are you all today?'

'We'll, it's a bit noisy. I wish that lot over there,' he waved his hand in the direction of the enemy lines. 'I wish they'd shut up and give us some peace.'

'Well, you know what they say, "If wishes were horses…"'

'What?'

'You know, "beggars would ride".'

'That's a new one on me Padre. As far as I'm concerned only Colonels and above get a horse.'

James laughed, waved and carried on.

He arrived at the RAP and joined in with the preparations for casualties in the next day's big offensive – the battle where the taking of Vimy Ridge, the highest part of the Arras area, was a vital part of the Allied plans.

That night after dark, James went to the Front line. All was quiet. It was as though both sides were waiting, resting, even contemplative. Yet, James knew that even in the quietness, men on guard were waiting, alert, men at the listening posts, ready for every sound.

It was very cold. Although officially spring, it didn't feel like it. Apart from the enemy that they were there to fight, Northern Europe was slowly coming to the end of the longest coldest winter many could remember. The days had been bad enough but when the temperatures dropped at night it was difficult to sleep because of the cold. James had forgotten how many layers he was wearing. Most wore all the clothes they had. A few individuals had been issued with sheepskin jerkins which helped a little – but they were few and far between. One soldier told James how he had broken the rules one night, taken off his boots and wrapped his feet in a sheepskin. Even a night in a heavily sand-bagged and insulated latrine, despite the stench, could offer more warmth than usual. James shivered then carried on working his way along the ice-slippery duckboards set in the trench. Now, with slowly rising April temperatures, the ice would melt and all would be mud again.

James looked around carefully. The Front line was an intensely dangerous place to be. This was where men went 'over the top' and into no man's land, that terrible place of wounding, death and destruction, and barbed wire, placed as much to defend a position as to repel the enemy. At the other side of no man's land which could be anything from thirty to hundreds of yards away, lay the enemy trenches.

Both Front and support lines ran in a series of sections or dog-legs, creating bays. This was a safety measure: if a shell exploded inside a bay or 'traverse', or an enemy entered one, it didn't affect so many men. In addition to the man-made dog-legs the lines went with natural land contours. This also made it slightly safer, and now and then you could gain a quick view of the enemy lines. The trenches joined up with other Front line trenches across France and Belgium. From early in the War the Front line stretched in a continuous trench for approximately four hundred miles from Switzerland to the North Sea with no way round. Some Front line trenches, especially the permanent ones like the one where James was, were about head high – the men could stand fairly upright – and gave reasonable cover. But, height-level varied and depended upon how quickly the trench had been dug. Some, speedily dug as the line was moving forward, were shallow, temporary, and men in them had to crouch and crawl.

Every man on the Front line had to remain on high alert. Even when not in an acute battle-phase snipers were watching at all times for a lapse in concentration, a head above the trench, an unwary movement. Opportunistic shelling went on at any time.

Although James was not posted to any one of the Scottish battalions in particular, the heavy concentration of Scots to the north-west of Vimy Ridge, the high ground lying to the north of Arras, suited James. While he could hardly say that he was 'delighted' to be anywhere in this War, if he had to be in it, he would choose to be with the men from home. It was to be their job with the Canadians, to take Vimy Ridge when the time came.

The time is just about with us, thought James. Some of them are along here I think. He walked swiftly along, identifying himself to any sentries and found a group of the Black Watch cooried into a small dugout. Their fire was on; they were cooking.

'Padre. Good to see you. Come and have your tea.' Sergeant Dodds got up to greet him.

'Thanks.' James stopped and slung his haversack to the ground. 'I have a tin of McConochie's here – can we add that to the mix?'

'Just what we're having. Here Corporal,' the Sergeant took the tin of stew and handed it to the corporal with the tin-opener. 'Better than bully-beef any day.'

'Smells fine, anyway.'

'Fills a hole,' said a slightly disgruntled voice.

'Oh come on now, Fleming, what are you wanting – salmon or caviar?'

'No, just fish and chips, or, an Arbroath smokie.'

'Arbroath smokie – well now, that's something else. Anyway, give up, it's McConochie's stew or want it.'

'Stew then, please.' Fleming held out his tin. 'At least it's better than that Australian meat paste.'

'Well, this,' the Corporal paused dramatically, 'this, comes from Aberdeen. It's bound to be good. Padre,' he continued, 'where's your mess-tin?'

'Here,' said James. 'Thank you.'

'Now boys, get tore in – oh wait a minute. Padre, seeing you're here, why don't we have a wee prayer?' The Sergeant looked at him.

'Would you like that?'

'Yes, Padre, let's do that. Don't take your helmets off, boys. I'm sure you can be excused, given where we are.'

The group sat in silence. James looked into the firelight, up at the stars and bowed his head.

'Lord, at this Easter time, give us courage and strength to face the ordeal that is before us. May we acquit ourselves as soldiers of our country and we pray that we may come through this safely. Let us join in the Lord's prayer. Our Father, which art in heaven...'

At the final Amen, a silence fell.

'Thank you Padre. Every little helps.' Sergeant Dodds picked up his fork and shovelled a large amount of McConochie's into his mouth. 'Mmm, delicious. Now, Padre,' he continued. 'How have you been getting on? You'll be quite busy, I'm thinking...'

James stayed there talking for a while before getting up. He dug in his pouch and handed out the cigarettes.

'Jist like 'Woodbine Willie'' Sergeant Dodds said. 'They say he aye has fags for the boys.'

'So I hear,' said James. 'I must get on now. I'm glad to see you all in such good fettle. God bless you all.'

'You too, Padre. Good luck tomorrow.' Sergeant Dodds got to his feet and saluted. 'Thank you for stopping by.'

'And you too.' James returned the salute. 'Thanks for tea. Take care.'

He moved on down the line. The spring return to the usual mud and slime was very obvious here. The stench of dead bodies and parts of bodies, latrines and unwashed humanity, for weeks masked by deep-freeze conditions, was returning. The rat population was on the rise again. In this, officers and men lived, moved and fought.

All along the line there were soldiers waiting, taking it in turn to be on sentry duty, some out in the saps, some from a vantage point in the trench. Waiting for the morning when the whistle would blow. One officer per company was on duty at all times and he took hourly reports from his NCOs. Each NCO had to move up and down his assigned part of the trench, checking all the time that sentries were alert, equipment was ready, and the men were as comfortable as they could be under the circumstances. It was very crowded.

James stopped at one group of men. They were hunkered down around one young private, lying on his side at the bottom of the trench. He was shaking, and crying.

'I canna dee it, I canna...'

'Och, come on now, son,' said the Corporal in charge. 'Come on, you'll manage fine. Jist pit yer heid doon an gie them laldy.'

'I canna. I'm that feart. I nivver kent it wid be lik this. It's been, ye ken, sic an afa bangin, an noise an sheetin fur days noo. A canna imagine fit it's gaan tae be lik the morn.'

'Ach, nane o us can tell,' said the Corporal. 'We jist dinna ken.' He turned round at the sight of James approaching and looked up with relief.

'Oh, here's the Padre – hae a wee craic wi him. He'll mak ye feel better.' Then, addressing James, 'See here, Padre, here's Thomson here. Ye need ti spik till him. Tell him something, onything – jist sort him oot, please.'

'All right, Corporal. Give us a wee bit of space, please.' James bent down beside Thomson as the others in the group shuffled down the line a bit. He waited quietly. After a few minutes he put his hand on the boy's shoulder. The crying grew less.

'Thomson, I'm Padre MacLeod. I've just come over to say hello and see how you're doing. Do you think you can talk to me now, Thomson?'

'A dinna ken.'

'How old are you?'

'Eighteen.'

'Where do you come from?'

'Stanley, jist ootside Perth.'

'That's not far from where I'm from – Perth is my home town.'

'Oh, A ken Perth. We eest ti gang there fur the dancin – but noo,' the boy stopped and closed his eyes.

'Thomson, open your eyes and speak to me,' said James. 'Tell me, when did you leave school?'

'Oh, a whilie ago. A went ti be a fairm loon when A wis fourteen. A likit it. A'm nae feart o hard work ye ken.'

'I ken that. I can see that. Ye're well set up. Div ye hae a lassie?'

'Oh ay. Wait a minty – A hae a photie. A keep it next ti me. She's an afa fine lassie.' He struggled into a sitting position and dug in his inner pocket. 'See, here she is.' James looked.

'She is indeed a bonnie lassie.' He handed the photo back. 'You keep that photo safe and keep thinking about her. What's her name?'

'Margie. She's really Margaret but her mother's Margaret as weel, so they ay caa'ed her Margie. A think we'll maybe get mairrit when aa this is bye.'

'Sounds like a great idea. She'll be very proud of her sodger laddie, won't she?'

'Mebbe.' Thomson sounded doubtful. 'A dinna ken if A can dee it though. A'm afa feart.'

'Thomson, do you think there is anyone here who is not feart?' He thought about that.

'Well, no, I suppose not – what about you Padre? Are you feart?'

James swallowed. 'Yes,' he said slowly. 'Yes, if you put it that way, I'm feart as well. But, now we're here, we have to get on and do what we have to do. Not just for ourselves, but for the folk at home and for the ones we love the best. I ken your Margie will be proud of you. Have you written her a letter telling her you love her?'

'No, I wrote her but I didn't exactly say that.'

'Would you like to do that?'

'Ay, wid ye tak it fur me?'

'Yes, I'll wait if you want to do it now. Do you need a pencil?'

'Ay, thanks Padre.'

James got out his notebook and indelible pencils and handed them over.

'You write the letter, don't tell her where you are, and give me the address and I'll see that it goes tonight. And tell the lassie you love her. Just see how pleased she'll be.'

He waited quietly while the laborious letter was written. At length Thomson looked up.

'Finished,' he said. 'Here ye are Padre.' He handed over the letter along with James's pencil and notebook. He got to his feet. The tear-stained face looked James straight in the eyes.

'A'm aa richt noo, Padre. I'll dae it fur Margie.

It was after 3am before James got back to the dugout. He was very tired. The last group of men that he saw had gathered, waiting for him and asked for Communion. With permission to have a fifteen minute break from the line they had moved to an area just behind the support line. Some men, realising what they were about, joined in as they went along. A few offered bread from their rations. They stood in the group. James looked round. He had never before served Communion in this situation. He could feel the emotion rising, the tears in his eyes, the lump in his throat. His hands trembled slightly. Come on, he said to himself. Be strong. He cleared his throat, looked at the men, raised his voice.

'Christ is risen.'

'He is risen indeed.'

'The Lord be with you.' To his amazement and delight the answer again came back in a rumble of voices.

'And with thy spirit.'

'Lift up your hearts…'

When the time came to pray, they all with one accord knelt on the ground and stayed there as the bread and wine were passed round and for the final Benediction. No one moved. James spoke again:

'Go forth in peace,' he said, 'and may you have strength and courage. Amen.' Slowly the men got to their feet and returned to their places in the line.

James watched them go, then, picking up his haversack, walked back to his dugout. His notebook contained men's letters, names and addresses including Private Thomson's. Carefully he addressed and matched envelopes to letters and set them aside until he was ready to take them to the dispatch point.

Then he started to write again.

Chapter 28

Birkenshaw

APRIL 1917

Charlotte woke in the early morning light and stretched. It was a quarter past six. When she listened carefully she could hear noises downstairs, muted voices. Edie and Meg were up. She sighed. She kept telling Meg to take things more easily but staying in bed in the morning was one thing Meg seemed unable to do. She was always around early. So Charlotte, seeing she was not going to win that argument, had insisted in employing Mrs Bertha Halcrow to come in for a few hours three times a week to do the floors and other heavy work usually done by Meg. In vain Meg had protested. Charlotte won this domestic battle and Meg gave in as gracefully as she could. Bertha was now an accepted part of the household and considered Angus to be her especial pet. This he accepted primarily because, well, he liked Bertha, she was comfortable to be with and didn't nag even though she was a woman, but she also brought in her bag such delights as tablet and treacle toffee and home baking specially for him and often what they called a 'fine piece' for him to take to school for playtime.

Charlotte got out of bed and ran downstairs to where Alexander lay in his new room. Ever since he had flitted downstairs he had been happier, less depressed, more optimistic, walking more, going outside on fine days. True, he hadn't managed the Birkenshaw front steps but then, they nearly all used the back door routinely. It was easy, sheltered and sunny, especially in these spring mornings. Charlotte daily felt a lighter heart as far as Alexander's health was concerned. She opened the door gently.

He was sitting up in bed with a large mug of tea.

'Good morning.' She kissed his forehead. 'You're awake early.'

'Yes, but so's Edie – see, she's been in already. Tea's up.'

'I'll go and get some and join you for a wee while. Then I'll have to waken Angus.'

On her return, they sat in silence for a minute, contemplating the day.

'I need to write Magnus,' Alexander said. 'That's the first thing I must do after breakfast. Where do you think I should send it to? He's on his way to Glamis Castle. He'll only get it when he arrives there.'

'Well,' Charlotte said, 'we could send it to Glamis. We know that's where he's going, Glamis Castle, and I think it's in a wee village called Glamis and Glamis is in Angus. So, I think we could safely send it there.'

'Is there really a village called Glamis?'

'Yes, and it's about four miles from Kirriemuir, you know where that book *Peter Pan* by J M Barrie was written – remember we bought a copy for Hannah when it was published? Nice book, beautifully illustrated.'

'How d'you know that Glamis is near Kirrimuir? I never knew that you'd been there.'

'I haven't,' said Charlotte. 'But when we knew that Magnus was going there I looked it up in my atlas. So that we'd have some idea of where he was going to be.'

'Oh – well anyway, Charlotte, about Magnus, you see, I really need to…'

'Alexander, I'm sorry to interrupt you but can we talk about this later? Please,' as she saw him frown. 'Please Alexander, I must go and waken Angus for school. You know what he's like if he has to rush.' He sighed and gave in.

'Oh all right. If you must.' She got up.

'What would you like for breakfast?'

'Oh, just porridge and toast, please.'

'I'll tell Edie.'

Angus was asleep. Charlotte looked at him. What a shame to waken him. She always felt this. She thought that children should be left to waken naturally, in peace with no rush. She pulled back the curtains; sunlight streamed in. He stirred.

'Angus. Hello. It's time to get up.'

He stirred, flung his hand over his eyes, opened them, peeked through his fingers.

'What day is it?'

'Wednesday. It's time to get up for school. It's a fine day,' she added, looking out of the window.

'Oh good.' Angus, suddenly remembering, got out of bed and joined her at the window. 'Mr Gear said if it was fine today I could go down to their house and see their rabbits. Can I do that Mother? After school?'

'Yes, if he said so, but are you sure he did?'

'Yes, don't you remember? It was the day Father came downstairs and Mr Gear, he said I could go some day. Well I saw him yesterday and he said I could go today if it was fine.'

'Very well,' said Charlotte. 'How many rabbits does he have?'

'I don't know but I hope it's lots. Mother,' Angus's voice took on his persuasive note, which Charlotte knew very well.

'Yes?' Knowing what was coming.

'Mother, do you think I could have a rabbit, or even two, if Mr Gear offers? I'll look after them myself. Honestly.'

'One maybe, but two – well I don't think so. You know what two rabbits make?'

'No, what?'

'Two, four, six, eight and so on little rabbits. No, Angus, not two.'

'But we could have two boys,' said Angus.

'No, they would fight.'

'Fight?' said Angus. 'Do rabbits fight?'

'I'm sure they do. Not two buck rabbits, not two any rabbits. I *might* think about one rabbit …'

'Ooh goody –'

'I said might, but we need to think about lots of things first, like, have you thought of a hutch for it? And where would we keep it? And what will you feed it on? And who's going to clean it out?'

'Well,' said Angus, throwing his arms out in a grand manner. 'I'll see to all of that, of course.' Charlotte had to hide a smile.

'I'll tell you what,' she said. 'You go as you've arranged tonight to Mr Gear, see his rabbits and if he suggests that you might have one, thank him very much, say you'll have to discuss it with me and come home and make out a plan for keeping a rabbit. Then we'll talk seriously about it. What do you think?'

'Is that a deal Mother?'

'Yes, said Charlotte. That can be a deal. No deal, no thinking about a rabbit.'

'All right, it's a deal.' Then he said, 'I think we should shake hands now. That's what you do in a deal.' They shook hands solemnly.

'Now,' said Charlotte, 'would you please get ready for breakfast. You're going to be late if you don't hurry.'

Downstairs, Edie said, 'What was all that about?'

'Rabbits. He wants one.'

Later, in the still time after Angus had rushed off to school to spread the word that he had made a deal with his mother, true and solemn with shaking hands and all that, Charlotte sat down beside Alexander with her second cup of tea.

'It's quiet when he's gone.' Alexander drained his mug and set it on his tray.

'Yes, he's a lively lad.'

'Now that he's gone could we go back to Magnus? I need to talk about him.'

'Yes, of course. I'm sorry I had to go away earlier. There just wasn't time then.'

'I know, I know. But we can do it now.' He fiddled with his sheet.

'Alexander what is it?'

'I need to write him today.'

'Yes.'

'I need to write him today, and I want to tell him – no, *ask* him to come home when he's able to leave Glamis? I need to see him so much.'

'But, we have mentioned it in a couple of letters …' Charlotte began.

'Yes, yes, but I want to make it clearer, that I want him home. His place is here.'

'Alexander, he may be very touchy about this – after all he had no choice at the time. Could you put yourself in his shoes and try and think how he might be feeling?'

'I know that you're thinking about his feelings and all that, but I keep saying to you, it's all in the past. My mind is quite made up. I'll write to him once I'm up.'

Later, he sat in the parlour window at the table there with his pen and paper.

Dear Magnus

        Well, here I am, now feeling much more mobile than hitherto. I can move about freely now I'm downstairs. I'm glad now that I have made the move.

By the time you receive this I hope that you will have settled down in Glamis. I hope that your journey went smoothly and did not affect your health too much. How long will you have to be there do you think? And, what happens next? I feel strongly that you should come home to Birkenshaw now. You have done your bit for the country. Your place is here now and we are all looking forward to seeing you.

May your health improve rapidly and we will see you ere long.

Yours affly.,

Father.

Charlotte to Magnus,

Dear Magnus,

This is just a note to go in with your Father's. We are all getting on fine. Angus's latest ploy is to acquire a rabbit. We have a sort of 'deal' going about this. We'll see.

As you see we are sending these letters to Glamis. We look forward to hearing from you when you have arrived and settled in. I wonder if the Lady Elizabeth Bowes Lyon is in attendance. They say she is very 'charming' but I wouldn't know, not really being aware of what 'charming' really is.

Your Father is making good progress – even outside conferring with Dod the gardener who is doing very well and taking good care of the trees.

Tale care. The children send their love.

Yours affly.,

Charlotte.

Chapter 29

Christina stirred. She sighed, opened her eyes, looked around, noticed the unfamiliar blanket. She turned and then, as she saw Lowrie beside her, she remembered. I'm in Lowrie's bed. What will he think of me?

She lay watching him. He looked so peaceful, so much less stressed. She put out a finger and traced the little lines round his eyes, ran her hand gently down his cheek. He put his hand up and impatiently scratched, as though brushing away a fly or, thought Christina, some other insect irritant that he might have met in the trenches. His eyes flickered and opened. Blue eyes looked into the grey ones studying him so closely. He smiled.

'Hello.'

'Hello.' She looked down.

'What's the matter? You look worried.'

'Lowrie, we're in bed. Your bed. Together.'

'So? So what?' He leaned up on his elbow. 'You were asleep when I came through from the bathroom. I was tired and got in beside you. What could be more reasonable?'

'Well, other people might not see it as reasonably as that.' She looked at him. His face was straight but she could see the laughter there.

'Lowrie, you're laughing at me.'

'Not at all, I'll get out of my own bed at once.' He made to jump out at his side.

'No, no, I didn't mean that, not really. It's just…' her voice trailed off.

'Yes, yes, all the old wifies would spik. I know, I know. But the answer is, we just don't say anything. All right? And anyway, it was a good sleep, don't you think?'

'Yes.' She stretched her arms out of the blanket. 'Did you cover me up?'

'Yes. You looked so lovely the way you were but you needed to be kept warm.'

'Thank you,' she said. 'It was kind of you not to waken me. I was so tired.'

'My pleasure. And now,' he added, 'that we've got all that sorted out, could we decide what's next on our agenda. For instance where are we to have dinner tonight?'

'Dinner? Are we thinking about that already?'

'Well, we can at least talk about it. But before we do, there's something else I want to do?' He moved closer and gently put his arms around her. He kissed her, so gently and tenderly at first, and then as she responded, with a greater passion that grew quickly.

After a few minutes, she drew back.

'Lowrie, Lowrie, we must stop, stop now while we can. I don't want to, but we must.'

'I know, but I love you so much.'

'I love you too.'

They drew apart, looking at each other.

'Christina,' said Lowrie. 'Did I hear you say what I think you said?'

'You might have.'

'Could you say it again please?'

'Why?'

He made a grab for her.

'Because you little besom, I want to hear again what you said.'

'Well, that's not very romantic.' She wriggled away.

'All right, Christina.' He was serious now. 'Please could you say again what you said.'

'Lowrie …' a little hesitantly.

'Yes?'

'Lowrie, I – I love you too.'

Lowrie's 'Ah-h,' came out as a breath of joy. Once more they were in each other's arms. Holding closely, loving, touching.

'I can feel your heart beating,' he whispered.

'Beating for you.' She ran her hands up the back of his head.

'Christina.'

'M-mm?'

'Will you marry me?'

'Oh, Lowrie…'

'Is that a "yes"?'

'Oh, Lowrie, yes. Should I say "please"?' He burst out laughing.

'You always were a well-brought up girl.'

'A minute ago you were calling me a besom.'

'Well, you can be both if you like. More entertainment…'

'Lowrie.' She picked up a pillow and hit him with it.

'Only joking,' he held up his hands. 'Now Mrs Harcus-to-be. When will we get married?'

'Seriously,' she said, 'you really want to marry me? I'm only me, you know. Little me from Jarlshavn. Not like the city girls.'

'You're the one I love, the one I've been looking for all those years and now I've found you I'm not going to let you go. And as for the "little me from Jarlshavn", don't make me laugh. You're worth ten of these city lassies. Let's make a date.'

'Lowrie, I would marry you tomorrow if I could, but let's – let's be sensible about this. There's a War on. And I don't think hospital rules will let me work on if I'm married.'

'But you've just said, "there's a War on". Can't they bend the rules?'

'I don't know what they'd do.'

'Don't you know anyone working there who's done it? I mean got married? And stayed on?'

'There was one nurse who got married but didn't stay on – but she – she was having a baby. That was really too much for Matron to accept. She left and no-one mentioned her out loud again.'

'Poor lassie. But what about, well, married? It shouldn't make any difference to your working practices. Could you find out?'

'Yes, I'll do a bit of quiet asking? Would that do? But, oh, Lowrie,' she said, 'what about our parents? My father. You'll need to ask him. We're doing this the wrong way round.'

'I did wonder, briefly, about waiting to ask him, but Christina, it's you I want to marry, not your father.'

'Yes, I know but you know what some older folk are like, and, especially Father. He's really quite strict.'

'Yes, I know,' Lowrie agreed, thinking of Magnus and his father's management of him when he fell short of parental expectations.

As if she could read his mind, Christina said, 'Father was very strict with Magnus. He sent Magnus away to Canada, you know.' She looked at him. He nodded gravely.

'I don't know why,' she said. 'I did ask Mother, when I was up for that week, when Father had his first stroke.'

'What did she say?'

'Well, the strange thing is, she didn't say anything. I just eventually felt that there was no use going on about it. So, I left it. But,' she added, 'I felt very out of it when he went away. He did say good-bye to me and that he would always love me. I missed him so much and I still miss him. I still don't know why he had to leave.'

Lowrie held her hand. He didn't speak.

'Lowrie,' she said suddenly. 'Do *you* know? You and Magnus are best friends. He must have told you. Could even have mentioned it when you visited him in Royaumont?' He still didn't speak. She gave his hand a little shake.

'Lowrie, you do know something, don't you? Won't you tell me please?' He put his arm round her.

'Christina, my dear, I don't believe in couples having secrets from each other, But, this is not mine to tell. Yes,' he admitted, 'Magnus took me into his confidence at the time...'

'And?'

'Christina, you of all people know about patient confidentiality.' As she nodded, he continued.

'Well, this is very similar. Lowrie told me about this problem in deepest confidence and I – I can't tell anybody – not even you. You do see that don't you?' She sighed.

'When you put it like that, yes, of course I see what you mean. Don't worry. I won't nag you about it anymore.'

'Let's go back to what we were talking about – us and getting married.'

'And my strict father.'

'How about I go and see your father and mother when I'm in Shetland this leave? I could go along, speak to your mother first, tell her our news, ask her advice on whether or not your father is able to hear our news and would he give us his blessing and work from there. What do you think?'

'Oh, Lowrie, would you do that? I'm sorry I can't be with you but...'

'No, no, I realise that. Now, now that we've got that settled, could we organise ourselves for something to eat. I know just the right restaurant, not far away. And tomorrow, he said, what do you think we're going to do tomorrow?'

'I can't possibly imagine.'

'We're going on a ring-hunt.'

Chapter 30

4 APRIL 1917

It took a long time, the hospital train from Creil to Le Havre. A matter of around one hundred and ten miles could have been achieved relatively smoothly in normal times. But these times weren't normal. The narrow-gauge railway from Creil to Le Havre had been bombed and repaired many times in the last two years. Now the rails were shaky and loose, very hazardous for trains moving over the junctions – there had been many derailments – journeys were of necessity slow and with frequent stops to clear debris off the lines. It seemed interminable.

Magnus was in the seated area of the train, Iain Dawkins close by. Every now and again Magnus stole a look at him. His eyes were closed but Magnus, looking at his constantly fiddling fingers doubted that he was sleeping. He looked out of the dirty window at the countryside, trees winter-bare but there was more than just the season to contend with. The trees looked War-torn, bereft of life possibly. The ground looked muddy-brown, almost grey. It had an air of misuse calling out for care and attention. It would take a few years to get the land back to its pre-war growth and green. People they passed looked incuriously at the white train with its bold insignia. They had seen too many now to get excited. Occasionally someone would raise a hand in greeting or acknowledgement perhaps. In the main, the train trudged on into the gathering gloom of the evening. Magnus sighed and turned to his book.

A while later Iain spoke. 'How are we getting on? Have you any idea how long this is going to take?'

'Well, it's seven o'clock now. I can't see us being there before tomorrow afternoon.'

'What?'

'Yes, I know it's long but we're not going very quickly. The railway track is in a very bad state and they won't want to take any risks of derailment with so many injured men on board. How are you feeling?'

'I'm not too bad.' Magnus noted his twitching fingers and tight lips.

'It's just past your medication time. I think I'll grab the next passing orderly and ask him to speak to the Sister about it.'

'Oh don't bother. They'll have enough to do without worrying about me.'

'That's all very well but you must have your meds – you must take them regularly.'

'Yes, well, I just don't like to be a bother.'

'You'd be even more bother,' said Magnus, 'if you didn't take your meds and then became more ill. Now, where's that orderly?'

He looked back along the carriage. Past the small seating area, he could see tiers of bunks, all occupied. Sisters, VADs and orderlies worked non-stop. Many of the casualties were still very ill and in great pain. To make things more difficult, there was little room to move, and it was very difficult nursing in such tight circumstances and with three levels of bunks. Magnus bit his lip as he remembered the cries of men in agony as they were moved from stretcher to bunk in Creil. An orderly hurried past.

'Hello,' called Magnus. 'Could you stop a minute please.' The orderly stopped, turned, saw his hand up.

'Yes, what can I do for you? Sorry we haven't been along before.'

'That's all right. We can see you've got your hands full.'

'You can say that again. It's the same all along the train. It's packed. Then we sort everyone out at the railhead at Le Havre, and clean the train and run back for more. It's never-ending. Anyway,' he paused, 'what can I help you with?'

'Thank you for stopping,' said Magnus. 'My colleague here, Mr Iain Dawkins,' he indicated Iain, 'is due to have his medication. Do you think you could speak to the Sister-in-Charge about it please? He really should have it.' The orderly looked at him, taking in the RAMC badge on his hat balanced on his knee.

'Yes Sir, I'll tell her immediately.' He took a note of where they were sitting. 'She'll be along.'

'Thank you very much.' The orderly hurried off.

Five minutes later the Sister-in-Charge came down the aisle.

'Good evening. I'm Rosemary Jones, in charge of this coach. How are you both getting along? Now, let me see,' she consulted her list. 'You'll be Mr Iain Dawkins and Captain Magnus Sinclair – that is, if my list is keeping up with the folk we've got on board.'

'Yes, Sister, that's correct.'

'Right, I have a list of medications here and my meds case here. Let's see, Captain Sinclair, you can have analgesia *prn* – how are you feeling?'

'I think I'm all right for the moment. Maybe something later, please.'

Yes, that's fine. Now, Mr Dawkins, I see that you're written up for your tablets every four hours. Here you are. Have you your water-bottle?'

'Yes,' Iain had it ready. 'Thank you.' She watched as he swallowed the tablets.

'Please don't miss a dose. We'll come to you if we can but even if you think we look very busy, just stop someone passing. Now, what else can we get you? Have you got rations?'

'Yes,' Magnus dug in his haversack. 'I was just thinking about food. But, first, how's Private Fletcher? He was with us – he's on this train. How is he?'

'He's been in a lot of pain – we had to re-dress his wounds and it was all very difficult. He's heavily sedated now. When he comes round, I'll let him know you're asking for him.'

'Thanks,' said Magnus, relieved. 'I was worried about him…you know…'

'Yes, I know. Now, you two, time to eat. How about some tea to wash it down?' She smiled as their eyes lit up. 'I know there's a tea round in a few minutes. I'll make sure that you're included. By the way where have you come from?'

'Royaumont.'

'Oh it's a lovely Abbey isn't it? How did you end up there? Where were you wounded?'

'The Somme.'

'Ah, the Somme.' She shook her head gravely. 'A sad time.' She looked at Iain who was sitting with his eyes closed. 'Was Mr Dawkins there too?'

'Yes,' said Magnus. 'We've both come via Royaumont. I'm going on to Glamis for convalescence.'

'Scotland – will you be glad to get back?'

'Yes…but…'

'But that's not where you come from is it? You have a Canadian cap-badge.'

'Well,' began Magnus, 'well…'

'No, I've heard your sort of voice before. I have a friend who speaks just like you. She comes from Shetland – a long way north. We trained in Aberdeen together. She's working in Edinburgh now. We both were. Then I came on to France. She stayed in Edinburgh to sort out the men who are sent home. Anyway,' she paused, 'I must get on. You see what it's like. Have you worked on the hospital trains?'

'No,' Magnus shook his head. 'I was on the RAPs and CCS, until I was wounded.'

'You must have gone through some very stressful experiences then. I'm glad you're here. See you later. Oh,' she paused again. 'You can tell me why the Canadian cap-badge some time. Everyone's got a story to tell.' She went on down the train.

Magnus settled back in his seat. That's one story I'm not going to tell, he thought. Nice lassie, though. Funny she recognised my accent. He opened his eyes – what was it she said? She said she knew, had trained in Aberdeen with someone who spoke the same way. I wonder who that was. It could have been Christina – I wonder. That would be a coincidence.

Tea arrived. He nudged Iain.

'Tea up. Where's your rations?'

They sat in silence nursing the familiar thick white mugs of hot strong tea.

'That's better.' Magnus took a big bite of his bully-beef sandwich. Mouth full, he asked, 'How are you now?'

'Better, I think. It's all such a muddle, so distant and yet so close sometimes that I can hear it, see it, smell the trenches, the bodies, the rats in amongst them.' Iain shuddered. 'It all goes round and round in my head until I think I'm going mad. That's why I'm going to Craiglockhart, you know. They said shell-shock. I never thought it would happen to me.'

'I'm sorry, sorry, that is, that they say you've got this. How do you feel about going to Craiglockhart?'

'Well, at least it's being acknowledged – that shell-shock exists, I mean. I don't know how they can help, though.'

'I think you'll need to wait and see,' said Magnus, treading carefully. 'However, at least you'll find that you're not alone, that there are others with the same illness, you'll meet some who are getting better which'll be encouraging and of course there are doctors there who will help you get through it.'

'But,' responded Iain, 'in the end, I'll still have to face a Medical Board. I'm dreading it.'

'But that's a long way down the line. The War could be finished sooner than you think.'

'Do you think so?'

'Well, things are going a bit better recently. I think the Somme taught the powers-that-be a lot – I hope so anyway. Keep hoping. We must do that… Oops,' as the train gave a lurch. 'We're stopping again. What is it this time?' He looked out of the window. A few soldiers, recruited to man the train were running along the side of the track towards the front end.

'Something across the line, I think. Maybe a tree.'

They fell silent. Iain dozed. Magnus picked up his book again. Later, the train moved off again, slowly gathering a little more speed as it moved towards Le Havre.

At last, many hours later the dawn light began to show in the east. Rays of sun filtered through the grime on the windows. They could feel the atmosphere in the carriage lightening as the daylight grew. Surely they couldn't have much further to go. They were running into a large built up town, they could just discern buildings, houses, churches, the train slowed as they entered a tunnel. At the other end, the train slowed further as they approached a large station.

'Where are we?'

Magnus peered out of the window. 'Wait a second, here's a sign – ah, now we're getting somewhere. We're at Rouen. I feel a bit more hopeful now.'

'Hopeful of what?'

'Of getting to Le Havre.'

'What – did you think there was a problem?'

'No not really. I'm only joking.' Magnus stretched. 'But you must admit it's felt a long way. Here's Sister coming now. Good morning.' He looked at her tired face. 'Been a reasonable night?'

'Busy, but all still with us, I'm glad to say. Now,' she went on. We stop here at Rouen for fifteen minutes. There is a Red Cross buffet if you want anything different to eat. Magnus, I'm happy for you to get out as long as you report back. Iain, I would rather you stayed on board if you don't mind.' Iain nodded.

'I'll get something for you,' offered Magnus. 'What would you like? A croissant? Two? Apricot jam?'

'Now you're talking – but, just anything you can get. Here.' Iain reached in his haversack. 'Money.'

'Never mind that just now.' He looked at Rosemary. 'What about you, Sister?'

'My order's been taken, thanks. You'd better be quick.'

Ten minutes later, he was back.

'Here we are, croissants and coffee. What more could a body ask for?'

'Have you told Sister you're back?'

'Yes, I waved as I was coming on again. They're loading up the goods end of the train with supplies for No 2 General Hospital at Le Havre. Apparently Rouen is the Base Depot for No 2's supplies and transport.'

'How did you find that out?'

'I asked what was going on. The station's full of supply trucks. So, we'll stop at No 2 to offload supplies and of course transfer the patients bound for there and then at some

196

point we head for the quayside. We may get a break at No 2 – I'm not sure. Drink your coffee before it gets too cold. They said to leave the mugs on the train and they'd be picked up – seems to be standard practice.'

'Thanks very much.' Iain took a large bite of croissant and washed it down with a slurp of coffee. 'Best I've ever tasted. There's the train moving now.'

Three hours later they neared the outskirts of Le Havre. Rosemary Jones came up.

'We're nearly at No 2. What will happen is this. The train staff need to stop here to unload hospital supplies. All patients will disembark. You could have gone on to the railhead with the train but orders are for you to go into the hospital for a few hours, have some lunch, a shave, you might even get some clean underclothes if you're lucky. You can have a rest. The Red Cross will transport you to the quayside in Le Havre in time to get the hospital ship. Is that satisfactory?'

They grinned back at her smiling face.

'Yes, thank you Sister. It sounds far more than we were expecting. That's fine, don't you think Iain?'

'Yes,' Iain rubbed his stubbly face. 'I could do with a shave.'

'By the way, Sister,' Magnus added, 'when you said yesterday that you had a friend, a colleague from Shetland, in Edinburgh, can you tell me her name. I might just know her.'

'Yes, it's Christina Sinclair. We're great friends.'

'But,' said Magnus, delighted. 'That's my sister. I wondered when you mentioned it but you had gone before I could say. What a coincidence.'

'That's amazing, wonderful. We've been friends since we started nursing. Of course, I didn't put two and two together. She's told me all about you.'

'*All* about me?'

'Well, I suppose not quite. Almost. But…'

'Well you've landed on your feet, Magnus,' put in Iain. 'Fancy being friends with the Sister-in-Charge. Some folk have all the luck. I wish I had a sister there too.'

'Do you have any sisters?' asked Magnus, diverted.

'Yes, but they're not there, both married. They can't supply me with an instant girlfriend.'

'All right, all right,' Rosemary Jones voice cut in. 'I need to see some of the other men. Here's No 2 General, I think. Good to meet you both and all the best. Magnus, I'll write to Christina to say that we've met.' They shook hands and she went off down the carriage.

'Here we are then. We'll need to be ticked off on a list and then ticked into the hospital.'

Some of the convalescent men were able to walk the short distance from the platform to No 2 General Hospital. As they walked, a long line of ambulances carrying the recently wounded men from the train to the safety of the hospital drove slowly past. At the door, orderlies pulled the stretchers bearing the men usually four at a time – from the ambulance and inside to await attention. The empty ambulance returned to the train for the next four.

197

Magnus said little. He knew this could go on for a long time until all were admitted. Iain, too looked on in silence. At length he spoke.

'Is it always like this?'

'Yes,' said Magnus. 'The numbers are enormous. They do their best but admitting a trainload of wounded personnel is a colossal task. Come on, I think it's this way. Be careful where you're going.'

In the street outside the hospital grounds some soldiers had set up their stone and brick fireplaces. Immediately Magnus thought back to Royaumont. It's just the same. It's as if they look on hospitals as safe havens and cluster round.

Here their mid-day meal was in progress. The locals seemed relaxed, smiling at the soldiers, one or two even offering a few eggs. Magnus and Iain walked past acknowledging the cheery 'Hullos' of the soldiers, for once in a state of rest and relaxation, and went through the hospital gates. Once again, like Royaumont, the grounds were a mess of broken-down military equipment, a couple of vehicles, including another old ambulance, nothing of any use as it was.

Running the length of the front of the hospital was a verandah-type structure, glass-topped and open in front to the fresh air and spring sunshine. It was full of soldiers, now able to be up and dressed. Many of their uniforms were shabby, torn, slashed, and blood-stained, dried and dark. All looked muddy, clarted sometimes with mud, dried on telling an unspoken story of days and nights in the trenches and not enough replacement uniforms. A few wore the standard issue hospital blues. Most of the soldiers wore bandages. Arms in slings, limbs swathed in gauze and crêpe, some heads and faces heavily wrapped up, crutches lying beside men with amputations. Above the initial impression Magnus noted the buzz of chat, here a burst of laughter, there a snatch of song. A haze of smoke hung in the air. Here and there a man slept or dozed, apparently oblivious to the general hubbub.

They walked inside. The difference in atmosphere was striking. The beds lay in the usual long rows, neat, tidy and clean. A VAD came forward with a list of names.

'Good afternoon,' she said. 'You'll be for the ferry tonight? Let me see. I've got to tick you in and then someone will tick you out tonight, to make sure you go.' She smiled. 'Only a joke, but we have noted that visitors in transit are often so happy with their wee rest here that they don't want to go. Now, come,' she added. 'Lunch is being served through here.'

The Red Cross vehicles came for them at seven o'clock that evening. It was dusk and by the time they crossed Le Havre, diverting as they came to roads closed through enemy action, it was completely dark. Street lighting was minimal. His Majesty's Hospital Ship *Donegal* lay alongside, large, two funnelled, painted white, with a green band running from stem to stern. On either side was painted a huge, unmistakeable red cross. For further identification at night, the *Donegal*, in common with other hospital ships, carried on the rail at either side of the stern, a long row of lights, red on the port side and green on the starboard.

'Come on Iain. Time to go now.' Magnus descended the steps of the Red Cross ambulance and turned.

'Yes, yes, I suppose so.' Iain joined him. 'It's a funny feeling, in a way. Almost unreal. I can't believe it's happening. Are you sure we're safe in that boat? I mean, ship. It seems pretty vulnerable to me.'

'It's as safe as houses.' Magnus smiled ruefully as he realised what he had just said and remembered all the shattered houses they had seen.

'Well, you know what I mean. It's as safe as anywhere. And, it's got all these red and green lights showing and the hospital ship insignia. We'll be fine. It's only for a few hours. We'll be in Southampton before dawn.'

The other men bound for the ship streamed past them, one or two looking back curiously as they went up the gangway with their bags.

'I don't know, I think I'll maybe just stay here, somewhere.' Iain looked around vaguely.

'Iain, you can't stay here. Come on, up the gangway with me and we'll find somewhere to sit.'

'No, I really don't want to do this.' He turned away.

'Iain, it's time you had your tablets again. You'll feel better then. I saw the Sister at No 2 General check them on the list and give them to the driver. The Sister on board will have them now. Come on.' Magnus took his arm and tried to steer him towards the gangway.

'Is there a problem?' They turned to see a Sister approaching, white veil and red cape fluttering in the breeze. She carried the usual clipboard and list of names. 'I'm Sister Wheelhouse – yes, I know,' as a flicker of an amused smile crossed Magnus's face '– it's a good name for being on a ship. Blame my father.'

'Good evening Sister.' Magnus saluted, relieved to see her. 'I'm Captain Magnus Sinclair and this is Lieutenant Iain Dawkins, both walking patients. We're due to join this hospital ship tonight.'

'That's fine,' she said. 'I'll just check this list. Yes, here you are, Lieutenant Dawkins and now Captain Sinclair, just a minute –' her finger hovered over the names – 'the S's are always at the tail-end aren't they? Ah yes, there you are.' She ticked his name with a flourish. 'Now, gentlemen, shall we embark?' She took hold of Iain's other arm and between them they walked him to the gangway.

'But, but,' Iain pulled back. 'I don't want to do this. I don't think you can make me.'

'Now Mr Dawkins, it's important you take these few steps up the gangway. Captain Sinclair and I'll help you but you need to do it.'

'Captain Sinclair?' He turned to Magnus holding his other arm. 'Are you Captain Sinclair?'

'Yes,' said Magnus. 'Now let's go.'

'So, who are you?' Iain turned to the Sister.

'I'm Sister Wheelhouse, *Major* Wheelhouse. Now Mr Dawkins, I'm ordering you to get up that gangway.'

199

It was slow, but they made it. At one point Magnus thought that Iain was going to refuse again, but Sister Wheelhouse was made of stern stuff, brought up in the old school that stood no nonsense.

'Come on, Sir, one foot in front of another, up you go, it's not far. There we are. No bos'un to pipe you on board I'm afraid. You'll have to put up with me. Now, you're due meds I think, according to your details.'

'Yes please,' said Iain, quite subdued, looking around. 'Is this where we sit?'

'Well, I think we should go into our ward sitting area inside, don't you? I'm afraid we don't have berths for you – they're all full up with the folk who are heading for further acute treatment but our reclining seats are very comfortable. I'll show you. Mind your heads at the low doorways.'

She led the way into a large area half-full of men sitting in groups. Now and then there were small cubicle-like areas. It was to one of these that she led Magnus and Iain.

'These are your seats for the voyage.' She looked directly at them. 'I'd be grateful if you'd stay here as much as you can please. You've a bell here directly connected to the ward office which is quite close. Please ring the bell if you've any worries. Orderlies will be round every now and again to see that everyone is all right and bringing night-time drinks. And, I will be doing my own rounds. Is that clear?'

'Yes Sister.'

'Now, if you would wait here please Mr Dawkins, I'll get your tablets. Captain Sinclair, could I have a word please?' Magnus followed her to the ward office.

'Thank you for coming through Captain. I understand that you've been accompanying Mr Dawkins on your journey from Royaumont.'

'Yes, that's right, on an unofficial basis. There were staff on the first ambulance and on the train and then here in Le Havre.'

'How's he been?'

'Not too bad, as long as he has his meds on time. A bit shaky in the Royaumont ambulance, but quite co-operative. In fact, trying to get him on the ship here is the first instance I've seen of more or less refusal. I was glad to see you.'

'Yes, I could see that you were struggling. We're grateful to you for doing this. Now, in the meantime, I'll see to his meds, and would you mind being with him for a few more hours until Southampton. I'll keep a watch on you both and please ring the bell at any time.'

'Yes, of course. That's no problem. He's a nice boy. He needs a bit of help.'

'Yes, but I'm very aware that you also have had a very bad time. Did you rest today?'

'Yes we were able to stretch out for a while at No 2 General.'

'That's good but, you need to try and sleep tonight too. You've a long road in front of you. Which reminds me, although you'll be booked on to a special carriage for returning wounded on the troop train, I'll arrange for Mr Dawkins to have an orderly escort him to London and then to Edinburgh. I think that's the best thing.'

'Thank you very much Sister.' Magnus felt a great feeling of relief. He was very tired.

'I'm only doing my duty Captain Sinclair. I'm concerned about you both. Now, Mr Dawkins' meds. I'll see to them, and *you* need to sit down and forget you're a doctor for a wee while and try and be a patient. Understand?' He looked at her and saw the twinkle in her eye softening the stern words.

'Yes Sister.'

'Right, thank you for your time, please go and rest. I'll be with you in a minute.'

At the same time as HMHS *Donegal* was quietly slipping out of her berth in Le Havre, Sister Rosemary Jones headed for the telephone exchange in No 2 General Hospital where she was spending the night.

The telephonist, a Corporal in the Signals Corps turned from his switchboard and smiled.

'Can I help you, Sister?'

'Yes, please. At least I hope so.'

'I can try.'

'Do you think you could get me this number please? It's Edinburgh, the Royal Infirmary of Edinburgh. Would that be possible?' She held out the number.

'It should be. I don't see why not. May take a few minutes.' He took the slip of paper and turned again to his connections.

Ten minutes later, he turned back to her. 'It's ringing now. I'll wait until they pick it up and speak, then you can speak on that telephone over there.' He pointed to a telephone hanging on the wall a few yards away.

'You know what to do, do you?'

'Yes, I think so.'

'Right, oh they're picking up now, just a minute. Hello, hello,' he said into the mouthpiece. 'Hello, is that Edinburgh? I'm speaking from No 2 General Hospital, Le Havre, France. Hold the line please. I have a call for you.' He nodded to Rosemary. She picked up her telephone.

'Hello?'

'Hello,' the voice said. 'Hello, can I help you.'

'Yes, please. I'm trying to get a message to Staff Nurse Christina Sinclair.'

'OK, just a moment please. I'm just looking for her name on the list … yes, I've got her now. She's in Ward 16 male, on nights. She'll be there now. Will I give it a go?'

'Yes please.'

Rosemary could hear the connection being made. This was more than she'd expected. She could even hear the conversation.

'Call on the line from France for Staff Nurse Christina Sinclair. Is she there please?'

'Mercy me, from France you say? Whatever next? Anyway the staff are not supposed to receive calls on duty.'

'Sister,' Rosemary heard the operator say. 'Sister it's from France, I expect it's important. And time's running out.'

'Ye-s, yes, I suppose so. Oh well, hang on – Staff Nurse Sinclair, telephone. Now. Come along, and don't be too long blethering.'

'Yes, Sister. No, Sister.' Listening, Rosemary smiled to herself.

'Hello?' Christina said.

'Hello Christina, it's Rosemary, Rosemary Jones.'

'Rosemary, in France? Is everything all right? Lowrie, Magnus – are they all right…?'

'Christina, listen. Magnus is on his way to Scotland. He should be in Edinburgh, the day after tomorrow on the troop-train. I just thought you'd like to know.'

'Oh yes, thank you. That's wonderful. I'll find out when the train's due and try and meet him. Oh Rosemary, thank you so much for letting me know. Is he all right?'

'Yes, he's doing well. He left here…oh there's the pips. Bye…' They were cut off.

Rosemary hung up and returned to the switchboard Corporal.

'Thank you very much.'

'Get your message across, did you, Sister?'

'Yes, thank you, just.'

'They don't give you long, do they? Just three minutes.'

'No, but I'm glad to get that. Do I owe you anything?'

'No no, between hospitals. No problem.'

'Thank you. That was important to us both. Good night.'

'Night, then, Sister.' He turned back to his switchboard with its flashing lights.

Chapter 31

'Lowrie, what a surprise.' Edie opened the Birkenshaw back door to his quick knock. 'It's great to see you. How are you? You look well.'

'I *am* well, Edie, thank you. And you? All well here?'

'Yes, we're all fine thank you. Come in. See Meg, look who's arrived.'

'Don't get up Meg.' Lowrie went over to her and shook hands. 'You look fine too.'

'Ach, I'm fine, Lowrie, but they keep telling me to sit down.'

'Oh, Meg, you do a big share of the work.'

'Well, I don't know, since Mrs Sinclair got Bertha in to help, I just feel I'm not pulling my weight.'

'I can't imagine you not pulling your weight Meg,' Lowrie said. 'You keep this ship going.'

'Ay, well, I'm getting so heavy with all this sitting around, I'm likely to sink the ship.'

'Come on Meg, if you think like that we'll all go down with you. Now, Lowrie,' Edie turned to him. 'Are you going through to see Mrs Sinclair?'

'Is she free?'

'Yes, she's in the wee sitting room. Come on, I'll take you through.'

'See you later Meg.'

'She's all right really,' whispered Edie as they went through. 'Just gets a bit touchy about what she thinks is not doing enough.' She knocked on the sitting room door, and put her head round.

'A visitor, Mrs Sinclair.'

'Thanks Edie.' Charlotte looked up from her letter-writing.

'Lowrie, hello, where did you spring from?' They shook hands, then she said with a choke in her voice, 'No, no, I need to hug you, I'm so pleased to see you back safely.'

'Now, how are things here? How are you, Mrs Sinclair? You've had quite a winter, I'm thinking.'

'Yes,' she said, 'but I think we're coming on now, especially now that the spring is with us, sort of. Shetland spring, you know. It's a long time coming.'

'Ay,' he agreed. 'I was sorry to hear about Mr Sinclair's illness.'

'Thank you. He's up and about most days now, and getting outside, and walking further each day. It's wonderful what can be done nowadays. Would you like to see him? I'm sure he'd be delighted to see you.'

'I'd like to see him too, but, first, could we talk for a minute?' Lowrie hesitated.

'Yes of course. Lowrie, what is it? Is there anything wrong? It's not, not Magnus again?'

'No, no, and anyway if there were, you'd have heard long before I could get here with any news.'

'Yes, of course, you're right. Well, what is it?'

'Mrs Sinclair…'

.Couldn't you just say Charlotte as Magnus does?'

203

'Charlotte,' he said.

'There, that's much better. Now,' she looked at him.

'Charlotte, I was on my way to Shetland on leave and,' he took a deep breath.

'Yes,' she said encouragingly.

'I stopped off at Edinburgh.' Get on with it thought Lowrie. You're behaving like a love-sick swain.

'That was a good place to stop. Was it busy? At least it would have broken your journey. How long did you stay?'

'Two days. Charlotte, I need to say this.'

'Sorry, Lowrie. I won't interrupt again.'

'I stopped off in Edinburgh and Christina met me off the train.' The last came out in a rush.

'Christina met you off the train? But that's a lovely thing to do. How did she know you were going to be there? Is she well? She always sounds so well in her letters, but you never know. I sometimes feel she works so hard that she might be pulling the wool over our eyes.'

'Christina is very well,' said Lowrie firmly. 'Very well, indeed. Charlotte, I knew Christina was going to meet the train. I stopped in Edinburgh especially so that we could meet.'

'O-h-h, I see, or, I think I see. What time of day was this?'

'Morning, about five days ago. I got into Lerwick on the boat yesterday morning.'

'So what did you do when you got off the train?'

'Went and had breakfast in the North British.'

'You what?'

'Breakfast in the N.B. What could be better? We were both starving. Christina'd been on duty all night and I'd been on the train from London.'

'Of course,' said Charlotte. 'Just what one does. Go and have breakfast in the poshest hotel in town. What did you have to eat?'

'Eggs Benedict.'

Charlotte raised her eyes to the ceiling and laughed.

'No ordinary scrambled eggs for you then.' Lowrie watched her and then joined in.

'Well, it was a special occasion,' he said when he was able, 'and, I'd just been paid.'

'Yes, of course.' Charlotte remembered where he had been. 'Do they always keep your pay until you get back?'

'Yes, or for when we go for rest behind the lines, which happens on a sort of rotational basis. There's nowhere else to spend it. It's better, safer this way, I think.'

They paused for a moment then Lowrie spoke again.

'Charlotte there's something else.'

'Yes, Lowrie?'

'Christina and I, well, we love each other very much. We want to get married – soon.'

'Lowrie.' She stood up, walked to the window and looked out. When she turned back to him, he could see the tears on her face. He got up to face her.

'Lowrie, this is such good news. I can't think of anyone I would rather see Christina marrying. I am so happy for you both. Is it official yet? Do your parents know?'

'Well, I told them when I arrived home but swore them to silence so that I'd time to come here and speak to you, and, also, I need to speak to Mr Sinclair. Christina was very sure that whatever we have agreed between us, *he* needs to be given his place as her father. If he's able, I must ask him for Christina's hand in marriage. How is he Charlotte? Do you think that he could cope with this, today?'

Charlotte considered.

'The first thing is, yes, Christina is right. I know that she's over twenty-one but fathers still like to be asked and some fathers would be very offended or even angry if they weren't. I think Alexander will appreciate your acknowledgement of what he'll see as his right, as Christina's father. You just need to do it. Would you like to go through now?'

'How is he?'

'Well, he's quite fine today. He's up and about, been out for his constitutional, sitting through there in the sunshine with the paper.' She walked to the door.

'Would you like me to come with you?'

'Yes, please, please come.'

'Very well, just one thing before we go through...' He stopped in mid-step.

'Yes?'

'What you've just told me today has made me very happy. I just want you to know.'

'Thank you, Charlotte. I'll tell Christina.'

'Now, let's go.'

Alexander was coping with the pages of the *Shetland Times*. His weak arm was not co-operating and the broadsheets seemed to have taken on a life of their own as he tried to wrestle them to a new page. One or two had reached the floor by the time Charlotte and Lowrie entered.

'Alexander, here's a sight for sore eyes – mercy, what's happened to the paper?' Charlotte went to him to help.

'Ach, I'm just a useless old man,' he groused. 'Can't even handle the paper.'

'No you're not and here's someone else who doesn't think that. Here's Lowrie, home on leave.'

'Lowrie?' Alexander was instantly diverted. 'Come in my boy, never mind the mutterings of an old man. How are you? Let me take a look at you. You look not too bad considering. Grown a moustache too, I see. Must be the fashion nowadays, I suppose. All the photos have men with mousers. Used to mean a sign of dignity and being grownup.' He stroked his own bristly top lip. Lowrie laughed.

'Hello Mr Sinclair. It's good to see you looking, and sounding, if I may say so, so well.'

'Good to see you too, my boy. How long are you home for?'

'Just a few days. I have to go back next week.'

'H-mm. To France?'

'Yes, but I do believe, you know, that the tide is turning in our favour.'

'This does seem to be the general consensus.' Alexander nodded. 'The papers try to give us an account but of course they're all censored and you have to try to get, well, the feel of the thing. I hope you are right, and, that the whole thing doesn't take too long.'

Charlotte slipped out as they settled to their discussion and opinions. She returned a few minutes later with coffee on a tray followed by Edie.

'This is the last of our coffee,' she said. 'No more till the next rations come through. And Edie has made scones.'

'Edie's scones.' Lowrie smiled at her. 'Do you remember giving me scones at the back door of Da Peerie Skulehoose when Magnus and I were boys?'

'I remember it well,' she said. 'I think you knew when I was baking.'

He took a bite and nodded happily. 'You haven't lost your touch. You'll need to give lessons.' She laughed at him.

'Will that be all for the moment, Mrs Sinclair?'

'Yes, thank you Edie.'

They sat for a moment.

'When do you think you'll be back again, Lowrie?'

'It's difficult to say. Sometimes you get home-leave reasonably regularly but sometimes it's a long time. There's no real reason, and no real pattern that I can see. It's even worse for the men.'

'Where are you going to be next?'

Lowrie shook his head. 'I can't say,' he said. 'We're not allowed to say. All I can tell you is France.'

'Yes, yes, of course. One has to be so careful. Sorry, my boy, I didn't want to put you on the spot.'

'That's all right,' said Lowrie. 'It's natural for people to want to know where their friends are. It must be very difficult, not… knowing…' his voice trailed off.

'Yes,' said Charlotte. 'It was bad when we were so anxious about Magnus. The not knowing, I mean. But you saw him, didn't you? In Royaumont?'

'Yes, that was a wonderful meeting,' said Lowrie. 'We had lost touch, you see, at the beginning of the war, and then I heard, quite by chance that he might be there. I borrowed the CO's horse, called appropriately enough, Dobbin – we were behind the lines at the time – and went along to find out. And there he was. Large as life,' he added, swallowing the emotion that always hit him when he recalled that meeting.

'That must have been important for you both,' said Alexander. Lowrie nodded.

'It was.'

'And now, he's coming to Glamis, to get fit again. I want him to come home, to Shetland. It would be good, very good. What d'you think Lowrie, don't you think he should come home?' Lowrie didn't know what to say.

'Well, I – well, I think he'll need a bit of rest and recuperation at Glamis before he's able to think of further travelling. He and the medical staff need to see how he is and how he gets on.'

'Yes, but, I really think…' Alexander started.

Charlotte moved in to steer the conversation away from troubled waters.

'Alexander,' she said, 'Lowrie was in Edinburgh the other day. Who do you think he saw?'

'Edinburgh? Why did you stop in Edinburgh and not come straight home?'

'I stopped in Edinburgh,' repeated Lowrie, 'because I wanted to meet somebody.'

'Oh, I see. Well that's interesting.'

'Yes,' said Lowrie. 'I met Christina. Or rather, she met me, off the train, the other day, in the morning.'

'In the morning? Shouldn't she have been in her bed? She's on night duty.'

'Yes, I know,' said Lowrie patiently, 'but she came to the station to meet me and we spent the day together. She had the time off.' Keep going, he said to himself.

'Mr Sinclair,' he said. 'I've come to ask you for Christina's hand in marriage. I want her to be my wife.'

'Your *wife*? Her hand in *marriage*?'

'Yes, em, please?'

'But she's only a girl. Not old enough.'

'She's nearly twenty five now,' Lowrie reminded him. 'She's grown up now.'

'And you, how old are you?' Lowrie sighed inwardly.

'Thirty-five,' he said.

'Hmph. Well,' Alexander admitted in a grudging fashion, 'I don't suppose difference in age matters, does it Charlotte?' She smiled at him.

'But,' he went on, 'marriage, in the middle of a War...or...' he looked up. 'You'll be wanting to wait until the War ends of course.'

'Well, no, not exactly,' Lowrie took a deep breath. 'We really want to get married on my next leave.'

'But, you might get killed. And then she'll be left a widow.'

'Yes,' said Lowrie, 'but I might get killed anyway, and she would be left anyway.'

'Yes, but at least she wouldn't be a widow.'

'Is there something wrong with being a widow? Apart from one's husband being dead?'

'No, no,' said Alexander, hastily. 'Not exactly. But it does mean that the widow is, well, less likely to get married again, she's, well – well, you know what I mean … what would her chances be of getting married again? Some men don't want, well, you know, someone who's been married before. And,' he added, 'she could be left with a child. What would she do then?'

'Look, Mr Sinclair.' Lowrie leaned towards him, biting back swift angry ripostes. He spoke firmly, with conviction.

'Christina and I love each other very much. We want to get married as soon as we can. We are fully aware that difficulties could lie ahead. We want to make the most of our lives together – however short or long that may be and I've come to you today as Christina's father, to ask for your blessing.'

Alexander sat, lost in thought. He thought of his doctor-son Magnus, so brave going down the cliff and saving Alfie Williamson's life, so stubborn, so wilful sometimes. He's like me, the realisation hit him. He remembered the day of his final row with Magnus, the day he had sent him away to Canada, with orders not to come back. He would give a lot to undo what he'd done that day. His actions had lost him his son. Was he to lose his daughter too? He surely would, just as if he'd shut the door on her himself. Just because he wanted to dictate, organise, tell them what to do. And why? Because of some outdated attitudes? He couldn't risk it. Come on, he said to himself. Grow up. Show Lowrie you're happy about this. Give them your blessing. Don't have another lot of unhappiness hanging over us.

He looked up, struggled to his feet to face Lowrie.

'Lowrie, my boy,' he said. 'I give you and my beloved daughter Christina my blessing to get married any time that is suitable for you. Just,' he stopped and swallowed. 'Take care of her, won't you?'

The last came out in a rush as he groped for a handkerchief. Charlotte tucked one into his hand and he wiped his eyes.

'Margery would be so pleased.' He looked round. 'Wouldn't she Charlotte?' She nodded, smiling, remembering the loving mother who had wanted so much to see her children grow up.

Lowrie guided him back to his chair.

'Mr Sinclair, I will love, respect and care for Christina for the rest of my life. Thank you for your blessing.'

Chapter 32

APRIL 1917

For once the troop train was on time. Christina stood and stared. This is even worse than the last time. I haven't seen Magnus for about nine years. I've no idea how much he might have changed. If I was worried about recognising Lowrie, I'm twenty times more worried now. Stupid of me for wanting to surprise him. But, I couldn't have got a message to him anyway.

The hundreds of men disgorged from the front of the train, walked past, some in groups, some alone, some standing around, a little lost, awaiting their next step. At the other end were three hospital train carriages, easily identifiable by their big red crosses.

That's where he'll be, she thought. He's a patient in transit. He'll be with the walking wounded, the convalescents. As the crowd from the front of the train thinned she noticed platform staff beginning to open the other doors. Slowly men began to disembark on foot, leaving those on stretchers until last. She watched closely.

It took a long time. Many of the 'walking wounded' were quite incapacitated and needed help to negotiate the step to the platform. Orderlies stood at regular intervals along the length of the carriages. Others stood with wheelchairs awaiting a specific person. At one door there seemed to be some confusion, or – reluctance, it seemed to Christina as she watched. A pale young man stood at the open door. Outside, on the platform with his hand up to help stood an orderly.

'Come on, Sir,' Christina heard him say. 'We're in Edinburgh now. It's all fine here. I think a car's waiting for you in the station forecourt. If you'd just come now please, Sir.'

'No, no, I think I'll just stay here. I'm quite comfortable on the train.'

'But you must get off, Sir. The train is going to be cleaned. And then more troops are getting on. It's going to London tomorrow with men going to France.'

'France?'

'Yes Sir. Come on Mr Dawkins, please, you're holding everyone else up. Are you all right Sir?' he called to a man standing behind.

'Yes, I am, thanks,' said a voice. 'Come on Iain, let's get off this train. It's only you and me at this door now. Everyone else has given up and gone to another exit.'

'Sorry Magnus, I just can't. I can't cross that gap.'

'That's what you said in London, Iain. You managed then. Go on, give it a go. Look, I'll oxter you, and Corporal MacPhee can take both of your hands. Like we did the last time. Corporal …'

'Sir?'

'Shall we do that?'

'Yes Sir.'

Christina watched all this with interest, and delight that her quest for Magnus had been simplified so suddenly. With Magnus behind, supporting Iain under his arms and the orderly taking both hands, they persuaded him to put one foot on the step.

'Now the other, Sir,' encouraged the orderly.

'I…I don't think I can.'

'Yes you can,' said Magnus's voice. 'Lift it up, move it forward and down.'

'Now I've got both feet on this tiny step.'

'Well, move one, Sir. That's it. And the other. There, Sir.' The Corporal looked up at Magnus.

'Thanks for your help, Sir. I think we could almost say, "With one bound he was free". Come on now Mr Dawkins, give Captain Sinclair space to get down the steps himself.'

'Oh, sorry Magnus.' Iain moved along. 'Sorry. I'm all right now. It's just crossing that gap, so frightening.' He shuddered. Christina felt sorry for him. She had seen men with shellshock before. Magnus came forward to the carriage step, trailing his kitbag.

'Here,' said the orderly, 'let me take that.'

'Thanks.' He handed it over and then stepped down. He looked around.

'I'm here…Scotland … Scotland. I haven't been here for nine years. I can't believe I'm back.' He put a hand over his eyes. The other searched his pocket. He blew his nose loudly.

Christina couldn't bear it. She looked at her once well-known and still loved brother, now thin and grey and ill-looking, so changed from the stalwart young man he once had been. She stepped forward.

'Magnus, Magnus. It's all right.' He looked up sharply, saw her standing there. He frowned.

'Who, who, are you? Do we know each other? Have you…?'

'Magnus, it's me.' She couldn't keep him guessing any longer. It was too much.

'It's me, Christina.'

'Christina?' he repeated. 'Christina. By all that's wonderful. Where did you spring from? How did you know I was here, today, now?'

'I had a wee telephone call telling me you'd be on the train and I decided to come down and give you a surprise. So here I am.'

'Surprise? You've nearly knocked me over.' He turned to the puzzled looking Iain and Corporal MacPhee. 'Sorry, I'm getting distracted here. May I present my sister, Miss Christina Sinclair. Christina, Lieutenant Iain Dawkins and Corporal MacPhee. We all travelled together from France.'

'Now,' said Corporal MacPhee, after the salutes and handshakes were over, 'if you don't mind sir, I expect Mr Dawkins's car is waiting and I think,' he nodded tactfully, 'there's someone with a clipboard waiting to tick you in and give you further information.'

'You're quite right Corporal. Thank you for your help.' Magnus turned to Iain.

'All the best.' They saluted each other, shook hands then Magnus clasped Iain's arms.

'We've been through a bit together.' Iain nodded unable to speak.

'Take care now. Hope to see you sometime.' Iain raised his hand in farewell and, with the orderly following, walked slowly away towards the exit.

Magnus turned back towards Christina.

'Sorry about that. Poor man. Shellshock. Hope he gets on well in Craiglockhart.'

'Is that where he's going?'

'Yes, do you know it?'

'Well, not to work in. I've escorted patients there and I've a couple of friends who work there.'

'Excuse me, Sir,' a voice interrupted. 'Are you Captain Magnus Sinclair going to Glamis Castle?'

'Yes, I am. I'm sorry to have kept you waiting.'

'That's all right sir. It's interesting, watching the troops come back and all that. Now, Sir, I'll just tick you off and I need to tell you Sir, that your train to Dundee leaves Waverley, platform 6 at 11.10. Here's your ticket Sir. That gives you about two hours to wait, Sir.'

'Thank you,' said Magnus. 'Do you know where we can get breakfast while we wait?'

'Yes Sir. That brings me to the next instruction I have to pass on to personnel in transit. We would prefer it if you didn't leave the station'– the man looked up – 'we don't want to lose you Sir. A very good breakfast buffet is available in the station. I'm sure your young lady will be welcome there too.'

'She's my sister.' Magnus smiled at her. 'I didn't know she was coming.'

'Well, that's very nice Sir. You're very welcome, Ma'am . Is that everything Sir? Any questions?'

'Yes, what happens at Dundee, have you any idea?'

'Oh yes, Sir, that was the other thing. A car will be there to meet you and take you to Glamis. You're the only one today.'

'Thank you very much.' Magnus saluted.

'Good bye Sir.' The man moved away.

Magnus turned towards Christina.

'My wee sister, all grown up. Come here. I can't believe you're real.' His voice was muffled in her hair as he held her. 'I thought I was hearing things when I heard your voice. That hasn't changed.'

'Isn't it funny,' she said. 'That's what I recognised too. Your voice from the train, trying to get Mr Dawkins to step off.'

'Have I changed so much?'

'Magnus, from what I've heard, you've been very ill. You're bound to look a bit bleary-eyed.'

'Bleary-eyed? I haven't had a proper drink for, well, ages.'

'Well, you've been up all night and travelling for days I should think. Give yourself time. Anyway, I'd know those blue eye eyes anywhere. Come on,' she added, 'let's find that buffet the clipboard man mentioned. I'm starving.'

'Nurses always are – look,' he pointed. 'I see the sign from here. Let's go.'

'Now, tell me,' he asked when they were settled at a small corner table at the window. 'Tell me about how you are. No, firstly, tell me how did you know I was going to be on that train?'

'Rosemary Jones.'

'Rosemary Jones – aha, yes, she knew, of course. And she said you're friends. She's a witch, magicking a meeting.'

'A very good witch. Careful what you say about my friends.'

'Yes, she might be flying about on her broomstick. No, seriously, she was excellent on the hospital train. A great nurse. So helpful. Now,' he said, 'tell me how *you* are. How's work?'

'Magnus, I'm fine. I love my job. I feel I'm doing something to help the War effort. The men seem to be happy to come to Edinburgh. Mind you,' she said. Her voice wobbled. 'It's all a bit awful sometimes. Tragic to see some of the wounds and damage that some won't recover from. What will they do with their lives? We may be throwing men at the War but we're not ready to deal with what comes after. As a country I mean. The Government hasn't thought it through. They're safe in hospital but what happens next?'

'They send them back to the Front?'

'Yes, before they're able. And for what? Magnus, will you have to go back? How are you really?'

He looked down and sighed.

Christina reached over and touched his hand.

'Magnus?'

'Christina, I feel so bad about this. I…I don't think they're going to let me go back.'

'But, Magnus, why do you feel so bad about it?'

'I have such a lot of experience now. It's a waste. I should be there with the rest, working, saving lives – and I'm not going to be allowed to do it. Medicine is my life. I know I could do it if they'd let me – but they won't. I know. I had a batch of the high heid yins round, you know RAMC Staff Officers. They took one look at my X-Rays of my head, and internals with shrapnel still sitting there, and shook their heads. So that's me for Glamis to convalesce and then who knows what? I couldn't stand a damned desk job for life.'

'Oh Magnus, I'm so sorry.'

'Thanks.' He held her hand tightly. 'Sorry for that. Shouldn't feel so sorry for myself. Lowrie said in his last letter that I should accept that I've done my bit. He's probably right but at the moment it's very difficult. Talking of Lowrie, have you heard from him, by the way?   It was very good to see him in Royaumont – what a surprise. And, how we reminisced. We had lost touch you know,' he went on. 'Now we've resolved never to lose touch again and remember always we're best friends and all that…   Anyway, *have* you heard from him? Christina?' He tapped the table. 'Wake up.'

'Sorry,' she jumped. 'I was just thinking…'

'Well?'

'About Lowrie, I suppose. And yes, before you ask again, I *have* heard from him.' She smiled a small secret smile.

'Christina. Why are you smiling like that? Have you any news about him?' He remembered the day when Lowrie so tentatively told him about his feelings for Christina.

She picked up the teapot. 'More tea?'

'You can be most annoying you know – just like you were when you were wee. You were always throwing toys out of the pram just for me to pick up.'

She refilled his cup and her own and set the teapot down.

'Lowrie's fine,' she said. 'He's very fine. He's just gone back to France from a week's leave...'

'Oh yes, I knew he was going sometime. You mean he's been and gone?'

'He stopped off in Edinburgh.'

'Pity I missed him,' Magnus went on. 'I would have liked to have seen...what did you say? He stopped off in *Edinburgh?*'

'That's called hearing but not listening.' She laughed at the expression on his face.

'All right, I'll tell you. Not everything of course – just the basics...'

'Christina...'

'Lowrie and I,' she went on. 'Well, we've been writing now and again since last year. We arranged to meet in Edinburgh on his leave, which we did. He asked me to marry him. I said "yes", he went on to Jarlshavn and asked Charlotte and Father if he could have my hand in marriage – what a stupid expression. Father should have said, "Take all of her while you're about it". Anyway I just had a letter from him, Lowrie I mean, a quick note really, saying Father was reasonably happy, a few caveats but eventually said "yes" and we'll get married on his next leave and well, that's all really.' She stopped.

'Christina...' Magnus stopped too. His handkerchief was out again.

'Why do I keep crying?' he complained. He sniffed loudly, gulped some tea. 'Oh I'm so pleased. That's the best news. Lowrie and my wee sister. I'm so happy for you.'

'Are you sure? I don't want you to feel I'm taking Lowrie away from you.'

'Oh that's quite different. Don't worry. When's his next leave? Can I come to the wedding?'

'Of course. You must come. Not sure when – even if he got a week-end pass. I'd a letter from Mother telling me about Lowrie's visit from her point of view. She's delighted and said Lowrie and Father were fine together. Mind you,' she said. 'I don't think they'll be able to come to the wedding.'

'How *is* Father?'

'I think he's all right as long as he sticks to his routine and areas and situations where he feels safe. I can't see him going anywhere on the *St Clair*. Are you going to be able to go to Jarlshavn?'

'I don't think so at the moment,' he said. 'I'll need to see how things are at Glamis.'

'Well, all right but when you're able I think they'd be very happy to see you.' He sighed again.

'I know, but it's one for the future. Now,' he said, changing the subject. 'D'you think we should be moving to Platform 6 to see if my train's there. It's about ten to eleven. I'd better get the bill.'

'Heavens, is that the time already?' She jumped up and started gathering her things.

'Can you manage your kitbag all right?'

'Yes, if I don't have to carry it too far. It depends on the weight. I don't have that much stuff here. Some is in store for the duration. Goodness knows what state it will be in when I get it back. Here's Platform 6. Now, where's my ticket?'

213

They stood outside the carriage, awkwardly, not quite knowing what to say.

'Christina,' Magnus began. 'I just want you to know…'

'Yes?'

'I just want you to know, I'm so proud of you, so proud of my wee sister, and so pleased that you're going to marry Lowrie. You've made me a very happy man. Whatever happens, remember that.' He held out his arms to her.

'Magnus,' she sniffed into his coat. 'What makes you say that? You sound so serious.'

'I just want you to know,' he said. 'And another thing,' he added. 'I'm so glad you came today. Will you come to Glamis?'

'I will indeed. If only to see that you're behaving yourself.' She sniffed again. 'I'll need to find out the train times.'

'Well, we know this one goes at 11.10. And, saying that,' he looked at his watch. 'Oh yes, here's the man with the clipboard.'

'All present and correct, Sir?' said the man.

'Yes, just getting on.'

'Thank you Sir.' The man moved on, ticking his name off.

'Is it always like that?'

'Not usually, but they need to keep tabs on freedom-loving patients. They don't want us to escape. Now, my dear, I must go. I can see steam coming out of that funnel.'

'Take care, Magnus. Keep in touch.'

'I'll tell you all about life in a castle.' He saluted and climbed on board.

She waved until the train ran out of sight in the tunnel leading from the station.

Chapter 33

17 APRIL 1917

Edie came in with the empty washing basket.

'There, that's it all out now. What a lovely day it is. Now, what else is there?'

'Sit down and have a cup of tea,' advised Meg. 'It's newly made. The soup's on. Have a break before you start yesterday's ironing. There must have been a lot for you to be washing on a Tuesday.'

'Yes, there was, but no more than usual. I just didn't have time yesterday, with taking time to go to the knitting group.'

'How's it going?'

'Very well,' said Edie. 'They fairly make you feel proud. I think everyone in the village now is knitting for the troops. They're going to get a lot of helmets and socks in France and Flanders. Some even have Fair Isle knitted in.'

'I'm sure that's not regulation. And it can't be in khaki or it wouldn't show.'

'No, but they look good. Mrs Gilbertson puts in a wee bit moorit in everything she knits and Mrs Isbister has put in a line of fawn, but Annie Reid has even put in a touch of red.'

'Do you think they'll get past the London inspectors? They're meant to be khaki'

'Ay, ay, but why not? Give the lads a laugh –hello Mrs Sinclair – tea?'

'Yes, thank you, in a minute, but I've just noticed Jimmy coming with the mail. It's all right Edie, don't get up. I'll get it.'

Charlotte met the postie at the front door.

'Morning Mrs Sinclair. A few the day for you.'

'Thanks Jimmy.'

Charlotte went back in, looking through the letters. A couple for Alexander, one or two bills and one Army one, addressed to herself. That's funny, she thought, from France, for me? She frowned, slipped it into her pocket, went through to Alexander.

'Here's your mail.'

'Oh, thanks,' he said. 'Anything else important? Nothing from Magnus?'

'No, nothing.'

'Ah well, he'll barely have arrived, I suppose. Needs to find his way about and all that. Still, I wish he'd let us know.'

'He will as soon as he can, I expect.'

'Ay.' He returned to the previous week's *Shetland Times*.

Charlotte slipped away. Alone, upstairs, she took the letter from her pocket, turned it over. The censor's stamp partially covered the sender's name but –

'It's James,' she breathed. With haste, she tore it open, pulled out the flimsy sheet.

My dear Charlotte,

I'm writing to you alone today and I'd be grateful if you could keep the fact that I have written between ourselves. I can't say where I am or what we are doing. However, I feel a strong urge to write to you tonight. Charlotte, I am stretching my hand out to you over the miles and I feel that I'll get through today more easily if I write to you and communicate my thoughts to you before the day breaks.

Today will be a big day in the course of the War, whichever way it goes. You have been much on my mind. It is 04.00 hrs. Before I go, I need to write to you to let you know that I love you. I have always loved you. I know that you're not free for me to have and to hold but I need to make my peace with you. If I don't come back to Scotland, if I don't see you again, please believe that you are the only woman that I shall ever love.

I would give anything to undo the wrong that I have done to you. I have always loved you, even when I was at my most angry and stubborn and when I walked away from you and out of your life. Again I say it. You are the only woman I shall ever love. I know that it is too late but I need you to know this and that I am sorry.

Charlotte, I shall try and do my duty – in my mind it will not only be for the sake of our Lord, but also for you. I hold a picture of you next to my heart.

If you have read thus far, I thank you for that. Take care of yourself.

Always your loving,

James MacLeod.

Charlotte read the letter, gasped , then read it again.

'Oh, James, James, where are you,' she whispered, tears running down her cheeks. 'What can I do? When did he write this?' She looked at the letter.

The ninth?   But, today's the seventeenth. That's eight days ago. He could be, she couldn't believe it – he could be dead. What can I do? I could look at the paper – but he won't be in the Shetland paper. How else can I find out? I can't tell anybody.

'That's funny,' remarked Edie to Meg a while later. 'Mrs Sinclair didn't come back for her tea. It's cold now. Oh well, she maybe forgot.' She took the cup and poured the tea away.

Chapter 34

Magnus stepped out of the train at Dundee and looked around him. The station was busy, with soldiers coming home presumably on leave, others getting off and more getting on, women with baskets, men with brief cases, a few children holding tightly to the women's skirts, a couple of babies, one yelling lustily. The train picked up speed again as it steamed out of the station on its way further north. The disembarking people scattered. Magnus walked along the quickly emptying platform and looked around him. He had passed through Dundee in the past but always on his way somewhere.

A porter came hurrying up to him.

'Are you for Glamis? The Castle? I'm looking for a Captain Sinclair.'

'That's me.'

'Aha, found you. Good,' the man ticked his name on his sheet with relish. 'I like to see things tidied up. Your transport to the Castle is outside. If you go out, Sir, I'll tell your driver. He's just inside having a blether.'

'Thank you.'.

Magnus picked up his kitbag and walked slowly out of the station to find a small motor car waiting outside. The driver was nowhere to be seen.

'Sir, Sir, A'm coming.' He looked round. A medical orderly came limping towards him, stopped, and saluted.

'Sorry Sir. A'm driver the day. Burnett's the name. I was just in the office having a wee fly-cup. It's mair than a wee bit chilly. Let me cairry your kitbag for ye.' Magnus returned the salute.

'Thank you Burnett. Is this our vehicle?'

'Yes, Sir. It's nae muckle but it gets us aroon and,' he added, 'it's better than the gig and that bad-tempered horse. At least this is less open, even though it's a bit draughty. D'yc want to sit in the front or back, Sir?'

'I'm quite happy in the front, thanks.'

'That's fine Sir, good to have company.' He opened the door with a flourish. 'Now I jist have to get her stairted.'

He got the starting handle, rammed it into the front of the engine, and turned vigorously. The engine gave a few coughs and lapsed into silence. Another try, another few coughs.

'Sulky besom,' Burnett muttered. 'Sorry Sir,' he called to Magnus. 'Aye haippens. Gangs like an angel when naebiddy's here, then plays up and shows me up when A'm looking for perfect behaviour.'

'There might be a lesson there, Burnett.'

'What's that, Sir?'

'Don't look for good behaviour.'

'Ach Sir. Div ye ken aboot cars? They're jist like wimmin. Thrawn.' He swung the starting handle again, the engine roared into life, creating a judder that rippled through the car.

'There she is, she must have heard me and started just to spite me. Tellin ye – jist like wimmen.'

They started off with a jerk, away from the station, through the city and out into the countryside. Magnus gave a sigh of relief.

'Div you nae like the toon?'

'Not really. I prefer the wide open spaces.'

'Ay, ay, sae, div A, bit it's a peety ye still have tae come intae the toon fur messages and aa that.'

'Like meeting folk from trains?'

'Weel, Sir, at's different.' Burnett glanced at him.

'Are ye jist back fae the Front Sir?'

'Yes, you could say that. I was in hospital for a while.'

'Far aboots wis aat?'

'Place called Royaumont, in the north of France. It's a sort of converted Abbey. Run by women, actually, started by an Edinburgh doctor. It's got women doctors, sisters, VAD nurses, They, they saved my life.'

'Wimmen, aa o them?'

'Ay.'

'Fit haippened?'

'Well, I was unconscious for five weeks and had what seemed like a lot of shrapnel wounds. Not funny. But I'm a lot better now.' Magnus, anxious to turn the conversation, looked at his driver.

'Were you at the Front? I don't think you're far from home now, though, listening to you.'

'Na, na, Sir. A'm fae near Aiberdeen, up the Dee a bittie. Ay, A wis at the Front. At the Somme, ye ken.'

'Mphm.'

'Weel, A got een, a great dod o yon shrapnel, richt in the knee. Smashed it. That wis me. Man it wis afa sair. Onywey, the surgeon, an afa clivver mannie, he says tae me, "we're going to do our best and save this knee for you, Burnett". An he did. It took a lang time mind ye. A wis in plaister fur wiks. Bit A kin walk noo, wi a bit o a limp mind ye, bit A'm here an A can get aboot an they hinna pit me oot o the Airmy. A winna gang back tae the Front tho.'

He braked as a rabbit ran across the road.

'Ach, rabbits an pheasants, they're ay wi us.'

'How do you feel about not going back to the Front?'

'Weel Sir, whiles A hear aboot it an A feel a bit guilty that a'm nae there. Then A remind masel that A widna be ony gweed onywey, an jist be a scunner tae abiddy else. Here, bein an orderly, A can be o some help an A'm able tae dee it.'

'Well said.'

'Are ee gaan back?'

'I'm not sure…' Magnus hesitated, unwilling to give a definite answer.

'Weel sir, A can see ee're a doctor. Ee'll be able tae be o eese onywey.'

'I hope so.'

'A ken so. They're cryin oot fur doctors. Noo, Sir, here we are. Jist a wee bittie noo. Haud on. It's an afa rough road. Naebiddy's touchcd it fur years.' He negotiated a pothole and continued, 'Watch oot fur Lady Elizabeth. She's only seventeen bit she's an afa fine quine, posh ye ken, bit likes a craic wi the sodgers. A think her faither the Earl, is aroon as weel, ye ken the Earl o Strathmore? Glamis Castle is his hame. It's an afa grand hoose – castle A shid say. There wis a big fire a whilie ago – fit a stramash. A'biddy that could wis fechtin it. An ye ken fit? Lady Elizabeth got aa the fire brigades roon aboot including Dundee tae come, an afore they arrived she organised aa the walkin sodgers an local fowk tae form a chain tae pass pails an watter doon the line. Onywey, the fire wis pitten oot, bit ee can still see far it wis. Here we are noo, Sir. He drew up with a flourish in front of the castle.'

'But this is the front door.'

'Ay Sir. The faimly said we hid tae eese it. Then when their loon Fergus wis killed at Loos – at wis back in 1915 – the sodgers aa stairted eesin the side entrance. They wis tryin tae be respectful-like, ye ken. Onywey, fan the faimly fun oot they said, "na,na, ye must keep using the front door". So we dee. They're afa kind.'

By this time, Burnett had stopped the engine. Magnus looked up. The front door was open and a young woman stood waiting.

'I think I'd better get out.'

'Ay Sir, that's Lady Elizabeth waiting. A'll get your kitbag.'

'Thank you,' said Magnus. 'You've been a great help.'

'Dinna fash yersel, Sir. At's fit A'm here fur.'

Magnus walked forward and saluted Lady Elizabeth.

'Good afternoon, Ma'am,' he said.

'How do you do? Now, you must be Captain Magnus Sinclair, is that right?'

'Yes,' he said, shaking the small outstretched hand. 'You're expecting me?'

'Oh, yes, we're all ready for you. I'm Lady Elizabeth Bowes Lyon,' she added. 'Just call me Lady Elizabeth. They all do. Now do come in out of the cold – hasn't it been a long, tiresome winter? But, spring is really here I think. You should see our primroses in the wood. Now,' she carried on. 'I have tea in here for you. You'll want some after your journey. Thank you, Burnett,' she called. 'Could you please just take Captain Sinclair's things up, room number four. Thank you so much.'

'Nae problem, your Ladyship.'

She turned to Magnus.

'That man's an absolute treasure. Will do anything for anyone. I dread the thought of losing him. Now do sit – you must be exhausted after your journey.'

'Thank you.' Magnus sat, overtaken by the flow of chat. What I really want, he thought, is to lie down. I'm so tired. But now I must take tea. And, in polite company.

'How do you like your tea, Captain Sinclair? Or, may I call you Magnus? I always like to use first names, if I can,' she continued as he nodded his acquiescence. 'Papa, I mean

219

the Earl you know, isn't so sure. He's frightened I sound 'fresh'. But I don't mean to. You don't think I do, do you Magnus?' She looked at him, eyes wide open.

'No – no, of course not.'

'That's settled then. I value your opinion. Now, enough about me. Here's your tea. I hope that it is *exactly* right for you.'

'Thank you.' He helped himself to milk.

'How was your journey. I do think long journeys are so tedious. Unless, of course, one has someone interesting to talk to. Did you Magnus?'

'Well,' he said. 'Yes I did. For part of the way. As far as Edinburgh. He left me there.'

'Oh dear, who was he? Where was he going? Was he wounded?'

'I really can go no further with that Lady Elizabeth. You see,' he continued as he could see that she was about to ask further. 'You see, I'm a doctor and as such I must respect my fellow passenger's privacy. I'm sure you understand.'

'Well…I suppose so. But I do like to hear every teensy-weensy bit about the War. I do so admire our boys going out to fight and so sorry when they get hurt. We do all we can for them here at Glamis you know.'

'I know you do,' Magnus reassured her. 'From what I hear, I think you all do a wonderful job.'

'Do you really?' She gazed at him.

'Yes, I do. How many members of hospital staff do you have?'

'Well, really, I can't remember, but they're all so good. Of course we have a few changes every so often. In fact our Sister-in-Charge is leaving. The QAs seem to change and post Sisters in and out very suddenly. They give us, and them, no warning. So, dear Sister Williamson is leaving for France within the week and someone else from France is coming here. Let me think, what's her name?' She felt in her jacket pocket and pulled out an official-looking letter.

'Dear Lady Elizabeth, um, um, ah, here it is … and Sister Rosemary Jones, (Capt QAIMNS) is to take up post as Sister-in-Charge, Glamis Castle Auxiliary Hospital … We would be grateful if you would supply transport to meet the appropriate train etc etc.'

'So, there you see it. I'm sure she'll be very nice – they all are – but one gets used to people you know. Why are you looking so surprised? Would you like more tea? And do have some of this shortbread. Cook makes it specially.'

'Thank you.' Magnus hadn't the strength to argue.

'But why,' she persisted, 'are you surprised?'

'Well, I was just thinking. I've met Sister Jones. Quite recently. She was on the hospital train I was on. In France. In charge of the coach I was in.'

'But what a co-incidence. How jolly. You'll be able to meet up again. Oh, what fun. Oh,' she added, 'talking of letters, I think I have one here for you. It came a few days ago, after you would have left your last hospital, I think and I just set it aside for you. Here you are. A Shetland postmark, I see?'

'Thank you.' Magnus took the letter. 'Yes, it's from my father.' He stuffed it into his pocket. 'Thank you very much for tea. It has been very good to meet you. I think your castle is beautiful.'

'How kind of you to say that. Glamis *is* lovely isn't it? We did have a fire not too long ago, of course. Everyone did so well.'

'Yes, I heard about that,' said Magnus. 'I also heard that you had a very large part to play in the fire-fighting.'

'Oh, well, one tries to do one's bit, you know. I do like to be a part of things.'

At last Magnus was able to escape to the privacy of room four and collapse on to one of the two beds there. The other looked empty. No evidence of anyone else, he thought with relief. He slept immediately, a dreamless in-the-depths unconscious hour.

He came to with a persistent knocking at his door. He squeezed his eyelids together and opened them.

'Who is it?'

'It's me, Sir. Burnett.'

'Come in.' Burnett's head came round the door.

'A'm afa sorry to waken ye Sir. Just to say, that it's seventeen thirty hours Sir and we have dinner early here at eighteen thirty. There's a bathroom here Sir, if you want to freshen up.'

'Thank you Burnett.'

Magnus sat up cautiously and swung his legs to the floor.

'Are you aa richt Sir?'

'Yes, thank you. I've just had an amazing sleep. Just as well you woke me.'

'Can I unpack for you Sir?'

'Well…'

'It's aa richt Sir, I aften dee it.'

'Thanks, then. I might even have a clean shirt. I think there's one there.'

Dinner was served in the Crypt of the castle. All ranks together. As Magnus approached he could hear the hubbub of voices. Anyone who was mobile and able to carry a plate of food stood in a queue at a closed hatch. As Magnus watched, at 18.30 precisely the hatch doors were opened from the other side to reveal the kitchen beyond and staff standing behind the serving-counter ready to dish up.

'Evening Sir.' The dinner orderly for the evening hurried forward. 'Able to queue, Sir?'

'Yes, certainly.'

'Right Sir. Just feel free. Your cutlery's on the table.' He moved on.

Magnus fell into line. The crypt felt like a long refectory, overtones of Royaumont, stone walls. He liked it. A table set for dinner ran along its length. He collected his lentil soup and settled himself towards the far end and opposite a blond young officer with his left arm immobilised in a sling. Later, Magnus was to see that the man's left leg was plastered from ankle to above the knee.

'Evening.'

'Evening.' Magnus tried the soup. 'Just like home,' he observed.

221

'They do well here.' The blond officer put his spoon into his empty plate. Held out his hand. 'Name's Johnnie Dingwall, 4th Seaforths.'

'Magnus Sinclair, RAMC.' They shook hands.

'Ah, a medic.'

'You could say that. The boot's on the other foot for the moment, though.'

'Bad luck. Where did it happen?'

'Somme.' Magnus was brief. He knew he hadn't got over it yet. Knowledge told him that these things could take a long time but, dear God, it was difficult. Johnnie Dingwall shot a look at him.

'Not easy is it? I still don't understand what hit me and why.'

'Can I take your plates?' A voice broke in. A very young-looking girl stood there.

'Hello Mary.' Johnnie Dingwall looked up. 'You're plate-collector the day.'

'Yes, Mr Dingwall. And I'll bring your main course if you're ready. It's mince and dough balls. Your favourite. What about you Sir?' She turned to Magnus. 'Would you like that?'

'Yes please, but…' he hesitated. 'I can easily get it.'

'No, no, don't worry. I can just as well carry two as one.' She went off.

'That's Mary – a local lassie. Not long out of school. Ah, here's Burnett. On a mission, I think.'

'Excuse me Sir. Colonel Fulton presents his compliments and would like to see you after dinner – say in about twenty minutes? In his office. Just off the main hall, it is.'

'Yes, of course, thank you. I'll be there.'

'Thank you Sir. Everything all right?'

'Yes, best dinner for a long time.'

The doctor was brief.

'I just needed to satisfy myself that you are all right after your journey. It's quite a marathon coming all the way from France like that. Are you very tired?'

'Nothing that a day or two's rest won't cure. I'll sleep well tonight, I should think.'

'That's fine. I'll put you on the breakfast in bed list for three days – no, no,' as Magnus protested. 'You're here to convalesce and that includes immediate recovery from the rigours of a long journey. It also includes obeying doctor's orders, and by the way, those of the nursing staff. So, please take things very slowly. I have a record of what's happened to you and we don't want to undo all the good that's been done. We want to build upon it.'

'Yes, Doctor. Thank you.'

'See you in the morning, say 11.00, for a further chat. Sleep well.'

The next morning's medical appointment was quite different. Lieutenant Colonel (Retd) Neil Fulton, very experienced in army ways in both peace and war, put Magnus through a run of tests both physical and mental to see how far his new patient had to travel before any consideration regarding his future.

222

'We can't make any decision,' he said. 'Not yet. I know you've been formally seen at Royaumont by the top docs and frankly, I agree that for you a return to the Front is not on. I can't see your health standing up to that. You know what it's like yourself. But,' he said, 'if you take your time and convalesce properly, and rest and exercise in appropriate degrees of difficulty, then,' he paused, 'I think you might be able to remain in the army on a home posting.'

'I just find it very difficult to accept – that I'm finished.' Magnus rested his elbow on the table and put his hand over his eyes.

'You're certainly not finished. There's masses of work to be done,' Neil Fulton declared. 'Isn't that right Sister? He appealed to Sister Williamson, who had joined him for part of Magnus's assessment.

'Yes, indeed. They're crying out for good, experienced doctors. But you must get better first.' With that, Magnus had to be content.

'Come and sit with me for lunch,' Sister Williamson suggested. 'The others'll be nearly finished. It's past one o'clock. They always keep some for the latecomers. I want to hear a bit more about France. You see,' she said, 'I'm not being entirely altruistic. I've had a sudden posting to the hospital trains in France. That's one thing I've never done. I'm quite excited about it. You've been on one as a patient. I'm sure there's a lot you can tell me. Did I hear Lady Elizabeth say that you know my replacement here, Rosemary Jones?'

'Yes, she was on the hospital train coming up to Le Havre. She handed me over, if you see what I mean, to the Sister-in-Charge of the hospital ship. But not only that, she turned out to be a friend of my sister – they were students together – and telephoned Edinburgh to tell her I was on my way north. Wasn't that good of her?'

Sister Williamson smiled at his enthusiasm.

'With all this going for you, she said, I can see your recovery really speeding up.'

Later on that afternoon Magnus remembered the letter. He was out taking a gentle stroll around the castle garden, looking at the trees ready to burst into leaf. I wonder how far on the Birkenshaw trees are. It's a long time since I've seen them. They'll be bigger than they were – not so far on as these though. Oh, Birkenshaw, the letter, what did I do with it? He tried one pocket, then another. Finally he found it, a bit crumpled. I'd better read it I suppose.

Damn, his eyes read over his father's letter. 'Your place is here now.' He's made that clear enough. And Charlotte's, so kind as always. I wonder if Angus got his rabbit. I'd better write back.

Glamis Castle Auxiliary Hospital,
Glamis,
Angus.

Dear Father and Charlotte,
Thank you very much for your letters which I received when I arrived here yesterday. I think they came a day or two before I did and were set aside by Lady Elizabeth Bowes Lyon to give me on my arrival. It's good to hear from you.

I'd a reasonable journey to Edinburgh from Southampton via London. Who should be there on the platform at Edinburgh but Christina, my wee sister whom I hadn't seen for years. We went and sat together in a café until I'd to get the Dundee train. I was so pleased to see her. How did she know? Well, her friend (they trained together) Rosemary Jones who is a QA, was Sister-in-Charge of the coach I was travelling in from Creil to Le Havre and after she saw me off on the HMHS *Donegal* at Le Havre she'd the goodness to telephone Christina and let her know when I was arriving in Edinburgh. Wasn't that good of her? I'll never forget her kindness.

This is a beautiful place – very peaceful and I'm sure I'll get on well here. I've seen the MO twice. He's insisting that I obey orders and take things very slowly. He says no decision can be made at the moment regarding my future. So I must be content with that and be a good patient. Difficult for me but there you are. I feel well on the whole, was out for a stroll this afternoon and am probably going to have some sort of exercise régime to get fit again. I do not foresee any leave in the near future – however let us wait and see what the long-term future brings.

Yes, Charlotte, Lady Elizabeth is in residence, and I 'took tea' with her on my arrival. She talked a great deal but means well and helps the Sisters and VADs in the wards. She also, I understand, sets up entertainment for patients and parties and that sort of thing.

Thank you again for your letters. Is there any news of James MacLeod? You know, the minister? I know that he went back to the Front but haven't heard how he's getting on. He's been a very good friend to me.

Love to you all,

Yours affly.,

Magnus.

PS Did Angus get his rabbit?

He addressed the envelope and put it in the 'out' tray in the hall on the way to the crypt for dinner.

Chapter 35

APRIL 1917

James was in a dream – a nightmare, a maelstrom of memories. He remembered the bumpy ride in the motor ambulance to the ADS. Bates, the medical orderly was with him. That in itself was unusual, he noted in his befuddled brain. I must be ill, not just injured.

A juddering stop, the noise of the engine died. He remembered Bates calling, 'Sucking chest wound. Please don't move him. I'm worried about him.' He heard a voice of authority beside him in the stationary ambulance, looking at his chest, rolling him over on the stretcher to make sure that the wound on his back was sealed, applying yet more dressings and putting up an intravenous drip.

'Take him straight to CCS,' the voice said. 'Don't waste any time. Keep him warm.' James tried to thank him but couldn't raise a finger. His brain chided him. Mother always told me to say thank you. What will the man think?

The CCS was another mile or so. Another jolting painful mile of very nearly impassable track. James thought, 'a lang Scots mile'. It felt like that. Lying on his injured side was very painful even with the morphine, but when he muttered, Bates said he had to be like that to allow his other lung to do the breathing for the injured one. He wanted to go home. He thought he said it. He didn't know. His mind went blank. He heard more shouting.

'Come on man, we're losing him.' Shouting at him, too.

'Sir, Padre, hold on, stick with it. We're nearly at the CCS. They'll see you right.' With an enormous effort he opened his eyes. He looked at Bates.

'Phew, that was close, Padre. Don't give me a fright like that again.'

A voice shouted from outside, 'We're here.' James could hear other voices, doors opening, a sliding as eager hands pulled the stretcher carrying his supine body out of the ambulance. Then running, more jolting. Then,

'Straight to theatre. Move, please.' He felt himself land on the table.

A voice. 'Let's have a look.' Then, 'Right,' the voice ordering, 'get an intravenous line into his other arm as well. Keep him warm. He's a very poor colour. Let's see the dressings.'

James felt himself going down a steep dark tunnel as everything went black.

Then there was a rumbling and rhythm. I wonder what that is. It doesn't matter. It's quite peaceful, lulling really. I wish I could breathe better. I'm so tired. He coughed.

'A-ah,' he groaned, grimaced, felt a gurgling in his throat.

'Well done,' said a voice, a woman's voice. 'Well done.' Someone wiped his mouth.

'Do you think you could cough again?' He coughed, groaned with the pain of it all, felt the gentle but firm wiping again.

'Good,' said the voice. The rhythm that had been so lulling changed to a lurching. The carriage shook.

'Oh, o-o-h, that's so sore.'

'I'll get you some more morphine in a minute.' The voice came again. I'm sure that's a woman. Where on earth am I? Or maybe I'm not 'on earth'?

'Am I dead?'

'No. Not dead. And not if I can help it. Can you open your eyes, Padre? James?'

He dragged his eyelids open. Lights shone, not too brightly but enough for him to see.

'That's better. What can you see?' He turned his head a little and groaned at the effort. He saw a slim figure with a Sister's white veil, apron and red cape standing beside him. That must be the owner of the voice. He voiced his next thought aloud, or that was the intention but it came over in a strained whisper.

'Where am I?'

'You're on a hospital train.' Sister Bernadette O'Flaherty observed him as he struggled to speak.

'What happened?'

'Can you remember anything?'

'The sniper… shooting ... being wounded. The RAP.' His brow creased in the effort to remember. 'Not much else.'

'Don't worry. You'll remember more as you go on. You're on a hospital train.'

'Where to?'

'We took you on at Arras. The ambulance got you there from CCS. You need surgery but they felt you'd be better in a General Hospital where you'd have time to recuperate. We're heading for Étaples, No 7 Canadian General, the old No 23 General Hospital, if that makes any sense to you.' She smiled as he screwed up his face in response.

'I know, it doesn't matter as long as they get you better.'

'What are my chances?'

'Padre, James, you know the score. You've been shot through your right lung. So far, you've had a rough ride. But, you're still with us, I'm happy to tell you. Now, I'm going to give you some more morphine to help the pain and make you sleep. You know that we're looking after you. We'll get you to Étaples as quickly as we can. You don't have to do anything except think positive.' She took the syringe that the orderly was holding, checked the dosage, administered the injection.

'Thanks.' He closed his eyes.

He slept through that train journey. He didn't know it but the Royal Engineers had only the previous few days been occupied repairing, yet again, bomb damage to the line. For once the train ran relatively smoothly. The seventy two kilometres or so from Arras to Étaples were accomplished with no major hiccups.

Bernadette O'Flaherty heaved a sigh of relief as she saw the buildings of the town come into view. She fingered the rosary beads in her pocket.

'Thank God,' she breathed. She looked anxiously at James. He lay very still on his injured side. She could see the left side of his chest rising and falling. Occasionally he coughed in his morphine-induced sleep. The sputum was frothy, blood-stained but, no smell, no infection yet, thanks be to God. She wiped the bloody sputum away. The MO came along from a coach further up the train.

'How is he?'

'So far so good. How is everyone else?'

'Well, all alive, I'm glad to say. We had three men die on the train on my last journey. I was beginning to think I'd a jinx. But today's been better. This Padre – MacLeod is it…?' she nodded… 'and some men in the next coach are very ill but at least they're alive.'

'What's the date? I've lost all track of time.'

'It's the 12th.'

'Have you heard how Arras is going?'

'Well, they took Vimy Ridge, I'm glad to tell you. The Canadians and the Scots did very well. But there are significant casualties I hear. The battle for Arras itself – well, they're still at it.'

The train's rhythm slowed as it neared Étaples station.

'Here we are,' Bernadette said. 'I can see orderlies waiting with stretchers.'

At No 7 Canadian General the staff awaited their latest train-load. Beds were clean and ready, spotless operating theatres awaited, sterilised instruments lying on trolleys in serried ranks under their green dressing towels. Many patients had been discharged the previous days, either back to support lines on the battlefield, or if that were not a feasible option, sent over the Channel to the big ports on the south coast of England for onward transportation and convalescence. Now in No 7 there was a renewed atmosphere of expectancy, a controlled jumpiness, a knowledge that more challenges lay ahead.

'It's always like this,' said Sister Rhoda Fiddes to her latest recruit, VAD Jenny Spencer. She'd been working at No 7 for a week but had not yet participated in an intake. 'Receiving' it was sometimes called when a trainload of wounded came in. Sometimes if hospitals were reasonably near each other in a big town, they rotated the job of receiving. Jenny Spencer looked at Sister now and bit her bottom lip.

'Don't worry. Just do as we ask and you'll be fine. Then you find you're doing things off your own bat as you get used to it. You've done well this last week – I know this is new for you but just think of the men and what they need and you find that you stop worrying about yourself.'

'Yes, Sister.'

'That's fine. Now, I think I can hear the first ambulance. Yes,' as she looked out of the window. Here they are.'

It was, or appeared to be chaotic for the first hour as more and more men were unloaded. Those on stretchers came first, as usual, four in an ambulance. Staff members went out to help orderlies bring them inside. Walking wounded followed and were ushered into a large common room until they could be organised into ward groups. The wards steadily filled with occupants in beds, fifteen or so down each of the long sides, and sometimes more in the middle of the floor. There were further mattresses ready to be placed on the floor between the beds should they be required. Theatres thrummed into action.

James lay, at last in a bed, only half-aware of what was going on around him. He had no idea of time. He remembered being put there, the pain of being rolled about as someone checked his dressings, his colour, his breathing, his intravenous drip, when he last had morphine. That information was tagged on to him. He thought someone spoke to him but he couldn't remember. He knew that someone with a friendly voice had given him a sip of water. He sensed over-all a feeling of activity, not particularly happening to him, but surrounding him. It was quite noisy too. He tried to switch his attention. Think of something pleasant. What's the nicest thing I can remember?

'No, no,' he muttered. 'I don't want to do that.' He was in Shetland. In the Manse garden in Jarlshavn. Charlotte was with him. They were standing close together. They were in love, kissing, talking of marriage.

Charlotte. Dear Charlotte. Am I going to die without seeing you again? He tried to shake his head.

'Don't want to do that…'

'Don't want to do what?' Another voice beside him.

'Die.'

'Whatever put that into your head, Padre? We're just about to take you to theatre to have a look at your chest. You don't think we'd do that if we thought you were going to die, do you? You know our ways better than that. Look, here are the boys with a stretcher for you.'

'Who are you?'

'Sister Rhoda Fiddes. Canadian Army Nursing Service, come here especially for you. I'm scrub sister today and I just came through to check that you're ready. I'll go now and they'll get you sorted. See you in a few minutes.'

The operating theatre was brightly lit. His eyes were dazzled by the glare.

'Hello Padre. Can you hear me?'

'Yes.'

'I'm Ernest Warnock. I'm going to be dealing with your chest today. Can I call you James?'

'Yes, that's fine.'

'Makes life easier doesn't it?' Without waiting for an answer he went on. 'I've been reading your notes and I want to have a close look, tidy your wound up a bit, I think and see where we go from there. I'll do it under a local – we'll do a block of the phrenic nerve with 1 percent procaine hydrochloride. That'll help for a while afterwards too. I'm sure you've seen this done on other people.'

'Ye-es.'

'Yes, I know it's different when it's yourself, but it'll be fine. Just relax and think of the nicest person you know.'

James sighed. Minutes later he could feel the pain disappear as the local anaesthetic took effect.

'Let's see now. Could you take the dressings down now, please?' James could feel the 'dirty' nurses undoing the bandages around his chest, working their way down through layers of gauze and padding until they reached the sealing dressing.

'Shall we open the wounds up now completely?'

'Let's look at the back first. Then we can put a seal on that while we attend to the front. It'll mean a bit of rolling about James, but you shouldn't feel it too much.'

'Needs a good clean, but it's not bad,' he murmured. 'I'll clean it out,' he added, swabbing briskly. 'There, now, that's the easy one. Now, seal please. We'll come back to it later. Now, roll James over please so that I can get at the front. Thanks. Let's have the sterile dressing and the seal off please.'

The final dressings came off with some difficulty and a fair amount of dried blood, but eventually they revealed the extent of the exit wound for inspection. James did his best not to cry out but even the phrenic nerve block couldn't stop the feeling of pulling as the adhering seal, giving every appearance of staying *in situ* for ever, was persuaded to part with his skin.

'Ouch,' said James. 'That hurt.'

'I know, James,' said one of the 'dirty' nurses. 'I'm sorry.'

'Now then.' Ernest Warnock scrutinised the wound closely. 'What d'you think, Sister? You're the one with the good nose. You can always sniff out infection. What a reputation to have.'

She bent over the wound without touching it. She sniffed, a few times. She looked, closely.

'It's a bit of a mess,' she said. 'Needs a good clean up, but, I can't smell any infection.'

'Good,' said Ernest. 'Do you hear that James? No infection that we can see, or smell.'

'Thanks,' breathed James with relief.

'Yes,' the surgeon looked at him sympathetically. 'It's a big hazard. I bet you've seen a few.'

'You can say that again,' said James.

'Right, now, these next few moments might be a bit rough but we must clean up to give you the best chance.'

'Go on.'

It was very uncomfortable. As quickly as they could the surgeon and Rhoda Fiddes worked together to investigate and examine James chest wound.

'Let's get rid of that old blood and exudate, then we'll be able to see better.' They worked on.

'Hmm, I think you might have a bit of bone damage.' He looked again. 'Yes, two ribs bashed a bit. A few bits and pieces to remove. We don't want them lying about causing trouble. He sounded casual but his movements as he picked about were precise. Each piece of bone, he dropped into a metal receiver.

'Now,' he said, 'let's do a bit of debridement now that we've got rid of the loose rubbish. We've managed quite far back, though. Right back to the narrowing of the entry wound. It all looks quite clean.'

'Are you coping, James?' Rhoda asked.

'Yes. Just a bit drowsy and you lot are stopping me going to sleep.'

'That's the morphine – lovely stuff. Just see us out. We're just going to remove some old tissue that you don't need, a bit of flesh, tissue damaged by the bullet. Then you'll heal more quickly. Scalpel, Sir?' She lifted her prepared Morgan Parker scalpel handle and blade and handed it to him.

'Thank you. Forceps too please.'

Skilfully he cut away the damaged flesh. Carefully he probed far into the wound, excised what he could, leaving pink healthy tissue to heal.

'I can see you're not a smoker, James,' he said. 'Your lung is very healthy-looking. I think you're going to get away with this.'

James closed his eyes, but could not prevent a tear squeezing out from under his eyelid.

'James?' Rhoda said. 'Here,' she called to Jenny Spencer the new VAD, in theatre for the first time. 'Come and stand with the Padre, give him a bit of support while we finish off.'

'Swabs please,' said Ernest mopping busily. 'A bit of bleeding.' He watched. 'It's not too much though. That's fine. Now, antiseptic cleanout.' She was there at the ready.

'Now, sutures.' He sutured in silence for a time. James lay as still as he could.

'That's fine,' Ernest said at last. 'Look's OK don't you think?'

'Very nice,' she agreed. 'Ready to finish the back now?'

'Yes. We'll roll you again James – just to put a few sutures in the entry wound. Here we go.'

'It's looking fine. Just a wee bit more. Now, dressings and chest bandage please. Quite firm, plenty padding, thanks everybody.' He bent over James.

'That's it done James. The pain will be away until the nerve block wears off in a few hours. They'll give you more morphine then. I can't pretend that it won't hurt. You've two badly broken-up ribs there which have to settle down. Keep breathing as deeply as you can. Best sitting up. Thank God you're fit. I'll come and see you tomorrow.'

'Thanks very much.'

'My pleasure. You did well.' He hurried off to prepare for his next patient.

Chapter 36

Lowrie to Christina

> Captain's dugout
> Somewhere in France

My dearest Christina,

This must as usual be brief. I've just done my official dispatches and saved the best (writing to you) till last. As we agreed, I went to see Charlotte and your father. I told Charlotte first about US and she was very pleased and happy. I am so glad that was her reaction. No arguing at all. Then she helped me to go to your father. She's wonderful – I've always thought so and I felt that she was really on my side. Anyway, your father was, on the whole, pleased for us. He put up a few challenges but I could see him thinking about it and then he stood up and gave me his permission. And, I promised him I'd be a good husband to you etc. So there you are. I expected a more difficult run-in but he was fine.

The other thing is, I had to ask permission to get married from my CO. Yes, we have to do that too. So I went along to the CO's HQ dugout. Our friends across the wire must have been having their dinner because all seemed quiet. He was sitting looking at a newspaper at least a week old. I asked permission to have a word, told him what I, or rather we, wanted. He actually seemed delighted for us. Said, news like this cheers up the boys. He also said I could have weekend leave reasonably soon. He'd have to discuss timing with his adjutant.

So, all is going in the right direction even down to the word 'soon'. I feel like going out and cheering but of course can't do that. But, I am very, very happy.

Any news about whether or not you can carry on at work after we are married?

I love you so much.

Always yours,

All my love,

Lowrie.

Christina to Lowrie

> RIE Nurses Home

My dear Lowrie,

I was so happy to receive your letter saying Father has said 'yes'. Thank you for doing that. I'm delighted that Mother was so helpful. I knew she'd be fine with this. I think she had an inkling of what was afoot.

Now it's my turn to give you some news. I made an appointment with Matron, put on my best apron and went to see her yesterday. She was sitting there behind her desk in this great office that she has. I don't know why she does it because she's quite nice underneath all the pomp. I told her why I'd come to see her, who you are, that you're in France, we want to get married and didn't want to wait until the war ended but to get married on your next leave if that were possible. I said, 'I love my work, and I would like to keep working as usual, please, Matron.' She looked at me through those glasses of hers. I really don't think she's that old, you just get that impression. But she's quite strict about Rules and I thought she was going to turn me down flat.

But she said, 'You know the Rules of this hospital, Staff Nurse Sinclair?'

'Yes, Matron,' I said. I didn't dare say, 'But...'

'Well,' she said, 'I know the Rules too. However...' and she took a long time over this. 'However, I always think there are times when Rules should be relaxed a little, and I think when this country is involved in such a War, then this could be one of those times. And anyway,' and I could see her face relaxing as well as the Rules, 'You Staff Nurse Sinclair are one of my best nurses and I wouldn't want to lose you to a Rule that I had no hand in making. I give you my blessing my dear.' And then she shook my hand. I couldn't believe it. But it's true.

'Thank you very much,' I said.

She said, 'My pleasure. I hope that you will be very happy. Do you know when the wedding day is to be?'

I said we hoped on your next leave but we didn't know quite when it was. And she said she hoped all would go well. Isn't that grand?

I won't blether any more – but just wanted to let you have the latest.

Stay safe.

Your always loving Christina.

Alexander to Christina   Birkenshaw.

My dear Christina,

I do hope you are well, not working too hard and getting enough sleep. I'm always concerned about you living in a city and missing the fresh sea air.

Lowrie came to see us and spoke to me very well about his love for you and that he and you wanted to become man and wife. I was a little hesitant to begin with. However on reflection I decided to say 'Yes'. Lowrie is a good man, we have known him and his family for a long time and as a lawyer he will be able to keep you in a manner which I would want for my daughter.

I was a little perturbed about your wish to become married before the end of the War while Lowrie remains in France. It seems a little precipitate. However I am persuaded that this is what you both very much want to do and I would not wish to be seen to be standing in your way.

So, my dear daughter, I give you my permission and my blessing for your marriage. I hope that you will have a long and happy life together.

Yours, affly.,

Your Father.

Charlotte to Christina:

I was so happy when Lowrie came when he was on leave and told me that he and you wanted to be married, and, as soon as possible. I felt and still do feel very emotional about this. It's just wonderful and we like Lowrie very much – always have done.

Lowrie and I went to your Father so that Lowrie could ask permission. Don't worry. All was well. He just feels it a bit, his daughter being married and, as he sees it, leaving him. He likes Lowrie.

Have you found out if you will be able to work after you are married while Lowrie is in France? It would be good for you if you could – and I pray that the War won't last much longer.

Be happy, Christina. We're happy for you and know that your birth mother, Margery would be as well.

With love from,
Mother.

Christina to Alexander and Charlotte:

Thank you both for your lovely letters. Lowrie and I are very happy and want the world to be happy too.

I'm glad to tell you Matron was very helpful about my continuing to work after we are married – so that's all right.

Lowrie also had to ask his Commanding Officer's permission. That was fine, and he's going to see Lowrie gets a weekend's home leave soon. We'll be married in Edinburgh. I'm sorry we won't be able to come to Jarlshavn but under the circumstances there won't be time. We'll hope to see you soon.

With love to you both and Hannah and Angus.
From
Christina.

Chapter 37

'Postie's here,' called Hannah. 'Have you any mail for him to take, Mother?'

'Thank you.' Charlotte took the letters. 'No, I haven't anything ready to go today, thanks.'

'I'll away down the road then.' Postie slapped down the flap of his bag. 'Are you all fine? Mr Sinclair getting about better now?'

'Yes, he's out in the garden, looking at where he's organising creating space for growing food, not flowers, to help to feed folk. Everywhere's getting very short of food now that the Germans have decided to try and starve us all into submission.'

'It's an awful thing.' Postie shook his head. 'We're short enough here but I wonder what it's like in the big towns and cities. The poor wee bairns.' He went off still shaking his head.

Charlotte

I took the mail inside, a few bills, always bills, a letter for Alexander and one addressed to both of us in Magnus's handwriting, postmarked Glamis. His writing was much better – it was unmistakably his hand now, not like the shaky first letters he'd sent us.

I found the paper knife always there on the hall table, slit the envelope and sat down in a sunny spot out of the breeze. It didn't take long to read and or to understand that a journey by boat to Shetland was not going to happen for Magnus in the near future. Magnus's health was not up to it and I'd no reason to doubt this, whatever his personal feelings were about returning. It worried me that he seemed so far from being fit. But then, I had no real idea of War wounds and head injuries. It seemed that in some cases recovery took a long time and I reminded myself that Magnus had been in a coma for five weeks. I was thankful he was alive. We all were but as a family we wanted to see him. I felt quite concerned for him.

I was also concerned about Alexander. It had taken him a lot to tell me he was sorry about what had happened and he wanted to say so to Magnus. He was carrying a burden of guilt – he was sure that he personally had sent Magnus on a road to War, destruction, injury and illness.

I felt guilty too in a way. I don't think I openly encouraged Magnus except for that one visit to Lerwick when I went with the express purpose of meeting him. But could I have stopped him from saying the things he did? Perhaps I could have – I did try when I felt things were beginning to get a bit out of hand. But that scene with the dolls' house so long ago could have taken a very different turn if Alexander hadn't come in when he did. I think in a way we were all culpable to a degree.

234

As I thought about it all, tried to analyse what we each had done and said, I began to realise something else. It dawned on me I was thinking about Magnus as Alexander's son, the boy I had known so well, tried to comfort when his mother had died. This was different from the good-looking young man to whom a very young version of me had been attracted and with whom I'd thought I felt a connecting spark. I hadn't noticed this change in me till now. I still did not feel motherly towards him – our age-gap was too close for that. It was more a feeling of friendship. I was concerned for his well-being. I loved him but as a very close friend. Any other feeling was just not there. I felt as though I had grown through a phase in my life and come out the other side. I felt lighter, happier in a way. Now, I wondered, does Magnus feel the same way?

Alexander walked slowly round the house. I went to meet him with the letter. The May sunshine felt quite warm and we sat on a bench together.

'How's the digging going?'

'Not too badly. The ground is warming up nicely and we'll get some tatties in very soon, I hope. Then we'll have a tattie-howking session in October. They'll be a contribution to the Jarlshavn food stores. We'll show them, these U-boats and so on that we can't be starved out. We're doing cabbages and leeks and carrots too. I've quite a few volunteers. What's the letter?'

'Magnus. From Glamis. He's settled in, seen the doctor twice since he arrived and…'

'Is he coming home?'

'Well, no, not just yet. He's not fit enough yet.'

'Ach, surely…' He was beginning to protest when I put the letter into his hands.

'Alexander, read the letter. You'll see what he's saying.'

He took the letter from me, adjusted his spectacles and sat reading quietly. When he'd finished, he sat there, letter in hand. The silence stretched from seconds to minutes.

'Ach,' he said again. 'Charlotte, you'll need to go.'

'What?'

'That's it. He can't come to us. It's quite obvious he's not able yet. I can't go to him – I'm not able either. Charlotte, please will you go for my sake and see that he's all right.' His voice shook. He pulled his handkerchief out of his pocket and blew his nose violently.

'I'm a silly old man,' he said. 'But he's my son and I love him.'

'But Alexander,' I said. 'I don't know if he'll want to see me.'

'Of course he'll want to see you.'

This was a whole new idea. I hadn't thought that far. There were so many 'buts' to it.

'But Alexander, I don't want to leave you alone. What if…?'

'What if, what if – what if none of us ever sees him alive again? And,' he continued, 'he's within visiting distance now. You need to go.'

I could feel myself weakening.

'I'll have to go on the boat – alone,' I said, feeling foolish even as I said it.

'So what? Where's the girl who came all the way to Shetland aged nineteen and a bit alone on the boat?'

'I'm a lot older now.'

235

'You don't look it.' He took my hand. 'Please Charlotte, please do this for me. I'll be fine here. Edie will be here and Meg, and Angus coming in and out and Hannah at the week-end. Go and see him for me. Please?' What could I say? I had to give in.

'Well,' I conceded, 'I'll write Magnus tonight and ask him if he'd like me to visit. How about that?'

'Could you *tell* him you're coming? Rather than ask?'

'But Alexander, that might be the wrong way of doing it. Please, let me do it this way. At least I've said I'll go.'

'All right.' He patted my hand. 'Thank you for that. You're sure you'll write tonight?'

'Yes, yes, I will – now here's Hannah, with Angus's new rabbit.'

'Look, isn't he sweet?' She came up and placed the rabbit carefully into my lap.

'Does Angus know that she's out?'

'Oh yes, he's charged me to look after her while he cleans out the hutch.' She looked at us and giggled. 'He's taking his duties very seriously. That was quite a deal you made with him, Mother.' Then, changing the subject, 'Do I see Magnus's writing? Is that a letter from him? Is he in Glamis now?'

'Yes, to all,' said Alexander. 'What a lot of questions you ask without waiting for answers. Don't your teachers teach you anything at that school?'

'Yes, Father, but it's so nice to see a letter.'

'Here, you can read it.' She read in silence.

'He *is* all right, isn't he?'

'Yes, we think so, just got to take things slowly. Your Mother is going sooth to Glamis to see him.'

'Mother? Are you? On the boat?'

I wished that Alexander had not said anything until it was settled.

'Well, I'm going to write him first to see if visiting is a good idea.'

'But why shouldn't it be? It's a wonderful idea. *I'd* be delighted to see you.'

'Well, I'm just going to ask first.'

I could have done without children knowing until I was sure that I'd be going.

'Now, Hannah, please don't mention this yet and especially to Angus. He'll get all excited about it and we're not at that stage yet.'

'No, no,' she said. 'I won't say. Don't worry. I'll take wee rabbitie and see how he's getting on.'

That evening I wrote to Magnus. I told him what was going on, about our vegetable-growing contribution to 'The Home Front' as people were calling it, Angus's rabbit and so on – little bits of home news. Then I said:

I've been thinking about a trip sooth and a visit to Glamis to see you if you would like this. Your father has suggested this and I'd be very happy to come. Please do consider this and let me know if this sounds feasible. Also, is there anywhere I could stay for a night or two?

With best wishes,

Yours, affly.,

Charlotte.

236

Once I had posted this I sat back and waited. The reply didn't take long. Magnus must have written by return.

Dear Charlotte,

Thank you for your letter. It was very good to hear from you and all about the Birkenshaw goings on. I was especially interested to hear about the vegetable-growing. It's the same here at Glamis. So much cultivation. So much need. Everyone is concerned about the U-boats sinking our supply ships and losing all these vital food supplies.

Life here at Glamis is good – for the moment. I'm getting what I need in the way of help, exercise, medical attention and company. I can go off by myself and read, rest, think and so on. I know I may become restless but for the moment it's seems to be what I need. Dr Fulton (Lt Col, Retd) MO in charge here is very firm that patients toe the line and I'm quite content to do so.

The nursing staff are good too. Quite a few VADs and about three QA sisters. The Sister-in-Charge has recently changed. It's a real coincidence. When I arrived, in charge was a Sister Williamson. She'd just had a sudden posting – apparently the QAs are often posted with little notice. She went to the hospital trains in the north of France and was replaced by Sister Rosemary Jones from the trains. I think I told you about her in my last letter. I couldn't believe it when I heard she was coming. She arrived a couple of days ago, came straight up and gave me a hug. When some of the others said, 'Oh, Sister, that's not fair,' she said, 'I always hug old patients.' The others laughed – I am, of course one of the oldest here – and I said 'less of the old, thank you.' She's such a nice girl and so helpful.

I'm very pleased to hear that you're planning a visit. I'll be delighted to see you. I told Dr Fulton and he suggested you stay in the guestroom here. This is standard practice. If you're happy with that it's easy to arrange. Let's know the dates and it will happen. Burnett the orderly will meet the train when you arrive.

Looking forward to seeing you.

Yours affly.,
Magnus.

I read it through and handed it to Alexander.

'He seems happy,' he commented. 'When do you think you'll go?'

'What about in say, ten days? That gives me time to pack, book the *St Clair*, see about train, organise the children, speak to Meg and Edie and Bertha Halcrow, tell Dr Taylor you'll be alone…'

'Stop, stop. I'm not going to be alone. I'll have all these women around. And the children.'

'Well, I know,' I said, 'but I, I really don't like leaving you.'

'Ach woman, I'll be fine.'

'I know.'

'I'm glad you're going to see him. It means a lot to me. But,' he paused. 'Come back soon, won't you.'

237

'Yes, Alexander, I will.' I tried to speak lightly but with an impulsive squeeze of hands, a moment of eye contact, there was a sudden sense of looking back together at long ago rocky waters.

'All right?'

'Yes,' I said. 'It's very all right.'

But all the time, at the back of my mind I'd the thought of James writing that letter in his dugout an hour before he went to his place next to a Front line fraught with danger. And, I did not know what had become of him.

Chapter 38

The grounds of No. 7 Canadian General Hospital, Étaples, northern France were in full spring mode. Early May sunshine shone down on patients fortunate enough to be outside. The verandah on the south side of the building stood with all doors and windows wide to the warmth and brightness.

James came through from his session with the physiotherapist. This old profession had come into its own in the War. It was well recognised as an important phase of a wounded man's programme of reconstruction and rehabilitation, both physical and mental. It meant that more men were more able to return to military duty as soon as possible. However, when this could not happen, the hope was that a patient's ability to cope as a civilian would be at as high a level of fitness achievable.

James quite enjoyed these sessions. The physiotherapist, Michael Ramsay, who himself had been wounded in 1915, was keen, almost fanatical, about getting and keeping fit. He was known for rounding up all who were able, for an early morning exercise class on the courtyard in front of the hospital.

James wasn't at this stage yet. He was still learning to breathe properly again and found his initial daily half-hour with Michael tiring and painful. The first session took place a couple of days after surgery.

'I don't really feel able for this,' James said, when Michael walked in, introduced himself and proposed that he 'should learn how to breathe a bit more deeply instead of these wee shallow breaths you're doing just now. And,' Michael continued, 'you should be sitting more upright.'

'But I keep slipping down.'

'Come on. Just try.' James tried. An orderly came in to help and between them, Michael and he helped James well up the bed with his pillows arranged at his back.

'Now,' said Michael. 'Let's breathe. Just take it slowly. Take a breath in… and out… and in… and out… Now, this time, hold it at the top of the breath… and then out. Good. Well done. Now …'

The next day was the same.

The day after that the physiotherapist and Sister Rhoda Fiddes persuaded James to get out of bed and do his breathing exercises sitting on a chair.

'That's great,' they said. 'You're breathing better all the time.'

'I am?'

'Yes, your pulmonary elasticity is improving each time you breathe, and as for your intrapleural relations…'

'My what?' James's face was such a study they burst out laughing.

'It's not funny,' he protested. 'It's damned sore.'

'Ah, ah, Padre, you shouldn't swear.'

'You two would drive anyone to drink.'

'Yes, sorry for laughing, James. All we're saying is that this is helping your injured lung expand and you're breathing better. That's increasing your blood flow to your pleural cavity, and you'll heal faster. You've a lot of healing to do but the faster you heal the less chance of infection. The better you breathe, the better quality of life you'll have in the future. Seriously.'

'Michael's quite right,' Rhoda chimed in. 'James, listen, looking at your notes, they nearly lost you a few times on your journey here. Back at the RAP, they didn't give much for your chances. So we're delighted to have you at this stage. And, we're determined to get you better.' James looked at the two of them, so earnest.

'I see,' he said. 'Thank you both for explaining.' He sat up straighter. 'Come on, then. What are we waiting for?'

After a few days of breathing like this, Michael added more concentrated breathing and body exercises, persuading James to expand his lungs and then to strengthen his legs, arms and shoulders. As the days went on, his morale and confidence grew, he was able to walk, slowly at first but gradually more confidently.

He chatted to the other patients. They learned he was a Padre. They found in him a confidant, called him to their bedsides to hear their stories, their problems, their worries over past mistakes. Their respect for him grew.

He had letters from his parents in Perth. His mother wrote first.

My dear James,

We have just had a very kind letter from Captain Robert Duncan RAMC giving us further details of your being wounded and how this happened. My dear boy, we are a whole mixture of emotions. When we got the telegram it said 'seriously wounded' and we were in despair. Then we got this letter. He told us you'd been shot in the chest by a sniper while you were out saving others. He also knew you were being taken to Étaples. We're so very proud of you, James. Please hold on and get well.

Will go and catch the post so that you get this quickly. We both send all our love.

God bless you,

Love from Mother.

For once James was not able to write his own letter in reply. As he had done for so many others, he asked VAD Jenny Spencer to sit down beside him in a quiet moment and dictated a note for her to send for him. It was a strange feeling.

Dear Mother and Father,

Thank you for your letter Mother. I'm in Étaples and am being well looked after. Jenny is writing this letter for me as I'm not quite able yet. I've had surgery to my injured lung and am a bit sore but my wound is not infected. I might be allowed to get up tomorrow if all is well. I'm having breathing exercises to teach my lung to breathe again. I hope you're both well. I'll write again when I can.

I love you both. May God be with you.

Your loving son,

James.

240

His father wrote.

Dear James,

We're so thankful to receive your letter in your words even though not your writing. Please thank Jenny for us for being your scribe.

Have you any idea what happens next? Is this a 'Blighty one' as they say in the newspapers? You know your bed is here for when you are able. Your mother is very keen to get a chance to look after you.

We're both fine but of course worried about you. I know that you will say, 'don't worry' but that's what parents do. Everyone around here sends best wishes, love and hopes for a speedy recovery. The folk in St Fillans have heard about you and keep wanting to hear more. They send their best regards.

Take care my dear boy. Keep doing the exercises.

From your loving Father.

After that, James was able to write his own letters and it was with this in mind that he carried with him his notebook and pen as he headed for the hospital garden and the sunshine. He was surprised at how well he felt. Michael warned him.

'I don't want to be a spoilsport, but please don't try to run before you can walk.'

'But I feel so much better.'

'It's only three weeks or so since you were wounded. You were very fit at the outset I'm glad to say. Just don't overdo it now. I'm glad you feel better, but just imagine all that torn tissue inside you healing nicely. If you overdo things you could really set yourself back.'

So James's first forays into the spring sunshine were slow, measured, but developed into more energetic walks as he felt his strength return.

He walked through the garden to his favourite seat in a sheltered sunny corner – so pleasant that James was surprised it was so little used. He sat down. He had just opened his writing pad when round the side of a large magnolia in full bloom came one of the QA Sisters, Anna French.

'Hello,' she said. 'Am I disturbing you?'

'Not at all'

'I love this magnolia, don't you? I've been watching it come out for weeks.' She went on, 'I see you've found this little hidey hole. I often come here on my tea break – just to get outside for a while.'

'It's a good seat. The others don't seem to get as far as here.'

'No, most of the boys are not fit enough.'

They chatted on then she said, 'I've just heard that one of our hospital ships was sunk by a torpedo in the Channel. Can you believe it? They'd all their green and red lights on show. It was quite obvious what it was. I'm so angry. I'm glad we don't have any German soldiers here just now. I don't know how I would cope with them.'

'You'd cope as you always do,' he replied, 'because you're a nurse and they're patients.'

241

'I suppose so.' She sighed.

'When did this happen?'

'Over two weeks ago, at least. On 17 April. I don't know why I didn't hear before. Sometimes we don't get the news.'

'Which ship?' he asked. '*Which ship* was it?'

'The *Donegal*. Why?'

'How many drowned?'

'About forty, I think. James, why? Do you know someone on that ship?'

'I know someone who was going on the *Donegal* but I don't know if that was the date. You never quite know which crossing you're going to be on. Oh, *Magnus*.'

'Who's Magnus?'

'He's a friend of mine. He was at Royaumont and was heading for Scotland to convalesce, on the *Donegal*. What can I do?'

'You could trace him by the Red Cross, but it sometimes takes ages. Do you know where his family is? They will know.'

'That's it. I didn't think for a moment. Of course – Charlotte.'

'Who's Charlotte? His mother?'

'No, not exactly. She died and Charlotte married his father. I have their address. I could write to them and ask if he was on that crossing. How awful.' He blew his nose.

'James,' she touched his arm. 'Look, we don't know he was there. When did he leave Royaumont?'

'Well, early April, then – but you just don't know – they might have been held up somewhere. You know what it's like.'

'Yes, it's possible. But,' she said standing up and smoothing her apron. 'The only way to find out is to write and ask, em, Charlotte. Now, I must go back to the ward. If you write the letter, I'll see it goes into the mail today and I'm sure you'll get an answer by return. I'm very sorry about this, but you mustn't give up hope.'

'That's *my* line,' he said. 'But, thanks, Anna.'

'See you later.' She hurried off.

James started a new page, a new letter.

No.7 Canadian General Hospital
Étaples

Dear Mr and Mrs Sinclair,

I hope you're both well.

I'm writing to you because I've heard today that the HMHS *Donegal* was torpedoed on 17 April between Le Havre and Southampton with forty lost. Magnus is much on my mind, as I saw him before I returned to the Front and I know he was to be on the *Donegal*. However I don't know if that was the date of his passage. I'm hoping he was on an earlier crossing.

I'm sorry to add to your burdens as this will if he is lost. Please could you let me know what has happened to him? We became very close while he was in Royaumont.

I can be contacted at the address above where I am currently a patient after being wounded. Thank you very much. I appreciate your help.

Yours sincerely,

James MacLeod.

At lunchtime Anna French came into the dining area.

'Excuse me.' James got to his feet and went over.

'Here's the letter. Thank you for seeing it goes into the mail.'

'You're very welcome, James. Are you feeling all right?'

'Well, better now I've done something about it. Thanks.' He returned to his table.

'Everything hunky-dory?' His neighbour Peter Sanderson, also wounded at Vimy Ridge, struggled to cut up his chicken with his bandaged hands.

'Here, let me do that.' James took the plate and cut it up into bites.

'Thanks – I'm sure I go short when you're not here to do that. So, is everything all right? You look a bit over-serious.'

'I was just giving Anna a letter for the mail. She told me about the *Donegal* and …'

'What about the *Donegal*?'

James told him what he knew.

'It's horrible when you don't know. That happened with me – with a friend. I didn't hear for ages.'

'Was he all right?'

'No, he died. It was about two years ago. We were brought up next door to each other. Anyway, I was posted and you just have to get on with it. But, it doesn't go away.'

James went up to his wee side-ward after lunch. He took out his photograph of Charlotte, his one and only memento of her. The photo was a little tired-looking after spending days and nights in his inside pocket. The eyes looking out at him were as steady as ever. He kissed the photo and fell asleep with it in his hand.

A few days later, a morning of pouring rain and wind, Jimmy the postie came in with the mail.

'Here you are. Another from France. He put the slightly crumpled letter down on the kitchen table. 'Sorry it's a bit damp.'

'You're a bit damp yourself,' said Meg. 'Want some tea? It's just poured.'

'Thanks,' he took the mug. 'It's pouring.'

'I'll take this through to Mr Sinclair.' Edie propped up her iron and went away.

Alexander sat, as usual reading the latest War news in the paper.

'Excuse me, Mr Sinclair, a letter for you and Mrs Sinclair.'

'Thanks Edie.'

The outside door banged. Charlotte came in. 'Sorry about the noise. The wind is quite high today. Any mail?'

'Yes. There's an odd one from, that James MacLeod. You know, the minister. Apparently he's worried that Magnus might have been lost with the *Donegal*. Funny that. I was reading about it in the paper just the other day.'

'What about it?'

'Well, It's a hospital ship and was crossing from Le Havre to Southampton on the 17th and these damned U-boats torpedoed it. Can you imagine, a hospital ship, with its special green and red lights on?'

'And they torpedoed it?'

'Yes, that's what I'm saying. It was in the paper but by that time we knew Magnus was at Glamis and I didn't think anything about it in relation to him.'

'How terrible. But why does he think Magnus might have been with it?'

'Because it seems Magnus was expecting to be on the *Donegal* and Mr MacLeod doesn't know which crossing he was on. He wants us to write to him?'

'Of course,' said Charlotte. 'Poor soul, he must be so anxious. Does he give a current contact address.'

'Yes, some hospital in Étaples. More or less on the French coast. He's a patient there.'
Charlotte took a breath. 'A patient?'

'Yes, he's been wounded.'

'Oh. Does he say how he is?' Charlotte kept her voice cool, disinterested.

'Well, if he's able to write a letter, he can't be too bad. Look, Charlotte, you write him for me, would you? After all, you went to his kirk. You know him. Tell him Magnus is alive and reached Glamis safely – you know the kind of thing to say. Thank him for his concern.'

Another deep breath.

'Of course. I'll write after lunch.'

'Thanks.'

Charlotte

I held myself together as I picked up the letter and went out of the room. I made for the bathroom and locked myself in before I felt able to read the letter. I sat down, opened up the one sheet. It was so formal, so correct. But of course it had to be.

'He's alive,' I whispered into the towel I was holding. 'He's alive. Oh thank you, thank you.' I sat and cried into that towel, with relief, emotion, I don't know what else. All the worry of so long seemed to come to a head with the few words on that piece of paper.

I had to pull myself together. It was nearly lunch time. Angus would be in from school. I ran water into the basin and bathed my face and eyes. I wasn't impressed with my looking-glass reflection. Cold water helped a little, then, some cream and a little powder. I could hear Angus talking as he came in. I went downstairs, the letter in my pocket.

At lunch the action against the *Donegal* was uppermost on Alexander's mind. It dawned on him how dangerous Channel crossings seemed to be to Allied soldiers, brought home to him by what he saw as Magnus's near miss. He talked about the perfidy of the enemy, and when Angus asked about 'perfidy' he explained at length about treachery and cheating. Angus thumped the table about the wickedness of the enemy and went back to school ready to tell his friends.

After lunch I took myself to the peace and quiet of the bedroom to write the letter to James.

Birkenshaw,
Jarlshavn.

Dear Mr MacLeod,

Thank you for your letter, received today. I'm writing by return as this must be a great worry for you and we're anxious to put your mind at rest. I'm happy to tell you that Magnus was not on the HMHS *Donegal* on the night of that particular sad crossing. He crossed to England on that route but on the week previous to the one in question. I'm sorry you were anxious about this.

Magnus arrived recently at Glamis Castle Auxiliary Hospital, Glamis, Angus. His health is not bad I think, considering what he has been through although he still has a way to go before he's well again. Christina met him at Edinburgh Waverley Station and they had a happy two hours together while he waited for the Dundee train.

We were sorry to note from your letter that you have been wounded and hope that this was not serious and that you'll be on the mend and out of hospital soon.

Thank you from us both for your care shown to Magnus in Royaumont. Magnus has told us by letter what a help and support you were and we appreciate this deeply.

With very best wishes to you and a speedy recovery.

Yours sincerely,

Charlotte Sinclair.

How I wished I could relax and write him a 'proper' letter from myself. But this was not to be. Before going out to catch the post I tucked James's letter into my special box along with his letter to me sent on 9 April 1917 before he went to face whatever that day would bring, and the old handkerchief with *JM* embroidered in the corner.

Then I went out into the wind again to catch the post.

Chapter 39

Sister Rosemary Jones's morning tea-break was a much appreciated pleasure. The staff had all discussed this phenomenon of regular tea-breaks and wondered if the powers-that-be understood more than they let on and moved staff away from acute battle areas where working days were long and arduous and tea breaks were almost unknown, to less stressing situations and then back again. They were all aware that this wouldn't be for the staff's sake alone. Nursing staff at a peak of fitness and wellbeing were more able to provide an excellent and sustained level of service to their patients. Like running a stable of race-horses they all said.

In her short time in Glamis, Rosemary's personal tea-break habit had progressed. Now, on a fine day, after saying where she was going, she went out to the garden, complete with mug to sip as she strolled along. About ten days after her arrival, she was strolling and sipping and looking at the plants and trees. She loved the new spring foliage and wondered how much further on they would be in Wales. She turned a corner and came upon Magnus sitting on a seat in the sun.

'Oh, Magnus, sorry, I didn't know you were here. How are you today?'

'I'm fine thanks, I'm fine. Sit down.' He moved along to make space for her.

'Thanks.' There was silence for a moment.

'Are you settling in all right?'

'Yes, it's so good, just for a time to have the space to breathe, to look around, instead of always rushing. And yet be doing my job too.'

'I wish I could do my job.'

'Magnus, give yourself time.'

'Yes, I know, but I'd like to get back to work. I need to immerse myself in work.'

'Why Magnus? '

'Ach, I don't know. I've made such a mess, of everything.'

'Have you? You mean by being wounded? You couldn't help that.'

'No, no, I realise that. But, well, just my life really…'

'Do you want to speak about it?'

'I don't know.' He put his head in his hands. 'I don't know.'

'Magnus,' she said, 'I noticed on the train from Creil to Le Havre you wear a Canadian cap-badge. That's quite unusual – a Scot, or rather a Shetlander, wearing a cap-badge from another country. I sensed there was a story behind the cap-badge. D'you remember I commented on it at the time?' He nodded.

'Has that got anything to do with this problem?' He looked up.

'You're very perceptive.'

'Well?'

'I suppose,' he began reluctantly. 'I suppose that's part of it.' He sighed. 'But,' he went on, 'it all began before I went to Canada.'

'Do you want to go back to the beginning?'

'I could, I suppose.'

'Magnus, I don't want to interrupt, but I see Èlise over there heading inside. I'll go and tell her when my break time is over, I'll be here with you. Stay here. I'll be right back.' Magnus watched as she walked swiftly over and spoke to Èlise who nodded and waved. He raised a hand to her.

'Sorry about that.' Rosemary sat down again. 'Now we've plenty of time. I don't want to create an artificial situation but I'd have had to go back soon otherwise.' There was a pause as he gathered his thoughts.

'It'd be good if I could tell someone,' he said. 'Someone not involved. It's very difficult.'

'Where's the beginning? How old were you when you think all this began?'

'I suppose I was about thirteen, maybe fourteen. My mother was very ill. Consumption.' Rosemary nodded.

'I didn't know that at the time – I just knew something was very wrong they weren't telling me. Then Charlotte appeared on the scene. She was the new teacher.'

'Charlotte?'

'Yes.' He half smiled. 'You'll meet her. She's arriving tomorrow.'

'O-oh, Mrs Sinclair. Of course, Charlotte.'

'Yes. Charlotte was wonderful. Such a support. So keen to help and such a friend to Mother. Mother, she died a few months later. I found it very difficult. I was old enough to be part of the funeral, understand what was going on. Christina didn't really understand. I don't know if she ever said anything about our mother to you. She was only three.'

'She only told me that her birth mother had died when she was very young. I don't know if she remembered very much at all. She calls Charlotte, 'Mother' doesn't she?'

'Yes, that's right. I couldn't call her that – sorry, I'm getting ahead of myself…He paused.

'Anyway,' he continued. 'Life had to go on. Then I found that there was gossip going about regarding my father and Charlotte. I was so angry. I suppose I must have been about sixteen when I thought I must be in love with Charlotte myself. The very idea of my father with her didn't bear thinking about. I got through school and got myself to Medical School in Aberdeen. The holidays were awful but I thought I could cope.'

'Did anyone else know?'

'Lowrie, my great friend Lowrie, jaloused – sorry – suspected, early on. Then I eventually told him, one day when I was very upset. It came to a head when my father found out. I was working in the Gilbert Bain Hospital in Lerwick and trying to keep away from her. But pressure to go home on days off was coming from all sides. So I did – go home, I mean. My father caught me trying to persuade Charlotte to come away with me. Stupid, I know, but there you are. He was furious, ordered me off to Canada. To cut it all very short, I finished up with a job in Calgary. Then the War started, I joined up and now I'm here. My whole life's been a mess because of this.'

'Magnus, how do you feel now about Charlotte?'

'Well,' he said, sidestepping the question, 'my father keeps pressurising me to go home and stay with them. My place is there now and all that. But, to be fair, I think he's

247

quite concerned about me and I'm sensing that's why Charlotte's coming, apart from trying to get me to go back.'

'Yes, but how do you *feel* about her?'

He hesitated. 'I don't know…I'm still very fond of her, of course, but…'

'But?'

'Well, Lowrie came to see me in Royaumont. I was still in the early stages of recovery, very emotional and all that. It was good to see him – we'd lost touch with each other. Because of the War. He was behind the lines, heard I was there, borrowed his CO's horse and rode over one day.'

'Heavens, that was resourceful.' She smiled at the thought.

'Anyway,' he went on. 'We talked about Charlotte and I went on and on, but with hindsight, I was a wee bit over-the-top. I've thought about it all since. I truly thought I was in love with her, when I was younger. But, now, well, she's a lovely woman. She happens to be married to my father. I love her as a dear friend who has helped and strengthened me in many times of great need.'

He took a deep breath, hesitated then continued.

'I think I may have mistaken that for,' he lifted a shoulder, 'a lover's love, a long term being together forever love. It's taken me months, since Lowrie's visit, to think this through. I'm still working through it. It's been very difficult. Do you want to know what has helped?'

'Yes, what was that?'

'Meeting you on the hospital train.' She looked down at her hands. Then up at him and smiled.

'Then,' he said. 'Then I thought I'd lost you at No 2 Hospital at Le Havre. Then, I got to Edinburgh and who was there but Christina, informed by you. I knew you were flying about somewhere. Then I arrive here and what do I hear but you've been posted in. I said you were a witch when I saw Christina in Edinburgh. Now I think it's true. He put his hand out to cover hers.

'Are you? A witch?'

'No Magnus,' she said. 'I'm not a witch. Just an ordinary human being doing what I can.' She carefully drew away her hand.

'But Rosemary…'

'Magnus,' she interrupted. 'You're a patient and as it happens, a doctor. I'm a nurse. You *know* that I must keep a professional distance from my patients.' He sighed.

'But Rosemary…'

'But me no buts, Magnus – not in this instance. No flirting.' He was silent. Then,

'You've squashed me.'

'No I haven't,' she said. 'Magnus, I'm not squashing you. I'm just trying to get us to take a step back. Look how far you've come this morning. You were worried. You've been able to speak about your problem. How do you feel now?' He considered.

'Better, I suppose. Ye-es, better.' He smiled. 'That's one positive thing.'

'How do you feel about seeing Charlotte tomorrow?'

'Well, I was very anxious about it but now…'

'Now?'

'I think I can cope a bit better now. I was worried about what she would say. I don't want to hurt her.'

'I don't know Charlotte of course, but has it ever occurred to you that she might be having similar worries? About you?'

'Do you think so?'

'I don't know. But it's possible. You'll just have to wait and see.'

'Now,' she stood up, smoothed her apron. He looked at her and smiled.

'You all do that.'

'All do what?'

'Er, smooth your aprons.' He laughed. 'Every nurse I've ever seen does that when she stands up.'

'Well, from the truly serious to the truly ridiculous, you are a master.' She self-consciously smoothed the apron again.

'Rosemary,' he said, as they were walking back.

'Yes?'

'A wee while ago, you mentioned the word, "us" and "taking a step back".'

'Magnus,' she warned.

'Yes, but, does that mean that there ever could be an occasion when we could take a step forward?'

'Let's just wait and see, shall we? Your priority at the moment is to get well. Mine is to help you do it.'

The train toiled into Dundee station about fifteen minutes late. Charlotte picked up her case and handbag and looked out. She heard the stationmaster shouting, 'Dundee-ee', Dundee-ee,' up and down the length of the train. In a sudden fluster, she opened the door. People milled about, either getting off or waiting to get on for the next stop over the Tay Bridge and all stops through Fife to Edinburgh. She stepped down carefully. She never had liked the gap between train and platform. She felt safer once she was down.

She looked about her. She'd never been to Dundee before. People headed purposefully for the exit. She supposed she should too and hope to find her lift to Glamis.

'Excuse me. Hello.' Footsteps came up behind her. She stopped, turned, came face to face with a man in uniform. He smiled and saluted.

'Are you Mrs Sinclair?'

'Yes, I am. Are you…?'

'Burnett, at your service, Ma'am. I'm here to convey you to Glamis Castle. Please, come this wey.' He led her in the opposite direction from the sign-posted exit. 'This is a quick wee wey that A ken, far they let me park ma car sometimes. It's handy when folk I'm giein a lift tae sometimes canna walk that far.'

'Did you think that of me?'

'Well, I wisna sure – so I thought it best to err on the safe side.' He smiled sideways at her as they walked along. 'But noo, I can see that you're eesed wi steppin oot wi the best o them.'

She smiled. 'I suppose I do walk a lot one way and another.'

'Here's wir car,' he said, pointing out the elderly vehicle. 'Nae luxurious-like but gets ye there. Front or back, Ma'am?'

'Oh, front I think please. Then I can see where I'm going. I've never been here before, you see.'

'Well I'm glad you've managed a fine day. Can be afa in winter but May can be afa fine.'

'I think you come from my part of the country – north east?'

'Ay, Captain Sinclair picked that up as weel. A'm fae Deeside. Fit about ee, far aboots div ee come fae.'

'Donside, Glenbuchat.'

'Man aat's afa bonny up ere. Bit lainly, though.'

'Different anyway.'

There was silence for a time then she said, 'But tell me, how is Captain Sinclair?'

'Well, he's deein weel as far as A can see. A bittie slow ye ken, bit A think ilka day he's comin on. We winna be lang noo. We're jist comin tae the afa driveway. They ca it a driveway bit A caa it a wee roadie – that's jist fit it is. He stopped talking as he negotiated the old car round the potholes. Eventually they drew up in front of the castle with a flourish and a squeak of brakes.

'Here noo. An there's Sister Jones waitin fur ye. A'll take yer bag in and then ging awa and ile that squeak.' He handed Charlotte over to Sister Rosemary Jones with a, 'Here she is, A'll tak the bag up. Nice tae meet ye, Mrs Sinclair', and he was off.

'Mrs Sinclair, hello, I'm Rosemary Jones. I'm so glad to meet you. Did you have a good journey? And, did Burnett collect you with no problems?'

'Yes, thank you, all was fine. It was very good of him to come and meet me.'

'Oh, he enjoys doing it. It's all part of his job. Come, I'll show you where your room is, and a little of the geography of the castle so you find your way about.'

Ten minutes later Charlotte descended the stairs.

'Have you everything you need?' Rosemary waited at the foot of the stairs with a tea tray in her hands.

'Yes, thank you. I feel fine, and I've washed the train off my hands.'

'Good. I've made some tea. Magnus is outside in the sunshine. I'll point out where to you. Shall I carry the tray out or would you like to take it out yourself? Perhaps you'd like to do that?'

'Oh yes, please. Just show me where he is.'

'Look over there. You can see him sitting on the seat. He's reading, I think.'

Charlotte walked carefully over the grass, tray in her hands. Her feet made no sound and she was quite near before he raised his head.

'Tea-time, Magnus.'

'Charlotte.' He turned, rose to his feet and stepped towards her.

'Charlotte…' he stopped. Looked at her. His face crumpled.

'It's all right, Magnus.' She put the tray down on a nearby table and held out her arms.

They stood for a long time, just holding each other. When they drew apart they looked at each other. Both faces were wet, eyes shining with tears. Simultaneously, they pulled out handkerchieves, wiped eyes, blew noses. They smiled at each other.

'After all this time,' she said, 'and all we can do is cry. Now,' she said when they had come to themselves a little. 'Let me have a look at you.' She scrutinised the man, seeing little in common with the young boy she had once known, let alone the young man she remembered working in the hospital in Lerwick. He squirmed under her steady gaze.

'I know I'm not a fashion plate…'

'You never were, Magnus. But – you've had a bad time I'm thinking. I don't think we who are left at home can ever imagine what it's like. How are you, really?'

'Well,' he said. 'You know about the injuries. The head injury left me out cold for about five weeks. It was James MacLeod who finally identified me. He was such a support, at Royaumont. He came as often as he could to visit and to help. He even worked on the wards to help the nursing staff.'

'Did he really?'

'Yes, they said they would give him a job if he was ever stuck. He had to go back to the Front. I wonder how he is. I haven't heard. Have you? I don't know whether he's dead or alive.'

'Yes, I do know how he is and he's alive.'

'He's alive?' Magnus nearly cried again. 'Oh, I'm so thankful. 'But, how do you know?'

'He wrote to us.'

'He wrote to you? But why?'

'Because he was worried about you.'

'But he knew where I was going, that I was all right.'

'Yes, but you see, Magnus, HMHS *Donegal* was torpedoed with forty drowned on the same route that you were on, the week after you. James knew you were going on the *Donegal* but didn't know which crossing and feared the worst. So he wrote to us.

'Is he all right?'

'Well, he's wounded and in hospital at Étaples but,' as Magnus gave a gasp of dismay, 'he wrote the letter himself, so seems to be all right.'

'Have you written back?'

'Yes, I wrote back and told him you were here.' Magnus heaved a sigh of relief.

'I'm so glad he's alive.'

'Yes, we all are.'

'I'll write him soon and give him the craic. Well, that's one load off my mind. I'm sorry about the *Donegal*, though. These ships did a great job.' He changed the subject.

'Are you seeing Christina while you're sooth? It was great to see her at Waverley. She looked very well.'

'No, I'm not seeing her this time. My primary purpose is to see you. She knows I'm coming. I wrote her as soon as we agreed to my trip. She quite understands – we'll probably see her soon when she gets her leave.'

'That's fine.' There was a pause and then he looked at Charlotte a little nervously, almost shyly. He looked down at his hands.

'What is it, Magnus?'

'I've been thinking…' He stopped. 'Ach, this is very difficult.'

'It is, isn't it?'

251

'What?'

'Thinking and – then, speaking out loud what you've been thinking.'

'You mean, you've been thinking as well?' he asked.

'It would surprise me if we hadn't both been thinking about... about ...'

'...what happened,' he finished for her.

'It was a long time ago. Can we come to terms with what went on then? Do you think we've moved forward a bit? It must have been very bad for you. How do you feel about it all now?'

He glanced at her, as slim as ever, the dark hair a little greyer in places now, her face showing signs of the strain over the years. The eyes were still the same. They looked at him thoughtfully, taking in the changes in him that time, war and stress had wrought. His fair hair was faded, thinner, his face lined and tired, his body too lean. Recent months had taken a severe toll. She felt her mouth tremble and bit her lip firmly. It wouldn't do to cry now.

Magnus saw the tremble and spoke gently.

'Charlotte,' he said. 'If you'd asked me that question eight or nine months ago, my answer might have been different. But, I've had a long time to think; to realise while I still have difficulty with being shown the door by my father, at the same time I must have put you and my father in a very awkward position. For that, I apologise to you. I think...I think...' he stopped.

'What do you think, Magnus?'

'I think I've had a time of growing up, if you can call it that.' He finished in a burst. 'I will always love you, Charlotte. There are just a hundred ways of loving.' She picked up his hand.

'My turn now?' And as he nodded, she continued.

'Magnus, I think we've *both* grown up a bit in the last ten years or so. We've looked back and looked at ourselves. I don't think we can call it all silly – perhaps misguided or letting things get out of hand might fit. I've no doubt we've thought about each other and been concerned over the years. And you, you vratch, have certainly added to my grey hairs by going missing and turning up half dead.'

'But,' she continued. 'More seriously, I'm sorry, too, for things I did to add to your burden. We're both older, hopefully wiser. Can we learn from this? I'll always love you too. You're right about love – so many different kinds of loving.'

They sat peacefully in the afternoon sunshine until they heard a bell ring from the Castle.

'Come,' he said. 'That's the half-hour bell.'

'What's the half-hour bell?'

'It must be six o'clock,' he said. 'The sound resonates for quite a distance and lets everyone outside know that dinner is in thirty minutes.'

That evening after dinner they watched the sun go down from the shelter of the verandah. No one else was there. The billiards table and darts board had claimed the attention of many of the men.

'It's peaceful,' she commented. 'It was much busier earlier.'

'Yes, some chaps will be having their dressings done and some their physical jerks. And then there's the games area, and of course Lady Elizabeth will be in the sitting room and some go in there and hang on to her every word.'

'What about you?'

'Oh, I do my exercises mostly in the mornings. I get up quite early.'

'And the Lady Elizabeth?'

'Charlotte, she's just a lassie – she's seventeen.'

'Well, she's a lucky lassie to live in such a house, the crypt, where we had that lovely dinner – I don't know how they manage in war-time – it's very atmospheric.'

'It's a good place isn't it? The whole castle is impressive. Much of the gardens is given over to vegetables for folk round about now that supplies are so short. We all eat a lot of home-grown produce.'

'Yes, it's the same at home – the Home Front – everyone's involved.'

A telephone rang in the distance. A minute later VAD Janet Mackay appeared. 'Excuse me, but there's a telephone call.'

'Oh,' Charlotte jumped up. 'Is everything all right?'

Janet put out a staying hand. 'It's all right. It's Christina, she said to say Christina. Will you take the call?'

'Of course, thank you.'

'The telephone is over here.'

'Hello, hello…'

'Mother, hello, have you arrived safely?'

'Yes, it's lovely to be here.'

'How's Magnus?'

'He's making good progress. He was delighted to see you at the station in Edinburgh.'

'I was glad to be there. Mother I haven't got long. Could you tell Magnus something for me please?'

'Yes, what is it?'

'Mother, he was asking in a letter about James Macleod.'

'Yes, he asked us too. I was able to tell Magnus today that he's in Étaples.'

'Mother, James is here in Edinburgh now.'

'In Edinburgh?'

'Yes, I saw his name on the admissions list from France and it said Chaplain after it. I knew it was him. I thought Magnus would like to know. I'll pop in and see him. He's been wounded, sniper fire in the chest. He's getting on fine, lucky man, no infection, making good progress.'

'Oh, poor James.' Charlotte groped for a hanky with her free hand. There was a silence.

'Mother, are you there?'

'Yes, yes, I'm here.' Charlotte pulled herself together. 'I'm glad he's reached Edinburgh. That's a good sign.'

'Yes, isn't it? Sure Magnus is all right?'

'Christina, he's getting on fine, but slowly. It will take a while I think. He's had a rough ride.'

'Poor Magnus.'

'Don't say that to him, whatever you do.'

'No, I won't. I must go, Mother. Take care.'

'Bye, Christina. Thank you for phoning.' She hung up.

VAD Janet MacKay was in the hall. 'Everything all right?'

'Yes thank you. Just getting some good news about an old friend.' She blew her nose, and went to tell Magnus the latest news.

'That was Christina.'

'Christina? What did she want?'

'To tell you about James. She didn't know you know he's all right. But now, she's seen his name on the Edinburgh admission list. So, he's back here. He has a chest wound but no infection.'

'Oh, that's good. He'll be fine if there's no infection. Nothing else?'

'No, I think she's just found out. Good of her to telephone and let us know.'

'That's families for you.'

'Yes. Good things to be a part of.'

'Ye-s, as long as everything is going smoothly.' He shifted in his chair. 'Not good if you feel you've been pushed out.'

'I can understand what you mean,' said Charlotte, remembering her own childhood when she was sent to her grandparents to be brought up and educated.

'Yes, I'm sorry,' said Magnus who had known about this for a long time. 'But it was different. You still felt cared about. I felt bereft.'

'And yet you were able to take a grip of yourself and get on with your new life. That shows real courage, Magnus. Many young men in your position would have gone to the dogs.'

'Well, I had a job to go to remember, thanks to Mr Sanderson at the Gilbert Bain, and perhaps as a sort of loyalty to him too, well I felt I couldn't let him down – nor you. Anyway, I'm thrawn as you know. I wasn't going to let my father beat me.'

'How do you feel about that now? You know, your father ...?'

He sighed. 'I may have mellowed a bit. It still hurts.'

'You managed to keep the contact going, though.'

'Ah,' he said, 'I consulted Lowrie about that.'

'You did? And what did he say?'

'He said to write to you all together as a family. Open communication. Then I could include you too.'

'Sensible.'

'Oh, and practical. Saves postage.' He smiled at his small joke.

'So, now,' Charlotte persisted. 'Your father. I need to tell him how you are. He's very anxious about you – yes he is.' She turned to Magnus as he looked ready to argue.

'Whether you believe this or not, or like it or not, he has had and still has huge guilt feelings about what happened that day. He wants to say sorry to you himself. He loves you. He said that, and as a reserved, sometimes proud man, he doesn't say these things too

254

often. I know he comes over didactic and stiff-necked. But inside, he's hurting. It's time to heal, Magnus, not just physical wounds but mental ones as well. I can understand your not wanting to come back to Birkenshaw for ever. You've your own life to lead. I went through a parallel event in a way at the Milton.'

'You did?'

Yes. I forgot you didn't know this part of my story. After my mother died, my father wanted me to go back, marry one of the farm workers so that I could keep house at the farm and therefore Dad would be fed, the farmworker would have a wife, the hens would be fed and butter made and so on.' She laughed and Magnus joined in.

'Is that really right?'

'Yes, but it was so long ago, I just look back and smile when I think about it. I was angry at the time, though.'

'I'm sure you were.'

'And I have been back. Of course I've been back for visits. And Glenbuchat doesn't stop because I'm not there making the butter.'

'Magnus,' she continued. 'Please will you consider coming to see your father? He's had two strokes. He can't come and visit you, however much he wants to. He'd give much to change what happened. He can't do that. None of us can go back. He wants to say sorry and make his peace with you. Can you give a not very well old man that?'

He paused. His pride, his thrawn-ness stood in his way. That's what it boiled down to. He looked at her.

'We're so alike, my father and me.' She didn't speak.

'What should I do?'

'What do you feel like doing?'

'I don't know. I could – I suppose I could get a few days' leave when I'm able.' Charlotte's relief was almost tangible.

'Do you think that would be possible?'

'I don't see why not. I'd have to be passed fit, of course – to go on the boat overnight.'

'Would you need an escort?'

'I don't know.'

'Magnus,' Charlotte said. 'Just a thought. If you're serious about coming for a few days…' He nodded as she looked at him.

'Christina will be on leave soon. Could you come together?'

'That's an idea that might work. And the doctor here would agree to that, I'm pretty sure.' They smiled at each other.

'You're a genius,' he said. 'A persuasive genius.'

Rosemary Jones came through to the verandah looking for them.

'Sorry Rosemary.' Magnus pre-empted her. 'We're just coming. Time ran away with us.'

Two days later they stood together on the platform at Dundee waiting for the Aberdeen train. Magnus had special permission to be there.

'Please don't go anywhere else,' Dr Neil Fulton had instructed. 'A run in the car to the station and back with Burnett as escort is fine. Anything else would set you back.'

The station master walked up and down shouting.

'The next train to stop at Dundee, platform two is the ten fifty to Edin-burr-ugh.' A few minutes later it puffed in to the opposite platform. Doors slammed.

What about James? Charlotte was tempted. She wanted to see him, hold him, help him, go on the train to him. She stayed firmly on platform one.

'Are you all right?' Magnus asked. 'You look a little pale.'

'No, no, I'm fine. Just, thinking…'

'It'll be all right you know,' he said, misunderstanding. She squeezed his hand.

'Yes, I know. Now, here's the train.'

'The next train on platform one is the eleven o'clock for Aberdee-een.'

She waved good-bye to him until it was out of sight.

Chapter 40

'Staff Nurse Sinclair.' Sister Ross's voice cut through Christina's thoughts as she crossed the hall. She stopped guiltily. Why did one always feel guilty when Sister Ross called like that?

'Yes, Sister.'

'There's a telegram for you. It came in a few minutes ago.'

'A telegram? For me? But who would send me a telegram?'

'Better open it and see.' Sister Ross was well used to nurses receiving telegrams and picking up the pieces in the aftermath of bad news. But not this time.

Christina tore open the envelope, scanned the contents of the telegram and gazed at Sister Ross with such shining happy eyes that the older woman smiled back at her.

'Well, go on then. Tell me.'

'Oh Sister Ross, it's from Lowrie, my fiancé. He's got a weekend's home leave and we can be married a week on Saturday. That's 26 May. Oh, do you think I'll be able to change my off-duty?'

'I think, on this very special occasion, Sister Johnston should manage that. Congratulations, my dear. I think this is news we've been waiting to hear – ever since Matron said "yes" to your marriage.'

'Thank you, Sister, Oh,' Christina looked at her watch, 'I'd better go. It's nearly time. Sister's on, so I can ask her today. Thank you Sister.'

James sat in a chair beside his bed in his ward with the *Scotsman*. The War news was not particularly good. He didn't know when it would end at this rate. He was glad and thankful that the attack on Vimy Ridge had apparently been successful, even though at a price. However, the battle of Arras – here they were in May and the *Scotsman* was still reporting battles at the Scarpe, the French army in disarray and morale at rock-bottom, countless casualties, and the Americans still not on the scene although there were statements of their plans to enter the conflict. A big battle at Bullecourt was ongoing. It all made for depressing reading. He hoped and prayed that this last battle would see the Arras offensive over. It had taken a month so far.

'Morning Sir, here's your mail.' It was the new VAD. 'Just one today.'

'Thank you.' James looked at the scribbled name and took a deep breath.

'Magnus – ouch,' he muttered as his shattered ribs and the wound surrounding them protested in unison.

'Everthing all right Sir?' the VAD paused.

'Oh yes,' he said, 'just breathing.'

'Keep doing that Sir.'

When she had gone he looked at the letter dated a couple of days previously.

Glamis

Dear James,

Firstly, I was delighted to say the least, to hear that you are alive. What a relief. When you left me at Royaumont I was very bothered about you. Then when there was no news and the fighting at Vimy was so bad I feared the worst. I asked my father and Charlotte, but, nothing. Then, and it all gets a bit confusing, they received your letter asking about me and the *Donegal* and realised that because you had written it, you were alive. They wrote me in Glamis to tell me. I was so glad. I was really worried.

And, I wasn't on the *Donegal* the night she was torpedoed – I sailed the previous week. I'm sorry you were worried about that.

The next thing was that Charlotte came sooth to visit me. While she was there Christina telephoned and told us the VG news that you're in Edinburgh. I'm sorry you were wounded but very glad that you're going to be fine.

I want to tell you about Charlotte. You may remember we had a long conversation in Royaumont about my problems. I won't discuss it fully here but I wanted you to know that since that day and a later session with Lowrie, I've done much thinking and soul-searching. I needed to. Charlotte and I talked a lot during her visit and cleared up many things. All is well. We are agreed that what is past has passed, and life can go on. When I'm able, I'm going to Shetland for a week to see my father. I know that Christina has leave soon and we could go north together on the boat. This would allay any fears that the doctor may have about my balance on board.

By the way, did you ever meet a QA Sister Rosemary Jones on your travels? I met her on the hospital train I was on. She's now here at Glamis. It's very good to see her.

I hope to see you soon before long. We're not so very far away here in Glamis. In the meantime, keep going and be nice to the nurses.

Yours,
Magnus.

James sat, letter in hand. 'Charlotte,' he said quietly into himself. 'I love you.'

Christina went to see James that day when she got off duty. They were getting to know each other well. When he first arrived in Edinburgh she'd called into the ward.

'Would you like to say hello?' said Sister.

'Is that allowed? Is he able?'

'Yes, I'm sure. Come on, I'll tell him he's got a visitor.'

'Hello James. Someone here for you.' She went away.

James looked up. 'Hello, I don't think we've met. I'm at a disadvantage.'

She stood by his bedside. 'Hello Padre, we have met, but it was a long time ago and I don't think you'd remember me. I was very small. In fact I don't think I remember you either. I'm Christina Sinclair, from Jarlshavn.'

'Christina, the wee ...'

'Besom,' she finished. 'Yes, I think I was. I hope very much I've grown past the besom stage now. So, how are you, Padre?'

258

'I'm getting on fine thank you. My recovery's just moved on by meeting up with such a breath of what was a very happy home. How did you find out I was here?'

'We knew you were alive because of your letter to Mother and Father from Étaples. Then I saw your name on the admission lists. Mother was at Glamis so I telephoned and told her. She was away to tell Magnus. I expect he was delighted. He appreciated all you did for him in Royaumont.'

'How was Charlotte when you spoke?' He tried to keep his voice casual.

'She was fine I think. Mind you, I think when I told her you're in Edinburgh, she might've been crying. There was a sort of silence and I ... well I just think this War is getting to her a bit. She was fine after that though.'

She went to see him most days and was pleased to see his progress. They became firm friends. He was very happy to hear about her engagement to Lowrie.

'I remember him as a boy,' he said. 'He used to come to the Kirk with his parents. He and Magnus were very close. They were a great pair.'

'They probably still are.'

The day of Lowrie's telegram, Christina was a woman with a mission. James was sitting in what was known as the 'balcony'. His bed had been moved to this area at the end of the ward a couple of days previously – a tangible sign of improvement: definitely promotion, its inhabitants felt. It was light, airy, windows on three sides and had a relaxed atmosphere that the long nightingale-type ward full of significantly ill patients could not supply. He looked up from his book as he saw her.

'Hello, nice to see you. Had a good day?'

'Not bad.' She pulled up a chair and sat down beside him.

'How about you?'

'Good, I think. Had the consultant's round. He's pleased. The physiotherapist has been and mauled me about. He's pleased. Sister's pleased. If they're all pleased, then I'm pleased.'

'Well, I hope you're going to be pleased with my news.'

'What's that?'

'I had a telegram from Lowrie...'

'And?'

'He's got a week-end's home leave in ten days' time and is coming up – to marry me. He wants me to organise it.'

She looked at him. She was smiling but creases ran across her forehead.

'That's grand,' he said. 'Why do you look so worried?'

'Where do I begin? James,' she said, 'can you help, please? For a start, d'you think you'd be able to marry us – please?'

'I don't see why not. I'd be honoured.'

'Oh James,' she leant over and kissed him on the cheek. 'Thank you so much.'

'Where do you want to be married?'

'We could have it in the hospital. In the chapel? Or, here? In your ward?'

'The ward's a good idea,' he said. 'But you don't know the patients in this ward. What about asking if your wedding could be in your own ward. That'd be a real boost to patient morale to be at their very own Staff Nurse's wedding.'

'That's a wonderful idea. I'm sure Sister Johnston would be happy for that. Would Sister Brown allow you to go along there?'

'Yes, sure she will allow that. She might insist on a wheelchair to get me there but I can walk the rest.'

'Now,' he continued, 'supposing that's all agreed with, there are certain things you need to attend to. There isn't time for all the banns to be cried. In Scotland, we don't have what's called in England a Special Licence. So...'

'What do we do?' James thought for a moment.

'Right,' he said. 'You need to go to the minister of the Parish Church where you live, explain the situation, identify yourself and that you are resident here. I'll give you a note verifying who you are. I'll also inform him I'm going to marry you and Lowrie here.'

'Do you have to do that? Will he mind?'

'No, no. It's just a courtesy because I'm planning to marry a couple in his parish. You need to take some sort of ID for Lowrie, like a letter from him showing evidence that he is in France. Ask the minister if he will agree under these circumstances to dispense with the full Proclamation of Banns. Once that's done, then you take a Certificate of Proclamation of Banns that the minister will give you, to the Registrar. He'll give you a Marriage Schedule which you and Lowrie must bring to your wedding for me to attend to. 'And,' he added, 'You'll need two witnesses. Have you any idea whom?'

'Well,' she said, her mind in a whirl. 'I wondered if Magnus would be able. What do you think?'

'That's a good idea. I wonder if they'd let him do it? It would mean a day away on the train. Is he up to it?'

'I don't know.'

'Well, you can ask. He might require an escort from Glamis. There's your second witness perhaps. Oh, and one other thing.'

'Yes?'

'Keep your mother and father in the picture.' He spoke seriously. 'They'll be feeling quite out of it. They love you very much.'

'Yes, you're right. I was going to send a telegram today after our talk.'

'That's fine. I'm glad. Well.' He smiled at her. 'We've covered a lot of ground today. I'm delighted. Thank you for asking me to marry you and Lowrie. This is quite special. From the sublime to the ridiculous, I'm glad now I got measured for my new uniform.'

'Not ridiculous at all. What happened to the old one?'

'Oh, they cut it off me,' he said. 'Gone, weeks ago. That's why I'm wearing these old bags.' She took his hand and held it.

'James,' she said. 'I'm so glad you're here. Thank you for doing this for us.'

'Right, away with you, you besom. I'll see you to the end of the ward. Mind and do what I said.'

Edie met the telegram boy coming up the lane the following morning.

'I'll take it for you,' she offered.

'Thanks, I've a lot today.' He swung his bike round and was off.

'Telegram Mrs Sinclair.'

'Thank you.' Charlotte took it, gingerly as usual. She turned it over and scrutinised it as though its contents would leap out and tell her their news. Addressed to both of us – I'd better open it.

Lowrie arriving Edinburgh 25 May stop wedding planned 26 May stop James MacLeod officiating in ward stop writing stop love you both stop Christina

'Alexander,' she ran into his bedroom where he was planning his day. 'Here, from Christina…'

'Has she had an accident?'

'No, no. It's good news. Read it.' She thrust the paper into his hand.

'Hm, hm,' he scanned it. 'Well, we knew it was coming, I suppose. My lassie – and I won't be there to give her away.' He looked at it again. 'See who's doing it. James MacLeod. Your old minister.'

'Yes, I'm glad he's able to do that. We'll miss the wedding Alexander but she'll be up here soon for her holiday. She can tell us all about it.'

'Yes, but it won't be the same.'

'Alexander, we talked about this. It's going to happen. We can't grudge Christina this.'

'No, I know. I'm just being an old – well, father, I suppose…' He held out his hand to her. 'Bear with me.'

'Ay, ay.' She squeezed his hand. 'Now, I must go and tell Edie and Meg.' And, pause for a moment. She stopped and looked out of the open door. Her mind's eye saw the young dog-collared James walking with loping strides up the cliff-top path with the Isle of Foula in the background. How long ago that seemed.

Magnus too, had a very similar telegram.

Lowrie arriving Edinburgh 25 May stop wedding planned 26 May stop James MacLeod officiating in ward stop can you come stop hope so stop love Christina stop

'Have a read of this,' he said to Rosemary Jones who had just entered the verandah.

'Well?' she said. 'Are you going?'

'How do I go about it? I'd like to go, but…'

'There's that 'but' again. If you want to go I'll consult with Colonel Fulton, see what he says and come back and tell you. I don't see reason why not.'

Her interview with her CO was brief. He was keen to see Magnus doing something outside Glamis.

'He'll need an escort of course. It'll be a long day. Morning train into Edinburgh then early evening return.'

'That sounds feasible.'

'Yes, but, who to be escort? Needs someone responsible. I know,' he said. 'You could do it yourself.'

'Me?'

'Yes, why not? Sister Ellis can act up. She does it anyway on your day off. You can have a day at the wedding with Magnus, keep him in order, don't let him get drunk whatever you do and come back in the evening. We'll put Burnett on driver-duty – he won't mind, he likes Magnus – and you. And, we'll probably manage train warrants for you both. There you are.' He swished his hands together. 'Done and dusted.'

Later that day Christina received two telegrams.

Very happy for both stop hope all well stop thanks to James stop writing stop love Father and Mother stop.

Coming to nuptials stop expect two stop arriving morning train Saturday 26 stop writing stop love Magnus stop.

The next few days passed in a blur. Christina, on duty every day to ensure a long weekend off for the wedding, consulted her 'to do' lists every five minutes. Sister Johnston was co-operation itself. She was delighted to have one of her Staff Nurses being married on her ward. It had never happened before. Perhaps this would start a trend. The news had certainly rippled round the ward – the patients who were able, could talk of little else and whether or not they had clean shirts to wear.

'What about lunch?' she asked. 'Let's ask the kitchen if they would do a buffet-lunch as well as the usual dinners. This is an important event.'

'Do you think they would do that?'

'I don't see why not. This is once in a lifetime.' She looked at Christina and laughed. 'I hope. And, it's good for the patients.'

Christina visited the local minister to sort out the business of Banns.

'No problem,' he said, 'what a happy story. I'm delighted to help. I'll call the Banns on Sunday and do the necessary paperwork. Could you come back and collect the papers – no, wait a minute. I've a better idea. I'll be visiting in the Infirmary on Tuesday. What ward are you in?'

'Sixteen.'

'Right, I'll come up when I'm there and hand the papers in to you. Will you be there? In the afternoon?'

'Yes,' said Christina. 'Thank you very much. That's a great help.'

'Well, you won't have much spare time, with all this running around and your work. Are you quite sure that's everything you need?'

'Yes, I think so.'

'Which ward is your Padre in? What's his name again?' He scanned the paper she had given him.

'James MacLeod. He's in ward twenty.'

262

'I can visit him as well when I'm in. We'll probably find out that we were at university together or something. No, probably I'm a great deal older. But I'll just check when I'm there that he has everything he needs.'

James kept a watching brief on the proceedings. He liked her earnestness. He was sure she'd leave no stone unturned to get things right. He was delighted to see the Rev George MacEwan walking down the ward towards his bed. They conferred in a ministerial way about weddings in general and this one in particular.

'She's a very nice young lady,' said James. 'I knew her first when she was about three, in Shetland. It's good to see her again, all grown up.'

'What about the 'groom?'

'Oh, he's a Shetlander as well. In France at the moment. He should arrive at Waverley on Friday. I remember him as a boy. He ran around with Christina's brother. He's currently a patient in Glamis but coming to be a witness.'

'Do they allow that? Patients out for this sort of thing?'

'If it's at all possible, it's encouraged. Morale must be kept up if possible. It's difficult – it's very bad out there. The public are not fully informed, they just don't understand. When the men do get home on leave, they say that folk say things like, "What, home again. You must be having the life of Riley out there. When are you going back?" They have no conception…'

'Would you come and preach in my pulpit one Sunday? It might help the congregation to understand. When you're able, of course,' George added hastily.

'I might do that, thanks,' said James, after a moment's hesitation. 'Once I'm able to walk further.'

'I'd come and get you of course, but thank you. I would appreciate that. Now, have you everything you need for the marriage?'

'Yes, I even have my Order of Service book. I've been reading it and …'

'What about robes?'

'Well, I have a new uniform – with the right buttons…'

'The right buttons?'

'Yes, they're black with the Chaplains Department insignia on them.' James laughed at the other man's face. 'But my robes and scarf are all packed in some quartermaster's store. That's what happens when you're wounded. Everything possible is kept safely for you.'

'I'll lend you a robe,' said George.

'All right, thank you. That's good of you.'

'I'll hand it in later this week.' George got up. 'I must go. I've a couple of old parishioners to see.'

263

Chapter 41

Friday came at last. Christina arrived early at the station and joined the waiting crowd. It was the same night train as before, due at 8.30am.

This time she saw him first. He was looking for her, hanging out of the window, hand on the door-handle ready to jump down the moment the train stopped. She moved through the crowd. The train slowed and stopped. As he opened the door he looked up and their eyes met.

He was first off the train. For a moment there was no-one else on the platform. They lost all sense of anyone else. They stood in a long silent holding of each other as others, shouting and hullo-ing, pushing and shoving, mingled past. They saw none of it.

'Are you all right?' He spoke at last.

'Yes,' she said. 'Are you?'

'I love you so much. It took me all my time to get through the last few days I can tell you. I'm so glad to see you.'

'Me too.'

'How have you got on with the admin?'

'Fine, no problems. I'll tell you in a minute. Are you hungry?'

'Yes. I wrote Mrs Dunn a few days ago and she is getting in some bread and things. Would you mind very much if we just go home for breakfast?'

'Home,' she said. 'That sounds lovely.'

'It is home,' he said seriously. 'At least, I hope you want it to be like that too. To begin with anyway, you know, when we're married.'

'Oh Lowrie, can we be there, this week-end? Tomorrow…'

'That's what I was hoping.'

They held hands as Lowrie hailed a taxi, gazed at each other as they drove along with no eyes for the streets of the New Town. The Stockbridge Colonies were not far. Mrs Dunn was waiting.

'How lovely to see you both again. The kettle's on, your breakfast's laid, just as you asked Captain Harcus.'

'Thank you very much,' Mrs Dunn. 'You got my letter, then?'

'Oh yes, and I've done your shopping, milk and bread and so on. Any time, Captain Harcus.'

'You're very kind. Are you and Mr Dunn both well?'

At last they were alone. They greeted each other all over again until Christina heard the kettle-lid rattling as the kettle boiled and ran to turn it down.

'So what like a week have you had with all the work to do?'

'It's gone well – couldn't have been better as long as you're happy with what I've arranged.'

'Go on then. Where, who, what, when and why?'

'Well, the Banns were called in the local church on Sunday. That'll do under the circumstances. We're getting married in my ward on Saturday…'

here.

vard:
ring,
the

pital

were

hich

are

'll

'What? Is that allowed?'

'Yes, good for morale and Sister's very happy – but you asked all the questions in one sentence and I'm just trying to tell you.'

'OK, sorry. I think you're at who?'

'The Reverend James Macleod…'

'What – James, who used to be in Jarlshavn?'

'Yes, he's a patient here, but he's a lot better,' she added quickly. 'He's very pleased to be marrying us.'

'That's very good, so much better than having somebody we don't know. How is he?'

'Improving every day – but we're at 'What?' – well it's a wedding. 'Why? – well, why does anyone get married?' She looked at him, her eyes full of mischief. 'I don't know if I'm prepared to answer that one. Any more questions?'

'Yes. How did you manage to get all this done in such a short time? I was quite concerned about landing you with it.'

'I was concerned too. Delighted of course, but I didn't have a clue where to begin.'

'So…'

'So, I went to James. He's been such a help. He pointed me in all the right directions. Oh, and another very important thing.'

'You mean there's more?'

'Lowrie, we need witnesses,' she paused, 'and, you know who's coming?'

'No,' he said patiently.

'Magnus.'

'Magnus? Magnus?' He put his head in his hands as his eyes filled with tears. 'Here I go again,' he said, pulling out his handkerchief. 'Every time I get away from that blasted Front, I start crying. Did you say Magnus? Is he able?'

'Lowrie,' Christina put her arms round him. 'He's able to come on the train tomorrow with an escort. She telephoned the ward yesterday just to check on timings. Her name is Rosemary Jones, she's Sister-in-Charge of Glamis and they'll be in Edinburgh on the morning train in time for the wedding.'

'That's perfect. We know a lot about each other, you know. We go back a long way. I can't think of anyone I'd like better to be there. What about this Rosemary – Jones did you say? Will she be the other witness?'

'Yes, I think that will be fine. Now, how have you been getting on? '

'I… well I've done a bit too. Behind the scenes.'

She tickled the hair behind his ear. He wriggled.

'You'll spoil my concentration. Come here, besom.'

'What have you been doing?'

'Organising the ring. I've got it.'

'Oh, Lowrie. How did you manage that?'

'Well, I hope this is all right with you, but I spoke to my mother and she said we could have my grandmother's ring if we'd like it. I liked the idea. It's a plain gold band. Here I have it in my pocket.' He took out a tiny old heart-shaped box and showed Christina the ring. She stared at it in silence.

'I know it's not new,' he said, 'but …'

265

'Lowrie, it's perfect, I don't want a new ring if I can have your Granny's one. That means so much to me. Thank you so much.'

'I'm glad. You'd better try it on.'

'Do you think I should?'

'Just to see that it fits. Here, I'll put it on for you.' It fitted perfectly.

'It fits. How did that come about?' He looked very innocent.

'Lowrie?'

'Well,' he admitted, 'I wrote down your engagement ring size. So it was easy to have this one altered to fit. I'll give it to Magnus in the morning and then you can have it for ever.'

That evening they went to see James. He looked Lowrie up and down.

'You've grown.' They burst out laughing.

'Just a little. I remember Magnus and me doing strenuous exercises up the back of Jarlshavn to get ourselves bigger, taller, fitter. It was all the rage.'

'I remember that place well – a great place for walking. Now,' James asked, 'how are you? Are you both ready for tomorrow? Christina, are you exhausted after all your running around?'

They went over the Wedding Service together making alterations in the wording here and there. 'After all, it's your wedding,' James said, 'If there's something special you want to say, well let's put it in.'

'I'm glad we're not saying "obey",' said Lowrie.

'I'm glad too,' said James. 'Forward thinking. Time they gave women the vote too.'

'You're quite right,' said Christina. 'Mother's all for it as well.' She returned to the service. 'I like the "to love and to cherish" bit.'

'Good words, yes. And, they're words for both. Now,' James sat pencil ready, 'anything else?'

'I think,' said Christina, 'given the circumstances, we might put in "far and near".'

'Yes,' said Lowrie. 'I like that. Brings it home to you.' James wrote the note into the service.

'Till tomorrow, then. You know, this is the first marriage I've done for a while. We don't get to do much marrying in the trenches. I'm very privileged.'

'It's we who are privileged. Good night James.'

They said a quiet good night to each other outside the nurses' home.

'Till tomorrow.' She watched him walk down the road. He turned back at the entrance and waved. The door opened and closed behind her.

Tomorrow came as it always does.

It came, too, for Magnus and Rosemary. Both in clean, pressed uniforms, they smiled at each other like a pair of excited schoolchildren set free for the day. Burnett, driver for the day sensed the excitement. They stopped outside the station.

'Here ye are,' he said. 'Mind and hae a gweed day. An dinna miss yer train hame. A'll hae the Colonel tae answer til if yer nae there.'

'That's all right, Burnett,' said Rosemary. 'We'll be there. And thank you very much for the lift.'

The train was on time. It arrived in Edinburgh at eleven o'clock. They were early at the Infirmary.

'How d'you feel? D'you feel able to walk all the way to the ward or shall we have a wheelchair. I'm sure they'd lend us one.'

'No thank you,' said Magnus. 'I'll walk.'

'It might be a long way. I know about hospital corridors.'

'I'll walk,' repeated Magnus. 'I'm fine. I've been taking walks for days.'

'We'll take our time then.' They strolled through the gate to the Porter's Lodge.

'Ward 16 is it?' The porter came out of his Lodge to point. See, you just go through the Main Entrance over there, and then along a bit and you'll see the signs – you can't miss them.' He smiled – 'how many times have I said that and people have come back saying they can't find the signs? Some people don't look.'

'That's all right,' said Magnus, 'we'll look. Thanks very much.' They walked on. Through the entrance, along the corridor.

'There's the sign, keep going, then up I think.'

This was the main corridor. It was busy, porters with trolleys of all sizes, orderlies pushing patients in wheelchairs, trolleyed stretchers with nurses aiming, Rosemary thought for the operating theatre, doctors in white coats, uniformed nurses, people. People everywhere.

'I'm glad I'm in Glamis,' said Magnus, looking around.

'Yes, but places like this are very necessary. It's busy, though.' They stood aside to let a large trolley past.

They climbed slowly to the first floor where they stopped for Magnus to get his breath back.

'I think Ward 16 is on this floor,' said Rosemary. 'There's the sign. It's through there. Take your time. It's not far.'

Below them they could hear feet climbing the stairs quickly. As they came round the curve of the stair Magnus looked down and smiled in recognition.

'I thought it was you in front of me,' Lowrie exclaimed. He took the last few steps two at a time and clasped Magnus to him.

'Oh it's good to see you. How are you?'

'I'm fine. And,' turning to Rosemary, Magnus said, 'may I present our bridegroom for today, Lowrie Harcus. Lowrie, this is Sister Rosemary Jones who is here to keep me in order.'

'I'm very pleased to meet you,' said Lowrie, saluting. 'You must have an awful job with him. I know him of old.'

'I'm glad to meet you too. I've heard a lot about you.'

'I don't know what to say to that.'

'I think we should walk on,' said Magnus.

'I need to give you the ring,' said Lowrie, digging in his pocket. 'Before we get there. Here it is. You won't lose it will you?'

'Safe with me.'

'I'll watch him.' Rosemary promised.

They walked past the busyness of the corridor, past the noise of the working ward: voices, feet, cries, screens being trailed from bed to bed, trolleys, trays clattering, sterilisers bubbling, opening and closing with clanging lids, instruments dropping in the sink for scrubbing.

'It's a noisy place,' said Lowrie, who had not, fortunately, he thought, been a hospital patient.

Rosemary had been looking around her with interest. 'Yes, it's so busy. They were probably receiving last night. Ah, Sister...'

Sister Johnston came forward. Her cuffs were off, her sleeves rolled up.

'Welcome to you all. How very good this is. I'm Mary Johnston, Ward Sister. Which of you is the bridegroom?' Lowrie stepped forward, saluted, and introduced all round.

'I'm so glad to meet you all. Staff Nurse Sinclair – Christina, and Padre MacLeod are in here.'

'Lowrie,' Christina hugged him. 'You made it.'

'Why, did you think I wouldn't? He stood back, admiring her in her uniform. 'You scrub up really well.'

'Lowrie.' She waved her bouquet at him. He put his arm round her and kissed her. 'Only joking.'

'Look, here's Magnus.'

'Magnus.' Her voice broke.

'Now.' he said, 'No crying, this is a happy day. Here's Rosemary.'

'Hello Rosemary. Thank you for helping Magnus come to my wedding. And, here's James MacLeod our Padre. I don't think you've met.'

'How do you do Padre? It's good to see you here.'

'James,' said Magnus. 'I couldn't get to you for this noisy lot.' They shook hands.

'How are you,' they said to each other in chorus, and then started laughing.

'Let's talk about that later,' said James. 'How's our time Sister?'

'It's ten past twelve. I was thinking that seeing the ward is so very busy at this end, you could go to the far end, near the balcony entrance, where all the fitter men are. They're really excited and looking forward to this. You can leave your outer things here and there is a looking-glass here if you wish but you all look pretty good to me.'

Rosemary went over.

'I'll just change my outdoor hat for my indoor.' She stood at the mirror and carefully pinned on the regulation QA Sister's veil.

'No use in a wind, this thing,' she said.

'Padre,' said Sister Johnston. 'Would you like to come with me and I'll show you where I've put the table for you.'

'How are you?' she said, as they walked through the busy ward. 'You're not overdoing it, are you?'

'No, I'm fine, Sister Brown insisted I have a wheelchair, but really I'm fine.'

'Well, I've put chairs near in case anyone, and that includes you, should need to sit down.'

'Thank you. That's very considerate.'

He put his Order of Service book on the table along with a small hand-carved wooden Cross.

'One of the soldiers carved that,' he said, 'and gave it to me. The next day the poor soul was dead. He'd be glad that it's used for this sort of thing.'

The small wedding party entered the ward a few minutes later. The patients watched with interest.

James looked at Lowrie and Christina.

'Ready?' He said quietly. They nodded. He took a breath and began.

'Dearly Belovèd, we are gathered here…'

Rosemary was very moved. I'm so glad I came, so glad. This is one of the most beautiful ceremonies I have been to – and yet it's so simple. She stole a look at Magnus. He was standing very still watching his sister marry his best friend. He turned as he felt her gaze and smiled at her, such a happy smile that her heart leapt.

Sister Johnston sat in her chair at the side, relieved to get the weight off her feet for a wee while, glad to be involved, and for 'her' men to see a better side to the War. As she watched she thought as well of her own 'soldier laddie', 'somewhere in France'.

Magnus stood, listening. Watching, waiting for his cue from James, to present the ring. He felt Rosemary's gaze and turned to meet her eyes. What he saw there gave him such scope for hope in the future that he smiled across to her. He instinctively wanted to take her hand. He pulled himself together as he heard James's cue and carefully took the ring out for James to bless and hand to Lowrie.

Lowrie carefully put the ring on his bride's finger. Then he held on to the ringed hand as well as the other. Like that they kissed. Like that they received the special Blessing.

Suddenly it was over. The Register signing, the congratulations to the happy couple, the buffet lunch provided by the Infirmary kitchens, the wine provided by Sister Johnston (her contribution she said), the parade round the beds, the smiling clapping men sitting clean-shirted, in beds, on chairs, one young lad on a window-sill.

Christina slipped away into the office where she had put her clothes for 'going away'. Her best gown hung at the back of the door. She slipped it over her head and wriggled it over her hips. Lowrie's seen this before but he likes it, he likes me in this green – and this hat, I think. She looked at herself in the mirror. The baby-blond had gone long ago. In its place her hair was very fair but with a slight reddish tint to it which suited the green dress. It had what she called a bend in it and tended to escape in tendrils around her face. It was doing that now. She tucked them back up and put her hat and coat on quickly. She picked up her bag and weekend case and went through to the ward.

She wasn't expecting the burst of applause and admiring calls from the men. She blushed, laughed and looked round for moral support before taking a step forward and waving to her admirers. Lowrie came over.

'You look beautiful.' He kissed her. This brought another round of applause. 'Maybe we should go now. Let's escort James back to his ward on our way.'

Christina shook hands with Sister Johnston, then leaned over and hugged her.

'Thank you so much. That's been perfect.'

'As I said, good for morale. Listen to them. Be happy. See you next week.'

James was glad to reach his bed. He lay down with a sigh of thankfulness.

'Now, don't speak to anyone for at least two hours,' said Sister Brown.

'No Sister.' He closed his eyes.

'When's your train?' asked Lowrie as they walked to the entrance.

'Half past five.'

'What about heading for the North British for afternoon tea and champagne?' We've time to do that and then just walk into the station. What do you think? My treat.'

'Sounds good,' said Magnus. 'Rosemary, I'm in your care. Are you happy?'

'Well,' she said, 'you'd better behave. I have strict instructions not to let you get drunk, but...'

'It sounds like a good plan,' said Christina, 'please come.'

'Are you able Magnus? Not too tired?'

'Certainly not,' he said. 'Anyway if I do get tired, I'll just lean on you. That's what you're there for after all.'

'He's very cheeky,' Rosemary turned to Christina. 'I don't know how you lived with him as a boy.'

'Come on,' said Lowrie. 'Here's a taxi. He put up his arm and the taxi stopped at the gate.'

'North British please. Come on you lot, get in.'

The same doorman was on duty. He recognised Lowrie.

'Ah, Sir, back again? Very nice to see you again. And your young lady.'

'My wife, now.'

'May I present my congratulations? Madame, I hope that you both will be very happy. Now, how can I help you?'

'We'd like afternoon tea and champagne, please, for four.'

'Certainly Sir. Please, just follow me.'

'Mercy,' said Rosemary when he had gone. 'What have you done to receive such treatment?' They told about the breakfast with eggs Benedict.

'What a show off.' Magnus rolled his eyes at the two of them sitting laughing at him.

'Certainly not,' said Rosemary. 'If any man took me to this hotel at half past eight in the morning and fed me eggs Benedict I'd be delighted, so don't you scoff. Here's the tea and the champagne glasses.'

Given time, the wedding party could have gone on all evening. They concentrated on the day: they toasted the bride and 'groom, then the 'groom toasted the witnesses whom he insisted on calling the bridesmaid and best-man To which Magnus replied and rolled out old stories of when Lowrie and he were boys. Not to be outdone Christina toasted Rosemary, and told of their time as student nurses living in the Nurses Home. She finished by standing up and looking at Rosemary.

'It's the custom I believe for a bride to throw her bouquet for someone to catch. I won't do that here – I might break the chandelier. But Rosemary, please have my bouquet and thank you for coming and bringing this brother of mine with you.' She handed the bouquet over, kissed Rosemary on the cheek and sat down.

'Speech, speech,' called Lowrie.

'Thank you very much,' Rosemary said, with a catch in her voice. 'I've had a wonderful day and I'm glad that Colonel Fulton ordered me to come.' She stopped. Magnus helped her out.

'Let's all toast Colonel Fulton.'

'To Colonel Fulton.'

'Now, look at the time,' Magnus said. 'Here, you're supposed to be looking after me. That's your job to get me on the train.'

'I'll square up.' Lowrie went to the desk. 'Thank you very much,' he said, to the waiter. 'That was just what we needed.'

'I'm very glad to hear that Sir.' He handed over the bill. 'Oh, and by the way, Sir, champagne on the house. Congratulations on your wedding, Sir. She's a lovely lady.'

'Thank you very much. That's very kind.'

'Our pleasure, sir.' The waiter bowed. 'We respect you military people very much.'

'Thank you.'

He walked to the entrance where the others waited.

'Everything all right?' asked Christina.

'Yes – yes, that is, do you know, the champagne was on the house. Wasn't that generous of them?'

'Yes, how unexpected.' Magnus was impressed. He couldn't resist saying, 'It must be the mouser.'

'Come on, the train,' implored Rosemary. They hurried into the station. The train stood at the platform. Magnus and Rosemary collapsed into their seats and as the guard waved his flag the train gave a burst of steam and headed slowly out of the station.

People milled around as usual.

'It's just an ordinary day for them,' said Christina. 'They don't know about us.'

'Do you want them to know?'

'I don't think so. It's good to be just us and this is our wedding day and all these people don't know.'

'Come on,' he said. 'Give me your arm. Time to go home. Shall we walk?'

They set off in the direction of the Stockbridge Colonies.

Chapter 42

MID JUNE 1917

Rosemary knocked on Magnus's door. She knew he'd to pack for his trip with Christina to Jarlshavn. She also knew he might require help to remember or find everything.

'Come in.' She opened it and looked in.

'Are you all ready?'

'Yes, I think so. I'm just trying to remember where I put my other socks.'

'What about these?' She pulled a pair of clean socks from under a pile of clothes.

'Yes, of course, there they are thanks. I should have looked there first.' He stuffed them into his case.

'Now, what else do you need?'

'I don't know.' He looked around.

'Let's look at the list.' They went through the list. He seemed to have everything.

'That's fine. Tickets in your pocket?'

'Yes.'

'ID and papers?'

'Yes.'

'Hat?' He put it on his head.

She looked out. 'I can see Burnett coming round with the car. Let's go.'

'Are you coming too – to the station?'

'Certainly. I'm coming to make sure you go.'

'Oh Rosemary, I'm not *that* bad am I?' She smiled at him.

'No Magnus – in fact, mind you come back, or I'll be up to Shetland in that *St Clair* of yours and drag you back.'

He looked at her then, the longing in his eyes so clear that she looked down, away from the direct blueness of them.

'Magnus,' she said. Her voice was soft. 'Don't, not yet. Don't say anything. You go to Shetland, make your peace with your father. Have a good week. Enjoy your time, rest and sleep when you can.'

'But it's so difficult.'

'D'you think it isn't difficult for me?' He looked at her.

'You mean…?'

'Magnus, I'm saying no more. I've probably said too much.' She picked up his suitcase. 'I think Burnett will be wondering where we are. Let's go.'

They arrived at the station in good time. The train was two minutes early. Christina was there, exactly where she said she would be. The seat opposite her was vacant, booked for Magnus. He gave Rosemary a touch on the arm in farewell and went forward.

'Hello,' he said, climbing on to the train and kissing Christina on both cheeks. 'How's Mrs Harcus?'

'I'm fine thank you, I think. Just a minute, till I say "hello" to Rosemary before we go.' She leaned out of the window.

'Rosemary, thank you for coming. How are things with you?'

'Fine, thank you. Are you busy in Edinburgh?'

'Yes, very. I'm glad to have my leave. A few of our current men will eventually get to Glamis I should think. I think the train's about to go.' Rosemary waved.

'Good bye, Magnus, be good.'

'Bye.' He waved back. 'See you soon.' He turned to Christina as the train picked up speed.

'Listen to her,' he said. 'Be good.'

'She probably has a point. Anyway, how are you?' She settled down in her seat again and looked him up and down. 'Seriously.'

'I'm all right you know. Getting fitter every day.'

'I'm really beginning to believe it. You do look better, more colour in your face.'

'That's the outside life. Walking in the Angus countryside. We've even been to Arbroath in a charabanc for an outing. We had a great walk along the cliff top. It starts at Whiting Ness and up along the cliffs. They're red sandstone – a lovely colour. We're going again soon for our summer outing. When we came back we had fish and chips.'

'I thought you were putting on a bit of weight. I'm glad. You were away to a rasher of wind.'

'Thank you for these kind words. Now,' he said. 'How about you? How have you been since your big day?'

'It was a good day, wasn't it?' He nodded.

'We had a lovely 'just us' weekend. We were so happy.'

'And now?'

'Well, now Lowrie's gone. I saw him off on the train that Monday morning. I could hardly bear to part with him. And I went straight to work.'

'Probably the best thing you could have done.'

'Yes, I know. Sister and the patients have been very helpful. Probably the men have been over-solicitous. They say things like, "never mind lassie, he'll soon be back" and pat my hand, and really that doesn't help to stiffen the spine. Sister's much more practical. She looked at my face that Monday, gave me a quick private hug in the duty room and then gave me a whole list of things to be attended to. Since then I've had a lot of extra responsibility and it's been very good for me. She says that she'll have certain aspects of Ward Management lined up for me for when I get back.'

'She certainly seems to understand.'

'Yes, I think there's real empathy there – she also has someone out in France and she gets through it by working hard and well and encouraging others to do the same.'

'Is Lowrie in touch?'

'Oh, yes, he writes every day, and I write to him. I'm not sure where he is exactly but I just keep hoping and praying he's safe.' The train slowed.

'Here's Montrose. A bonny place they say. Another nice place within striking distance of Glamis. Acres of flat sand when the tide's out. A great bird place.'

'I have sandwiches,' she said. 'And a flask of tea. Now or later?'

'Now, please. I'm starving.'

'Don't they feed you?'

'Yes, but it seems a long time since breakfast.' He took a bite of sandwich. 'Mmm, this is excellent. Did you make them?'

'Yes. I went home last night and made them. Nice to go home when I can.'

'Home,' he said. 'It's good for you to be able to say that.' She smiled, nodded, said, 'Yes, it's a lovely feeling.'

'But, Magnus,' she said, 'tell me more about you. How are you and my old friend Rosemary getting on?' He drew in his breath sharply. His brow creased as he sat silently. She leaned forward.

'Magnus? What is it? Have I…have I said something wrong?'

'No, no, Christina, not at all – it's just …'

'Just what? Have you had a row?'

'No, we haven't had a row. Anything but…'

'Well, why did you look so, well, *conscious*, when I asked about you and Rosemary? Is it, could it be, have I – oh Magnus, have I hit the nail on the proverbial head?' As he groaned, leaned back in his seat and closed his eyes, she exclaimed,

'Oh Magnus, I'm sorry, I didn't mean to push you like that.' He opened his eyes.

'It's a bit late for that. *We're* not even talking about it. If there is an 'it' which I'm beginning to doubt.'

'I'm very sorry to upset you.'

'That's all right. You weren't to know.'

'H-mmm.' Christina looked over at him and waited.

'How *did* you know? We didn't say anything on your wedding day? We were just a patient going to a wedding with a nurse in attendance.' Christina's anxious face opened up with a big smile as she laughed at him.

'What's so funny?'

'If you could hear what you've just said. You make yourself sound like an aald mannie with a Sarah Gamp type person pushing your bath-chair. You certainly didn't come over like that.'

'How did we come over?'

'Oh, a nice professional couple going to a meeting.'

'Christina. Seriously.' She put her hand over and touched his knee.

'Magnus, do you really want me to say what I saw?'

'Go on.'

'I saw a handsome young couple, who deliberately kept each other at least six inches apart at all times. Who didn't touch each other unless they had to. I know that you were a step behind us at our marriage ceremony, but even so, I could sense you looking at each other. It was very strong.'

'But we haven't said anything – Rosemary won't. She's so professional. She's much stronger than I am. Is it so obvious?'

'Only to me, I think. I don't think Lowrie noticed. I can understand why Rosemary is holding you away, though. She's a nurse, you're a patient. Colonel Fulton would make sure she was posted away.'

274

'I know. That's the thing. I actually do know. It's just so difficult. For her too. She indicated as much to me this morning.'

'At least it sounds as if you both feel the same way.' She smiled as he nodded.

'I'm so glad.'

'Well, I think she does. Feel the same way, I mean. But, that's all very well but how do we cope?'

'With difficulty. At least you're not bed-ridden and you can get out and about.'

'Christina,' he suddenly said. 'You won't – tell anybody will you? After all nothing's been said between us…'

'Magnus, trust me. Not a word.'

'Not even to Lowrie?'

'Not even to Lowrie.'

The *St Clair* was very busy. Mid-June in Shetland meant mid-summer, long summer days, short, light nights of the simmer-dim, visitors declaring proudly on their postcards home they'd been able to read *The Shetland Times* at midnight with no artificial light, the inevitable disappointment if the weather disagreed with their expectations. Then there were cliff-top walks, bird-watching at fever pitch, boat-trips for the more adventurous, even as far as the Isle of Foula if you wanted to go to the 'edge of the world' and see the highest vertical cliffs in Britain and set foot on this most special of places.

It took a while to get organised. Fortunately Christina had booked their cabin. It seemed to be impossible otherwise. They could hear the complaints of people who'd turned up without booking. They didn't want to spend the night in the passengers' lounge.

'I've slept many a night in that lounge when I was a student,' said Magnus with little sympathy. 'It's quite all right. No problem at all. And, you can be first at the serving hatch in the morning for the porridge. Nothing like it.'

'Do you want to offer to swap your cabin if it's that good?'

'No,' he admitted.

'Come on then, let's find it. We'll be away in a wee while.'

The cabin was small, but at least they were together and by themselves.

Magnus closed the door, surveyed the bunks, top and bottom.

'Christina.'

'Yes?' She was busy opening the straps of her case to get out her washing things.

'Christina, this sounds really stupid…'

'What? What sounds stupid?'

'Would you mind if I have the bottom bunk?' He looked upset.

'Magnus, of course I don't mind. I'd have thought you'd be wanting the top one to feel a bit more free.'

'Yes but you see, I need to be able to access the floor, sometimes quickly.' He looked at her, pleading for understanding.

'Magnus, is this something to do with being injured, or, in the trenches?'

'I knew you'd get it. Sometimes…sometimes…'

'Yes?'

'In the nights I'm there – not actually, of course, but in my dreams. When I waken I'm on the floor because I've dropped to the bottom of the trench to avoid the shells and sniper-fire.' He sighed. 'Maybe it'll stop eventually. They say it will. So,' he added with a wry smile, 'you can see why I don't want to go leaping out of the top bunk.'

'Magnus, thanks for telling me.' She put up a hand and stroked his face. 'You can most certainly go into the bottom bunk. You've had a rough time haven't you?'

'Everybody who goes out there has a rough time. When's it all going to stop?'

They had dinner at a window table in the dining room as the *St Clair* was crossing the harbour bar. Beyond the bar the shelter of the harbour gave way to the wind and waves of the open waters of the North Sea.

'It's a beautiful evening,' said Magnus. 'It's quite noisy and stuffy in here. D'you fancy a bit of fresh air?'

'Come on then. It looks quite breezy. I'll take my coat I think.'

The deck was quieter. A few folk were out feeling the sea breeze, walking, holding on to hats, watching the east coast of Scotland with hills beyond, slip past in the evening sunshine.

'This side seems to be more sheltered,' said Magnus. 'Would you like to find a seat? Look, here's wee corner with nobody in it.'

Christina sighed with pleasure as she looked around. 'I can hardly believe I'm on my way north again. I love it so much.'

'Where do you think you and Lowrie will live eventually? Would you go back to Shetland on a permanent basis?'

'I think we'll have to wait and see. Lowrie has a contract in Edinburgh to which he'll return after the War. But, then, who knows? What about you? Will you go back?'

'Christina, I don't know. You know how much I care about my homeland. But...'

'But what Magnus? Why did you go away in the first place?'

'Nobody has ever told you?'

'No. It was horrible when you went. You said "Good bye" but you didn't say why. Then you were gone. Mother disappeared to Towie and Father was barely speaking to anyone. I asked Mother why but she didn't tell me. I also asked Lowrie, quite recently. I was sure he'd know, but he wouldn't say either.'

'He's a great friend. We know many things about each other. Christina, I'm glad he didn't tell you because it shows yet again how much we trust each other. The other person I've discussed this with is James.'

'James? When was that?'

'In Royaumont. When I was at one of my weakest points. He's a very thoughtful listener. I really unburdened to him, poor soul. However, I think *you* have a right to know why I went, and that it should come from me.' She waited.

'I was very angry, and confused, I think,' he continued, 'firstly, when Mother died and then when the spik of the village began to link Father's and Charlotte's names together. This escalated for me until I realised, or thought I realised, that I was in love with her myself.'

'Oh, Magnus. What did you do? Wait a minute – did that fight you had with Alfie Twatt in the playing-field have anything to do with it?' Magnus made a face.

'D'you remember about that?'

'Only just. I remember hearing you and Father shouting. Anyway, sorry to interrupt – go on.'

'Well, by the time I was practising in Lerwick ...' He told her the rest of the story... 'You do see, don't you?' he said eventually. 'I could hardly say to you at that time I was in love with the woman you called Mother, now could I?'

'No,' she said. 'I see that, of course. You poor soul. But, Magnus,' she said, 'what about now? How do you feel about this visit?'

He took her hand and held it. 'It's all right,' he said. 'I've had a lot of time in the last few months to think. I've accepted that I've grown past this. Charlotte and I had a long talk when she came to Glamis and we cleared the air. Father wants to see me. I think we both need – want – to make peace with each other.'

'Magnus.' She sighed. 'I said earlier you'd had a rough time. Now, I see that was only a part of it. Thank you for telling me.'

'I'm glad you know. You're not angry, are you?'

'Not angry, only sad for you – and Mother. It must've been a dreadful time for you all – including Father. No wonder he was so morose.'

'How do you think he is now?'

'Physically or mentally?'

'Both.'

'The two strokes have left their mark. He's a bit disabled and was unwilling to move downstairs as you know. But the morale-boosting side is now he can go out to the garden and deave Dod Halcrow with his organisation and plans.'

'How does Dod manage?'

'Mother says he does very well. We'll see tomorrow.' She shivered. 'Shall we go in? It's getting a wee bit chilly.'

As they strolled back along the deck they stopped at the railing and took a last look at the evening sun sparkling on the dancing waves.

'Christina,' he said. 'Thanks for listening. I'm glad I told you.'

'I'm glad too.'

'Do you think the boat will be on time?' Alexander gazed anxiously at the blue morning sky.

'I'll just go and test the wind.' Angus rushed outside. They could see him standing with a finger wetted with spit held aloft into the light wind.

'A slight breeze coming from the south-east,' he reported breathlessly. 'D'you think that'll be all right for them?'

'Yes, that's fine. They should just be coming through the Sound of Bressay now. They won't be long.'

'But Angus,' reminded Charlotte. 'I don't think they'll be here before you go to school. In fact I'm sure of it.'

'Oh Mother, can't I stay?'

'No Angus, what would Mrs Manson say if every person whose brother was coming home wanted a day off school? Now, are you all ready? Got your bag?'

'Yes,' he sighed.

'And your coat? Here it is.' He put it on in a resigned fashion.

'I'm really wanting to stay.' He tried one more time.

'And I'm really wishing you could too. But we can't all get what we want. Never mind Angus, you can come home for lunch today and you'll see them then. Now, I hear Edie coming to tell you it's time.' Eventually he was away.

'Shame. I can understand how he feels. It's been ten years. He'll have no memories of Magnus. Hannah just remembers someone who came to play sometimes.'

'Ten years.' Alexander sighed. 'What a long time.'

'And a lot of water has gone under the bridge. Alexander, we must try and be happy for today and not look back. We need to make it as easy as possible for Magnus. And,' she went on, 'remember Christina's coming too, and she's been married since we saw her last. We mustn't overlook that. She's Mrs Lowrie Harcus.'

'Yes, of course. I get so wrapped up in things. I forget the happy side sometimes. We must give her a big welcome.'

A little later, Alexander put down his newspaper as Charlotte paused in her letter-writing.

'Is that the gig I hear coming now?' he said.

The gig rattled through the Birkenshaw gate. Both Magnus and Christina were up in front beside Dod. Magnus said little. All the six miles from Lerwick his eyes had drunk in the views, of lochs, and voes running in from the sea with little isles lying here and there. Shetland sheep with frisking lambs, white and creamy, moorit and other browns; shaggy ponies watching the passing gig with the well-groomed pony in the shafts. Whatever else might be happening, little here seemed different. The same peat rik; the same kishies on the backs of women walking by the road, all the while, fingers busy at their knitting. Nothing has changed. But I've changed. Now, at last, I can feel glad to be here. He sat up straight. Christina squeezed his hand.

'All right?' He smiled and nodded.

'Thank you Dod. That was good of you.' They swung their bags down. Dod, a man of few words, smiled, said that was fine, he was glad to see them back and took the pony round to give him a nosebag.

'There they are, I knew they'd come by the back door. They always do.' Charlotte ran through to the kitchen, arms wide for the two of them.

'You're here. Magnus, Christina, come on in.' Edie and Meg waited patiently.

Magnus smiled at them. 'I'm glad some things never change. How are you both?'

'We're well.' Meg looked him up and down. 'You look as though you need a bit of food on your bones though. What do you think Edie.'

'Mmm,' Edie began. 'Well…'

'Oh come on Meg. Christina's just said I was putting on weight.'

'Where's Father?' Christina was already away through to him.

278

'Hello Father.' She stood in the doorway.

'My dear Christina, how are you?' He walked awkwardly towards her, dragging his foot a little. He put his arms out and kissed her. 'My newly-married daughter. We've thought about you so much. Did you have a happy day?'

'Yes, it was very happy – but, we missed you and Mother. I'm glad to be here and see you now. And, look, here's Magnus.'

He stood there in the doorway, his uniformed son, a little hesitant, biting his lower lip, greying, still thin despite the recent weight gain.

'Magnus,' said Alexander. 'Come in.' He held out his arms. 'Oh, how I've missed you. What a mistake I made. I'm so sorry.'

They held each other, the elder, frailer, weeping in relief on his boy's chest. Magnus cried too as he supported his now-old father for a few moments before, very gently, moving his arm round his shoulders and helping him to a chair.

Un-noticed, Christina slipped away to the kitchen where the kettle was on the boil.

'I think we should give them a few minutes.'

'That's fine.' Charlotte understood at once. 'So, how are you? And, how was the wedding?'

'It was a wonderful day.'

'What's your dress like?' asked Edie, always wanting to hear about the Edinburgh fashions. Christina laughed.

'Well, Edie, I was married in my uniform.'

'Your uniform? But why didn't you have a frock?'

'Edie, I didn't have time to go shopping. Everything was done in such a rush. And I knew Lowrie and Magnus and Rosemary would be in uniform and I thought it would be better so. But I did change before we left the hospital into my best frock which is a lovely green.'

'That would suit you,' said Meg.

'Yes, it's a bonny dress. Then we escorted James back to his ward and the four of us went to the North British for afternoon tea and champagne. And, the waiter recognised Lowrie from before and the champagne was on the house.'

'That was very generous,' said Charlotte. 'How did they know to give you that?'

'Because Lowrie said, "My wife now",' said Christina, smiling at the memory. 'I think that was the first time he said "my wife".'

'It was a good day,' agreed a voice from the doorway. But,' Magnus said plaintively, 'aren't we going to get any coffee today? I thought you would have saved it specially.'

'Oh Magnus, I'm sorry.' Edie leapt up. 'It's just ready. We were just hearing about the glamorous life in Edinburgh.' She turned her back on his tear-streaked face pretending not to notice but in reality hiding her own tears from him. He looked so much older, so careworn. Not the boy she used to know. Meg looked down at her knitting. Christina went back to the parlour to her father.

Charlotte turned towards Magnus as he spoke, saw his face, rose to her feet immediately and went to him.

'Come,' she said, 'just till the kettle boils again.' He followed her to the back door, open to the sunshine. She passed him a handkerchief and applied another to her own eyes.

279

'Nobody said it would be easy.'

'No, I know, but, dear Lord it's difficult. He's so vulnerable-looking. So frail.'

They stood there as he dried his eyes, wiped his face and took a few deep breaths.

'Coffee,' called Edie. 'Going through.'

'Coming. Ready?'

'Yes. Thanks Charlotte.'

'Oh, I've an unending supply of hankies. They've been used for everything over the years. Come on.'

In the parlour Christina sat holding hands with Alexander.

'All right, now?' she whispered, as she heard the rattle of cups.

'Yes, I'm fine. Don't tell, will you. Grown men don't cry.'

'Oh, I don't know about that. I think grown men *should* cry – it would do them good.'

He smiled tenderly at her and patted her hand.

'My girl,' he said. 'Always, my girl.'

Chapter 43

James sat in the day-room of his ward reading the *Scotsman* and an overview of the previous few weeks and months of the War. Although the Battle of Bullecourt had ended on 16 May and was widely taken to be the end of the Battle of Arras, many observers did not consider the whole Arras Offensive to be complete until the middle of June.

He was further horrified yet not surprised in a way, to note that during the month of April the 51st Highland Division had a total of 214 officers and 4,382 other ranks killed, wounded and missing, men with whom he worked, lived, prayed with, gave Communion to, and, was wounded alongside. It was an upsetting thought. He had picked out some names from the lists but the numbers were too many to take in. And that's only in the Arras area. It's the same elsewhere. He flung the paper to the floor.

Christina came to see him later.

'See if you can cheer him up,' said Sister Brown. 'He's very down today.'

'What's the matter? That's not like James.'

'I know. Between you and me,' Sister Brown said, 'I think he's ready to move on. He needs to go and convalesce somewhere.'

'He couldn't go to his parents. They're too old and he'd finish up worrying about them.'

'What about a convalescent hospital in Perth?'

'I don't know. It's an idea. Shall I speak to him?'

'You could find out any way. Sound him out, gently.'

Christina found him reading by his bed. He looked up at her approach and half-rose.

'Don't get up,' she said. 'I'll pull in a chair.'

'You spoil me. My manners are getting to be atrocious, if, I ever had any. It's good to see you. How was Shetland?'

'Fine,' she said. 'A good week, I think. How are you, James? I haven't seen you since before we went. How have you been?'

'Not brilliant,' he said. 'My wound's fine, I think. The dressing's off. It still looks pretty drastic and,' he added, 'it's very tender. I don't like being touched on the right side. But, well, I'm all right really.'

'You don't sound too enthusiastic.'

'Sorry. I can't work up any enthusiasm. I think,' he paused. 'I think, Christina, I'm just marking time now.'

'D'you think you need a change?'

'Yes, I do. I suppose they'll say convalescence next, but where? I know my mother wants to have me there but she's not able to housekeep for me and they'd both be watching my every move. St Fillans is out of course as I left – that would have been great but it's not an option.'

'What about convalescing in Perth or thereabouts so that you knew your surroundings and could see your parents but wouldn't be on top of them?'

'That might do I suppose. Do you know of anywhere? I suppose Auxiliary hospitals are springing up all over the place.'

'Yes, they are. All the wards have a list – which I may add is growing by the day. What about speaking to Sister Brown and Dr, what's his name…?'

'Collins, Major William Collins…'

'Yes, Major Collins. Speak to them about it. If he and Sister agree that you're ready to move on then they can find out about Auxiliary hospitals in Perth. Shall I tell Sister on my way out, what you're thinking'

'That'd be helpful. Thanks.' He looked brighter. 'See, I just needed you here to gee me up a bit. Now,' he said. 'Your turn. How about you? How's your father, and – and Charlotte? Was Magnus – em, all right?'

'It *was* a very emotional homecoming,' she admitted. 'But they've made their peace, and yes, Magnus will return another time.' Her grey eyes met his. 'Magnus told me,' she added, 'on the boat. He said I should hear from him why he left and there is no problem now.'

'I'm glad,' said James. 'I'm very glad. Good to hear some things work out. And your father too, all right is he?'

'He's slow, but gets about in the garden. I suppose, in a way, every day is a bonus.'

When she got up to go, he said, 'Would you come and see me?'

'Where?'

'In Perth, if I get there, of course.'

'Heavens you move fast once you get started. Yes, of course I'll come and see you. And Lowrie too, when he gets back.'

'How is he?'

'Very busy, I think, reading between the lines. He doesn't say too much. You know how it is.'

When she left him, Christina put her head round the duty-room door.

'How did you get on?'

'Fine, I think. He says he feels he's marking time. He doesn't want to go to his parents. He quite likes the idea of one of these Auxiliary Hospitals – there must be a couple in Perth.'

'Here's the list.' Sister Brown found it in her in-tray. 'If I don't want to lose anything it goes in there. Now, let me see. Goodness this list is growing – here we are though, Perth. There's the Infirmary but we don't want him to go there – he needs to see himself making a step forward. Ah, Rosebank Auxiliary Hospital – that might do. We could talk about it anyway. I'll speak to James and Major Collins and we'll see what we can do.'

On the day of the summer outing to Arbroath, Burnett took the charabanc, hired for the day, to the front door of Glamis Castle at half past ten. It promised to be another lovely day. The sun shone from a cloudless sky, only a slight breeze moved the treetops, thoughts of the War faded into the background. The men who were able came out, laughing and joshing, in uniform if they had it, if not, fresh army hospital blues, helped each other up the steps and headed for the back of the charabanc with much chatter and laughter. Sister Ellis in charge of the party, was assisted by two VADs and Burnett. Burnett did everything, or seemed to.

Arbroath beckoned. The drive through the countryside, a wander round the shops near the harbour, fish and chips at the pier and then the cliff top walk and home again in time for dinner.

'You've been before.' Ewan Dingwall settled himself beside Magnus. 'How far is it?'

'Where to? Arbroath?'

'Yes.'

'Oh, I think about twenty one miles, give or take a mile. Via Forfar, it's not too far. It's worth it for the cliffs and the view.'

'A bit like home, is it, for you?'

'Different cliffs, a different sea. Nice, though.'

Magnus fell silent, into his thoughts. Now that he had managed the trip to Shetland, made his peace with his father, returned to Glamis, he felt better, happier about himself. Even any residual anger with his father for ordering him out of the house, that he thought he'd never get rid of, had somehow dissipated. Perhaps it was the sight of and contact with his father whose appearance had affected Magnus deeply. It could have been the emotion of the occasion. Their response to each other after the trauma of ten years enforced separation had touched Magnus and Alexander much more deeply than either had imagined.

There were other sides to the visit north. After their time together at Glamis, Magnus found he was also able to greet Charlotte on home territory as the wife of his father and a trusted friend. They were easy now in each other's company. There was no tension, no stress.

It was good too, to be with Christina, almost like the old days. Together they restored their old relationship, re-traced their footsteps, walked again the old walks, looked out from the cliff tops at Foula, their island at the 'edge of the world', peaks sometimes clear and sharp, sometimes shrouded in mystery. It was time out for them. They made the most of it.

Then there was Magnus's meeting again with sister Hannah and brother Angus. On that first day, Angus came tearing in at lunch time only to be pulled up short by the sight of Magnus sitting at the kitchen table in his shirt-sleeves, podding freshly picked peas for lunch.

'Hello Angus,' said Magnus. 'Had a good morning at school?'

'Yes, thank you.' Angus stood at a safe distance while he took in the newcomer.

'Would you like some peas?'

'Not too many,' interrupted Edie. 'We need them for lunch.'

'Only one pod, then.' He offered it.

'Thanks,' said Angus, stepping closer to take it. All bravado gone, here was his *brother*. This was a hazy, spoken-about concept, now made real by the sight of Magnus sitting so normally at the kitchen table.

'It's all right, you know,' said Magnus. 'I don't bite. I'm very glad to meet you properly at last. You were only a baby – when I saw you last. We didn't know each other really, but I did carry you into the parlour to be baptised.'

'Did you?' Angus was impressed. 'Thank you.'

'You're welcome. I'm sorry I haven't been around very much to see you grow up.'

'I haven't grown up *that* much,' said Angus. 'But I do go to school in Lerwick after the summer. Did you know?'

'Well, I think you told me that in a letter. It was good of you to write. Oh,' added Magnus, 'and talking of that, em,' he lowered his voice and fished in his pocket, 'I've brought you a wee piece of shrapnel to show to your friends.'

'Oh, *thank you*, Magnus.' There was no holding Angus now. Shyness overcome, he stepped forward and flung his arms round Magnus's neck. 'The boys will really want to see this.' Angus was a slave to Magnus from then on. There was nothing he wouldn't do for him, fetching and carrying, anticipating his every need.

Hannah appeared on the scene at the weekend. Growing fast, she had Charlotte's grey eyes, which looked Magnus up and down before her face broke into a big smile and she gave him a hug. 'I do remember you,' she said. 'I didn't know if I would but I do. It's your eyes. The blue eyes. How are you?'

'All the better for seeing you, as the wolf said.' Magnus felt choked all over again as he regarded her. No longer the baby of three, here was a girl almost ready to fly.

'How's school?' He tried to be casual. His eyes gave him away.

'Magnus,' she said, puzzled. 'Magnus? Is everything all right?'

'Oh yes,' he said, 'just, well, you've changed a bit, that's all. I've missed your years in between.'

'I've missed you too,' she held his hand. 'Do you have to go away again?'

'Yes, I'm afraid so. You see I'm still officially on convalescence and I've to go back to Glamis Castle.'

'D'you like it there?'

'Yes, for the moment.'

'Will you come back here?'

'Yes,' he said. 'I will. But I can't say when. We just need to enjoy the moment. What about showing me the garden? By the way, I've brought you a wee souvenir from France.' He dug in his pocket and pulled out a small knife.

'Magnus, that's beautiful. What's it made from?'

'A soldier made it,' he said. 'In a trench. From a shell casing. They do a lot of this sort of thing.' He glanced at her. 'It's not all 'over the top' you know. Sometimes the soldiers are very bored and need something to do. They pick up stuff like old shell casings and carve and fiddle about and make things. He gave it to me for a few cigarettes.' She smiled at him and put it in her pocket.

'Thank you,' she said. 'This is very meaningful to me – because, of you. I'll treasure it forever.' They went out into the garden.

'I'll leave Father to show you the trees,' she said. 'For me to do it would be stealing his thunder. Let's see how the flowers are coming along.'

Ewan gave him a nudge. 'Wake up. You're away in a dwam. I think this is Arbroath now.' Magnus jumped and looked out.

'Yes, this is it.'

'We'll soon be stopping,' Burnett called from the front. 'We'll stop down by the pier. Sister says half an hour for having a look around then we'll get some of Arbroath's finest – fish and chips – before doing our walk. All right everybody?'

'Yes, thank you,' they chorused.

The charabanc stopped and they surged forward, rattling down the steps with eager feet.

'I hope they don't overtire themselves,' Edith Ellis, Sister-in-Charge, watched them doubtfully.

'They're only away for thirty minutes,' said VAD Ann Thomson. 'Surely they'll be all right?'

'I wouldn't trust them.'

Magnus and Ewan strolled along the sea front.

'D'you want to look at the shops?' said Magnus.

'Not particularly. I'd rather look at what's going on here. See, they've still got some of the wee fishing boats upended. They're working on them before they can take them out.'

They stopped to watch. The boat-menders were taking full advantage of the fine day. Sails lay spread out, to be examined for wear and tear and mending. Masts lay alongside. The men repairing the bottom of the boats went over each plank meticulously, looking for possible leaks, replacing a sprung plank here, patching there, before re-caulking with pitch to make the boat watertight for the season. This was their livelihood and, their lives.

Other boats were a stage ahead. The painters were at work. Coat after coat of paint or varnish went on before they were satisfied. And finally the name and identity number of the boat was re-applied if necessary, to comply with Harbour Rules.

They strolled back, impressed.

'You didn't go far,' said Edith Ellis sitting in the sun, waiting for the crowd to return.

'Too much to see here,' said Magnus. 'You can see shops any time. Here they come. Look at Ann and Vera. They're like a couple of sheep dogs.'

The two VADs had set out after the men to make sure that they didn't lose track of the time. They were all returning together, men in front with the VADs behind, not quite barking, but certainly keeping them grouped and moving.

'Here we are,' said Gerry Green. 'All present and correct, held together by these lovely ladies.'

'That's enough,' said Vera. 'You were the one heading for the pub. Once in there and we'd never have got you out.'

'Right everyone,' said Edith Ellis. 'Do you all want fish and chips?'

'Yes, please.'

'Have you all got your water bottles?'

'Yes, Sister.'

'Right, I'll go and place the order, and hopefully get them. Burnett, will you stay here please with Nurses Kynoch and Thomson? Ewan, will you come with me please, to help carry the order back?'

After their fifteen minutes post-prandial break, to allow the 'best haddock and chips they'd ever tasted' to go down, the party walked from the east end of the Victoria Park, past well-known Whiting Ness. The path then climbed above the red-sandstone cliffs, before levelling out. There were seabirds in their thousands – fulmars, herring gulls, kittiwakes and the rest all competed for space on the narrow cliff edges. Wild flowers hung on here and there, wherever they could get a hold, daisies and buttercups beside the path, thrift on the edge. Inland, lay the open cultivated fields of Angus. On the seaward side the waves danced in the sun. A few boats were out, sails up, more of a breeze out to sea. On the horizon a couple of cargo boats headed north.

The group took its time. These were men in varying stages of recovery from wounds, major surgery, fractures and other traumas. The convoy, as usual, could only go as fast as the slowest vessel. Most were quite content to do so. Apart, that is from Gerry Green, who led the throng – an ungainly, unlikely guide indeed as he had never been there before and was paying no attention to the condition of the pathway.

'D'you think he's after a stripe?' said Ewan quietly to Magnus.

'Well, if he is, he won't get it that way.' Magnus raised his voice.

'Green. Please go a bit more slowly and pay attention to the path.'

'Sir.' Green slowed his pace. Edith Ellis, looked round.

'Thanks,' she said to Magnus. 'I'll think twice before taking him on a cliff-top walk again.'

They came to the rock known as the Needle's E'e. They stood for a moment and marvelled at this before following the path left and looped round another viewpoint, Dickmont's Den. This deep narrow inlet allowed a view far below, of the sea frothing and bubbling as it surged back and forth in the narrow gap.

'I don't like that much,' muttered Magnus. He breathed a sigh of relief as the path led them round and back to the cliff-top. In front of them they could see the Deil's Heid.

'I think the Deil's Heid, that sea stack,' said Edith Ellis pointing, 'is as far as we'll go today.'

'Aw, Sister, can't we go a bit further?' said Green.

'No, we have to get back and that will be far enough.' She was quite final about it.

'Watch him.' said Magnus. 'He's a pain in the neck.'

The group walked on towards the sea stack. The gap between Green and the main body grew noticeably wider again.

'Green,' called Sister Ellis. 'Stay with the group. That's an order.'

He turned and gave her an insolent look, but did slow down. But within a minute he moved ahead again.

They were almost at the point where the cliff-top path curved away to the left round the headland at the level of the Deil's Heid when Green, not looking where he was going, slipped and fell over the edge. There was a united gasp of horror with an instinctive move forward.

'Halt,' shouted Edith Ellis. The men stopped. 'We don't want anyone else falling over.' Magnus and Ewan moved to her side.

'Well said,' said Ewan. 'Now, let's see what's going on. Magnus, already crawling forward to the cliff edge, looked over.

'He's on a ledge, I'd say about half way down. Green,' he shouted, 'can you hear me?' Green waved his hand in response.

'Green, don't move. Not at all. Wait, we'll get help.' He crawled backwards, to the path. 'He's about halfway down, lying down, waved his hand, but he's badly positioned. His leg's out of line. I need to go down and assess his injuries.'

'Magnus you can't,' Edith said. 'You're a patient. We'll send for help.'

'I'm a doctor, Edith. Yes, we need help, you're quite right. But I must get down there and assess his injuries. There's something badly wrong with his left leg. Probably his femur's gone but I need to check that there's a pulse in his foot. It's very twisted-looking. Also, we've no idea what's going on internally. I have to go, don't you see?' He paused for breath. 'Anyway,' he added, 'I've been down a cliff before, to a patient. I can do it.'

'Magnus,' Ewan put in, 'are you sure this is completely necessary? Because, if so…'

'Yes. If there'd been no doctor on the walk then we would take a different course but as I'm here, then it has to be this way.'

'All right,' said Ewan. He looked at Edith. 'I see Magnus's point, Edith. I'm sure you do as well. I acknowledge he's a patient and in your care but this is completely unforeseen.' She nodded.

'How about sending Burnett at the double back to Arbroath for men with ropes and instructions to send for an ambulance from the hospital? I'd go but Burnett's fit despite his knee – he'll make better time than I would. They'll come as fast as they can and pull him up and then Magnus. The ambulance can take Green to the local infirmary.' He turned to Magnus who was looking over the cliff edge again.

'Does that plan sound feasible to you?'

'Yes, thank you Ewan.' Magnus turned to Edith. He shook her hand. 'This I must do. I'm sorry to overrule you on this occasion.'

'I know,' she said. 'I understand completely. Be careful.'

'I will. May I have the First Aid kit please?' He slung the bag on his back, saluted, turned from her, shook hands with Ewan and returned to the cliff edge.

'Right everybody, gather round, back off the edge. The situation is this…' Sister Ellis gave out her orders. Immediately, Burnett started his run back to Arbroath. The VADs moved the men further back from the cliff edge, made them sit down on the grass, drink from their water bottles and handed out chocolate rations.

Edith Ellis walked as close as she dared before lifting up her skirts and, on her hands and knees, crawled to the edge and looked over. Down below she could see Green on the ledge and Magnus inching his way down the cliff towards him.

Magnus didn't dare look down at his objective. It took all his energy to stay on the cliff, groping for toe and hand holds and moving, creeping, towards the ledge and the injured man.

He didn't like it. As soon as he moved his hands from the top and on to the tiny crevices on the cliff and started feeling for toe-holds with first his right foot, then his left, he confirmed what he already knew, that his stamina was in poor supply compared to the fit man he once was. The sandstone seemed quite friable. He could sense the looseness of some of the crevices as he felt for a grip. Sometimes stones came away in his hands or slipped from under a questing foot. He stopped, panting, leaning against the cliff for support. Waves of nausea surged upwards from his stomach. He retched. Grimly he controlled the nausea, swallowing against the tide that threatened to engulf him. To heave and vomit now would surely cause him to fall. As the feeling passed he took advantage of the respite and moved again. Another crevice, another toe-hold. Inch by inch. Sideways and down. Over and over again. He was very tired. How much more?

Suddenly, he felt more secure. His feet were placed flat. He dared to look. He was on the ledge about ten feet along from where Green lay. He took his hands from the crevices. His legs gave way and he sat down on a bed of thrift growing in profusion on this wild place. The nausea now overwhelmed him and he no longer attempted to hold it back. He leaned sideways and vomited copiously, holding on to his wounds, so well healed yet internally still so vulnerable.

'Dear God,' he said. 'What am I doing?' He sat straight, wiped his mouth and realised that he felt better. He heard shouting from above and looked up. He could see Edith Ellis's head looking over the edge of the cliff. She shouted something. He couldn't hear. He waved his hand to reassure her then crawled, full of new purpose, towards his casualty.

'Hello Green.'

'Hello, Sir. Good of you to come down.'

'My pleasure, Green.' Magnus started opening the First Aid kit.

'Sir?'

'Yes?'

'Sir, I'm sorry.'

'That's all right, Green. Now, let's have a look at you. Help is on its way, but in the meantime I need to look at that leg and anywhere else. Tell me where you feel pain.'

'My leg, I think – I think that's worst. I had a few bangs on the way down.'

'I imagine you did. D'you think you were knocked out?'

'No, I don't think so. It all happened so quickly, but …'

'Right, I'll do your observations and then we'll look at the leg. Your pulse is not too bad, a bit fast; pupils fine, equal and reacting, no sign of a concussion, bruises to the face – I bet we find a few more of those and you'll have a nice shiner to show the boys. Now, the leg.' Quickly he cut up Green's left trouser leg to reveal the leg and foot displayed at an angle totally out of alignment.

'I need to check your ankle pulse.' It was weak, almost imperceptible.

'Green, I think you've broken your leg in a couple of places – the femur, the top bone, certainly, and further down. Your foot is lying squint and I need to straighten it as much as I can. It's important so that the blood will get through to your foot. You know the score.' As he was speaking he was getting the morphine out of the First Aid kit.

'I'll give you some morphine to help with the pain.' Green nodded. He knew full well that to leave his foot out of line as it was could result in a lack of blood supply with eventual loss of his foot. He felt the morphine sliding into his vein. Within a minute life looked more relaxed. He closed his eyes.

'Green,' said Magnus. 'I'm going to straighten your foot now. Ready?'

'Yes, Sir.' Green tried to breathe deeply but the pain when it came hit him suddenly and overwhelmingly. Edith Ellis watching and listening above heard the cries.

'Sorry,' said Magnus. He felt the ankle pulse. It beat strongly against his fingers. He smiled with relief. 'That's better.'

'Have you saved my foot?' Green's voice was slurred.

'I hope so, I think so. I just need to try and stabilise it in that position.' Magnus busied himself with heavy supports and bandages.

'There, I think that'll hold it until we get you to the Infirmary. Now, let's see the top. Yes,' he continued, 'that also needs hauling into line. I'll do that if I can, and support and bandage it. You really need a Thomas's splint but...'

He knelt astride Green's left leg and said, 'Ready?' again. Green nodded. Magnus put his hands above Green's knee, held tightly and pulled. He could feel the bone moving. Green screamed again. Magnus pulled until he felt the femur was a straight as he could get it.

'It's not perfect but we'll be able to support it with this,' he said. He arranged two temporary splints alongside Green's leg and held the lot together with heavy bandages. Then he bound both legs together as firmly as he could with a further bandage.

'There,' he said. 'That should do for the time being.'

Suddenly he heard more shouting from above. He looked up. Two more heads showed beside Edith's. He waved.

'Green, can you hear me? Listen, help is coming. They're here.'

'Who's here?'

'Men, coming to help. Yes, here's a rope coming down.' The rope landed beside them, followed swiftly by another.

'Here they come.' Two men came bounding down the cliff-face using the ropes hand over hand. Magnus watched, admiring their expertise.

'They've done that before,' he said. 'They're coming down like monkeys.'

'Ay, ay, how are you getting on?' The first man let go of his rope and called up to his mate, 'Come on slow coach, what's keepin ye?' He turned with a grin. 'Don't mind us. We keep a competition going. I'm Jim,' he said, 'and that's Peter.'

'I'm very glad to see you,' said Magnus. 'This is Gerry Green and I'm Magnus Sinclair.'

'You're the doctor?' said Jim.

'Yes.'

'And a patient too, I understand.'

'Yes, well, that's a side issue...'

'Well, believe me it's nae a side issue here. News travels fast here. As we speak it's going round Arbroath that we've got an accident on the cliffs and a doctor who is currently a patient has gone down the cliff wi nae rope tae help. Man, ye're a hero.'

By this time the second man, Peter, was with them. A man of few words, he merely smiled at Magnus and patted him on the back.

'Ay, ay Gerry,' said Jim.

'Hullo,' slurred Gerry.

'He's nae been drinkin?' Jim turned to Magnus.

'No, no, it's the morphine.' Swiftly he have them a brief outline of what he had done to alleviate temporarily the problems of the injured leg.

'So it's all straightened and supported now?'

'As far as I can get it.'

'That's great. And his arms are not injured.'

'Bruised but not broken as far as I can see. He's moving them well.'

'Right, Peter, we'd better get the rope on. He should be fine wi that morphine in him. Gerry,' he turned to the patient. 'Gerry, can you hear me?' He nodded.

'We're just tying a rope under your oxters to get you up the cliff. It'll be a bit bumpy but the lads at the top will do their best. More heads appeared at the top.'

'Right lads, pull away.' The rope tightened as it took the weight. They supported Green as long as they could. Then he was away, swinging and bumping on the rope until he reached the top into willing hands which grabbed and made him safe.

Within minutes the rope was down again.

'Now, Magnus, your turn.' Magnus got up but immediately felt so dizzy and disorientated that he sat down again.

'Sorry,' he said. 'I'm going to vomit again.' He leaned sideways, vomited, then sat, pale and shaking, before keeling over on to his side.

'I feel terrible,' he said. 'I don't think I'm going to make it.'

'You bloody well are,' said Jim. 'Come on, let's get the rope round your oxters, and we'll get you up the cliff. Gi'es a hand, Peter.' They started putting the rope around Magnus's chest but he shook it off.

'No, no,' he said, 'I'll be all right here. I'll just lie here. Just for a few minutes.' He tried to push them off and in so doing moved himself perilously near to the edge of the shelf.

'Pull him back, back,' shouted Jim. 'He'll go over.'

'I can't,' panted Peter. 'He's slipping.'

Before they could do anything further Magnus had gone.

'Damn,' said Jim. 'And blast.'

They lay down and looked over. Down below, they could see Magnus lying motionless at the bottom, just out of reach of the waves.

Chapter 44

Rosemary Jones looked at her watch. Half past six.

'The Arbroath party should be back by now. I wonder if they've had a puncture with these pneumatic tyres that they're all using. I hope they're all right.' The new VAD Janet MacKay looked up from her notes.

'Is there any way of finding out?'

'We could telephone the police station at Arbroath – I'll go and see what Colonel Fulton says. How's your reading going?'

'Fine thank you Sister. It takes a wee while for everything to go into place.'

'And, just when you think you've got something sorted, another thing crops up to flummox you. Keep going.' Rosemary went out and crossed the hall. Colonel Fulton was in. She knocked.

'Come in.' He was sitting at his desk, reading the casualty list in the newspaper. He set it aside.

'I think that list gets longer every day. Is everything all right, Sister?'

'I'm a bit bothered. The Arbroath party isn't back yet. They should be here by six thirty for their evening meal. It's after that now. They had plenty of time to do what they planned.'

'I see.' He tapped his fingers on the desk. 'I wonder. Who was driving? Oh, Burnett, of course. That should be all right. Sister-in-Charge?'

'Sister Ellis.'

'Well, how about giving them till seven o'clock? If they haven't returned by then we'll give the Arbroath Police Station a ring on the telephone. Agreed?'

'Yes, Sir. Thank you.' She checked the crypt to see that dinner was going out as usual to those who were left, informed the staff that there was a hold-up of unknown length and returned to her office.

The minutes ticked past. She couldn't concentrate, kept looking out of the window.

In the distance they heard an engine, the sound growing nearer until they could hear it revving as it avoided the driveway potholes.

'That'll be them.' She ran to the door and looked out, ready to remonstrate with them for their lateness.

Instead of the charabanc, drawing up with a rattle at the front entrance was the Arbroath Police car. A police sergeant got out of the passenger side followed by a constable who cut the engine, pulled up the hand-brake before climbing out the driver's side. Rosemary hurried forward.

'Good evening. Is there a problem?' The sergeant saluted. He spoke with a strong Orkney accent.

'Good evening Sister, I'm Sergeant Flett from Arbroath Police station. This is Constable Fergus.'

'Is there a problem?' she repeated.

'Well, yes,' he hesitated. 'Could we go inside please?'

'Yes, of course. Come into my office.' She led the way.

'Nurse MacKay, please go and ask Colonel Fulton to come through.'

'Yes, Sister.'

'Could we just wait a minute for the Colonel please? I can hear him coming.'

The two policemen jumped to their feet as he came in.

'Evening, Sir.' They introduced themselves.

'So, what's happened? Why have you come?'

'Well, Sir, Sister, it's like this. We understand that a party from here had an outing to Arbroath today.' They nodded.

'Yes, they should've been back well before now,' said Rosemary. 'We're quite worried about them.'

'Yes, indeed, you would be.'

'Is there any news? What has happened?'

'Well, they went out along the cliff top for a walk after having fish and chips at the harbour.'

'Yes, that was the plan,' said Rosemary. They've done that before. What has happened?' she repeated.

'Apparently,' said the sergeant carefully, 'one of the men went over the cliff at a well-known landmark called the Deil's Heid.'

'Oh no.' Colonel Fulton thumped his fist on his knee. He sighed. 'Is he all right?'

'Well, Sir, another of the party, another patient we understand, but he is also a medical officer...' Rosemary drew in her breath sharply. 'This doctor very bravely climbed down the cliff to him. We understand the casualty required immediate medical attention – otherwise he might lose the foot in the affected leg. Sister'– he consulted his notebook – 'Ellis was very clear. She gave a very good report. So, by the time help came, Captain, er, Sinclair had gone down and performed the necessary first aid – *very* necessary I understand. The men with ropes arrived, two went down the cliff, the casualty was pulled up and the rest should have followed.'

'*Should* have followed?'

'What happened then was' – the Sergeant cleared his throat – 'the plan was to pull Captain Sinclair up next. However, by this time the strain was telling on him, he was quite unwell, became disorientated, overbalanced and fell further.'

Rosemary, ashen-faced, got up and walked to the window. She gazed out, unseeing, then turned.

'Is he... is he, dead?'

'No, he's not dead. He landed near the bottom. The men at the top immediately sent for the Lifeboat and threw down longer ropes to allow the first two men to go down further to render assistance to Captain Sinclair. A short time later the Lifeboat came alongside, and they were able to get him aboard and back to Arbroath. We saw them arrive and noted his transfer to the ambulance. He was alive then and there was a doctor in attendance with the ambulance. He'll be getting attention in casualty right now. We came on here to notify you in person. The charabanc will be here soon.'

'May I just also say,' he added, 'Captain Sinclair has shown courage of the highest order. Arbroath was alive with the news that he'd gone down the cliff after a casualty. They'll be very sad to hear this news. He's a brave man.'

'Thank you,' said Colonel Fulton. 'I'm proud of him. I wish we knew how he is. And, of course, the other casualty. Do you have his name?'

'Yes, Sir,' the constable said. He looked at his notes. 'It's Green, Sir, Gerry Green.'

'Ah,' said Neil Fulton. 'Green. Yes, I hope he gets on well. It sounds as though Captain Sinclair saved his foot.'

'Oh, from what I hear there's no doubt about that. Now, Sir, if it'll help, I'll put a police call through to the Infirmary from here and find out how Captain Sinclair and er, Green are.'

'Yes please, I think that would be best.' They heard him speaking to the operator.

'Hello, Police here. I want a priority call to Arbroath Infirmary please. Yes, now. Thank you... Hello, Police here. Can you put me through to Casualty please?...'

'Hello, Casualty, hello, Sister? Ah hello. Sergeant Flett here. You admitted two men from the cliff accident today...'

Iain Fulton walked over to the window and stood beside Rosemary. She was very pale, silent, holding herself together.

'Are you all right, Rosemary?' She nodded.

'I should have been there.'

'Rosemary, you couldn't have done a thing. You know what Green's like.'

'Yes,' she said. 'I do. But I still wish... I might have been able to do something.'

'Rosemary, we both know Green. I'm not surprised he came a cropper. And, Magnus can be very determined I think.' He thought for a moment. 'It would help me very much if you went to Arbroath Infirmary and check out what is going on – with them both. Would you be prepared to do that?' He glanced at her. 'It would help me and perhaps put your mind at rest.'

'Could I do that?'

'You could go with Sergeant Flett and then, when Burnett is back and has eaten, I'll send him over later. Sister Ellis can take over as Sister-in-Charge until night sister is on duty. He turned, 'Sergeant?'

'Yes, Colonel?'

'Would you mind giving Sister Jones a lift to the Infirmary when you return to Arbroath please? It would be very helpful.'

'No problem. Can you be ready in about ten minutes, Sister?'

'Yes, thank you.' Rosemary went to get her coat and give a brief hand over to Edith Ellis.

The entrance to the Infirmary was quiet giving no indication of previous excitement. She thanked the two policemen, entered and looked about her. All was quiet. Save for a young man in a white coat at the desk writing up what looked like patients' notes.

'Can I help you?'

'I'm looking for the two men who were injured today on the cliffs. They're patients; of mine – I'm Rosemary Jones, Sister-in-Charge at Glamis Auxiliary Hospital. My CO has asked me to come and see how they are and to thank you for your help.'

'Ah, I know who you mean.' The young man smiled at her. 'Anything we can do – by the way I'm Duncan Fraser, Registrar.'

'How do you do? So, how are they?'

'Well, the young man with the fractures has been to theatre. He'll be fine, thanks to the excellent and timely first aid he had. Lucky he didn't lose his foot. If that doctor hadn't gone down to him he would have.'

'How is he? Dr Sinclair, I mean…' Rosemary's voice faltered. The Registrar looked grave.

'He was not at all good on admission. We stabilised him, put up blood, did some X-rays before taking him to theatre. We understand he's been badly wounded before?'

'Yes, he was comatose for five weeks and shrapnel wounding plus plus, during the Somme Offensive. He took a lot of orientation before he came to Glamis. He was just showing signs of regaining some strength.'

'Then he goes down a cliff. A brave man. He was conscious while he was here. He's taken some terrific bruising to his body. He'll be in a lot of pain. There may be some internal damage – not entirely sure yet. His BP was quite low. He was quite shocked. He lost a fair amount of blood – that's why we're giving him blood and they're operating.'

'What's his prognosis?'

'We can't say that yet.' The doctor noted her pallor. 'Don't give up. Come, we're not so busy in Casualty now – sit down and I'll get you a cup of tea.'

He came back with tea and cake for two. 'Here, you look as though you could do with something.'

'Thanks.' She sipped gratefully. 'How long do you think they'll be?'

'I can't say. It depends you know, on what they find. When he comes out he'll go to the Special Room in Ward 4, a sort of intensive care room.' She nodded.

'When will I be able to see him?'

'Let's wait and see. How do you feel now?'

'Rejuvenated. That ginger cake was delicious.'

'We have a very good baker here. We make good use of him. The folk are clamouring at the door to be patients because the food here is better than they can get at home.'

'Now,' he said, 'would you like to go and see the other chap – Green, I think his name is – while you're waiting? That'll be one of your patients off your mind.'

Green lay quietly, screens round his bed. A large bed-cradle raised the bedding off his affected leg. The ends of a Thomas's splint protruded from the bed-end, firmly fixed to its weights and pulleys. His ankle was heavily plastered and held in place. His face was bruised, particularly on the left side. His left eye was closed, swollen and discoloured. His right eye stared out from the bruises and lit up when Rosemary appeared behind the screen. She gasped inwardly – he could have come straight from a battlefield – but maintained a professional approach.

'Good evening Green. How are you feeling?'

'Hullo, Sister. I suppose, all right, thank you. Some contraption, that.' He nodded towards his leg and their attachments.

'All in a good cause.'

'Yes, Sister.' He paused. 'I'm sorry Sister.'

'Sorry for what, Green?'

'For not heeding Sister Ellis and Captain Sinclair.'

'Well, Green, when you're back at Glamis, you'll be able to say it yourself.'

'Yes, Sister.' He looked crestfallen.

'Rosemary said, 'I'm sure you won't be too long here. They'll probably allow you back for bed-rest with your splint and pulleys.'

'Sister, how is Captain Sinclair?' She took a deep breath.

'We don't know yet. He's still in theatre.'

'Oh.' He gave her his one-eyed stare. 'I'm truly sorry.' He held out his hand. She took it.

'I need to go now. I'll see you another time. I'm glad you're all right.'

'Thank you Sister.'

She went back to Duncan Fraser standing at the door.

'Is he all right, do you think?' she asked.

'Yes, he'll be fine. Nice black eye. D'you want to wait for Captain Sinclair to come out of theatre?'

'Yes, if that's allowed.'

'Oh, don't worry. You're in uniform. You're staff. I'll show you, then I must go back to Casualty. Someone's coming in. Here's Ward 4 and here's Sister.'

Sister Marian Webb treated her as a colleague.

'Here's our Special Room. He'll be here for the foreseeable future until we're satisfied with his condition.'

The room was quite small, spotless, an oxygen cylinder by the bed. The bed-ends were off, ready for any eventuality. Other equipment for any speedy resuscitation lay on a table. Sheets and blankets were folded back and out of the way ready to admit a post-operative patient.

'They won't be long now. Please have a seat. Can I get you anything?'

'No, but thank you.' Rosemary sat and prepared to wait.

What seemed a long time later, she heard the rattle and clank of a lift climbing laboriously. The gates opened.

Magnus lay on the trolley, so still, so bruised yet so pale that for a second she stopped breathing. Was he alive? And yet, he must be if they were bringing him back here to be specialled. She stepped back as busy, more impersonal hands, lifted, rolled, placed, checked the transfusion of blood still running into a vein in his right arm. Another bottle of saline dripped slowly into his left. Sister Webb stepped back after completing her immediate observations and motioned Rosemary forward.

'I'll just go and get the theatre report. I'll be just outside. He should be coming round. Do him good to see a kent face.'

Rosemary, hardly daring, took his hand. It was warm, alive. Tears coursed down her cheeks. She brushed them away with the back of her hand before anyone could see.

'Magnus,' she said very quietly. Then a little louder, 'Magnus, can you hear me?'

There was the slightest response in the vague frown on his forehead.

'Magnus, it's me, Rosemary. Can you open your eyes?'

There was no response. She looked round to see that no-one was there, then bent down and gave him a swift kiss on the lips. He lay still, then back came the slight twitch of the forehead. She squeezed his hand.

'Magnus, it's Rosemary. Can you hear me?'

The door opened and Sister Webb entered.

'Is he awake?'

'Not yet, but I don't think he's very far away.' Marian Webb came to the bedside.

'Hello Magnus. I'm just going to do your observations.' She glanced at Rosemary. 'I'll just do his obs then I'll tell you what's going on.'

'I'll go out and leave you to it for a minute. Magnus, it's Rosemary again. I'm just going out for a few minutes while Sister does your obs. I'll be back in a minute.'

'Thanks Rosemary,' said Marian Webb.

'I'll just go down and see if my driver has arrived and ask him to wait. I'll be right back.' She went down and looked out. There was no sign. She went over to where a nurse sat and explained the situation.

'He'll probably come in asking for me,' she finished. 'His name's Burnett. Could you ask him to wait please? Would that be all right?'

'Yes, of course. We'll give him a cup of tea. Where will you be?'

'In the Special Room in Ward 4.'

'We'll send a message to the ward, if we're not too busy.'

'Thank you very much. I'll go back there now.'

Marian Webb had finished checking Magnus over. She came to the door to meet Rosemary.

'How is he?'

'His obs are stable. The theatre report says he had a ruptured spleen – that's what was causing the bleeding so it's been removed. Also, his right kidney is badly bruised. That'll cause pain and problems for a wee while. He's on morphine for pain. He's not quite with us yet. I think he's trying but maybe you'll be able to get through to him.'

'No fractures?'

'No fractures. I think he probably banged his head. We're doing concussion observations. Given what he's been through now and before, I'm amazed that he's not a lot worse.'

Rosemary went quietly to Magnus's bed-side. Her legs suddenly felt very tired. She sat down, picked up his hand and held it to her cheek.

'Come on Magnus, speak to me.' The hand in hers moved.

'Magnus? Can you squeeze my hand?' The hand gripped – just a little. His eyelids fluttered, open, then closed, the puzzled frown re-appeared. His eyes opened again.

Magnus spoke. 'What…?' his tongue licked his dry lips.

'Wait Magnus, I'll wet your lips.' Then he tried again.

'What's going on?' Recognition dawned. 'Rosemary, what are you doing here? You're supposed to be at Glamis. Where am I?'

296

'Magnus you're in Arbroath Infirmary. There was an accident. You fell down the cliff.'

'I – what? The cliff?'

'You were on the outing – remember?'

'Oh, the outing. Yes, I remember. But it was Green, Green who fell.'

'Yes, he fell. You went down to help him. You saved his foot, Magnus.'

'Is he OK?'

'Yes, he's fine. D'you remember anything else?'

'I had a wonderful dream,' he said. 'I was asleep and you came and kissed me. And you held my hand. You wouldn't do it before. Can you kiss me now, Rosemary?'

She bent over and kissed him again. He smiled. 'This is not a dream is it?'

'No Magnus, not a dream.'

'Was it a dream before?'

'Well,' she hesitated. 'It maybe felt like one.'

'But it was real? You kissed me when I was asleep? No wonder I thought I was in the Garden of Eden.' He tried to move his arms towards her and stopped and looked at them.

'So, why am I here? Lying down? With drips – in both arms? 'Blood? he said urgently. 'Rosemary, why have I got blood up? What's going on?'

'Sh-hh, it's all right. Lie quietly and I'll tell you...'

She gave him a brief outline of what had happened, finishing up with his admission. 'And so,' she concluded, 'here you are, I'm afraid, and you need to do what you're told for a bit.'

'Concussion, no spleen, bruised kidney, and a body that probably looks as though it's been in a fight. I'm useless.'

'I'm telling you, you've been very fortunate. I think it was touch and go until they got your spleen out and the bleeding under control. Magnus, we nearly, nearly lost you.' She put her head on his bed and sobbed. 'I nearly lost you. And you would've been gone before I'd told you.' He took a big painful breath.

'Told me what?' As she realised what she'd said, he said again, 'What did you want to tell me?'

'I've wanted to tell you for ages,' she said. 'I feel so ... well, nurses shouldn't ...'

'Shouldn't?'

She sighed. 'Fall in love with their patients. There,' she said. 'I've said it. Magnus, I love you. I shouldn't have let myself do it but...'

'Don't you realise I've been wanting you to say this for weeks. Rosemary I love you, I've loved you since the hospital train and then I thought I'd lost you. And then you held me at arm's length for so long. Come, kiss me again.' They kissed and smiled at each other and she could see the tension going from him.

'I think you're very tired now.'

'Yes, I could sleep again.' His eyelids drooped. Rosemary gently extracted her hand from his grasp and found Marian Webb sitting outside the room writing her notes. She looked up.

'I heard you chatting. He sounds as though he's well round now.' Rosemary felt her face growing pink.

'Yes, he's quite lucid, but he's asleep again. I'm still not sure how much he remembers after he saw to Green.'

'I think that'll come back as he improves. That's fine to be going on with – that he knows you and is asking questions. Now, this is the natural sleep he needs. I'll go in and sit with him till the night-staff come.'

'Thank you very much. May I come back?'

'Yes, of course. Come when you can. You'll be good for him.'

It was late when Burnett turned into the Glamis Castle driveway. Colonel Fulton waited at the front door.

'Thank you, Burnett. Thank you for being so willing to wait.'

She walked slowly up the steps.

'How is he?'

'He's going to be all right.' She told him what had been done and the up to date news about Magnus.

'And Green.'

'He'll be fine. And,' she added, 'he's very apologetic.'

'So he should be.'

'Yes, well, he's paying for it now. He's going to be laid up for weeks.'

'I've telephoned Mr and Mrs Sinclair.'

'Who did you speak to?'

'Mrs Sinclair. I told her what had happened, and that he was badly injured. I also said there was every hope that he'd be all right.'

'How did she take the news?'

'She was upset, but seemed able to cope. She was away to tell Magnus's father. I told her we'd telephone if there was any news. She said to telephone any time. Would you telephone, please, and give her a first-hand report?'

'Yes, of course. I'll just go and get off my things.'

Chapter 45

Charlotte put the telephone down with trembling hands. Magnus had gone down another cliff, to help someone else. In his unfit condition. She sighed, put her head in her hands. I've to tell Alexander. How do I do it? What am I going to say? Magnus might be dying. How bare is that? Magnus is all battered and bruised. How can I say that? A sob escaped her. It'll kill him. Just after they've found each other again.

'Miss – Mrs Sinclair?' It was Edie. 'Are you all right? Mrs Sinclair, you're crying. What is it? What's the matter? Was it that telephone call? I heard it ringing. Who was it? Can I help you?'

'Oh, Edie.' Charlotte sighed. 'I've to tell Alexander…'

'What, Mrs Sinclair? What do you have to tell him?'

'I have to tell him,' Charlotte took a deep breath, 'about Magnus.'

'Magnus? What has happened?'

'Magnus,' said Charlotte steadily, as though saying something by rote, 'Magnus has gone down a cliff to help someone again. But, this time he fell.'

'Oh, Miss – Mrs Sinclair, is he, is he dead?'

'No Edie, he's not dead, but he's very badly injured. That's why, you see, I need to go and tell Mr Sinclair, to let him know and to prepare him.'

'Oh Miss – Mrs Sinclair. How do you think he's going to be?'

'I don't know.' Charlotte blew her nose. 'Put some more wood on the fire would you Edie, please? I won't go to bed yet. I'll wait up for more news. But, in the meantime, I'll need to go to Mr Sinclair.'

She walked through to the room that had become very much Alexander's since his move downstairs. Books lay in piles on the floor. The latest copy of *The Shetland Times* lay on the table with his spectacles on top of it. His favourite pictures hung on the walls. A bird-table sat outside the window where he could see the birds coming and going and log on a daily basis which ones and how many were visiting. His beloved trees he could see past the immediate garden, in the field. Even now, Charlotte saw, you could see the silvery shapes standing out in the simmer-dim, when the sun was never far away.

He wasn't asleep. He knew I'd come, she thought. He always hears the telephone. As if he knew what she was thinking he spoke.

'Who was on the telephone?'

'It was Dr Fulton, from Glamis.'

'What did he want? It's late to be phoning.'

'He telephoned about Magnus. There's been an accident.'

'What kind of an accident. They shouldn't have accidents at Glamis. It's a hospital.'

'Yes, but they went for an outing, today, to Arbroath.'

'How did they get there?'

'In a charabanc. They…'

'In a charabanc? So the charabanc had an accident. Is that it? Is Magnus all right?'

299

'Alexander, the charabanc didn't have an accident.' As he was about to interrupt again she put a hand on his and said, 'Just hear me out Alexander, and I'll tell you.' He subsided.

'They went to Arbroath and walked along the cliff top. Someone fell down the cliff and Magnus went down to give first aid.' His hand gripped hers tightly.

'And, they're not going to telephone at this time to tell us that he's gone down a cliff to help someone. What's happened to him?'

'He was very brave, he went down, saved the man's foot, and then, he – he fell down the rest of the cliff. I think he didn't feel very well and lost his balance.'

'Oh God. How is he?'

'All that Dr Fulton could tell me was that he's in theatre in Arbroath Infirmary. He's expecting more news and I said to telephone any time.'

'Has someone gone to see him?'

'Yes, he said the Sister-in-Charge of Glamis had obtained a lift back to Arbroath with the police to go and see for herself. She'll report back and then one of them will telephone us.' They held hands in silence for a few minutes.

'My son,' he said. 'My eldest son. I threw him out. He came back and we made peace – we found each other again. And, and he's gone from me again. He'll never come back this time. He's going to die because he went to help someone.'

'Alexander, the doctor did not say he was going to die.'

'Ach, you know what doctors are like. They wrap up horrible facts in euphemisms.'

'He did not wrap anything up,' Charlotte insisted. 'He told me the facts.'

'What precisely did he say then?'

'He said, that Magnus fell, taking a few knocks on the way down and hit a place very near the bottom of the cliff. Immediately, two men went down on ropes, and gave first aid to Magnus till the Lifeboat came.'

'And he's in theatre now?'

'As far as I know. I know no more than you now. We need to wait.'

A long two hours later the telephone rang.

Charlotte hurried to pick it up.

'Hello.'

'Hello. Is that Mrs Sinclair?'

'Yes, speaking.'

'Mrs Sinclair, this is Rosemary Jones, from Glamis. I'm just back from seeing Magnus.'

'Yes, how is he?'

'Well, the first thing is, I'm happy to say he's conscious and speaking normally to me.'

'Oh, I'm so glad. Go on.'

'He was in theatre for quite a while. He lost a lot of blood. They've removed his spleen which was haemorrhaging, he has a very bruised kidney, concussion and bad overall bruising.'

'Will the kidney be all right?'

'Yes, they think so. He's in quite a lot of discomfort but they're giving him morphine.' She continued, 'Mrs Sinclair, the main thing to say now is that he's making very good progress. He was speaking to me before I left, and then he fell asleep again – a normal sleep. The Sister was pleased with his condition.'

'What about the blood loss?'

'They're giving him some more blood intravenously. I think he's doing well considering what he's just been through. I'm going back to see him tomorrow and will telephone again when I can.'

'Thank you very much. Just one more thing – how is the other man? I understand that Magnus …'

'Yes, Green, the other casualty, he's got a leg fractured in two places. Magnus did a wonderful job. He saved Green's foot by going down. Green's going to be fine.'

'I'm so glad. Thank you very much for telephoning.'

'You're welcome. I'll speak with you tomorrow.' They rang off.

Charlotte sat beside the telephone for a minute to gather her thoughts before going back. Alexander looked up. His good hand nervously fiddled with the sheet.

'Well,' he burst out. 'It's bad news and you don't want to tell me.'

'Alexander, no. It's not like that. Magnus is – I think he's going to be all right.' She sat beside his bed, leant over and wrapped her arms round him. 'He's awake, or been awake, and talking.'

'Tell me, tell me what she said.'

'Well, she started by telling me that he's conscious. And then she went on …'

Alexander's anxious questioning continued for a while until Charlotte said.

'I think we should both try and have some sleep now. Can I get you anything? Some warm milk? Help you sleep. It's very late.'

'Yes please,' he sank back. 'I think I might sleep with that.' She found Edie in the kitchen.

'Oh, Miss, Mrs Sinclair, how is he? I heard the telephone…'

'It's all right Edie. I think he's going to be all right.'

'Oh Miss, I'm so happy for you, for us all. I'll just go and tell Meg.'Charlotte went back to Alexander with his warm milk.

'I didn't make it too hot so you'd be able to drink it.'

When he had finished, she said, 'Do you think you could sleep now?'

'Yes, I'm tired. You do think he's going to be all right, don't you?'

'Yes, Alexander. I really do.'

'Then let us be full of thankfulness.' He put out his good arm and held her closely. 'I love you, you know, my girl-bride.'

'And I love you too Alexander.' They kissed. He smiled at her and closed his eyes, visibly relaxing as he settled for sleep.

Charlotte checked all was well in the kitchen, shooed Edie off to bed, looked in on Hannah and Angus, sound asleep, and went, at last, to her own room. Far in the north-east, already the simmer-dim was brightening to herald the new day.

301

Charlotte

I woke with a start. My heart was pounding. Early morning sunshine poured into the room. I looked at my clock – it was only five. I suddenly felt a surge of something, something very urgent. I got out of bed, reached for my dressing-gown, and flung it on. There was something the matter. I could feel it. Alexander. I ran down the stairs to his room.

He lay quietly, his last smile for me still on his face. It was with almost a feeling of reverence that I approached his bed. I knew before I touched him that he had gone from me. I picked up his hand, the hand that had held mine a short few hours before. It was still quite warm but limp and pulseless. I sat down beside him.

I don't know how long I sat there. I didn't hear the activity in the kitchen as Edie rattled up the big stove. I didn't hear Hannah's feet crossing the landing looking for me. I didn't even notice Hannah at Alexander's door. I just sat, holding his hand, then very gently kissed it and laid it down.

'Mother? Mother, is everything all right?'

'Hannah. My dear. Come in.' I got up and held out my hand. Hannah, Father's just died, so quietly…'

'Oh Mother.' We held each other closely. Hannah sobbed into my shoulder.

'When? When did he die?'

'I can't tell exactly when,' I said. 'I came down at five and he was gone then but not very long before. But look at him, Hannah. He's died so peacefully, so quietly I wouldn't wish it any other way for him.'

'But he's gone.' Tears ran down her face. 'He's my father and he's gone.'

'Who's gone?' Angus was suddenly in the room. He looked round.

'What's going on? Why are you standing here talking when father's asleep?'

'Angus,' I took his hand. 'I didn't mean you to find out like this.'

'Find out what?'

'Your father died a wee while ago. Look, he's happy, he's got a smile on his face. Come, and see him.' I led him over to the bed.

'Father?' He took his hand. 'His hand's cold, Mother. If I put it under the blankets will it warm up?'

'No, not now.'

Hannah touched his face. 'He does look happy,' she said. 'Like when he's watching the birds or walking in the garden.'

'Yes,' I said. 'Let's hold on to that. We need to be happy for him. Now we need to tell Edie and Meg. I think Edie at least will be in the kitchen.'

'I'll go.' Hannah slipped out. Angus cooried into me, saying nothing. She wasn't long. Edie came back with her.

'Poor Mr Sinclair. We'll miss him. Do you think it had anything to do with the news about Magnus?'

'What news about Magnus?' Hannah asked. I looked at them both. How much could they take.

'Let's go and sit down in the kitchen.'

As gently as I could I told them about Magnus's fall, how and why it had happened. I tried hard to give the positive side.

'The main thing now, is that Magnus is all right, he's in hospital in Arbroath and we'll hear more news later. I know all this is a lot in one day. Here's Meg. And Edie's here too.'

'Mrs Sinclair, I'm so sorry.'

'Thank you, Meg. This is difficult for you too. You've known him for so very long.'

'Ay, ay, he did well, but, well, there you are. I'm glad he didn't suffer. Now, Hannah,' Meg turned to her. 'Let's get the breakfast going. We all need to eat.' Edie was already putting the kettle on.

'And, I need to telephone Doctor Taylor.' I went through with Angus at my heels.

'Are you sure you want to stay?' I said. 'I'm going to tell the doctor about Father you know.' I didn't want to upset him. On the other hand, it might help him to take it in.

'Yes, I know. I'm staying with you.' He stood by me as I spoke to the operator.

'Yes, that's right, Jarlshavn 232. Thank you. I hear it ringing,' I said to Angus. 'Hello,' as someone answered the telephone. 'Hello, Dr Taylor? It's Charlotte Sinclair here.'

'Mrs Sinclair, good morning. How are you all? What can I do for you?'

'I'm sorry to give you bad news. I'm afraid Mr Sinclair has died.'

'I'm very sorry. When do you think this happened?'

'Sometime before five this morning, I think. I found him then.'

'All right. I'll be right round and you can give me the details then.'

'Thank you very much. Good bye.'

I replaced the telephone and took Angus's hand. He was cold and trembly.

'Come on, let's get you dressed and then you'll feel a bit better.' He cried then, when we reached his bedroom with the door shut. I held him until the first deluge of grief had passed and he was more relaxed, pressed into my breast, holding on very tightly. Every now and again he gave a shuddering sigh.

'Do you think you could manage to get dressed now?'

'I don't know.'

'Come, I'll help you. Then you can have some breakfast. You really will feel better.' Little by little we managed. He was very reluctant to let me go. We went together to the kitchen where Meg and Edie were dishing up. The doorbell rang.

'That'll be Dr Taylor. Hannah and Angus, will you stay here with Meg and Edie? Angus,' I said, as he made to come with me, 'I will come back, but I must see Dr Taylor about Father.'

'Yes,' said Edie, 'you stay with us and have your porridge.'

'Come on Angus,' said Hannah. 'Here's your bowl.' I caught her eye as I passed her. She smiled faintly. 'You go on, Mother,' she said. 'He'll be all right.'

I went to let Dr Taylor in.

Chapter 46

Rosemary tapped on Colonel Neil Fulton's door.

'Come in. Oh, it's you Rosemary. How was Mrs Sinclair last night when you telephoned?'

'She seemed fine, relieved I should say, thankful that Magnus seemed to have turned a corner. But, Neil,' she sat down on the edge of the chair opposite him. 'She's just telephoned this morning.'

'But surely she knew that you'd telephone when you had some news.'

'Yes, that's what we arranged. But, she was phoning to say that Magnus's father has died.'

'Died? When?'

'Early this morning. She says she told him about our telephone conversation. He seemed quite happy and settled down. It was probably very late by then. She went to bed and woke at five, and found him dead. She's had the GP to certify the death. He's had two previous known strokes so this wasn't entirely a surprise.'

'How is she?'

'Not sure. Coping well, but possibly too well. She's running around doing things. She's away to telephone her daughter, Christina. You'll remember that I escorted Magnus to Christina's wedding.' He nodded.

'I advised her,' said Rosemary, 'and I hope this is all right with you, to ask Christina not to contact Arbroath – and of course she'll also have to tell her about Magnus – until I've had a chance to tell him face to face. I hope that was the right thing to do.'

'Yes, of course,' he said. 'When do you want to go? Who's on with you? He looked at the list. I see for once you and Sister Ellis are on together. She can act up and – pity Burnett will be away in the car with you or he would be available here.'

'If you'd let me take the car,' she said, 'I can drive.'

'Can you?'

'Yes, the nursing sisters frequently drove ambulances and other vehicles in France. Not a problem.'

'Right, that's settled. Go and inform Sister Ellis and I'll get Burnett to bring the car round.'

'Thank you.'

'An hour and a half later she parked in front of the Infirmary and headed for Ward 4. It was busy. Sister Marian Webb, sleeves rolled up was instructing two young nurses on the laying up of sterile trolleys.

'Good morning,' she called. 'I'll be with you in a minute.'

'Rosemary sat and thought about her mission for the day. How best to tell an ill man that his father has just died. She'd had to do many difficult things in her day, but this one was particularly hard.

'Sorry to keep you waiting. Come into the office.' Marian Webb rolled her sleeves down as she spoke.

'How's Magnus?'

'He's doing well, I think. His blood's transfusion's finished. The other drip is still up but just very slowly to keep the vein open until we're absolutely sure. He's managed to take a little porridge and milk this morning, just a spoonful or two till we see how he goes. He's still on hourly obs which are stable and reasonably satisfactory on the whole. They improved overnight. Still in pain, but that's inevitable and we're covering that as far as we can with morphine. We hope to be able to start pulling back on that soon.'

'He sounds a bit better than yesterday.'

'Oh yes, he's definitely improved.'

'How do you think he'd cope with a piece of bad news?'

'How bad?'

'Very. His father died early this morning.' She told Marian what had happened. 'To make things worse, Magnus and his father had only recently made peace after a long separation. It'll be very hard on him. His mother's going to tell his sister this morning. She's a staff nurse at RIE.'

'She's bound to come here to see him when she gets time. You need to tell him now, if you can. Then he's ready for her when she comes.'

Rosemary tapped then put her head round the door. Magnus lay propped up on pillows, more alert-looking than the day before.

'Hello, how are you today?'

He lifted his free arm and waved it at her. 'Not bad, considering.' He dropped his voice to a whisper. 'Come and give me a kiss.'

'Magnus,' she protested.

'Come on now, you can't do it one day and not the next.' She gave in, walked towards him, looked round guiltily and kissed him.

'You sound and look better.'

'Yes, I think things are improving. That morphine is great.'

'Yes, I've heard other people say that.'

'You look a bit worried. What's the problem?' Rosemary looked down. Was it as obvious as that?

'Come, Rosemary, I can see something's bothering you. Is it to do with me? What have they not told me?'

'No, no, Magnus, it's nothing like that.'

'So there is something. What is it? Please tell me.'

'Magnus, I was speaking to Charlotte. Colonel Fulton telephoned her last night to tell them about your accident and I telephoned to say you were out of theatre and all right. Then Charlotte telephoned me today.'

'What did she want?' Rosemary took his hand.

'She needed to tell me that your father has died. Magnus I'm sorry.'

He said nothing. As if to shut out the bad news, he closed his eyes. For five minutes they sat like that. Tears squeezed out from under his eyelids. Rosemary stroked his hand back and forth between hers trying to make contact.

305

'Magnus,' she said. 'I'm here. What can I do for you? How can I help you?' He opened his eyes. Suddenly-released tears streamed down his face. His grief shook his pain-racked frame. She held him and he leant against her.

Marian Webb, concerned for her patient, looked unnoticed round the door and surveyed the scene before quietly withdrawing.

Eventually he sat back and wiped his eyes. 'Sorry, he said. I can cope now. Tell me what happened.' She told him all she knew. He sighed.

'I suppose it had to come. We all knew it. I'm glad it was peaceful at the end, or so it seems.'

'That's what Charlotte's saying.'

'How is she?'

'She's concerned about you. She was away to tell Christina. We felt it would be better if I told you face to face.'

'I'm glad it was you who told me. It must have been difficult.'

'It was. But it's done now.'

They sat in silence for a few minutes then he said,

'What happens next?'

'Well the GP will issue the death certificate and then I presume there will be a funeral.'

'But there will be the kisting before that and all the organisation. I should be there. Oh, Rosemary, I won't be able to go.'

'No, Magnus, I don't think so. Tell me,' she asked, 'What's the kisting?'

'That's a very old custom, a ceremony really. The joiner makes a kist – or coffin, then before the funeral the body is formally placed in the kist. It's a family occasion, usually done at home with the minister there.'

'That sounds like a good family custom.'

'Yes it is. That's the quiet bit. But, then there's viewing – folk come in the days before the funeral to view the body, and offer commiserations to the family. And have food and drink. They're all so kind and well-meaning but it seems never-ending at the time.' He paused, thinking, then continued.

'I remember when my mother died. I was very angry and upset that they all had a wake, a party the night of the funeral.' Charlotte was such a help. His voice wobbled. 'I should be there for her now. There will be so much to do.' There was a tap at the door and Marian Webb entered.

'Magnus, I'm very sorry for your loss.' She stood by his bed, taking his pulse. 'How are you?'

'Tired,' he said. 'Glad Rosemary came.' He squeezed her hand.

'Sister Webb, don't you think I would be fit enough to go to my father's funeral?'

'Magnus, have you any idea how near you came to bleeding to death?' He looked at her.

'I'm not joking,' she said, 'or exaggerating. We were very worried for a while, until we controlled the bleeding by removing your spleen. Your body's had to cope with that as

306

well as everything else. That was only yesterday. I'm very sorry, but you just won't be able to do this. Mrs Sinclair won't expect it of you under the circumstances.' He was silent. Then he looked first at Rosemary who nodded encouragement, then at Sister Webb.

'I know,' he said. 'I know what I would be telling anyone else. But it's difficult when it's so personal. It's all right. I won't argue.'

'Looking at you,' said Sister Webb, 'I'm thinking you could do with a nap.'

'I agree,' said Rosemary. 'I'll go away now, come back in a while, then I'll get back to Glamis.'

She looked back in an hour. He was sitting up, with a bowl of lentil soup in front of him.

'Smells good.' She sat down.

'It *is* good. Have you had any lunch?'

'Yes, I had a bowl of soup in the staff dining room..'

'Christina telephoned,' he said. 'She's got compassionate leave, is heading north tomorrow and will call in past on her way to Aberdeen.'

'You'll be glad to see each other.'

That evening, Christina went along to Ward 20 to see James.

'Hello.' He put down his book. 'Glad to see you. How are things with you?'

'I'm fine, thanks. How about you? Any news yet about moving on?'

'Yes, it's all settled. I'm being posted to the Rosebank Auxiliary Hospital in Perth to convalesce, probably next week. Sister and Major Collins and I had a confab and they went away and set it all in motion, and, there you are.'

'How do you feel now?'

'Well, it's a step forward and I'll be able to get out a bit…'

'You'll be under strict orders to behave yourself.'

'Yes, I know but I'll be able to walk outside and further – it'll all be less medicalised. I'll get fitter and then be more ready to go before an Army Medical Board.'

'You take it slowly, mind.'

'But you'll be back to see me before I go?'

'Well, James, there *is* something I need to tell you.'

'You look very serious.'

'Yes, we've hit a rough patch – oh not Lowrie and me' – she said, 'but the Sinclair family.'

'What's happened?'

'Magnus, he went on an outing with some of the other patients, to Arbroath. There was an accident on the cliff…'

But,' she continued when she had told him, 'by the time Mother had a chance to telephone me the following morning, she found Father had – died in his sleep.' She stopped. 'I'm sorry. I find it very difficult to say.'

'Oh Christina, I am very sorry. It must have been quite sudden. Was it another stroke?'

'I think so. It was almost half-expected but that doesn't prepare you does it?'

'Not really. It's a big blow. What are you going to do? And, how is Magnus? And Charlotte and the children?'

307

'Mother, I think, is coping. Hannah's very capable and is putting on a brave face. Angus will hardly let Mother out of his sight. I'm on compassionate leave from now. I go north tomorrow and I'll see Magnus in Arbroath Infirmary en route.'

'How is he?' She made a face.

'I haven't seen him but I understand it was touch and go. He's going to be all right though. Not sure how 'all right'. I don't know how he'd get on with a Medical Board now. He won't be able to go to Father's funeral. I spoke to Rosemary earlier today. She says he's very sad, but resigned'

'She's been in to see him?'

'Oh yes, the evening of the accident. She saw the other chap too then – Green. Magnus saved his foot by giving first aid, knowing what to do.' She got to her feet.

'I must go. I have to pack. But I needed to see you first. You're part of the family.'

'Thank you for coming. Just one thing, before you go, we've talked about the rest of your family Christina, but how about you? How are *you*?' She sat down again.

'Ach well,' she said. 'I do what I have to do. I'll be glad to see Mother. I miss – I miss, Lowrie so much. It's like a constant ache. I do so want him to come through this War but sometimes, sometimes, I wonder if we'll get out of it together.' She sighed.

'Try and stay away from fears like that Christina. Please, try and think positively for him and with him. Lift up your heart. Let his be lifted up too.'

'Yes, you're right, of course. Will you think about us – from a distance?'

'Yes, of course I will.'

'Thank you.' She got up. 'Thank you, James.'

'Tell Charlotte I'll write. I'm so sorry for her loss, for this loss which all of you are bearing.'

'Good bye James.' She bent and kissed him on the cheek, then walked away.

When she left James sat and thought for a moment then took his writing materials out.

Ward 20,
RIE

Dear Charlotte,

Christina has just been in to tell me your very sad news about Alexander. I'm so sorry to hear this – words to express the depth of feeling that I have are difficult to find. Please accept my deepest condolences.

It was good of Christina to find the time to come in and tell me. She was away to pack for her journey north to be with you. I'm sure that you will each be a source of comfort to one another and of course Hannah and Angus, and, Meg and Edie.

I was sorry too, to hear about Magnus's accident, but glad to hear that he is out of danger. I hope that he is on his feet soon and on the way back to good health.

I thought that you might like to know that I am being discharged to convalesce at the Rosebank Auxiliary Hospital, in Perth.

It would be good to hear how you are getting along sometime.

I am so sad for you in your loss.

Yours very sincerely,
James.

Christina walked out of Arbroath station and hailed the only taxi there.

'Where to, Miss? Here, let me take that for you.' He took her case.

'Thank you. Arbroath Infirmary, please. Is it far?'

'Not really. Save you walking in this drizzle. And, with that case. Have you been here before?'

'Passing through. I haven't stopped before.'

'Good place, Arbroath. Great fish, the smokies.'

'Yes, I know. I'm hoping for some for lunch.'

'Ay, ye'll maybe get that at the Infirmary – if not, ye'll hae tae heid for the Fit o the Toon tae buy some. Here's the Infirmary.' He slowed up at the entrance.

'Thank you very much,' said Christina, as he handed out her bag.

'A pleasure Miss. Mind and get the smokies.'

'I'll try.'

She headed straight for Ward 4. Sister Marian Webb was in her office.

'Hello, I'm looking for Magnus Sinclair. I phoned – I'm his sister, Christina.'

'Hello,' Marian Webb held out her hand. 'We're expecting you. I know you don't have too much time. Come on and see him.'

'How is he?'

'Getting along nicely. I wouldn't have given tuppence for him when he came in, and then yesterday he was better but very upset about his father. Today he's sorting himself out. Your visit will do him good. This is his room. Just knock and go in yourself.'

It was indeed a flying visit. They both knew that the *St Clair*, bound to a timetable, could wait for no-one. They cried at sight of each other, united in the sense of having lost an important part of their lives, however different that was for each of them.

'I would have liked more time with him,' said Magnus. 'Time to be friends and get to know each other. But time was just what we didn't have.'

'But, aren't you glad that you went? Magnus, think if you hadn't gone, if you'd been too late.'

'I know. From my own point of view, that's one thing I'm glad about in all of this. I'm glad I went and we made peace.'

'I'm very sure that he was glad too.'

'I hope so.'

'I know so. And,' she added, 'I know Lowrie thinks so too.'

'How *is* Lowrie?'

'He's doing all right. We write a lot. Sometimes the letters get through quickly, sometimes they don't and then I get a few in a bundle together. Then I have to try and read them in order. Otherwise I get all mixed up. He dates them all.'

She was chattering. She knew it. He looked at her and stopped her.

'Christina.'

'Mphm?'

'How are *you*. He sounds fine. But what about you? You'll be missing him, I'm thinking.'

309

'Magnus, don't say it. It just makes it worse. I, I can cope when I don't speak about it. James said I should try and think positively but it's difficult with the War news and the casualties keep coming in.' She twisted her hands together. He put his hands round hers to calm them.

'James is right. But keep going my girl, my wee sister. All will be well – you'll see.' They smiled at each other.

'Now,' he said. 'I've written a letter to Charlotte. It's not much, but could you take it to her, please.' She tucked it into her bag.

'I think I need to go.'

'Yes, you should. I'd hate you to be late for the boat.'

'Don't get up.'

'Don't worry, I won't. But by the time you see me next, I'll be on my feet.'

'I'm very proud of you – all over again. But – please don't do anything daft.'

'Away with you. As if I would.'

They laughed and she made for the door, turning round to give him a wave as she went.

In the middle of the following morning she walked in through the open back door at Birkenshaw. Drizzle and fog which had dampened the Isles and the spirits of their people over the last few days had cleared overnight. It was clear, bright and the world was drying out. She could hear Hannah's voice, and Meg's slower response.

'Hello,' she called.

'Christina. You're home.' Hannah held out her arms. 'I'm so glad to see you. Oh Christina, Father's dead. It's sad.'

'Yes, I know. I'm sorry.' She stroked her sister's hair. 'It's difficult for you.' She looked at Meg.

'Meg, Thank you. I know what a support you will have been.'

'Ach, Christina, we just do what we can.' The old woman walked stiffly over to her and rubbed her back in welcome. 'It does my heart good to see you.' Christina smiled and kissed the old cheek.

'Where's Mother?'

'Through the house with Angus. I think he's watching her write letters. He'll maybe be able to leave her for a bit now you've come.'

'He's being a bit clingy,' said Hannah. 'We'll all be better now you're here.'

'Well, let's go and see them. Is Edie here?'

'Yes, she's upstairs.'

'I'll see her in a while.'

Charlotte and Angus were in the parlour. Charlotte wrote at her desk. Her correspondence was mounting as the word spread of Alexander's death. She was amazed and humbled as the letters poured in. Angus sat beside her desk reading. Every so often he put his hand up and touched her. She would look up and smile and then, reassured, he returned to his book.

'Give him time,' Dr Taylor had said. 'He's just showing a wee bit of insecurity. He's lost one parent and he's checking that you're still there. Bear with it.' Charlotte looked up as Christina entered.

'Hello, It's good to see you.'

'How are you? And you Angus?' Christina put out an arm to him.

'I'm all right,' said Angus. 'Just, you know.' His face screwed up. 'Father's dead. I don't like him being dead.'

'None of us do,' said Christina. She looked over his head at Charlotte and raised her eyebrows.

'Angus is keeping me company when I'm writing letters,' said Charlotte. 'There are so many. And he's putting on the stamps.'

'Oh, that reminds me.' Christina rummaged in her bag. 'Here's another, from Magnus.'

'How is he?' Charlotte put the letter into her pocket for later.

'All right, thank Goodness. He's had surgery, but he's coping. He's being well looked after in Arbroath and then Rosemary's been in and out, from Glamis, the Sister-in-Charge. She's seen the other chap too – Green. The man who fell first. He's fine too. Our brother,' she said to Angus, 'is very brave. He went down a cliff to help a man and saved his foot from having to be amputated.'

'That's pretty amazing,' said Angus. 'I might be a doctor too.'

'I think the kettle might be boiling. I'm gasping. I had a very early breakfast on the *St Clair*.'

Later, Charlotte opened the letter. It was brief – but at least he was able to write.

Arbroath Infirmary

Dear Charlotte,

I was very sad to receive the news about Father. As you will know Rosemary told me – she is a great support. I'm glad to think that you'll have the rest of the family and Meg and Edie to be with you and help at this time. I am so sorry I can't be there. I'll come when I'm able. I know you'll understand and feel that Father would as well.

I hope that all goes well and that Father gets a 'fine day and a following wind'.

Take care of yourself.

Yours, affly.,

Magnus.

Charlotte

Then it was over. Alexander's funeral took place a week after he died. When the last visitor at the wake had walked down the driveway, the last person helping in the kitchen had gone with anxious questions of 'is there anything else I can do?', the last well-wisher had left for the time being – for they all promised that they'd be back to help with

311

anything we needed, we sat back and looked at each other. As usual, we were round the kitchen table, Christina, Hannah, Angus, Meg, Edie and I.

I looked round at them, my beloved family and dear old friends. We all missed Magnus's presence but it was good to have first-hand news from Christina and from his letter which she had brought.

Angus yawned loudly.

'Past your bed-time,' I said. 'Long past.' He looked at me sadly.

'I miss Father. He used to tell me about the trees.'

'I know,' I said, 'but just think, he would want you to carry on learning about the trees. And, he's left all his books on trees so that we can still learn about them.'

'It won't be the same.'

'We'll do it together,' offered Hannah. 'I need to do it too, and it will help my school botany.'

'Now,' I said. 'Bed, my boy.'

'Will you come up?'

'When you're in bed.' He went away.

'At least he's doing that by himself now.'

'I see quite a difference in the last day or two,' said Christina.

'He's recognising that he has to move on,' said Meg. 'We all have to.' She was right. It just took a bit of doing.

The past week had been so busy arranging things from the kisting to the funeral service with the minister, the wake and all the visitors in between that there was little time to think of moving on. When I remarked on this, Meg reminded me of when Christina's mother died.

'Folk want to come,' she said.

'I'm glad we've done it,' said Christina. 'But I'm sorry Magnus missed it.'

'Yes,' said Edie. Magnus was a particular pet of hers, even though he was thirty-five. She was quite doleful. 'He'll be very disappointed.'

'He'll understand,' I said.

'Yes,' said Christina. 'He was reconciled. He was more worried about not being able to help.'

Finally I encouraged them all off to bed. I went up to Angus and found him in bed with one of Alexander's books on trees.

'I think,' he said seriously, 'I think I'll need to go out tomorrow and check on the trees. Father's not here now to organise this so I'll need to do it. I've just been thinking about it.'

'That's good Angus. I've been wondering what we should do about that. Will you consult with Dod about them then?'

'Yes,' he said. 'He can show me what he does to keep the rabbits out and what needs to be checked. Don't worry Mother. I'll see to it.' He sounded so purposeful.

'Thank you, Angus. Do you think it's time to put your book down now and go to sleep?' We said our goodnights. I'd just reached the door when he called me back.

'Mother?'

'Yes?'

'Do you think Father would be glad I'm the tree-keeper?'

'I'm sure he would.' I went downstairs feeling heartened.

All was quiet. Birkenshaw was slowing down for the night. A little later I stood at my bedroom window, our bedroom once, before Alexander's move downstairs. Stars were visible to the south but the subtle glow further north outshone the would-be starlight.

'It's quiet now, Alexander,' I spoke aloud. 'Peaceful. You too, rest in peace. Go well.'

I got into bed and lay there, Eventually, I must have slept. When I next opened my eyes it was bright morning and I could hear Edie rattling the range in the kitchen.

Chapter 47

AUGUST 1917

It was a wild summer's day of east coast wind and rain when Burnett pulled up the Glamis car at the front entrance to Arbroath Infirmary. Sitting in a wheel-chair, Magnus waited just inside. He saw the car with Rosemary in the passenger seat and made to get up.

'Just take it slowly,' said Marian Webb down to see him off. 'Here's Rosemary. I'll hand you over.' She gave him a pat on the arm to soften the words. 'Just like a parcel.'

'All set?'

'Yes, I'm just telling Magnus I'm about to hand him over.'

'Nice, isn't it?' said Magnus. Rosemary smiled, accepted Magnus's medical notes and held out her arm.

'What are we waiting for?' Magnus turned to Marian Webb.

'I can't thank you enough for all you've done.'

'I'm glad we were able to help.'

'That's the understatement of the year. Thank you Sister Webb.'

'You're welcome. Now, go before your driver is asked to move on.'

Burnett got out at their approach, held the door wide, helped Magnus in the front where he had more room for his legs, humming all the while.

'A'm that pleased tae see you in ae piece.'

'Thanks, Burnett. Good to see you too.' Magnus sat back and shut his eyes.

It was marginally less windy and wet at Glamis.

'I can manage,' Magnus insisted, waving away offers of help. 'I've been practising.' He did manage but was very glad to get inside. His room had been changed to the ground floor.

'You can change back to the upstairs when you're ready,' Rosemary said. 'Burnett are you free just now?'

Yes Sister.'

'Will you please help Magnus to get comfortable? 'You should rest now Magnus, and then we'll see how you are. I'll be in to see you in a while.'

Later, she returned. She had been in to Colonel Neil Fulton and handed over Magnus's medical notes. They spent some time going over them.

'He had a close call,' said Neil. 'Thank goodness they got him to theatre in time. Poor soul, on top of all he's been through. He's going to take twice as long convalescing.' She nodded.

'Where is he now?'

'He's in bed, resting.' She looked at her watch. 'Probably having lunch. I'd better go and see that they've remembered.'

'Right, you do that and I'll see him in the afternoon and have a look at him.'

Magnus was finishing his lunch. 'Better food here than in Arbroath – it wasn't bad,' he added hastily. 'Quite good in fact. But this is better.'

'Have you had a sleep?'

'Yes, funnily enough, I have. I didn't think I would, but it's a lot quieter here.'

'So, how do you feel now?'

'Better, I think. More rested. It's amazing, a great sleep.' He stretched, winced, let his arms drop again. Not quite ready for big stretching.' Instead, he put out his hand and held hers, his blue eyes on her face.

She sat down on the bed.

'Magnus, we need to do something about this.'

'Mphm.' He tickled the palm of her hand.

'Magnus. Listen. I'm serious.'

'Right. I'm being serious too. What's the matter?'

'We need to talk to the Colonel about – about us.' He sucked through his teeth.

'You do see, don't you?'

'In principle, yes, I do. But, he may have you posted.'

'I hope not but we'll have to take the chance. I can't go on in this secretive way while I'm working here. Not in this job.'

'You're right of course. All right. Let's speak to Neil and see what he says.'

'He's coming up to see you after lunch. I could give you some time for that and then come through…'

'What should we tell him?'

'Er…'she hesitated.

'Well, could we make this more, formal, for instance? Like this: Rosemary, will you marry me?' She gasped.

'Magnus, I don't know what to say.'

'You could say "yes",' he said. His grip on her hand grew tighter.

'Go on Rosemary. Please say "yes". Just think how much more quickly I'll recover if you do.'

'That's blackmail.'

'Rosemary – please. I want you to say "yes" very much. I love you so much.'

'I love you too. It hasn't been very long but…'

'I think we knew from the time on the hospital train.'

'I think we did.'

'Then is it, a "yes"?'

'Yes, Magnus, yes. I'll marry you with all my heart.'

'Even though I'm a decrepit old thing with no future, no prospects?'

'I don't believe that but "yes" anyway.'

'Come closer then. You're a better mover than I am at the moment.' Their betrothal kiss left them both breathless. They pulled apart laughing.

'Help, Sister, I need oxygen. I'm not ready for such exercise.' He looked at her then said, 'I love you so much. I'll never stop loving you.'

'Nor I you.' He held her hand to his cheek.

'We need to get a ring on that finger. Leave it to me.'

'Where do we go from here?'

'We need to see the Colonel.' He sat back on his pillows. 'It's the only way. We'll surely manage some sort of agreement until I'm better.'

A short while later Neil Fulton visited Magnus in his room for his post-hospital check-up. He was a careful man and took his time. He observed his patient's heightened colour, raised pulse, sense of suppressed excitement. He made no comment except on the state of his splenectomy wound which had healed well with no infection.

'They've done a good job on you, but you'll be aware of that.'

'I couldn't fault them,' said Magnus.

'So, how are you feeling in general?'

'Well, I'm very slow, physically. I've gone backwards in that aspect.'

'That was inevitable having a fall like that. But, you'll get past that. We'll work out a new régime for you.' Neil Fulton paused then said, 'I was sorry to hear about your father.'

'Thank you. Yes, it's a big blow. It seemed quite sudden too but, in a way almost inevitable after two previous strokes. From my personal point of view, it was doubly sad.' Magnus paused. Neil waited.

'You see,' Magnus went on. 'We had just got back on real speaking terms again after years of separation. Just weeks ago, when I went to Shetland with Christina. We only had a few days together.'

'That's hard.'

'But, I'm so thankful I was able to go. And, he didn't have to lie long, not like some poor souls. His death seems to have been happy and peaceful.'

'I'm glad. It makes a difference to everyone. Rosemary spoke with Mrs Sinclair. How is she now?'

'I think she's managing – it'll take a while. She's a lovely caring person. She sometimes doesn't stop to look after herself.'

They heard the knock. Rosemary's head looked round the door.

'Can I come in?' Neil Fulton looked at Magnus.

'All right Magnus?'

'Yes, of course.' Magnus beckoned to her. She closed the door and sat down.

'You're quite satisfied with me aren't you?'

'Yes, you'll do. Just obey the régime and get outside when you can. I'll write you up for pain relief *prn*.'

'Thank you,' said Magnus. 'Em, there is one other thing.' He looked at Rosemary.

'Yes?' Neil looked at them. 'What is it?' They stopped, looked again at each other.

'It's like this,' Rosemary began.

'No, let me,' said Magnus. 'This is all my fault.'

'What's all your fault? Is there a problem?'

'Anything but.' Magnus suddenly launched into an explanation. 'As Rosemary said, it's like this. Rosemary and I, well we first met on a hospital train in France. I fell for her hook, line and sinker then, thought I'd lost her, then blow me down when I get here, find she's been posted in. That's serendipity, Sir. We'd like to get engaged, Sir.' He closed his eyes, unable to look at Rosemary.

Neil glanced at her.

'Rosemary? Have you anything to say?' She sat up straight.

'I feel the same way. It's been difficult being secretive, you know, a nurse and a patient.' He nodded. 'We felt a bit, underhand. Just wanted to be open with you.'

'I see.' Neil scratched his head. 'I knew there was something.'

'You knew?'

'Well, not exactly what, but, for a start, your obs this afternoon, Magnus, were not exactly what I would have expected of a convalescent man who's recently been sleeping for an hour.' Rosemary hid a smile. 'And you,' he turned to her. 'I smelt a rat at your reaction at the news about Magnus. You know, when Sergeant Flett came?'

'You're very observant.'

'It's my job,' he pointed out. 'So,' he continued. 'You've told me your news and firstly, I congratulate you both. I hope you'll be very happy.' He shook hands with Magnus, then said, 'May I kiss the young lady?'

'Be my guest,' said Magnus faintly, stunned at the way the conversation was going. Neil stood up and Rosemary pulled herself out of her chair.

'May I?' he said. She nodded. He kissed her briefly but firmly on the lips. 'Be happy my dear. Nothing like a good love story.'

'Now,' he continued. 'That's fine, but we need to think carefully. I should post you out,' he said to Rosemary. 'But you won't want to do that and I don't want to lose a very good Sister-in-Charge.'

'Thank you,' she said.

'I think this sort of thing is going on all the time in this War. You've been very honest and you shouldn't be penalised for that. You could have carried on behind my back and I'd have been bound to find out. As they keep telling us, "walls have ears".' He continued.

'There are too many men and women being killed and potential marriages and families being ruined because of this War. I'm not going to add to it if I can help it.' He was silent for a moment before going on.

'So, how about a compromise? You both stay here in your current roles. Rosemary you must undertake not to do any nursing care that Magnus might need.' She nodded. 'Magnus, Sister Ellis can do your dressing while it's necessary, Burnett can help you with your clothes and anything else. We'll be quite open about your engagement and you can see each other in off duty and so on. I'll expect you both to be completely circumspect at all times. I know I need say no more. We'll take any next step as it comes. Can you cope with this?'

'Yes, thank you.'

'Right, I'll leave you now. See you later. All the best to you both. I think I'll go and see if my tea's on my desk.' He left them and walked to his office. What have I just suggested? Heaven help us if the Brigadier and the Chief Matron don't agree. Well, I'll argue the case if it comes to it. He poured his tea and sat back. I think I need some home leave after that.

That evening Magnus wrote to Charlotte and told her his news.

… I want you to be the first to know…he embarked on his story…

Please be happy for us. This has all happened very quickly but we're very happy and we want you to be as well. I'll never forget the help you have given me over the years. I'm glad that your strength persuaded me back to Birkenshaw to make peace with Father. Our last days together were short but very meaningful. Thank you for that.

I wonder if I could ask for something else. I believe that somewhere Father kept my mother's engagement ring. Do you think I could please have this to give to Rosemary? This would mean a great deal, to both of us I think.

Hope to see you in the not too distant future.

Yours, very affly.,

Magnus.

Two days later the postman dropped the letter on the Birkenshaw door mat.

'Post, Miss – Mrs Sinclair,' Edie gave her the bundle.

'Thanks Edie.' Charlotte shuffled through the envelopes.

'Here's one from Magnus. I'll take it outside.'

Charlotte

I got up from my seat in the garden and went in and upstairs to my room where Alexander's chest of drawers still stood, empty of his clothes now. But in the top drawer lay some special items, mostly jewellery, which we had discussed one evening.

'I would like these to stay in the family,' he'd said. 'You'll know to whom to give them and when.'

I opened the drawer and removed the little box. The ring lay on its velvet cushion, the diamonds surrounding the emerald sparkling in the sunlight. I could remember Margery wearing it. I heard her voice, saw her smile. I went downstairs to tell the good news.

'Getting married? Magnus?' said Hannah. 'I thought he was a confirmed bachelor.'

'Well now you know.'

'Another wedding in the family,' she marvelled. 'Can we go to this one?'

'I don't know anything else yet. We'll have to wait and see. Magnus still has a bit of recovery to do.'

'Anyway,' said Angus. 'I suppose it's all very good, but weddings are really girls' stuff. That's what the boys at school say.'

'Angus, you tell the boys that weddings and marriage are two way. It's not just all about the woman.'

I showed them the ring that had been Margery's and was now going to be for Rosemary.

'It's beautiful. May I try it on please?' Hannah put it on her finger and held it up. 'See how it sparkles and shines in the sun.'

'See what I said,' said Angus. 'Girls' stuff.'

'We'll post it to Magnus today,' I said. 'Registered post. Let's go and tell Meg and Edie.'

Later, I sat down to write James. I had written him in thanks for his letter about Alexander's passing. Now I wanted to tell him the latest about Magnus.

Dear James,

I thought I'd drop you a line to tell you the latest about Magnus. He's now back at Glamis, has had a fair setback with the cliff-fall, but is being well-looked after. The good news – and I'm very happy to tell you this – is that he and Rosemary Jones whom you met at Christina's wedding, are engaged to be married. I'm so pleased for them. I thought you'd like to know.

Life goes on at Birkenshaw. We miss Alexander a great deal but are glad he went so peacefully. That knowledge is a great help. Hannah and Angus go back to school soon – both now at Lerwick as Angus starts year one there. He's looking forward to this although with a little trepidation. He's still a little clingy (to me). This started when Alexander died but has improved recently because he's looking after the trees and checks them on a regular basis. Woe betide any rabbit which enters our field. Mind you, he has a pet rabbit of his own, but 'that's different', he says. Anyway, things are improving. Working alongside Dod our gardener has helped too.

Hannah is fine and getting ready for school.

I hope you're well and enjoying being in Perth. Take care of yourself.

Yours,

Charlotte.

Mrs Chisholm, the housekeeper at Rosebank brought James's mail out to him along with his mid-morning tea. It was mild and humid. He'd had a walk and was sitting reading the paper.

'Thank you Mrs Chisholm.'

As she laid the tray down they heard a car door slam with an alarming thump, followed by the garden gate creaking.

'Here's Dr Donald from St Fillans. Is there any more tea in that pot?'

'Yes, of course.'

'Morning, Iain.' The doctor sat down with a sigh.

'Good to see you. Tea's on the way. You, all right?'

'Thanks,' said the doctor. 'Yes, I'm fine, had an early surgery and thought I'd drive over to Perth to pick up some medicines from the pharmacist but come first to you in the hope that you'd have some tea going. I time things quite well don't I? How are you?'

They sat and talked for a while.

'You're the talk of the village,' Iain said. 'What you did. They're all going on about it. I feel quite sorry for your replacement. He can't get a look in.'

'I'll be a nine days' wonder.'

'They're all a bit scared – nobody in St Fillans wants you to have to go again. As your ex-doctor,' he said, 'if it were up to me I wouldn't sanction your return to the Front. Not the way you were working.'

'But I had to…'

'Yes I know you had to, and we're all proud of you for doing it. But James, they're not going to let you out to the Front again. I'm sorry, but you won't have the stamina with that lovely lung you've got there. Fancy a staff job?'

'No comment,' said James.

'I've missed you, you know,' said Iain. 'We made a good team. Body and soul. Holistic care.' James nodded.

'That's why I wouldn't want a staff job. I'm better at the hands-on approach.' Iain looked at his watch.

'I've more than had my fifteen minutes. Behave yourself won't you? Thank Mrs Chisholm for the tea.'

'Thanks for coming.' The doctor waved and James could hear the crank of the starting handle. The car engine roared into life. James turned to his letters.

First off the pile was Charlotte's. He recognised the writing. The only woman he would ever love. I must have patience until she's ready, or, with a sudden doubt, until I hope she's ready. He read it, watching for any small nuance signalling any special feeling towards him. He was delighted to read of Magnus and Rosemary. But the letter was friendly, relaxed and did not betray anything other than ordinary friendship. He frowned, vexed.

He told himself off. She's probably stopped caring about you. It's twenty three years after all. Or, he told himself hopefully she's maybe just being careful, maybe waiting for me to make a first move. It's maybe too soon for her after Alexander's death. I'll write in a day or two responding to this. I'll play it by ear.

Chapter 48

It was nearly time for the school year to begin again. Hannah packed too much, insisting that she really needed the extras that made her case so difficult to close. Angus was only marginally better. As far as Blackie his black rabbit was concerned, he was very reluctant to leave him at all.

'Don't you think I could take him Mother?' he said. 'He wouldn't be any bother. I'm sure that Mrs Ratter wouldn't mind.' Mrs Ratter was the current landlady of the boys' boarding-house, successor to Mrs Blance whom Magnus knew so well.

'I'm sure she would,' said Hannah, with her two years' weekly boarding experience. 'The Rules clearly say, "No Pets. She would ask Mother to take him straight home.'

'Well, who'll look after him for me?'

'If you asked nicely,' said Charlotte, 'we might do it between us during the week. Then you can take over at the week-ends. It's the only way, Angus.'

'I suppose it will have to do,' he muttered.

'Angus, you can do better than that.' Charlotte felt sorry for him but wouldn't let him off.

'Sorry,' he said. 'Please will you help to look after him?'

'Yes, of course, with Edie and Meg if they agree. You've done very well looking after him, Angus. Now you need to arrange for when you're not here.' He leaned against her.

'I know. It's just all, well, a bit different – without Father.' Hannah came over and sat down beside his other side.

'I miss Father too, you know. It's a funny feeling isn't it? We know we can't keep crying. We would dry up. But what do you do instead?'

'I don't know,' he admitted. 'Do you feel it as well?'

'Of course I do. But I see you doing something instead of crying.'

'Do you? What do I do?'

'Trees,' she said. 'You do trees.'

'Am I doing that instead of crying?'

'I think so. What do you think Mother?'

I'd been sitting listening to this conversation with wonder. Leave it to the children, I thought. They sort themselves out.

'Mother? What do you think about doing something else instead of crying all the time?'

'Well, I think crying has its place. It's a necessary emotional release and it's important to be able to cry sometimes, and that goes for boys and men too.'

Charlotte eyed Angus as she spoke. She didn't like the 'grown men don't cry' idea. She knew that many boys thought it was cissy and didn't want Angus to be so buttoned up that he couldn't show his emotions. Angus went a little pink.

'I did cry a bit.'

'I know you did. I expected you to. I expect Magnus cried too.'

'*Magnus?* Do you think *he* cried when father died?'

'I'm sure he did.' He thought about this.

'Peerie Jim cried at school when his Granpa died and the boys said he was a cissy.'

'Don't you think that was a bit unkind?'

'Yes, I do'

'I quite agree,' said Hannah. 'Poor wee boy.'

To move on from the subject Charlotte said, 'What about taking a walk round the field and you can show us how the trees are doing?'

This was an instant diversion. He rushed to get his boots. For the next hour he treated Charlotte and Hannah to a guided walk and talk on his heightened knowledge of trees and their names and how he was looking after them.

Charlotte

When the day came, Dod came round with the gig and we piled the luggage on board and jogged the six miles to Lerwick. Hannah was delighted to be dropped off at the girls' boarding house first. She skipped off with her friends to look at the new counterpanes in her dormitory.

'See you on Friday, Mother.' Just at the end she gave me a special cuddle, and said, 'Don't be too lonely without Father, will you.' That was the thoughtful bit that brought a lump to the throat and I found myself blinking hard as I returned to the gig where Angus and Dod waited.

'Right, round a couple of corners and we'll be there.'

Then the parting was over. Our first real parting. He looked at me. I could see his eyes shining. He hugged me fiercely, my youngest, and went off with Mrs Ratter to find his dormitory with another couple of boys from Jarlshavn.

I went back to my quiet house.

All went well, I understand. Angus came bouncing in, followed by Hannah, at five o'clock on Friday evening shouting, 'I'm back and, Mother,' speaking very quickly, 'I've lost a pair of socks, one slipper and two pencils, already. Mrs Ratter says it's amazing I haven't lost anything else.' I looked at Hannah. She raised her eyebrows and smiled.

'Thank goodness he didn't take the rabbit,' she said.

Life dropped into a routine for the next few weeks. We all seemed to become used to the situation. Then a letter appeared from Christina that set me thinking.

15 September 1917

My dear Mother,

Just an extra wee note. Lowrie and I have managed to get (by a lot of hard work and negotiation) two weeks leave at the same time. In October. I can hardly believe it.

What we were thinking is this. Would you and Hannah and Angus like to come sooth in October for a break? It would be a good chance for you to take them to see Aunt Lizzie and Granny first and then continue on to Edinburgh in the train. I'm sure there'd be no problem getting the children off school in October – so many children go off anyway to go to the tatties.

I also wondered if you'd like to leave Hannah and Angus with us for a few days. We could show them Edinburgh Castle and other sights. Then you'd be free to go and see, for instance, James in Perth. I visited him the other day and he was asking after you. I think he'd like a visit. He's getting on very well, and he says his doctor is pleased with him but I feel he's lacking something. It's difficult to put into words. Almost, something to look forward to.

Then there's Magnus. He's been through such a bad time. He would love to see you.

Have no fear, we are here and happy to entertain Hannah and Angus while you go visiting. It will be fun for us too.

Please consider this. We think it's a very good idea and hope you do too.

Love from Christina.

PS No problem about accommodation. Mrs Dunn is going to lend us her spare room. Love, C

I sat back in my chair, letter in my lap and pondered. My immediate reaction was, no, it couldn't be done. I could list any number of reasons why: too complicated, too much to organise, it was too soon after Alexander's passing, it wasn't fair to take the children off school, I didn't want to leave the house... I could feel myself backing off. But then, what were all those so-called reasons? Yes, it was not long since Alexander died but by the planned date it would be well over three months. It would be good for us to have a holiday.

What about taking the children off school? As a teacher, it was usually a nuisance when parents did this. But this was October we were thinking about. Over half the children would be off at the tattie-howkin. October was the time for lifting the potatoes out of the ground before the winter frosts set in and turned the tatties to so much mush. Most children able and available went to the tattie-picking or howkin. So many went, most of the teachers thought it would only be a matter of time before the Scotch Education Department made it an official holiday. The timing was perfect to take Hannah and Angus for a break.

What was really holding me back? On an impulse I went upstairs to where I kept my special letters and, the hanky with *JM* in the corner. I took it out and held it for a bit. I took out the letter that James had written on Easter Monday and re-read it. '*You are the only woman I shall ever love*'. He said it twice. What could I do? Was it so difficult to go and visit him when he'd been ill? Was it wrong? Was I frightened of what people would think? That I would be the spik of the village? Or was I frightened of my own feelings? Probably all of these. However, it would be very good to go to Christina and Lowrie with the children and go and visit Magnus. And, I made myself say it, I want to see James too. I held the hanky and the letter tightly. I really do want to do this.

323

Chapter 49

Charlotte

It turned out to be so simple to arrange. I wrote Christina saying 'yes' in principle. I wrote James a note suggesting a visit, and, if he liked the idea, asking if he would book me into a local hotel. Both replied by return of post. The children were delighted and excited at the notion of going on the boat and on a train. I also contacted Magnus, and Rosemary immediately wrote and offered me hospitality at Glamis Castle again. Meg and Edie were happy about keeping the home fires burning at Birkenshaw.

It was wonderful seeing Lizzie again. She herself came to meet us at Alford station and came running on to the platform as the train was drawing in.

'Ay, ay, then. Foo are ye daein?' She hugged me then looked at my two growing bairns and said, 'A widna hae kent them, they've grown that muckle. Bit mind ee it's ten years.' She swept them up in a hug then pushed them on out of the station.

'Come on then folks, the gig's oot here. A left a wee loonie haudin the reins.'

She gave a sweetie to the wee boy standing stroking the horse's nose – 'een fur yer moo and een fur yer pooch'. We set off, first to see Granny in Towie before heading for the Glen.

She was waiting for us, as always. She looked good for a ninety-three year old. A bit thinner maybe but the old vigour still lingered. The children loved her at first sight.

'I've never met a Great-granny before,' said Angus as we left that day. 'May we call you "Granny" for short?' She nodded.

'May I come back and visit you, please,' he went on. 'I see you have plenty of trees here. I can tell you about the trees I'm working with. They were Father's you know, and now I'm looking after them, with Dod.'

'Yes, please come back,' said Granny. 'I'll be up to the Kirton before you go to Edinburgh. But next time you're sooth I hope you'll maybe come and stay with me. Would you like that? And you too, Hannah?'

'Good bye, Granny,' I said, kissing her cheek. 'I'll come back down by myself tomorrow,' if, I looked at Lizzie, 'I can borrow the gig.'

'Ay, ay, nae bother. If I ken bairns, they'll be oot aa day wi oor lot.'

We had two full days at the Kirkton of Glenbuchat after that first day. The time was spent talking, catching up, Hannah and Angus got to know their cousins Geordie and May who were twelve and ten. They spent the first few minutes giggling at the way each set of cousins spoke until they were used to the funny voices and became firm friends. Lizzie and I watched and compared and saw many family features, gestures in common.

'It's not just where you are,' we agreed as we watched. 'It's who you are.'

I went up to the Milton to see my father and Cathy his second wife.

'Ay ay, Lassickie. Foo'r ye daein? A wis sorry ti hear aboot yer man.'

'Thanks, Dad. I gave him a kiss on the cheek. I'm fine. So are the bairns. Here they are. Hannah, Angus, meet Grandad.' They shook hands. 'Fine bairns,' was his comment. 'Like ee, like Mary, bonny, bonny.'

Throughout the day, Lizzie's kitchen at the Kirkton was kept busy with folk coming in and out. The tattie harvest was in full swing but my brothers were at the Front and I missed their cheerful craic. Their children were around, though, and the three of them came shyly to meet these cousins and aunt from another world.

It was a good two days. The children went off out. Lizzie's two had been granted a holiday from the tattie-howkin but Hannah and Angus wanted to see what was going on and they all finished up in ancient clothes, up in the mud and the dubs and the dreels of the fields, following the horse-drawn machine throwing up the tatties and bending to fill their baskets. They found it fun, for a while. Their backs lasted longer than the grown-ups did, probably because they were nearer the ground.

Lizzie and I prepared food for the workers: pieces for the mid-day break and then for the family at night a big hearty pot of stew with tatties, carrots and dough balls with steamed pudding to follow. Anything to fill them up.

While we worked we talked. We talked down the years, confiding, opening doors long closed, laughing like silly lassies sometimes, crying at others. Lizzie told me how the loss of their third child Jeanie had happened.

'It wis an afa sair winter, about three year ago noo. It jist went on an on and she got the croup and jist couldna throw it aff. We tried aathin, bit it wis nae eese. Tom wis afa grieved ye ken. We aa were. The doctor, ye ken Leslie fa took ower fae Granpa?' I nodded.

'Weel he wis here, A dinna ken, it felt lik aa the time, the nurse wis here. And then it wis aa ower an we hid tae tak oor wee eenie up tae the Kirkyaird. It wis afa. A kent then fit ee must ha gone through fan ye lost yer first bairns. A wis afa sorry.'

We cried together for the gathered emotions of the past. Somehow, although it opened old wounds, it helped in a funny sort of way.

Eventually, inevitably, we came to the present.

'Fit are ye gaan ti dee noo?' I looked at Lizzie and said, 'Well I'm here now, and tomorrow we're heading for Edinburgh to see Christina and Lowrie.'

'An afa fine quine. Fit's Lowrie like?'

'We've known him for years. He's Magnus's best friend. They're about ages. I would trust him anywhere. He's been in France for a long time now. He and Christina are going to look after Hannah and Angus and show them some of Edinburgh, like the Castle and so on...'

'That'll gie ye time ti gang aboot by yersel.' I nodded.

'Fit dee ye hae in min?'

'Well, I'll go to Glamis to see Magnus. I'm not sure how fit he is yet since the accident. I'm just going myself. By the way,' I added, 'I haven't mentioned this to the children.'

''Fit wey nae?' I looked at her. 'Is there something ye're nae tellin me?'

I hadn't told the children because I didn't want them to know that I was going to visit James. Lizzie jaloused at once I was omitting something.

'Lizzie,' I said.

'Ay, fit is't?'

'Look, I'm not telling the children because I'm going to visit James.'

'James? Fa's James?'

So then the story came out. Going back to our unofficial engagement so long ago and how it had been called off.

'You can see why,' I said, 'I don't want my going to visit him to be known in Jarlshavn. Lizzie, I'd be the spik o the village. Again. So, I'm not telling the children.'

'But ye might, in the future.' Her eyes were alight, teasing.

'Lizzie, just let me get to this point.'

'But ye will let me ken fit haippens?'

'Lizzie, we'll probably say "hello, nice to see you" and that'll be that.'

'Ay, A believe ye. Aa richt, ma lips are sealed.'

I told Granny what I was doing when I went down to see her. I was glad to have some time alone with her even if it was short.

'I was sorry I couldn't come, when Granpa died. I wanted to be with you.'

'Charlotte, I didn't expect you to come. You know that. You'd enough on your hands, with Alexander being ill then.'

'I know. I couldn't leave him but a bit of me felt I should be here. How are you, really?'

'I'm very well,' she said. 'I'm so glad to be still here in this house. I'm busy, I'm happy, kept in order by Jessie who's stuck with me all those years. Lizzie comes in as often as she can – at least once a week. I miss Andrew, of course I do, but life goes on. I speak to him sometimes and think I can hear him answering.' She laughed. 'Don't mind me. Just an old woman's fancy.'

'You're an inspiration,' I said.

'No,' she said. 'Just normal, I hope. Now, how about you? What are your plans?'

I told her what we planned for the holiday and then what the children didn't know, the visit to James. She was immediately sympathetic.

'It would be a bit strange if you didn't go,' she said. 'Of course you must go and see him. I quite understand why you're not talking about it, given what happened. But you go and enjoy your time with him. Then, well, let events take care of themselves.'

'Thank you Granny. You're a comfort.'

I told the children on the train to Edinburgh that I'd be leaving them for a few days to visit the likes of Edinburgh Castle with Christina and Lowrie while I visited Magnus. I needn't have worried about leaving them. They were thrilled and excited at the prospect.

'Don't worry about us, Mother,' they assured me. 'We'll be fine.'

'Are we nearly there?' asked Angus.

'Yes, we are. Look, we're just about to go over the Forth Bridge. Take a look. It's a miracle of engineering.'

'It's amazing. When was it built?'

'It was finished in 1890. Look,' I handed over pennies. 'The thing to do, what everyone does, is throw pennies from the bridge into the water for luck.'

'Can we do it?' Angus asked. 'Now?'

'Yes, let's get the window down a wee bit. You have to wish a wish, mind.'

In excited solemnity, they flung their pennies out. I tossed a penny out as well, feeling a bit daft but they would have questioned me if I hadn't.

'What did you wish for Mother?' Angus asked.

'You're not supposed to tell your wish,' Hannah said.

'How do you know?'

'I just know,' said Hannah, smugly. 'Anyway, in no way am I telling anyone what I've wished. How about you, Mother?'

'No indeed,' I said. 'Never will my wish pass my lips.'

By this time we were at the other side of the bridge. Dalmeny went past then shortly the beginning of the city could be seen. Houses, buildings, churches, roads, traffic, far more than they had ever seen. We came to Haymarket. The train slowed and stopped.

'Is this where we get off?'

'Not yet. We have a wee bit to go before Waverley station.'

Then we were there. So were Christina and Lowrie, waving, smiling, greeting the children when the train stopped and they were the first to jump down.

'When are we going to see the Castle?' Hannah was very keen to visit and take notes for her school history. Seeing where the events she was learning about actually happened, she reasoned, would help her to make them real in her mind.

'I think the day after tomorrow after your mother's away. We'll save it until then.'

They seemed happy with this. I was delighted they seemed so relaxed with Christina and Lowrie. From my point of view, I could go away for a few days with a quiet mind. However I still felt concerned that Christina and Lowrie were giving up precious leave time for this.

'Mother, you mustn't think like that,' said Christina when the children were in bed downstairs. 'James and Magnus will love to see you and you'll have a lot of catching up to do. By yourself. Honestly we're happy to have them.'

'Yes,' chimed in Lowrie. 'I'm looking forward to having an excuse to go to the Castle and on the trams and so on. Let me play a little.'

'Now,' he said, presenting me with a neatly written sheet of paper. 'Here are your train times for your visits to Perth and Glamis. You go from Edinburgh to Perth. What could be easier? When you leave Perth you get the train to Glamis. What a wonderful system. Take a book to read, look at the scenery. Then, after you say "Good-bye" to Magnus in Glamis, on to Dundee by train and we'll meet you at Dundee station with the children and you all can get the train to Aberdeen.'

'Hannah and Angus have mentioned you're going to Magnus,' said Christina. 'But they haven't said anything about James. They just said "seeing someone else".'

'They never knew James,' I said. 'He was minister in Jarlshavn so long ago. I just felt…'I hesitated. I didn't quite know what to say.

'Can I say something?' said Christina. I nodded.

'Are you a bit worried about what the Jarlshavn folk would say? I love them but I know what they're like. Maybe a few wouldn't think it was "the thing" for you to be going and visiting James alone, however good he's been to us. Folk'll take any chance to spik, won't they?'

'That's pretty much it,' I said, relieved.

'Don't you worry,' said Lowrie. 'We'll not mention him.'

It was afternoon by the time the train chugged into Perth station. It was busy. The train was full of military personnel and many left the train here. Some boarded, bound for Aberdeen and beyond.

Charlotte saw him waiting on the platform. Even after twenty three years Charlotte would have recognised him, although time and War and being wounded had taken their toll. The hair was now grey, the face lined and thinner, but he was still a bonny-looking well-set up man.

He's seen me, she thought, as James, watching the train slow down and stop, caught sight of her and raised his hand. Her heart was racing as she picked up her bag and made to open the door. He was there before her. The door swung open, one hand took the case from her and the other took hers and helped her down. They stood there, awkwardly, not quite sure of protocol for such an occasion.

'Charlotte,' he breathed. Then, with a slight inclination of the head, 'Charlotte, I'm so pleased to see you again.' They shook hands formally.

'James, I'm happy to see you too.' She looked up, their eyes met, he noted the unshed tears, and recognising it was neither the time nor the place, swallowed down his own urge to sweep her to him.

'Come,' he said. 'Let's go and sit somewhere. I know a quiet wee place. Then I'll take you to the hotel I've booked for you. I hope it's all right.'

'I'm sure it will be fine. Is it near where you are?'

'It's on the same side of the river, not far away from Rosebank. I thought it would be easier that way and it's not far into the town centre. Here's the wee tea house.'

She went to 'wash the train off her hands' as she put it while James found a table in a little semi-enclosed corner. He was watching for her return.

'I'm here. I've ordered tea. Is that all right?'

'Yes, thank you. I'm parched.' As she spoke, the waitress arrived with tea and scones.

'Sit and rest yourself. Shall I pour?'

'Yes, please.' She sat back and watched him.

'How are the children?'

'They're fine thank you. They can't wait to get going on the castle and everything. Angus wants to drive a tram. It's very good of Christina and Lowrie to have them. They have so little time together.'

'They're a nice young couple. I was delighted to have the privilege of marrying them.'

'They were very glad to have you do it and, that you were able.' Charlotte's voice wobbled. She took a sip of her tea.

'Would you, would you have dinner with me tonight? I could walk over to the hotel and we could dine in the restaurant there, if you like.'

'Thank you, James.' Charlotte looked up. 'I'd like that.'

'Good.' Then, 'I was sorry when Christina told me about Alexander,' he said. 'So soon after Magnus's accident. It was a lot to bear. I wanted to help somehow, but there was nothing I could do.'

'You wrote a lovely comforting letter,' Charlotte said. 'James, please don't feel bad that you couldn't be there to help personally. I know,' she went on. 'I know from your letter that you were thinking about us. Everyone who could be there rallied round. We were all very thankful Alexander didn't suffer at the end. He was so peaceful. That's the comfort.'

She drank her tea then put her cup down and smiled at him.

'Now, tell me about you. How've you been? I'm sure you must be glad to be here. And to be near your parents. How are they?'

'They're getting older,' he said. 'Both in their eighties now. Both a bit slower and don't go out so much. I go down to see them when I can – but I'm officially posted to the Rosebank Auxiliary Hospital, you see, and therefore still under orders. Like Magnus at Glamis.'

'Yes, I think I understand. They keep a pretty close watch on him, don't they?'

'Yes, from what I hear. Until, he decides to climb down a cliff.' He looked at her and shook his head. 'There was probably no stopping him.'

'So I can't just run in and out at will,' he continued. 'I'm free to come and go to a certain extent but must sign in and out and if they thought I was doing too much, they would tell me and I'd have to obey orders. It's the Army's way of keeping tabs on convalescent personnel.'

'Is that why they instigated so many convalescent hospitals?'

'Yes. On the other hand, perhaps some of the men had nowhere else to go for a while.'

'Do you like it at Rosebank?'

'Yes, I do. I have a wee room to myself, the food is good and the staff are helpful. It's much less institutionalised than Edinburgh is. But then that's a big Infirmary. It has to be run on strict lines. And, the staff are very good. Just look at our Christina, for a start. She's a lovely young woman. For the moment,' he said, 'I'm fine.'

'What happens next?'

'I don't know. The hospital doctor was in seeing me yesterday. He didn't seem too sure about my return to the Front.' He made a face. 'I feel I should go back. But, he said quite bluntly that I'd probably have no choice.'

'It's difficult to imagine what it's like if one has never been there,' she said. 'We're given such a sanitised version in the newspapers.'

'I know,' he said. 'They say the first casualty of war is the truth and I'm telling you, the people are not being given the truth about what's going on. Apart from the casualty lists, and even they are incorrect, the population has no real idea.'

The hotel foyer was warm, carpeted, with comfortable chairs in quiet corners. A helpful young lady attended the reception desk.

'What time shall I come over?' James said. 'Would seven suit you?'

'I'll look forward to that. I'll book a table now just in case they're busy.'

He hesitated then said, 'I – I'll go now then, and, well, I'll see you later…'

'Yes, you go and have a rest. That's what I'm going to do. Thanks for tea. Good bye James. See you at seven.' She turned and with a little wave, walked towards the reception desk. James walked back to Rosebank and flung himself on his bed. Contrary to all his expectations born of a mind in turmoil, beating out a 'she love me, she loves me not' rhythm, he fell into a deep sound sleep.

Charlotte's room was on the first floor of the hotel. She looked out of the window to see the river Tay flowing past towards its Firth to the east where it spilled its water into the North Sea. The road below was busy with pedestrians walking along the pavements, buses, horses with gigs, farm horses and their waggons, their owners trying to get out of this alien town environment, some cars, charabancs loaded with trippers. This was one of the routes to the hills and turned eventually through the farms and hills and glens of Perthshire into one of the highest in Scotland, away north round the Devil's Elbow towards Braemar and Deeside and of course from there across another set of hills to Donside and her own Glenbuchat.

She sat down in a cushioned armchair, quite spent with, not just emotion, but with the effort of containing her emotions. It had been such a full week so far. She hadn't quite realised what it would be like, leaving Shetland even for a holiday with none of the family – no Alexander – at Birkenshaw. That was like leaving a part of herself behind. Then there was the coping with a whole lot of different experiences and encounters one after another culminating with the first meeting for many years with the man who had declared the she was 'the only woman I shall ever love'.

She felt in her bag, pulled out a small folder and opened it. Lying there were James's letters and his handkerchief given to wipe her tears so long ago. She spread it out on her lap and looked at the initials 𝓙𝓜 in the corner. She picked up his letter, the one written before Vimy Ridge and read it again. She held the two together, sat back and sighed.

Charlotte woke an hour later. It was six o'clock. She looked at the letter and hanky in her hand, smiled, replaced them in the folder and in her bag. The bathroom was near, the water was hot and plentiful, towels soft. She allowed herself the luxury of a bath and dressed in her favourite green dress and gold chain. She put her hair up with hands which trembled slightly, remembering the first time she had done this over two decades ago for her very first luncheon with James at the Manse in Jarlshavn. When she thought she was ready, she made herself sit still and breathe calmly until two minutes to seven.

He was there, standing in the foyer, eyes watching the stairs for her, eyes which lit up as he saw her descend. He came forward.

'Charlotte.' He kissed her lightly on the cheek.' Come, let's have a drink in what they call the parlour until our table's ready. The waiter'll bring us the menu there.'

He sat and fidgeted. The drinks order came. He made sure Charlotte had what she ordered, that it was satisfactory, he put a cushion behind her back, asked if that was comfortable, tied one of his shoe-laces which didn't need tying, sat on the edge of his chair.

'James,' she said, after a few minutes. 'You'll exhaust yourself. What's the matter? It's only me.'

'Yes, that's the point. It *is* you. I can hardly believe it. You, meeting me.' She smiled.

'It's been a long time hasn't it? How was St Fillan's? Were you happy there?'

'Yes, I was. The village and surrounding countryside is beautiful, the people are great, the church lovely. Just one thing missing – you weren't there.' She pretended not to hear his last sentence.

'Did you have to leave officially to join the Army at the start of the War?'

'Well, they would have kept the kirk for me, but I felt if I did that they might be without a minister for years and so I resigned my charge when I was Commissioned. It seemed the right thing to do. Then they were free to call a new minister – which they did.'

'But that would have meant that you had to leave the Manse.'

'Yes, that's true. My furniture is partly in storage and partly in a spare room in my parents' house in Perth. If I'd been married with a family, well things would've been different. It would've been their home.'

'But as it is, you've no home of your own.'

'Well, I can always go to my parents if I need to…'

'But it's not the same.'

'No, it isn't,' he agreed. 'But it won't be for ever. If I've to resign my Commission because of my injury then I'd hope to get a call from somewhere not too far away.'

'Excuse me Sir, Madam.' The waiter came up. 'Your table is ready for you. We apologise again for the somewhat limited choice for you owing to Wartime restrictions.'

'Thank you. I'm sure it'll be fine. We're looking forward to it.'

The meal was indeed fine. James regaled Charlotte with details of not just the quality but also the boredom of trench food (McConochie's tinned stew excepted) and they resolved to try and never complain again.

They returned to sit in the parlour for what turned out to be surprisingly good coffee.

'Do they have a curfew at Rosebank?'

'Well, in theory yes. But they know where I am and I think Sister wouldn't be that worried if I went past the witching hour. I really only go to my parents. This is my first proper night out since I came here.'

'It's been quite a bad time for you, though hasn't it?'

'Well, it wasn't funny to begin with.'

'What happened?'

He gave her an abbreviated version of how he'd been injured. She listened carefully.

'But I thought padres didn't carry weapons.'

'We don't.'

'So what were you doing out in the dark when there were snipers around? Were you forward from the Front line?'

'Charlotte, you shouldn't ask questions like that.'

331

'Well, were you?' When he was silent she said, 'James. You were, weren't you? Why?'

'Charlotte,' he said. 'Sometimes it just happens.'

'I've heard of this sort of thing,' Charlotte said. He looked at her, unspeaking.

'I've heard there are wounded men lying out in no-man's land with some trying to get back to their own lines after dark. Soldiers and others,' she looked at him meaningfully, 'go out and bring them into safety for first aid. They take a huge risk. The bravery sounds incredible. James,' she added after a moment. 'Was that what you did? Did you go out after dark into no-man's land?' He didn't answer.

'James. You did. I know it. Oh, what a mad thing to do, and how brave, and how proud I am of you. Oh James…'

She opened her bag and in her haste to reach her handkerchief, her little folder containing the letters and the 𝓙𝓜 hanky fell out, landed on the floor and opened. James bent down and picked it up as she blew her nose and wiped her eyes. He couldn't fail to see what the folder contained. He caught his breath and waited until she composed herself. She took a sip of coffee and swallowed. He held the folder out to her.

'You dropped this.'

'Thank you.' She took it. 'Did you – did you see what's in it?'

'Yes. It fell open on the floor.'

'Oh, what must you think of me? Bringing them with me. It's the first time I've taken them away from Birkenshaw.'

'Charlotte, Charlotte, I think it's wonderful.'

'You do?'

'Listen, you daft lassie, you remember in that letter, I said I carried a picture of you next my heart?'

'Yes.'

'What d'you think was beside the picture?'

'I don't know.'

'Well, remember that last day?' She nodded. 'I remembered I'd left the hanky with you that day. I couldn't go back for it, given the circumstances in which we parted. And anyway it was only a hanky. But what was "only a hanky" became a sort of talisman. I've carried an identical one next to your photo since then as a …a sort of memory – as a hope, if you like.'

She smiled. 'Who says ministers have no romance in them?' Then, seriously, 'I'm so glad you wrote, James. Not that the letter made me any less anxious, but I – I …'

'Don't say any more,' he said. 'Writing that letter to you was an important thing for me to do. I *needed* to do it, Charlotte.' Abruptly, he said, 'have you finished your coffee?'

'Yes. Why?'

'Let's go out to the garden. It's a lovely evening. You might need your coat, though.'

'Wait a moment.' On her return he tied her scarf round her neck.

'Let's go.'

They strolled round the side of the hotel to a small, hedged secluded garden. No one else was there. Discreet lighting showed up late roses displaying in some profusion round the edges. She leant forward and sniffed appreciatively.

332

'These are perfect. What a good idea – to come out here I mean.'

'Charlotte,' James said. 'That letter, I meant what I said. But I also wanted to put things right with you before I went, before the battle began. What I was trying to say was, you're the only woman I'll ever love and I was arrogant and took you for granted. I wanted to tell you this and say sorry. I needed to do it before I went into the Vimy Ridge situation because' – she waited – 'because,' his voice broke, 'I didn't know if I was going to be alive at the end of it.'

They stopped walking and turned to each other.

'Oh, James, James, it is a beautiful letter and I knew what you were saying. I kept it with the hanky because they are so special to me.' He held out his arms to her.

'Come, my dear.'

Their first kiss after so many years was as sweet as the first kiss given in the Manse garden so long ago. They stood then, with arms round each other, quietly, just resting, each thinking about the unspoken knowledge come alive in those moments of closeness.

Chapter 50

'Excuse me Madam,' said the waitress's voice at Charlotte's elbow. 'I can see your visitor just coming. Would you like coffee now?'

'Yes, please,' said Charlotte.

'Where would you like it? Our south east verandah is very pleasant in the morning. Would you like to go there? It's lovely and quiet.'

'Yes, thank you. That's very considerate.'

'I'll see to that, then.' The girl hurried off just as James came into the foyer.

'Good morning.' He smiled at her. 'How are you today?'

'Very well, I think.'

'Don't you know? I know how *I* feel…'

'James, we're having coffee in the south east verandah.'

'The where?'

'The verandah. I think it's through here. They say it's good in the mornings. Oh,' she added, as she entered the room lit with morning sunshine, thriving indoor plants in the windows. 'It's lovely.'

They sat down. She looked at him, suddenly tongue-tied.

He coughed then took a deep breath and winced. 'Sorry,' he said. 'Ribs and all that. 'Wait a minute, here's the coffee.'

'Now,' he said, when their waitress had disappeared. 'How did you sleep?'

'Hmm. Off and on.'

'Me too. I kept waking up and thinking. Charlotte.' He leant forward. 'I don't want to rush this – well, yes I do really – but I realise we need to talk. I meant what I said, you know. In that letter.'

'Yes, I know, James.'

'I'm so happy you kept it, and the hanky. Charlotte I love you. Can you possibly love me back?'

'James you're going too fast for me. I must remember Alexander. It's not four months yet since he died. I loved him – oh, not in the same way as I loved you. That was special, different. But what Alexander and I had was also important. We had a strong, stable, loving relationship, he was the father of my Hannah and Angus, as well as Christina and Magnus and our wee Alexander up in the Kirkyard…' she faltered.

'Here,' he moved his seat to come beside her. 'I don't want to rush you. I'm sorry if it appeared that way.' She took a deep breath and continued.

'It's all right James. I don't blame you after all those years. But I need time, time to recover, time to adjust and allow myself to move on. And then I have to consider the children and their feelings and – and you'll have heard me on this one before – I don't want you and me to be the spik of the village.'

'But,' she went on. 'In the middle of all this, there's you and me. You realise the fact I kept your *JM* hanky is saying something to you?'

'I'm looking on it as a coded message.' She saw the love-light in his eyes and smiled at him.

'I can't help it,' she admitted. 'I love you, James MacLeod.' He held her hand very tightly.

'Charlotte, will you marry me even though I'm an old bachelor? I love you very, very much. As I think you know, I've always loved you. There just hasn't been anyone else.'

She looked at him, so serious. She recalled his first proposal to her so long ago. The love declared was still the same.

'Yes, James, I'll marry you.' They kissed each other as token of this new loving pact.

'Oh, I'm a happy man.' James pulled his uniform straight, ran his finger round his neck to ease the starchiness of his dog-collar, caught her eye and said, 'When?'

'James.' He put up his hands in surrender.

'All right. I'm rushing again. Don't worry, Charlotte. I know the rules.' He got to his feet..

'I can't sit still. The sun's out. The 'silvery Tay' will be sparkling today. Let's go and walk along the river bank. We can make plans and I'll whisper sweet nothings into your ear.'

'Realistically,' he continued when they were outside and heading for the riverbank, 'we need to wait and be very circumspect until next summer at the earliest.'

'Yes, discretion has to be the order of the day. I wouldn't even tell the children yet. They need recovery time too don't you think?'

'Yes, to be quite honest we'll need to tread carefully, especially with Hannah and Angus. I don't want them to think I'm trying to usurp their father. What about Magnus and Christina? They might be quite sympathetic.'

'Yes probably, but couldn't we wait a wee while? Maybe until we hear about what you're going to be doing. When is your Medical Board anyway?'

'In about a month. I haven't heard officially but it should be November sometime.'

'What do you really think they'll say?'

'Let's sit down for a moment.' They sat on a bench by the riverside and were silent, watching the water, feeling the autumn sunshine, enjoying the peace. Then he spoke.

'In my mind, I think the end result of this is that I'll be medically discharged as unfit for Frontline duty.'

'You mean, not go back to France?'

'That's right.'

'Is that what you want?'

'Not really, at least,' he hesitated. 'Up until very recently, I was dreading being told officially what more than one doctor has said informally. Even though I know I'm not physically able to do what I was doing.' He held her hand tightly. 'Loving you, being allowed to love you, has given this a different perspective. Somehow the inevitable has become more bearable.'

'Is there anything else in the army you could do?'

'I expect if I really wanted they would probably find a home posting for me but – Charlotte, that's not for me. I became a Padre to be with and support those in the War zone.'

'So, what then?'

'Well, if I'm medically discharged, I'd be free to accept a call to a charge in the Kirk.'

'Where would that be?'

'I don't know yet. We'd need to think about it. How would you like living in a Manse? See,' he added, 'I'm not taking anything for granted.' They caught each other's eye. Charlotte shook her head.

'That was not one of our better days. I still hate remembering that – the horrible ending of it all.' She shuddered. He put his arm round her.

'We're not going to do any more of that. Once was enough.' He paused then said, 'You haven't answered my question. How *would* you like living in a manse?'

'It would be fine, I suppose – I don't have much acquaintance with manse-life.'

'I've enjoyed it so far. The St Fillans folk were fine, friendly, and it's a lovely place. But we can't go back. We must think forward.'

'I don't suppose you want to be too far from your parents.'

'No, in a way, but travelling for visits and checking up on them is getting easier with the trains. We could have a car, perhaps. We need to wait for the result of the Board, then if they want to offer me a medical discharge, I can notify the Kirk's HQ in Edinburgh and see what the next step is. How do you feel about that?'

'It sounds like a plan to me, in the short term at least. I can hardly believe it.'

He threw a stone into a pool and they watched the ripples.

'See those ripples? That's the way things happen isn't it. Just a few words and a whole new movement gets going. Oh, my dearest Charlotte, this is the right thing for us. I can feel it.' They turned closely to each other and for a few moments, time stood still as they responded to their joint need to show their love.

At last they drew apart. Charlotte settled her hat which had been pushed askew. James laughed at her.

'Sorry,' he said, putting out a hand to help. 'I'm no better. Mine's all squint too. Come on, let's walk. We should probably go back and get some lunch.'

'You won't forget me will you?' They stood on the platform waiting for the train.

'James, my dear. What are you talking about?' She saw that he was very near to tears. 'You've made me very happy.'

'I love you so much.'

'And I, you. But I must go now. See, here's the guard. Good bye James. I'll write.' They kissed gently then he saluted smartly as the train drew out of the station on to the branch-line heading for Glamis.

Charlotte

Burnett waited at the little station.

'Morning, Ma'am. Glad to see you.' He handed me down and took my bag.

'Hello Burnett. Thanks for coming. How are things at the Castle?'

'Nae sae bad. Captain Sinclair is getting on real weel. A widna hae gi'en muckle for him a whiley ago. Noo he's that busy deein his régime as he caa's it.'

'What's his régime?'

'Weel, it's fit the Colonel his set oot fur him ti get him fit again. A think it's workin, min. He's fair improvin. Ye'll be pleased ti see him, Mrs Sinclair. He's deein fine.'

'That sounds very positive.' We clattered on.

'The pot-holes hinna gaen awa,' he remarked. 'Ach, bit there's a War on an there's hardly ony money, let alane men ti mend it. We jist need tae ca' canny.'

'Here we are noo.' He drew up in front of the castle. 'A ken far he'll be. Doon in yon wee quiet neuk, doon the gairdin. Readin nae doot. Ay readin. If he's nae deein his régime, he's readin. A'll tak yer bag in if ye wint ti gang doon.'

'Thanks Burnett.'

I walked over the grass towards the still figure. My feet made no sound but he must have sensed my approach. He stood, turned, smiled in greeting.

'Magnus. I'm glad to see you again.' I looked at him critically. 'Hmm, better than I imagined, I think.'

'Charlotte.' He hugged me. 'How are you? I was so sorry not to be able to go to Father's funeral. I missed you all so much.'

'We missed you too. I felt particularly sad that you weren't there for your own sake, but there was nothing you or anyone else could do. We just had to get on with it. I think we were all glad when it was over though.'

We talked for a while about Alexander's death and the funeral and how we all were. It was important to Magnus. He still felt bad about not being there. He was the eldest son and he should have been present. Eventually I steered him on to a happier topic.

'Magnus, I'm very happy about you and Rosemary.'

'Thank you Charlotte. Thank you too, for sending the ring so promptly. We're delighted with it. It's very important to us.'

'Is everything working out – with her work and so on?'

'Yes, Colonel Fulton's been very helpful and now everyone here knows. We should probably go up. Have you seen her yet?'

'No, I came straight down here to see you.'

As they approached the house Rosemary came out with a tray in her hands.

'Burnett told me you had arrived.'

'I hope you two will be very happy,' I said. The happy couple looked at each other. I could see how much in love they were.

'Have you made any plans?'

'Not really,' said Magnus, 'Or nothing definite anyway. We're content to wait till I'm fitter, then there'll be the eventual Medical Board and well, we'll just wait and see. It's great to see you, Charlotte,' he continued. 'Now, tell us how are Hannah and Angus and Christina and Lowrie. I can hardly believe that you've left the bairns in their care.'

'Why not?' said Rosemary. 'They're grown-ups and perfectly capable. The children will have a lovely time with them.'

Chapter 51

The wedding day of Charlotte and James was a culmination of months of quiet discussion and thought, on the part of the bride and groom anyway. It had been difficult to keep their secret but on the whole they felt they had not done too badly.

Lizzie, of course, was quickly on the trail. The next time she and Charlotte met on a further flying visit sooth for Charlotte it was in Esslemont and MacIntosh's Tea Rooms in Aberdeen. It was January, the Christmas holidays were over and Charlotte had arranged go sooth, leaving Hannah and Angus in their usual routine of school and home at the week-end. They had asked questions.

'But what are you going sooth again for?' said Angus. 'I need you here.'

'Are you sure you'll be all right by yourself Mother?' said Hannah. 'Wouldn't you like me to come with you?'

'Thank you Hannah. I'll be fine. Angus, I'm going down to see Aunt Lizzie. She's coming into Aberdeen to meet me. Don't you think that's good of her, to come all that way? Then I'm going to see Magnus again. I hear he's doing well but I want to see him myself. I'll pop down to Edinburgh on the train to see Christina and hear the latest news about Lowrie. Then back to Aberdeen – I'll be home in no time.'

Charlotte

Then there was the question of Edie and Meg. They'd supported me through many ups and downs through the years and I trusted them. I couldn't go away this time without telling them, especially as I was leaving my children in their care.

One evening when all was quiet, I went to the kitchen where they sat knitting away at their 'comforts for the soldiers'.

'What are you making at the moment?' Edie looked up and shook her length of khaki knitting.

'Socks again,' she said. 'I think I could turn heels in my sleep.'

'I'm on another balaclava, with a wee bit of Fair Isle thrown in,' said Meg. 'The competition for variation is still going on. How's *your* knitting going Mrs Sinclair?'

'Not too badly. The Knitting Bees and First Aid classes are going well too. Em,' I said. 'I came to tell you something.' They put down their knitting.

'Let's have a cup of tea,' suggested Edie. I had to laugh.

'You always say the right thing.'

'Well, Miss, em, Mrs Sinclair, tea is always good when there's talking.'

'Yes, you're quite right. Thanks Edie.' I waited, chatting to Meg as Edie made mugs of tea and handed out flapjacks.

'Now,' I said when they were settled. 'What I'm going to tell you is very private. Not even the children. Not anyone. Can I speak with you on these terms, please?'

'Mrs Sinclair,' said Meg, puzzled. 'You know you can. We do not speak out and about regarding what goes on in this house.'

'No,' agreed Edie. 'Indeed not, and *never*, when you were at Da Peerie Skulehoose did I mention anything.'

'I know you didn't and I know I can trust you absolutely. I just needed to say it – I didn't mean to imply anything…' I was beginning to think that I had offended by asking so bluntly for confidentiality but Meg, ever-astute, picked up my confusion.

'That's all right, Mrs Sinclair,' she said. 'We understand. We know you didn't mean anything else.' They looked at me expectantly. I took a deep breath and began.

'You may both remember, a long time ago when I came to Jarlshavn first, that the minister at the Kirk here was Mr James MacLeod.' The both nodded.

'Oh yes, I remember him,' said Edie. 'He used to come and visit you, didn't he, with books, and vegetables from his garden. He was such a nice man. Do you ever hear from him now, Miss, em, Mrs Sinclair?'

'Edie, let Mrs Sinclair get on with saying what it is she wants to tell us,' said Meg. You'll put her off her stotter.' Edie, sat back, nibbled her biscuit, sipped her tea.

'Sorry, Miss, em Mrs Sinclair. It's just that I remembered so well…'

'Edie.' said Meg.

'It's all right,' I said. 'I'm sure you both remember him. Well, as I was saying, he was there when I was new here and as you remember Edie, he visited me in Da Peerie Skulehoose. We went out for walks too, and I once went to lunch at the Manse.'

'Did you?' said Meg. 'Well, Mrs Laurenson never let that drop. Mind you,' she said, 'quite right too. Confidentiality to your employer, I always say.'

'Thank you Meg.' I must get to the end, I thought. I keep getting side-tracked.

'Well,' I continued. 'Mr MacLeod and I became engaged to be married. Unofficially. Nobody knew.'

'What?' The pair of them gazed at me. 'What happened?'

'We had a row,' I said simply. 'And that was that.'

'Ahh,' said Meg. 'Was that around the time of that awful party that Christina had? The one when she tantrummed all over the place?'

'And the whole village was alive with gossip,' put in Edie.

'Well, that's wee villages for you,' I said. 'Now, I really want to get to the point of this story.' They waited. 'What I need to say is that Mr Sinclair and I have met up again. He was badly wounded and is now convalescing in Perth. I saw him in October when I was down.'

'How is he?' asked Meg.

'He's much better. He's not able to go back to the Front but will probably get a call from a Kirk. And,' I could feel myself slowing up. 'We're, we're going to get married, when the time is right.'

There was a short silence. Then Meg slowly pulled herself to her feet and came over to me and took my hand.

'Lassie, this is very good news,' she said. 'I, for one, hope that happiness will be yours all your days. Yes, we know that you loved Mr Sinclair, you were a wonderful wife to him but you have to move forward. You're doing the right thing.'

'Thank you. That means a lot to me.'

Edie, in her turn congratulated me, then, she said, 'I always thought he looked so good in that dog-collar of his.' We laughed then and Meg brought out the kitchen sherry and we toasted each other before going to bed and my journey sooth on the *St Clair* the next evening.

Aberdeen was busy, crowded with people and noisy with trams clanging, cars tooting, horses and carriages and carts rattling over the cassies.

'Mercy me,' said Lizzie as the two sisters met in Esslemont and MacIntosh's (E&M's) doorway. 'Fit a mineer. Gie me Glenbuchat ony day.' Without pausing she grabbed Charlotte's arm and ushered her inside. 'Noo,' she said. 'Come on. A hae a table aa ready. A hae a surprise fur ee inside.'

They made their way to the tearoom where a familiar figure sat at a corner table.

'Granny. It's you. You're the surprise. Don't get up. How wonderful to see you. Thank you for coming. Oh, I can't believe it.'

'Yes it's me. When I heard that you were coming sooth again and Lizzie was meeting you here I thought, well I'll come too.' She looked at me straight. 'I like to keep an eye on things.'

Charlotte sat down beside her and sighed with contentment.

'This is lovely. A threesome.' She pulled off her gloves and laid them on the table.

'I wish I could take my shoes off too. I think Aberdeen's pavements are getting harder every time I come. Mind you,' she added. 'It could be my feet.'

'It'll be your corns, wearing too tight shoes,' suggested Lizzie.

'I don't, on two counts, have corns or too-tight shoes. At least not since I was very small and we wore them until our toes were really squeezed.'

'A min it weel. Noo fit are ye haein?' The waitress approached and Lizzie made her request.

'I'm afraid scones are limited to one each,' said the waitress. 'War-time. The bakers are having difficulty getting flour.'

'If you can spare one,' said Charlotte, 'that would be fine.'

'This awful War,' said Lizzie. 'Foo lang dae ye think it'll last?'

'Your guess is as good as mine.'

'Nae first-hand knowledge then?'

'Well I don't think Magnus knows any more than we do. Lowrie's still in France, I don't know where. We're not supposed to know these things. The public is only told after the event and sometimes not even then. They think they're keeping up our morale by not telling us.'

'And fit aboot James?'

'He won't know, any more than the rest.'

'Ay, but fit aboot him? Come on Charlotte. Gies the craic.'

'You're a pain, Lizzie Gordon. Always ferreting out news.' Granny laughed.

'She doesn't change.'

'Come on noo Granny, ee wint tae ken fit's gaan on as weel.' Granny nodded. Charlotte sighed.

'Oh, well. Here we go. But only in strictest confidence mind. Nae spikken aboot this till I say.'

'Would we?' Charlotte looked at them.

'Hmm. I don't know about *you*, Lizzie. Anyway,' she gave in. 'Yes, James and I are unofficially engaged,' Lizzie jumped up, ran round the table and hugged her.

'Whssht, control yourself.' Lizzie sat down but raised her teacup in a silent toast. Granny smiled in a satisfied way.

'I'm delighted for you,' she said. 'Are you going to tell us anymore?'

'Well, that's it, really. He asked me and I said "Yes".'

'Come on Charlotte. I ken you. There must be mair ti'lt than that.'

'Lizzie, it's very personal…'

'Weel, foo's he gettin on?'

'He's much better. Still convalescing but he's had his Medical Board.'

'Fit dis at dee?'

'It assesses his fitness to go back to the Front.'

'And fit haippened?'

'Well, we weren't surprised when they said he wasn't fit to go back. James told me in a letter recently. He seems reconciled to it. And, I wouldn't want him to return unless he's fully able.'

'So, what happens next?' asked Granny.

'Well, he'll probably get a medical discharge.'

'So, you'll have a wedding in the offing?'

'I hope so.'

'My dear, I hope you'll both be very happy.'

Lizzie put her hand across the table and squeezed Charlotte's.

'I'm gled,' she said. 'Really gled. I winna say onythin until ye say. I quite understand.'

'Thanks, Lizzie. Granny, I'm glad you came. When was the last time you were in Aberdeen?'

'A long time ago. It has to be something special to get me out of Towie.'

The little train on the branch-line from Dundee pulled into Glamis station the following day. This time a surprise awaited Charlotte. Magnus was there with the Glamis Castle vehicle.

'Magnus, it's good to see you. How are you? Better enough to be allowed out with the car.'

'Yes, I've been out driving a few times now. As long as the roads are clear of snow and ice. It's made a great difference to my existence. Mind you, I can't go far and there has to be a good reason. Petrol rationing,' he added in response to her enquiring look. 'Don't you know there's a War on? You look well.'

'I am well, thanks.' They set off.

It was after dinner when they were relaxed and at ease in the quiet verandah that she confided her news. She started tentatively but with growing courage as she realised that Magnus was interested and supportive, not against her marrying James, as she had feared.

'No wonder you looked so upbeat when I saw you in October,' he said. 'You could have told us, Rosemary and me, you know.' She looked at him and shook her head.

'No, Magnus, it was too soon. It was very new and I had to take it all in myself. Forbye, it was only four months since Alexander died. Even now it's too soon to go spikken aboot it. You won't say anything about it, will you? Till I say?'

'No, no,' he reassured her. 'Can we tell Rosemary?'

'Oh, of course, Rosemary's different. But, Jarlshavn folk, you know.'

'I know,' he said. 'You don't want it getting about, till say, July?'

'Exactly.'

'But Charlotte, go back a bit. You and James must have got to know each other pretty well when I was a boy – when, when mother was so ill. Around that time.'

Charlotte hesitated. *I need to tell him. How is he going to take this? After all that he's been through, and our past history.*

'Magnus,' she began.

'Charlotte, what's the matter? Are you all right?'

'Yes, Magnus, but I need to tell you something. Something about what happened long ago.'

'Go on,' he said, puzzled at her serious voice. Another voice interrupted her as she took a deep breath to begin.

'Hello.' It was Rosemary. 'Phew,' she sat down beside them. 'That's everyone happy now, for a while. Late dressings are done, games room in full swing, early bedders reading.' She regarded the two of them and smiled. 'I'm sure that you've both done quite a bit of catching up.'

'Yes,' agreed Magnus. 'News you mightn't be expecting.'

'Really?' Rosemary turned to Charlotte. 'What have you dug up?'

'Go on Magnus,' said Charlotte. 'I said you could tell Rosemary.'

'I think you're going to be pleased at this, Rosemary,' said Magnus. He paused.

'Charlotte has just told me that she and James are going to be married.'

'O-hh.' Rosemary's hands flew to her face. 'That *is* news. She leant over, took Charlotte's hands and kissed her. 'I'm so pleased for you both. When did all this happen? Oh, I hope you'll both be very happy.' She smiled all over her face.

'Thank you. We're very happy, but of course as Magnus and I have just been discussing, we can't make it public until the summer. You understand don't you?'

'Of course. That's as custom decrees under the circumstances. I understand completely. How is James anyway? Has he had his Medical Board?'

'Yes, and he'll probably get a medical discharge. He can't go back to the Front.'

'Well, at least he knows officially,' said Magnus.

'Yes, it does help to organise.'

'But Charlotte,' Magnus said. 'You were about to tell me something about what happened long ago. Can you tell me now? And Rosemary too?'

'I'll go away if you like,' offered Rosemary, 'if this is something private.'

'No, no, stay,' said Charlotte. 'It *is* private but I'd be glad if you would stay and hear it with Magnus.'

'Right,' said Magnus. 'Fire away.' Charlotte looked at him, raised her eyebrows at him and shook her head.

'It's not as easy as that. It's actually a very sort of mixed up story.'

She went right back: to Margery's dying wish that she and Alexander would get married, to her and James falling in love and becoming secretly engaged, to Christina's request at her fourth birthday party that Charlotte should become her 'Mama', to subsequent gossip that she and Alexander were going to get married, to her row over this with James and the end of their engagement. Any hope of peace between them ended when he informed her about his call to St Fillans and he wanted her to accompany him as his wife.

'That finished it,' she admitted. 'I was angry that he hadn't consulted me and he'd taken it for granted that I would drop everything and go with him.'

'You know more or less about Alexander and me,' she finished. 'And I know that Magnus has told you Rosemary, where he comes into the story.' Rosemary nodded and looked at Magnus. He sat with his head in his hands.

'Magnus?' she said.

'I'm all right,' he said in a muffled voice. 'Just give me a minute.' He took a few deep breaths then sat up.

'Charlotte,' he said. 'I need to know. Charlotte, did you love my father?' He looked so upset that Charlotte's heart went out to him. Rosemary put her arm round his bowed shoulders.

'Magnus, I did. We had a stable, loving relationship. It wasn't the same as James, but then it wouldn't be, would it? No loves are ever the same. And I know you witnessed some bad times, Magnus, but no marriage goes problem-free. But I did love your father, and remember, we made Hannah and Angus, and the other little ones that … that I don't forget, and there's little Alexander John in the Kirkyard. Now, will you believe me and give James and me your blessing to go forward?'

In response, he rose from his chair and walked over to her. She got up to face him, meeting his eyes steadily.

'Of course I believe you and give you my blessing. I – we –' he held out his hand to Rosemary – 'hope that you'll both be very happy.'

They held each other then, the three of them, in a togetherness that sealed a special friendship they were to remember for ever.

'There's another thing I need to speak to you about,' Charlotte said. 'We haven't said much about Alexander's Will yet. Alexander has provided for all of you in a fair way. But, Magnus, as Alexander's eldest son, Birkenshaw officially belongs to you as part of your inheritance.' He made a move as if to speak, to protest, but she put out a staying hand.

'Wait a minute Magnus. I know that I have the life occupancy of Birkenshaw and I'd planned to live there with Hannah and Angus at least until they'd finished school. But now things have changed. James will undoubtedly get a parish in Scotland and we'll live in a manse. Hannah and Angus will be with us and go to the appropriate school. I know this'll be a big step for them, but there it is. So you see, Magnus, the house will be yours to have this year if you want.'

Magnus looked at Rosemary. 'Shall we tell her?' he said.

She nodded. 'Go on.'

'We weren't going to tell you this until we were sure,' he began. Charlotte raised her eyebrows again.

'Sure of what?

'If you wait a minute I'll tell you. We've been putting out feelers regarding work for me when I'm medically discharged which I know I will be. Shetland is the obvious choice for me and Rosemary's keen too. I wrote to my old boss Mr Sanderson at the Gilbert Bain Hospital. He wrote back saying there'd be a job for me there when I was ready – not my old job I hasten to add, but one to suit my needs and experience.'

'And,' chimed in Rosemary, 'he handed my curriculum vitae to the Matron and she has offered me a Sister's post for as long as I want.'

'Just right,' said Charlotte. 'For the two of you.' She sat back and smiled. 'So, can you see yourselves in Birkenshaw?'

'You don't need to ask twice.'

The last leg of Charlotte's journey sooth was to Edinburgh to Christina. As she had hoped, Christina took a practical attitude to Charlotte's news.

'Mother, I never expected you to remain single for the rest of your life. You're still young, you're pretty, you're nice. I did wonder who you might finish up with – I mean you could have married someone ghastly who we couldn't stand.'

'Christina. Do you think I'd do a thing like that?'

'We-ll you never know – no, no, Mother, I'm just teasing you. I'm delighted you're marrying James. He's a lucky man. I hope he realises it. I can just remember him when I was a wee girl. Nice man even then. Were you gone on him then, too?'

'What a way to put it.' Charlotte told her the story. She was a good listener, didn't ask too many questions but was horrified to hear of her own part in the drama.

'Oh Mother, I'm sorry. I remember that day. I was very over-excited and the other children were being very superior about having a Mama. I couldn't take it. I'm sorry,' she said again. 'If only I hadn't done that, then…'

'Then,' Charlotte said, 'we wouldn't have had Hannah and Angus, and Alexander and I would never have known what it was to love each other. Don't berate yourself about this, Christina. Life is full of, "if only". It's also too short to regret something that happened so long ago. Be happy with the "now" and not feel bad about what happened when you were so young.' Christina smiled.

'No wonder when James and I met first, in the Ward, I mean, he called me the wee besom.'

'Did he really?'

'More or less. Anyway, Mother, I'm so happy for you both. When is the big day?'

'We're not sure. We're not going public till, possibly July. But tell Lowrie of course. No one else.' She nodded in agreement.

344

'Will you be one of my bridesmaids, please. This'll be a very quiet wedding but I need my girls as bridesmaids. You and Hannah.'

'Mother, that's perfect. Yes, please. I must write and tell Lowrie,' she carried on. 'He'll be delighted. I wonder if he could get leave.'

'How is he?' She shrugged.

'All right I think. Tired. They're all tired. They say it's not going to last much longer but they're taking a long time about it.'

James stood on the platform at Perth station awaiting Charlotte's train –her diversion he called it. They had two hours together before the Aberdeen train was due. She stepped off the train into his arms.

'Let's go and sit down somewhere quiet. I was thinking the foyer of the Station Hotel. We'll get a cup of tea.'

'I haven't got long.'

'No, but it's very near.' He took her arm and ushered her in.

'Now,' when they were settled. 'How did the telling go? Is everyone happy?'

'Yes, I think so. Magnus needed a bit of reassurance but he's fine. Christina asked if I'd been 'gone' on you when you were in Jarlshavn.' He burst out laughing.

'What did you say?'

'Well, it was a good way into telling her about us now and the back story. Anyway, how did your parents take the news?'

'They're delighted. They want to meet you.'

'Of course,' she said. 'That's only right and proper. I've no doubt I'll be sooth again and I'll come to the hotel.'

'I'm so looking forward to the day when we can be together for always. When do you think?'

'Late summer could be a possibility. What do you think?'

A while later she looked at her watch.

'James, I must go. I mustn't miss the train.'

She reached the platform just in time.

'Good bye my dear.' He kissed her, held her hand till the last minute, waved as the train gathered speed and was lost to view, turned and walked from the station.

Charlotte spent a windy night on the *St Clair* and was home the next morning. It was a Saturday and her two youngest awaited her at the gate.

James to Charlotte

My dearest,

I've just heard from the Church offices in Edinburgh with a list of vacant parishes in Scotland. One of these is Towie. I wonder how you feel about my letting them know that I am available for their consideration? I won't do anything about this until I hear from you – I think I have learned that lesson…

Love always, James.

Charlotte to James.

…I'm glad you're not 'available' for a city charge. Towie – I know it well, bonny place, good folk, I was happy there. Can I say more? You have my blessing…

James to Charlotte

…The Kirk Session of Towie Kirk has invited me to preach on a Sunday suitable to both parties. Do you think you could come and be there please? We would have an opportunity to see the Manse, but more importantly, your support means a great deal to me…

Charlotte to James

… Of course I'll come. Just let me know when, and I'll make arrangements with Meg and Edie…We'll be able to stay with Granny at Trancie House.

Charlotte

By this time it was June and I felt that I had to tell Hannah and Angus what was happening. Although it was still less than a year since Alexander had died, I felt that they, and I, could cope with talking about the next step. One fine afternoon we were in the garden working at the weeds. We stopped for a breather.

'I want to tell you something.' Hannah looked up from her book immediately. Angus stroked his rabbit and waited.

'I want you both to know that I loved your father very much.'

'Yes, Mother, we know that,' said Hannah. 'Is that what you wanted to tell us? We've always known that.'

'I'm glad you do,' I said. 'I missed him very much when he died. I still do. But there comes a time when we have to make big decisions about our lives and I've come to this point. I am going to be married again to a man I also love very much. I've known him a long time and we have met up again recently.'

'Who is he Mother?' Hannah said. 'Do we know him?'

'No, you haven't met him yet, but I hope you will soon. His name is James MacLeod. He was badly injured in France last year and is just getting better. He's in hospital in Perth.'

'Perth,' she said. 'Isn't that quite near Glamis?' Then, with a flash of insight, she said, 'Did you go and see him, away back, when we were in Edinburgh?'

'Yes, I did. I had heard that he had been injured and I wanted to visit him.'

'Hm.' She sat a moment. 'So you didn't tell us what you were doing?'

'No.'

'Why not?'

'I didn't tell you because – I wasn't sure myself what was going to happen. It could have been just a very formal "hello" and "good bye". So I felt I should wait. And then,' I pre-empted the next question, 'I didn't tell you later because I felt it was a very big secret for you to be carrying around.'

'You could have – I'm quite trustworthy.'

'I know that.' There was a silence, then she spoke again.

'Is he all right?'

'Yes, and he's not going back to the Front. He's a minister and was a Padre.'

'How did he get injured?' Angus suddenly joined the conversation.

'He went out into no-man's land in the evening, in the dark, to help injured soldiers get back to the Regimental Aid Post and a sniper shot him.'

'That's *very* brave,' Angus said. 'Can I tell the boys at school?'

'I don't see why not,' I said. 'What do you think Hannah?'

'Och, let him tell them. It's as good a way of telling the village that you're getting married again as any.'

'You think so?'

'Oh yes, Mother, you know how people talk.'

When Angus had run off to settle his rabbit she said, 'You said, em, that Mr Macleod is a minister. Does that mean we'll have to leave Birkenshaw, leave Jarlshavn?'

'Yes. I'm glad you asked. I don't think Angus has thought that far ahead.'

'Where will we be living?'

'Well, James has spoken to the elders of a church in the village of Towie, in Aberdeenshire. We might go there.'

'But Mother, that's where you grew up. That's near where Aunt Lizzie lives, and our cousins, and Granny. We've been there. We would see them often. That would be all right. Here was me thinking that we'd have to go somewhere we don't know at all.'

'Would you be happy going there then?'

'Yes, I think that would be fine. I'd be sad to leave here and all my friends here and school – that's a point,' she said. 'Where would school be?'

'I'd have to sort that out,' I admitted. 'Towie is a rural village and only has a primary school. I think you'd have to go to, possibly Aboyne but I'm not sure of buses and timings. You might need to go into digs during the week.'

'How far is it?'

'It's about sixteen miles away. Anyway,' I reminded her, 'nothing's definite yet. But James is preaching on Sunday of next week and I should be there with him. I'm going to leave you for a few days again, I'm afraid.'

'That's all right,' she said. 'And don't worry about Angus. He'll be fine as long as he can take that blessed rabbit.' Then she added, 'Mother, can we meet him soon, Mr MacLeod?'

'Yes, I think he's coming up here for a visit in July. He's looking forward to meeting you two.'

'Of course you must come to me for James's preaching weekend,' said Granny to Charlotte over her new telephone. 'What would the people of Towie say if you didn't? Fit a spik. And anyway, I want to meet James. See this man that all the talk is about.'

347

She was standing at Trancie House front door as she had stood so long ago awaiting the arrival of Charlotte, the child she and Granpa had taken on. The car, Granpa's car, drew up. The years fell away but this time Charlotte was climbing the steps to her with the man she was going to marry.

The week-end was full. On the Saturday afternoon the Session Clerk, Graham Stein and another elder took them to see the Manse. It was a big house, built in 1819, standing on the south bank of the River Don, three storeys high and spacious with it. Mr Brown, the elder assured Charlotte that help in the house was available. The size of the house might put some folk off but they liked it.

James 'preached for the kirk' at morning service in Towie. After the Kirk scailed, the Session gathered and interviewed him. As well as asking about his previous ministries in Jarlshavn and St Fillans, the elders were particularly interested in the topical subject of his work as a chaplain and what it was like in France. One of them suggested that a series of sermons on World War 1 would be a good idea to bring the congregation up to speed with what it was really like and 'not the rubbish that was served up to them in the papers'. This was met with a rumble of agreement. They also wanted to meet Charlotte. A couple of the older ones remembered her as a girl.

'Oh ay, I min ye as a wee quinie livin here at Trancie wi yer Granny and the Doctor. Ye were aye dottin aboot.'

'A winner noo if this will help or hinner yer man's chances noo.' They laughed heartily at their wee joke before going on into solemn conclave with their peers.

James and Charlotte walked back to Granny's for a late lunch.

'Well?' she said.

'All went fine I think,' said James. 'What do you think?'

'Well your preaching was fine, service good, your hymns, they knew them. Nothing collapsed. It was very good. Just like before but...'

'But?'

'But better.' Charlotte said. 'You've developed. Experience.'

Later that evening, the phone rang. It was the Session Clerk.

'Mr MacLeod, we just thought we'd speak to you before you go. We are unanimous. Would you come and be our minister please?'

'Thank you very much. Please may I ring you back in a few minutes? I'd just like to consult with my fiancée.'

They waltzed round Granny's parlour.

'Is that called "consulting"?' She sat in her chair laughing.

'All right?' he said toCharlotte.

'All right.' He kissed her and went back to the telephone.

Hannah and Angus stood watching for them.

'They always do this.'

When they reached the Birkenshaw entrance, they got out of the bus and walked up the drive together.

'Good of you to come and meet us,' said James. 'Oh, and I see what you mean about trees. Now,' he said, 'you're the tree-keeper aren't you?' Angus nodded.

'I'll show you if you like. Hannah too,' he said. 'She does a lot of work, mulching them with the grass mowings.'

'Oh, so it's a joint effort.'

'And Dod,' put in Hannah.

'Who's Dod?'

'He's the gardener and our friend. And he knows all about plants and trees.'

'Come on,' said Charlotte. 'Meg and Edie will be wondering where we are.'

James's few days in Jarlshavn passed in a flurry of talking, meeting old friends, visiting the kirk for old times' sake, the current minister for good manners' sake, re-walking old walks.

On his last day they walked for the last time up their old cliff-top walk. They talked of many things, hopes and dreams, things past, present and what could be in the future. Then he stopped, still holding her hand.

'Listen,' he said. 'Listen, a lark. Look. Can you see it?' Up, up against the blue they could see and hear the lark, singing its heart out.

'"…*in the sky / The larks, still bravely singing, fly / Scarce heard amid the guns below…*" A Canadian wrote that at Ypres in 1915.'

'It's beautiful James,' said Charlotte. 'So right.'

They set off hand in hand down the path into their future.

The Press and Journal

Aberdeen Monday19 August 1918

The marriage has taken place on Saturday 17 August 1918
between
Major the Reverend James MacLeod and Mrs Charlotte Sinclair
née Gordon, at Towie Parish Church.
The Reverend Douglas Shand, Glenbuchat officiated.

The bride was attired in a full-length gown of deep green crushed velvet. She was attended by her step-daughter, Mrs Christina Harcus and her daughter, Miss Hannah Sinclair. Her attendants were in cream with floral head dresses and carried bouquets of summer flowers.
The groom was attended by Captain Lowrie Harcus,
the Gordon Highlanders
and Captain Magnus Sinclair RAMC.
Master Angus Sinclair, son of the bride, was also in attendance,

Mrs MacLeod was born at the Milton of Glenbuchat and lived for many years with her grandparents, the late Dr Andrew Grant and Mrs Margaret Grant of Trancie House, Towie. She attended Towie Primary School where she was Dux in 1888. She went on to qualify as a teacher at the Free Church Teaching College, Aberdeen before taking up a teaching post in Jarlshavn, Shetland.

Mr MacLeod hails from Perth, attended Perth High School and studied Divinity at the University of Edinburgh. Following ministries in Jarlshavn and St Fillans, he volunteered as a Chaplain with the Army Chaplains Department. In this role he served in different theatres of the War in France before being severely wounded while rescuing wounded personnel during the Battle of Vimy Ridge.

The P&J would like to wish the Reverend and Mrs James MacLeod
a long and happy married life together.
Mr MacLeod was recently inducted to the Parish of Towie,
in the Presbytery of Alford.

Chapter 52

The Manse, Towie

MONDAY 11 NOVEMBER 1918

The telephone rang.

'I'll get it.' Charlotte picked up the receiver.

'Hello? Hello Christina. How good to hear you. Is everything all right?'

'Hello Mother. Yes, everything's very all right. Mother, the fighting's stopped. They've signed the Armistice papers. At Compiègne. The Chief Medical Officer of the Infirmary had a telegram a wee while ago and is spreading the word. I'm hoping to hear from Lowrie today when he's able.'

'Christina thank you so much for letting us know. That's wonderful news. After all this time. I'll have to go and tell James.'

'Yes, and I'll have to get off the line. There's a queue for this telephone as you can imagine. Bye, Mother.'

'Bye Christina.' She turned to James hovering beside her.

'It's over. James it's over. They've signed.'

'Oh, thank God. At last.' He took her in his arms and hugged her fiercely. 'My dear girl, by all that's wonderful and amazing, let us remember this day.' She held him close, close to her, thankful all over again for what life had given them. Suddenly he moved, stillness broken.

'James?'

'I must ring the bells, or, find Bill the beadle to do it for me. Spread the news.'

The telephone rang again.

He picked it up.

'Hello? Ah, Constable. Thank you for phoning. Yes, we've just heard. I'm away out to get the Beadle to ring the bell. Yes. Thanks. See you later.'

'Where's my coat? I'll be back soon.' He rushed off.

At Glamis Castle Lt Col (Retd) Neil Fulton gathered all who were able, together in the Games Room. They stood, expectant, shuffling, nudging, waiting. He walked in and as he turned to face them he looked over his bunch of convalescent men, some dressed in regulation Hospital Blues, many in various items of handed-down clothing drawn from multiple stores or borrowed from each other. Here and there stood the QA Nursing Sisters in their red capes. VADs and other members of staff, sensing that something momentous was afoot, swelled the ranks. All who were able, were there.

'I won't keep you long,' Neil Fulton said. 'I have called you together to give you a piece of good news. An Armistice between the Allies and the Germans was signed today at eleven hundred hours. Therefore, I am happy, delighted, to confirm to you that the fighting has stopped. There will still have to be further negotiations towards a Treaty. However, for today, the Armistice is the good news.'

The Games Room sounded to the cheers and happy laughter and singing.

'And,' he said, when he could be heard. 'A ration of rum for everybody tonight. This brought even more noise.

Rosemary slipped out to the telephone. She asked for the Birkenshaw number.

'Magnus?' as the voice at the other end said 'Hello'.

'Magnus, it's me, Rosemary.'

'Rosemary, are you all right.'

'Yes, Magnus. My dearest, the Armistice has been signed.'

'Truly? Is that official.'

'Yes. I've no doubt bells will be ringing all over the place before long.'

'Thank God.'

'We can be together soon forever. In the meantime I'll be up for a few days' break in a week or two if Meg will act as chaperone again. Must go. Bye my dear.'

'Good bye. Thanks for ringing.'

Two days later

Christina sat in the sitting-room in the 'rooms' at Stockbridge Colonies. The fire was on and her shoes were off. She sat with the newspaper, reading the latest about the Armistice, the jollifications in the big cities and towns, the bells ringing out across the country, the reminders to spare a thought for those who would not be returning, those whose lives would never be the same again and those who had been left alone.

In the background of her mind she heard the front door opening and closing. A few minutes later she heard a step on the stair. Slowly the sitting-room door opened and Lowrie, rather worn and dishevelled, walked in.

He stood there and for a second all they did was look. Then she leapt up and, stockinged feet regardless, ran to him. They clung to each other.

'They've signed the Armistice.' he kept repeating. 'They've signed. The fighting's stopped. I just wanted to see you and tell you myself. The CO gave me a weekend. The fighting's stopped.'

Chapter 53

The Manse, Towie

SEPTEMBER 1919

'Hannah, Angus, are you ready? You need to go. Young Jock's outside in the car.'

It was Monday morning, the day Young Jock came with Granpa's car to take them the sixteen miles to school in Aboyne. They had become used to this: the early Monday morning start, the week in their digs in Aboyne with Mrs Lizzie Shand, sister-in-law of the Glenbuchat minister, the Rev Douglas Shand and the return drive on Fridays to Towie with Young Jock.

This plan was quickly put in place near the beginning of the 1918 winter term. When Douglas Shand had heard that the two Manse bairns at Towie required weekly digs to enable them to attend the Secondary school in Aboyne, he had come up with an immediate solution.

'My sister-in-law, Lizzie, she has lodgers. I'm sure she's had bairns before. I'll find out.' That was settled within hours. They all visited, saw what would be their rooms during the week, liked what they saw, Mrs Shand liked them. Everyone was happy.

'Just coming Mother.'

Doors banged, a rummle of feet on the stairs and they came running down.

'Have you got everything?'

'Yes Mother.' Hannah looked at her. 'Are you all right Mother?'

'Yes, I'm fine.' Perceptive girl. She knows the time is very near.

'Sure?'

'Yes, now on you go, the pair of you. Yes, Angus,' she said, in response to anxious instructions. 'We'll look after your rabbit. Have a good week.'

'You too. See you later.' They kissed her good-bye and ran out to Young Jock.

Charlotte waved them 'Good bye', exhaled slowly and sat on the stairs. Every Monday morning was like this. There was always a rush at the last minute. However much she planned. She felt herself relaxing in the quiet.

Now, when is this new wee one going to come? That'll be the next thing. She smiled and stroked the bump in her front as she felt the inner activity. James came through.

'All OK? What are you sitting on the stairs for?'

'Just resting. He, or she, is very active.'

'Shouldn't you be phoning Lizzie?' He helped her up and ushered her through to the kitchen.

'No, I don't think it will be today. Lizzie thinks it'll be sometime this week. She's standing by. She might pop in if she's time. I hope it's before they come home on Friday anyway.'

353

'What can I get you, Mrs MacLeod?' Jeannie Forbes came in from hanging out the washing. 'Good drying day.'

'A cup of tea would be good, thanks Jeannie.'

When Charlotte and James were married the previous year, they had not seriously considered adding a baby to the equation. At forty-three year of age, Charlotte was sure her day for that was over. James was so happy to be married, as far as he was concerned, his cup was full.

Some months later he discovered that his cup was brimming over.

Charlotte consulted Lizzie as the local midwife.

'Lizzie, tell me if this is 'the change' or something else.'

Lizzie listened, examined, looked, palpated and finally took out her foetal stethoscope. After listening intently she looked up smiling.

'I'm going to be an aunt again.' They burst out laughing.

'That's marvellous. I never thought I would – have another one, I mean. When, do you think?'

'Mid-September – give or tak a day. That's great. Now,' she said. 'We're sisters. Are you sure you want me – ye mebbe want to gang to some other midwife.'

'Lizzie, don't be daft. *You're* my midwife.'

'Ye'll need to be afa careful, min. Ye're nae spring chicken.'

'Thanks.'

'No seriously. Watch yer step. A'll hae tae tell Doctor Leslie. He'll be doon tae see ye.'

James was delighted. He kept looking at her, wondering at the new life growing within. He started treating her like some precious ornament until she showed her protest by threatening to run up Trancie Hill by herself. He brought in flowers, rushed to put her feet on a footstool, would have answered to her every whim if she'd let him.

'I'm not ill, James,' she said to him one fine evening.

'I know but I just want to take care of you. Did I tell you my mother's started knitting? She can't believe she's going to be a Grandma at last.'

'Granny's excited too. It's been a long time since the last great-grand-child was born. And Dad's happy. He'll get to know this one as a baby.'

'And all the others are so pleased for us. I see Hannah reading the baby book. I hope she doesn't learn more than is good for her.'

'She won't, don't worry. Anyway, now that we've made everyone happy with what we're growing, let's relax. How has your day been?'

Charlotte had a feeling that this labour wouldn't last too long. After all, Angus's birth hadn't taken long. Mind you, Lizzie had warned her it didn't always follow. That week on Friday morning Charlotte knew that the day had come. At half past five she was awake. By breakfast time she was pacing the floor.

'Oh, here's another one. It creeps from the back to both sides and then to the front at the same time.'

'I'll telephone Lizzie.'

This little one came quickly, gently, with no fuss at twenty-five minutes past eleven in the morning. James, sitting out on the stairs heard the cry. Charlotte watched in wonder at the pinking up of the velvety skin as the baby breathed.

'Fit hiv we got?' Lizzie asked. 'Are ye gaan tae hae a look?'

'It's a boy.'

'An he's gorgeous, aren't ye, ma bonny wee loonie?' He pursed his lips at her. Charlotte laughed.

'Give James a shout, will you?' He was there as soon as Lizzie opened the door.

'Oh, well done. That was quick. Are you all right?' He kissed her.

'Yes, yes, I'm fine. Meet your son, James.' She held the baby out to him. 'Here, wee laddie, have a cuddle from your Papa.' He sniffed in appreciation.

'Is that what they call the new-baby smell? It's quite special.' His face was a joy as he held his new son and looked over the baby's head at Charlotte.

'Thank you.' She smiled at him, at them both.

'You go and sit down with him over there,' instructed Lizzie, 'and we'll finish off here. Keep him warm now.'

'Yes, Lizzie.'

Later, after Lizzie had gone promising to return later, after lunch, after Charlotte had slept, the baby boy peaceful in his basket beside her, James put down his sermon for Sunday on which, unsuccessfully, he'd been trying to concentrate. He ran quietly up the stairs and looked round the bedroom door. Charlotte sat in bed, with the baby in her arms.

'All well?'

'Yes. I've just fed him again. Just look at him. Perfection personified.'

'He's beautiful. And so are you.' He sat down on the bed beside Charlotte and swung his legs up.

'Let me have another look.' He addressed his son face to face. 'Now, what are we going to call you?' The baby half opened his eyes and yawned.

'That's respect,' Charlotte said. 'What *will* we call him? After your father?'

'Ewan? Would you be happy with that?'

'It's a good name. Let's do it. Follow tradition, after the paternal grandfather.'

'All right – well, let's give him the works and call him Andrew after your grandfather. Ewan Andrew MacLeod. That sounds good.'

They sat peacefully together, holding hands, the baby lying cuddled in his shawl across their laps.

A tap at the door, then a cautious opening.

'Can I come in?'

'Granny. Where did you spring from? Come in.'

'A little bird told me I might find some news here. Young Jock drove me across. He's away to Aboyne a while ago to meet the bairns. They'll be back soon. I've had a wee fly-cup and a blether with Jeannie in the kitchen because it seemed so quiet up here.' She hesitated on the threshold.

'Granny,' James said. 'Don't stand there. Come in and see who we've made.'

He got off the bed, crossed the room and helped her over to the wee chair next to the bed. She bent over, kissed Charlotte and looked at the bundle in the shawl.

'Our wee boy,' said Charlotte. 'Ewan Andrew MacLeod.'

'Well done, my dear. I'm so happy for you all.'

Charlotte held out the baby to James who placed him carefully in the old arms.

'My new great grand-son. Ewan Andrew. I like his name. Andrew would have been very pleased at this honour. Thank you.' She sat back and held him close to her breast.

'Little Ewan Andrew, for the moment, we're the oldest and the youngest in this family. We'll get to know each other very well. We'll make a good team.'

The proud parents held hands and smiled at them.

'Crossing generations,' said Charlotte.

Here come another two.'

In the distance they heard a door slam and a rummle of feet running upstairs.

Glossary

Ben: through
Besom: broom; brush; term of reproach for a woman
Blessés (Fr): wounded
Blighty one; Blighty wound: a War wound that warrants repatriation to Britain
Boves (Fr): underground tunnels in the Arras area of France
Ca canny: take care; go slowly
Cassie: sett; rectangular stone paving block
Cheerie bye: good bye
Claik, claiking: chatter; gossip
Clarted: covered, usually in mud or muck
Coup, couped: upset; spilt
Craic: news; chat
Deave: annoy
Dee: do
Dod: piece
Dog-tags: identity discs; identity tags
Dreels: drills, as in ploughed field; rows of potatoes
Dubs: mud
Dwam: half asleep dream
Ee: you
Een, one; eenie – diminutive of 'een'
Eese: use; eest: used
Feart: frightened
Fit wey nae: why not
Flee stick to the wa: '…let that flee stick to the wa': let's not go any further with
    that; lit: let that fly stick to the wall
Flit: flitted: move, usually house; go elsewhere
Foo: how
Fushen: vigour;
Gaan: going
Gansey: guernsey; a seaman's jersey
Hae: have
Happit: wrapped; covered; happit up: very well covered
High-heid-yins: seniors; 'top brass'
Hinna: haven't
Hinner: hinder

Howdie: uncertified midwife; also in Shetland:
Hummel doddies: fingerless gloves; mitts with fingers covered and separate thumb.
Hunkered: squatting down
Jaloused: suspected
Kishie: hand-made basket for carrying peats (Shetland)
Kist: chest; coffin
Mairret: married
Mineer: mess; noise; fuss
Minty: minute;
Needle's E'e: Needle's eye. In this case, a large rock with a hole in it north of
    Arbroath
Neuk: corner, nook
On appro: on approbation/approval
Oxter: armpit
Piece: in the context of eating, something light to eat for lunch or school playtime.
    'Fine piece' is the same but something especially good to eat.
Pig: stone hot-water bottle
Piltock: a coalfish in its second year, eg Pollack
Poilu (Fr): soldier, 'tommy'
Pro re nata: as the situation arises
Quine:girl
Rummle: rumble
Sair made: hard-pressed
Sair: sore; afa sair winter: very bad winter
Scailed: emptied, eg 'the Kirk scailed': the people came out of church
Scunner: nuisance; sicken
Smoor; smooring: smother, smothering
Sodger: soldier
Sooth: south, as in anywhere south of Shetland.
Spik: speak; in this context, gossip.
Stotter as in 'off/aff her stotter': in this context, off the point; distract;
Stowed out: full up
Tablet: a peculiarly Scottish sweet (not fudge) made with variations of, sugar,
    butter, condensed milk with possibly different flavourings or additions.
Ti'lt: to it
Vratch: wretch
Winna: won't
Woodbine Wullie: a Chaplain, Geoffrey Anketell Studdert Kennedy MC, well-
    known in World War One, for giving out Woodbine's cigarettes to the
    soldiers along with spiritual comfort and hope.
Yours affly.: yours affectionately (eighteenth, nineteenth, occasionally early
    twentieth century)